T0193354

Sweet Obsession

THEODORA KOULOURIS

iUniverse, Inc.
Bloomington

Sweet Obsession

iUniverse books may be ordered through booksellers or by contacting:

iUniverse
1663 Liberty Drive
Bloomington, IN 47403
www.iuniverse.com
1-800-Authors (1-800-288-4677)

ISBN: 978-1-4759-4475-4 (sc)
ISBN: 978-1-4759-4477-8 (e)
ISBN: 978-1-4759-4476-1 (hc)

Library of Congress Control Number: 2012916955

Printed in the United States of America

iUniverse rev. date: 10/8/2012

With God everything is possible ...
even the impossible.

Acknowledgments

I owe a huge debt of graditude to all the people who helped me make my dream come true. First and foremost I thank my five "editors" who eagerly read my book and gave me friendly advice. My lovely daughter Eleni, who pushed me hard to finish my book and achieve my goals, my neice Xrisa, who was the first to read it, Irene, one of my best friends, who had excellent ideas, Maria, friend and neighbor who always found time for me, and my cousin Katerina, who always encouraged me to reach for the sky.

I want to thank my lovely daughter Yianna who helped me with all her computer skills.

I want to thank the "Cuz Club," my sister Kathy, my cousins, Katerina, Sofia, Paula, Kathy, and Patricia, for encouraging and cheering me on as I followed my dream.

Many thanks to my best friend Vasiliki, who from the beginning of my journey, listened to my story for months, has put in thousands of hours of her time to hear me tell it over and over again, and not once ever, has she complained. She now knows every word in my book by heart.

Many thanks to my cousin Tina who guided me, and her daughter Maria, who helped me start my blog.

I would like to thank my husband George. It is because of him that I felt inspired to write this story.

Many thanks to Nidal, my Prince Charming from high school.

Many thanks to my mother, who has dedicated her whole life to her children and grandchildren. A woman who knows how to love unconditionally. She is my hero.

I would like to thank my two sisters, Kathy and Maria, for all their love and support throughout our lives. You have been with me through thick and thin. *Ta athelfia then xorizoune, H mira toxi yrapsi, kai opios anamesa tous be, fotia na tous ekapsi.*

I thank all my nieces and nephews, Billy, Yianni, Demetri, Anastasia, Chrissy, Joanna, Nicky, Bobbie, Vickie, Robert, and my great-nephew Matthew, for filling my life with great joy.

Many thanks to my two brothers-in-law, George and Bob, who truly I say, act like brothers and not like in-laws.

I thank my three sons, Apostoli, Panagiotis, and Yianni, for their love and support, and my beautiful daughters, Eleni and Yianna, who pamper me so much that I truly feel like a queen. I love you all dearly. You are all the very air that I breathe. I cannot and will not live without you.

Above all, I thank the lord, my Heavenly father, who has made everything in my life possible, even the impossible. Thank you Father for reminding me to count my blessings and not my needs. I praise you.

Chapter One
Loula
Arabia 1877

There he was, looking as handsome as ever. He stared right at me, clearly distressed, with his big, beautiful, blue eyes. He was leaning against the stone wall, looking lazy. It seemed to everyone in the ballroom that he was listening to a few gentlemen argue about politics, but I knew him better than anyone in this room did. He nodded to the two gentlemen, as if he heard every word they said, but his eyes never wavered from me, as if I were the prize, as if I were the only woman on earth. *Some people say I have cast a spell on him. They do not understand his feelings for me.*

Even though a distance was between us, I could still feel his eyes on me, burning my skin, electrifying my body, and stirring strong feelings of lust deep within my soul. *Sometimes I wonder who this man is and why he loves me so. I do not have royal blood running in my veins; nor am I an aristocrat. I am but a poor commoner from America with no family or wealth to speak of.*

Every breath Nidal takes, it is for me. I see it, I feel it, and I know it without any doubt whatsoever. Sometimes his love scares me.

1

No one has ever loved me this way before. My prince loves with all his heart and soul. When I touch him, every fiber in his body comes alive. I have this unexplainable power over him.

His piercing eyes were still looking hungrily at me, and I looked back at him. I stared right into his soul, the same way he looked at me. Frustrated, he sighed and ran his hands through his hair, never once taking his glance away from me.

I know what he is thinking at all times, even before he thinks it. I know it is hard to understand what I am saying, but it is the truth. His feelings for me consume him. These feelings run in his blood, in his veins, like a drug that takes over his body and controls his every thought.

And if he does come to me now, I will have no way to control myself. I will tell him that I love him too. I have withheld from telling him this because I fear the way he will react. There's no telling what he might do in the name of love.

Nidal had been ridiculed for loving me this way. His people did not understand the hold I had on him. The king, Nidal's father, said he would lose the respect of his people. They were already questioning his obsessive behavior.

This country cried for him to find a wife from their country—not a woman from another world, a commoner who did not speak their language well and did not know their traditions. They wanted him to choose a wife with Arabian blood in her veins, a woman who could give him a son, an Arabian son. The people wanted him to marry royalty. They wanted him to marry the beautiful Princess Shaeena, someone who had been trained from birth to marry my prince one day. Nidal did not love her. He never had. He saw her as the sister he never had. Nidal, his cousin Billal, and Princess Shaeena grew up together.

He does not listen to anything anyone tells him, and he betrays everyone by loving me. He has loved me ever since he laid eyes on me many years ago. He has never loved or been with another woman. He is true to me and only me. The king has been patient with him all these years because he thought his son would eventually change his mind, but that did not happen. So the king stood back and allowed his son to follow his dreams. He had no other choice.

I could not take my eyes off him either. I watched him watch me. I knew he was losing his patience. Any minute now, he would come charging over here to stake his claim. He was very possesive of me and did not like it when men were around me, especially his cousin, Prince Billal, a handsome prince who showed admiration for me. I knew that my prince suffered deep inside his heart whenever I so much as glanced at Prince Billal. He told me so. Nidal felt threatened whenever his cousin was around. I had no idea why. I knew I had not given him any reason to feel threatened, and neither had Prince Billal so far.

Prince Billal walked over to me, and I did not know what to do. He flashed me a smile to die for, showing off even, white teeth and luscious lips that I was sure could seduce any woman he wanted to. He had dreamy eyes and long eyelashes. He had tied his lengthy black hair in a ponytail, and I knew without a doubt that every woman in Arabia would love to run her fingers through his thick mane. Billal's powerful warrior body stopped a few feet away from me.

I looked around the room and noticed every woman in the ballroom staring breathlessly at him. He reached out and pulled me close to him, near enough where I could feel his heart beat against my breast. He kissed me tenderly on the cheek, and then he whispered hoarsely for my ears alone, "Loula, you take my breath away," and at that moment I looked over his shoulder and saw Nidal lose all color in his face and charge right at us.

I felt Billal's body stiffen as a fuming Nidal barked, "Take your paws off my woman!"

The music halted. Everyone in the ballroom stared at us. I froze, not knowing what to expect next. I could hear whispering among the crowd, and I saw the people of this kingdom shaking their heads in disapproval. I braced myself for what I knew would happen. My prince swung his fist and knocked the stunned Billal off his feet. As he fell to the floor, everyone, including myself, stared at Nidal in disbelief.

Nidal turned and looked at me with accusing eyes, as if I had betrayed him, as if I had torn down his world. At that precise moment, his cousin stood up after stumbling a few times and raised his fist to swing back at Nidal, for he was angry and feeling humiliated. But the crowd kept him from doing just that. The consequence of putting one's hands on the crown prince was prison.

There was silence again in the ballroom. Everyone fearfully took a few steps backward. They did not want to be caught in the middle of the feuding cousins.

Nidal took this opportunity to threaten everyone at the ball. "If any man so much as touches, talks, or even looks at Loula, I will rip out your throat!"

Everyone stared at him, fearing he would do as he threatened. Nidal was a man obsessed. His hands shook as he looked around the room. I knew he was daring anyone to disobey him. He wanted me all to himself.

I am supposed to stand among this crowd at the ball all by myself? What is the point for me to be here in the first place if the men are not allowed to look at me and the women keep their distance out of envy and fear? No one has befriended me yet, and after this episode, no one will ever want to be my friend!

Nidal's accusing eyes stopped on me. I shrank back from the hostility I saw in them. Nidal grabbed my arm abruptly and pulled me swiftly through the disbelieving crowd, humiliating me to no accord. He angrily marched us both out of the ballroom with quick strides down the hall while everyone looked on.

I was racing to keep up with his long, angry strides, I almost lost my balance and tripped on the Oriental carpet that was so lavishly thrown on the marble floor. We reached the bedroom door, and Nidal kicked it, creating a two-inch gash with his boot. The door swung open, and he pushed me in the room as he also walked in and slammed the door shut behind him.

His chest was rising and falling and his eyes were blazing fire as he turned and faced me. He gave me a look that said, "I will kill you now."

But I held my ground. *I am not afraid of him! I know he loves me, and I know that I love him too.* So I only felt anger that he dared to embarrass me so. *How dare Nidal do this to me!*

He walked up to me. He was so close that I could feel his breath on my face. He was fuming, out of his mind with anger. I knew he wanted to throttle me, but I was angry too. Nidal had humiliated me in front of all his people. They already had a hard time accepting me, and now this would put an even bigger damper on things.

I did not do anything wrong. How dare he put me in this awful position!

I raised my hand and quickly slapped him hard across his face. It was a gut instinct. I did not even think about what I was doing. It just happened, and I immediately regretted my actions.

It caught him off guard. So much anger flickered in his eyes. Without thinking, I raised my hand to slap him again, and this time, he caught my arm in midair. Then he grabbed my other arm, and I thought he was going to push me to the floor, but he just held me with his strong arms as he stared deep into my soul, angry as could be. Then he brought his lips down to mine and kissed me.

At first, it was a hard, brutal kiss as his lips crashed down on mine. Then slowly, without warning, it turned into a sweet, slow, passionate kiss. He pulled me close to him and kissed me so sensually and so lovingly that I melted against him. I lost all sense of what was happening and collapsed in his arms. His hands slid down the arch of my back, pulling me closer to him. I could feel his manhood press against me, and I melted in sweet ecstasy in his arms.

I was completely in love with him, and at this moment, if he had asked me to carve out my heart and hand it to him on a silver platter, I would have done just that. I knew I could not live without him. He was my life now, as I was his.

Our bodies fit together as if God created us to become one. The closer he pulled me to his body, the heavier he breathed. I could feel his heart beating so fast that it felt like my own. This was the time, so perfect a time to tell him how I felt. My lips went close to his ear, and I whispered softly, "I love you."

His body stiffened, and he softly pushed me away from him. Confused, I looked up to his face and saw that his eyes were closed. I tried pushing my body up against his, but his hands blocked me from getting too close to him. Suddenly, his hands let go of me, and his arms dropped to his sides. He walked away from me.

I stared after him in disbelief. Nidal walked quickly into the bathroom and slammed the door shut. A million unanswered questions came to my mind. I felt faint. I put my hands up against the wall to support my body and tried to calm my beating heart before it burst from pain. I could still feel his burning lips on mine and his hands on my body. Imprints of his lovemaking were marked on my skin, proving to me that I was not dreaming. This was real. My blood was still in heat, my hands were shaking, and my heart was breaking.

What did I say that made him upset? Did he not want me to love him? Was he still mad at me for accepting a kiss from his cousin? How dare he drag me here, start making love to me, and then push me away like that! He never once considered my feelings! Today was all about him! He is conceited! Does he ever stop to even wonder how I am feeling? How I am hurting?

Fuming, I walked over to the bathroom and swung open the door. He had some explaining to do, but as I looked in the bathroom, Nidal was standing with his back turned to me, just staring at the wall.

"Nidal ... Nidal ... Nidal."

He ignored me.

I stepped a few feet closer to him and whispered, "Nidal."

Nidal turned around slowly, and his face looked tormented. "Explain yourself," I said.

He walked up to me in two strides and grabbed me by the shoulders. "Why did you lie to me?"

How ironic! After begging me for months to love him, when I finally feel the love he always craved, I tell him, and he has trouble believing me. He has no reason to doubt me. My heart belongs to him and him alone.

He was staring deep into my eyes. I knew he was waiting for an answer. Slowly, the tears in his eyes rolled down his beautiful face.

I looked up at him and whispered, "I love you."

He pulled back and, in a voice that sounded full of anguish, told me, "Do not lie to me. Tell me the truth."

I looked into his tormented, blue eyes and said softly, "I love you, Nidal." And I wiped the tears from his face. "I remember a day not too long ago when you told me that you could not live without me. I understand now what that means, for I too cannot live without you, Nidal." I told him, praying that he would believe that I speak the truth.

Finally, I saw the muscles on his face relax. He took me into his arms and kissed me tenderly. I tasted the salty tears that rolled down his face and onto his lips. I pushed my body onto his, letting him know that I also wanted him as much as he wanted me.

My prince lifted me up in his arms and walked over to the bed, where he gently dropped me on the mattress, and then he lay down next to me and took me in his arms again. We lay there, just staring into each other's eyes. Both of us had tears that threatened to spill over a river and drown us with love.

I understand now. It is simple. My prince wants to be sure of my love for him before he gives himself to me.

We stayed up all night talking. He had a million questions he wanted to ask me, and I also wanted some questions answered. I wanted to know every thought that occupied his mind. I thought I knew him well, but I was wrong. *I would spend the rest of my life, if I had to, to find out everything that lies in his heart.*

I desperately need to hear from his mouth that he desires me as much as I desire him. "Nidal, if you love me as much as you claim you do, then why do you hesitate to make love to me? Is there something wrong with the way I look? Am I not woman enough for you?" I asked, and I pulled away from him and looked up into his handsome face.

Nidal's eyes blazed with passion as he pulled me back into his embrace. "You think I don't desire you?" he asked hoarsely, as he pushed his body on mine. I felt his huge manhood piercing my thigh and electricity shot throughout my entire body. "Loula," he whispered, and he closed his eyes. I held my breath as I waited for him to speak. When Nidal opened his eyes, his hold tightened, and he sighed. "I want nothing more then to make love to you, but I will not, because I do not think it is the right time yet. I need to be 100 percent sure that you are ready for me." He said softly.

"You think I am not ready? I have never been more ready in my whole entire life then I am at this very moment, Nidal." I said, hopeful that he would believe me.

Nidal searched in my eyes for the truth. A few seconds later, he sighed, and said, "You are not ready, Loula. I have waited for you for too many years to act on lust alone. I need more from you and I can tell you are not ready yet. After waiting for you all my life, Loula, one more day won't kill me, but not waiting and rushing things will." He stopped for a brief second so I could comprehend what he was telling me. *I cannot believe I wasted all these years living without him, meeting all the wrong people, and not once thinking of this beautiful soul.*

Nidal's beautiful face inched closer to mine. I can feel his breath on my face. I am dizzy with want for him. I need him badly. Does he not realize this?

"I can tell you do not understand my explanation, Loula, which only proves to me that I am right. You are not ready for me. I have waited for you practically my entire life. I could not erase your image from my mind. I could not even kiss another without feeling as if I had betrayed you. I need for you to understand my feelings for you. It is very important to me that when I make love to you, your feelings will be as mine are for you. I will accept nothing less," he said passionately.

Wow! Unbelievable. Who loves like that? So many women are in this country, beautiful women who would die just to spend one single night with my prince, and he chose me. I can't even comprehend it. It is above and beyond human nature. How can a beautiful man like this remain a virgin for all these years, waiting for me?

"Nidal, if you love me as strongly as you say that you do, then how can you keep yourself from making love to me? Do you not feel an urge to have sex?" I asked.

"It is not without great difficulty that I refrain from making love to you, Loula." Nidal lowered his eyes and sighed. "I have mastered my thoughts and feelings, and know how to handle the situation when need be."

"Then please tell me how you are able to do that, so I too can do the same, because I am suffering from need for you and know not what to do," I said.

"I masturbate, Loula," he whispered, and his eyes were blazing with fire as he looked at me.

Fire shot throughout my entire body as I struggled to lay still. With trembling hands I cupped his beautiful face and said, "Nidal, all these years, why have you not taken to your bed a woman to fulfill your sexual desires?" and as soon as I said those words, jealousy consumed me and my heart twisted with pain.

"Would you prefer I do that next time, Loula?" he asked me, with a hint of a smile on his face as he waited for a response. His words were like a knife in my heart and I tried to wiggle out of his embrace, but he tightened his hold on me and threw his leg over my body and I was trapped. Not knowing what to do and feeling frustrated, I started to cry.

"Don't cry, Loula. I do not have any desire to sleep with any other woman besides you. I have never betrayed you and I never will," he said, his voice husky with passion, as he placed butterfly kisses across my face and down my neck.

I tried to understand his feelings for me. *Why would he do this for me? Who am I? I am not unique. Why does he insist on having me when he can choose any other woman in the world?*

I looked deep into his eyes for answers. The eyes are the windows of one's soul. He was not the only one with trust issues. I also couldn't believe all this, but all I saw in his eyes was love, adoration, and complete and total submission.

I felt his shaft swollen against my thigh. Every fiber in my body came to life. I was aching for him to take me and make me his. I needed Nidal to claim what belonged to him. My body was on fire, and it was desperately thirsty for his touch, but I knew that tonight was not the night.

I closed my eyes and pretended to sleep. He pulled me closer, and I could feel his hold on me relax. I could not understand how he was able to tame his body to lie next to mine with such ease when my body was aching to be touched by him. Thankfully, sometime in the peaceful night, I fell asleep.

In the morning, the sun splashed its bright light across the room. The window was slightly open, and a delicate, warm breeze softly teased my skin. I could hear the birds chirping cheerfully outside and the horses snorting and chasing each other while the people of Arabia went about their daily business.

I opened my eyes and saw my prince resting his head on his elbow, looking down at me tenderly. I wanted him so desperately that I slipped my fingers through his hair and pulled his head, bringing his lips down to mine.

Without warning, lust unleashed itself inside my entire body as heat exploded furiously, bursting with fire, and consumed all my senses. Nidal lifted my nightgown up over my breast, and his eyes burned with desire as they drifted over my breast and down my belly. He made a strangled sound as his hands glided up my thigh. Skillfully, his fingers worked their magic, sending electric shock waves throughout my entire body.

He scattered scorching kisses over my breast, and I trembled in his arms. My hands traced the outline of his body and found his enlarged bulge that was pressing against my thigh. I slipped my hand inside his undergarment and grabbed it. Immediately, Nidal froze, and in that instant, my world came crashing down.

Embarrassed once again, I looked up at him, questioning his behavior. In answer, he gently pushed me away and quickly jumped out of bed. I looked hungrily at his tall, lean body. Nidal walked slowly to the chair in the corner where his shirt lay, grabbed it, and put it on. With trembling hands, he struggled to button his shirt. His accusing gaze never once left my sight. His huge muscles threatened to rip the very shirt he wore as he bent over and grabbed his pantaloons from the floor.

Embarrassed out of my mind, I quickly threw the covers over my head to hide in the dark, and I tugged my nightgown all the way down to hide my shameless body. Maybe we could ignore what just happened for the sake of my sanity, but my body betrayed me. It was aroused and still shaking from the aftermath. These sexual feelings were new to me, and I knew not how to turn them off.

I peeked outside the covers just as my prince was finished dressing, and he smiled down at me wickedly. The look on his face said, "I'm going to make you pay for all the years I waited for you." I could tell that he knew what I was feeling, and he was going to let me suffer. That was not fair. He needed me to give him a taste of his own medicine. I threw back the covers, but not before I untied the lace from the nightgown that I was wearing. My left breast escaped playfully outside my gown, teasing the eyes of my prince, who just stood there frozen in time, staring at me. His smile now disappeared as lust took over. He looked like a wolf licking his chops. My right breast was exposed in the direct view

11

of the sunlight, and I took my time getting out of bed, pretending I had no idea what was happening.

From the corner of my eyes, I could see cold sweat on my prince's forehead as he swallowed hard. And I looked down and saw his bulge ready to burst the seams of his pantaloons. *Good! Let him suffer too. He deserves it!*

I marched into the bathroom and closed the door hard, causing an echoing sound to penetrate throughout the room. *Now what? What do I do now?*

And that was when I noticed the keyhole, and I peeked through it just in time to witness Nidal slam his fist into the closet door behind him, creating a hole the size of his fist. I winced, knowing the pain his hand must be feeling. I could tell it was throbbing.

At that moment, a servant knocked on the door, "Master, is everything all right?"

"Everything is fine," Nidal said gruffly, and he slid down in the chair that was against the wall, and dropped his face into his hands. I do not know if he is angry or just trying to kill the pain on his hand.

He got what he deserved! I was also in pain. My body ached from wanting him so badly. He made it happen, and then he punished me for it. *I feel so embarrassed. Humiliated!*

These feelings coming to life inside me were new to me. I did not know the ways of lovemaking. I was a virgin as well, and I felt as if my body had just betrayed me.

At that moment, the queen burst open the door to our room and marched in. Nidal quickly stood and walked over to her. He adored his mother, the only other woman he had ever loved. She was elegantly dressed in pink from head to toe, very fashionable in her gown. Her hair was swept up in an updo, showing off a beautiful pair of pink diamond earrings that dangled from her ears. She had a slender neck and striking facial features that resembled her son's. She was clearly an aristocrat and a very beautiful lady, even at her age.

Nidal took her hands in his and kissed them. The queen smiled up at him, "Where's Loula?" she asked, as her gaze swept across the room. Nidal remained silent. She pulled away from him and gracefully walked to the door, and turned around and said sternly, "I hate to tell you I told you so, but I did warn you, Nidal. Anyhow, lunch will be served in half an hour. Do not be late. You know how that irritates your father."

Nidal's jaw tensed up for a second, but he quickly ignored the comment and looked toward the bathroom. When the queen left the room, Nidal checked to make sure the door was locked. He walked over to the bathroom and tried to open it but could not because I had locked it. He banged on it a few times, and then he sharply threatened, "Open this door now, Loula, before I break it down!"

Knowing he makes good on his threats, I quickly opened the door, but I was not about to let him off that easy. So I played his game. Nidal's eyes appraised me from head to toe. He looked so darn sexy. I had to control myself before I did something foolish.

Nidal swallowed nervously and said, "I am going to the dining room. Come immediately. Do not be late!" His tone was cold.

I will not let him rule me. I am not his slave. I will take my time and make them all wait for my arrival.

I was very careful with my appearance, choosing a low-cut gown that revealed a small amount of cleavage. The gown, a soft brown satin, darkened my skin tone, giving the illusion that I was tanned. I let my hair down, and it dropped to my waist. I pinched my cheeks to bring some color to them, and when I glanced in the mirror, the lady who looked back at me appeared very sexy. Satisfied with the results, I slipped my feet into my silk slip-ons and hurriedly flew across the great hall.

I joined them in the dining room a few minutes later. The conversation stopped automatically as the guards opened the double doors and I walked in. The dining room was a beautiful room with elegant tapestries on all four walls, candle chandeliers hanging from the cathedral ceiling, and silk curtains that draped around the French windows. The dining table was a shiny, black cherrywood that could easily seat fifty guests, and its matching chairs were beautifully carved with an elegant flower design. The silverware was sterling silver, and the water goblets were made of fine crystal, as well as the wineglasses. A lavish Oriental carpet covered the marble floor. But then I did not expect anything less from royalty.

Everyone, except for Billal, was looking at me. He looked the opposite way. He sported a black eye. I could tell there was a lot of tension between him and my prince. Every gentleman at the dining table stood, and I walked over to my seat, which was next to Nidal's. I waited for the servant to push my chair in, and after I sat down, all the men sat too.

Everyone greeted me with a smile and a hello, except for Billal. He did not say one word to me. *How absurd! He isn't allowed to talk to me, yet he sits at the table with us. I will never understand the customs and traditions of Arabia.*

I glanced sideways at Nidal, and I could tell he was angry at his cousin's presence in the room. I lowered my gaze to his lap, and I saw Nidal clenching his fists. I just wanted all this to stop. Nidal's jealousy needed to stop. His actions were embarrassing the palace, and it was putting a strain on the crown. The king had already warned him to check his behavior.

This was not an intimate affair. I thought lunch would be a little less formal than this, but I was wrong. Altogether, twenty-five of us were sitting down for lunch. They all pretended to eat, but I caught the guests stealing glances at the prince and myself. The queen was staring at me too. I knew she disapproved of my presence in the palace. She had never smiled at me. She had never spoken to me, not once. She simply ignored my existence.

I had lost my appetite. I just wanted to get through this, excuse myself, and run to the safety of my room, where no one could see the pain I was feeling in my heart and the tears about to form in my eyes. I could seclude myself there in privacy and not be under the constant scrutiny of these people who already prejudged me unfairly.

The servants were taking their time serving us the six-course meal. The main course was duck served with red wine sauce, and there were roasted potatoes and three different kinds of vegetables. All this food was mouthwatering, and I was famished, having skipped breakfast.

Everyone ate in silence. No one dared say a word. Finally, the queen broke the silence, and asked the man sitting opposite her, "Have you ever visited the gardens? The flowers are in full bloom this time of year," she said sweetly.

The man just stared at her for a split second. Tiny balls of sweat formed on his balding head, as he was trying to decide if that were a trick question or if she truly favored his response. He decided it was the latter. Relieved, he quickly answered with a fake smile, "No, my queen, I have never seen the garden in all its glory, but would look forward to doing just that after we are finished with lunch."

Again, there was silence as the guests finished the last of their meal. The servants cleaned up the table and brought out the pastries and tea. The guests chimed in conversations again, and all spoke almost at the same time. The tension was gone, there was laughter and smiles, and everyone was drinking tea and having a good time. Even Nidal's tone was neutral, but he had a smile that was as dangerous as a cobra waiting to bite. His blue eyes had darkened as he glanced across the table at his cousin Billal.

He stole a side glance at me. His eyes were empty and sad. I looked away quickly. Tension was in the room again. Everyone's laughter broke off abruptly when all witnessed the look that Nidal had thrown me. It was suddenly very quiet in the room again, and it seemed like a lifetime later when the king quickly muttered something and everyone at the table picked up their conversation where they had left off.

I saw the queen take a deep breath and sigh as she gazed at her son and me with a disapproving glare. I felt so uncomfortable at the way she conducted herself. It was not fair that she judged me so. I felt a wave of sadness, and I wished things could have been different. I wanted to befriend the queen. We both loved Nidal, and it would be to both our benefit if we tried to be civil to each other.

At that moment, Nidal took my hand in his, and I looked up surprised and saw him staring blankly at the guests. He probably wasn't even aware of what he was doing. The fine lines on his face relaxed now, and he almost looked like he was having a good time. With his fingers, Nidal gently caressed my hand. His light touch felt warm on my skin, and I started wishing that things were different and that he was not a prince with a million responsibilities, but just another man who lived a simple life, a commoner who could come and go as he pleased. People thought the prince was born to a life of privilege, but they did not know that Nidal was a slave to his crown.

I stared at the wineglass that was sitting in front of me. I dared not look up. Billal was sitting almost across from where I sat, and I did not want Nidal to accuse me of glaring at his cousin. Nor did I want Nidal to punch Billal in the face again. So my eyes stayed glued to the crystal glass as I waited patiently for this fiasco to be over with and we could both be excused.

As the minutes ticked away, Nidal continued to playfully caress my hand. A second later, I felt his thigh brush up lightly against my thigh, and his hold on my hand tightened. I looked up and saw him looking down at me. Nidal stared deep into my eyes with passion or, one could say lust. I could feel my body temperature rise just thinking of what Nidal had in mind for me upon our return to our chambers.

It suddenly felt stuffy in the room. I needed some fresh air. Just then, Nidal stood and gently pulled me to my feet. He excused the both of us and pulled me along his side and out into the corridor from the side door. I could still feel the eyes of all the guests on my back as they all tried to guess what was about to happen to me as I disappeared from their view.

Nidal swiftly pulled me along, down the hallway, and into our chamber, where he closed the door behind us and scooped me into his arms, laying a wet kiss on my neck with trembling lips. Fire shot up my breast and down my spine. He had the power to turn me on as quickly as a snake bites its next victim. Only instead of venom, honey poured out of his mouth and sweetened my soul.

Dizzy with passion, I did not resist his lovemaking. Instead, I got drunk from it as he brought me closer to him, and I once again felt his bulge pressing against my womanhood. I knew he was just as much aroused as I was. In that instant, I relaxed my back and arched into total submission. He could do what he wanted to me, and I would allow it. I had no control of my senses. My heart was pounding a thousand times a second, and I thought I would burst into tears of joy.

Somewhere far away, I heard pounding on the door, but I was oblivious to reality as Nidal's kisses burned my lips. But the pounding on the door got even louder, and Nidal pulled away from me with a groan and asked angrily, "Who is it?"

There was no answer, so he opened the door to see for himself who would dare interrupt us at such a moment. A servant was standing outside and looked scared out of his mind. My heart went out to him as he nervously said, "The king wants you to visit his quarters hastily."

Nidal pushed the door and closed it in the servant's face, terrifying the poor soul even more. Nidal looked at me with an apologetic smile. With trembling hands, I ran my fingers through my long black hair and looked down at my toes so he would not notice how disappointed I was.

Nidal softly caressed my face and gently lifted my chin, and our eyes locked. No words were necessary at this moment. It was plain and simple. We both wanted to pick up where we left off, but we knew that was impossible. When the king gave orders, he did not like to wait. My prince whispered his love for me and quickly exited the room. Left all alone, I felt goose bumps all over my trembling body.

I wondered what would have happened if we were not interrupted. I knew I would have allowed Nidal to do what he wanted to me, but would he have done just that? I would never know the answer to that now. I felt cheated from the truth. A feeling of loneliness overcame me, and I tried to keep my emotions in check as I looked around the room for a comfort zone. It was such a huge room, and it was so elegantly decorated with its French couches and lavish Oriental rugs, beautiful silk curtains that trimmed the French windows, and crystal vases and bed linens imported from Italy. It seemed as if this room represented the whole world with all this beauty, but even though all this was breathtakingly beautiful, I could not appreciate anything. *They are just material things. Nidal is all I need to be happy.*

I changed into my nightgown and lay in bed with thoughts of Nidal on my mind. I dozed off, and when I next opened my eyes, the room was dark. *How many hours have I slept?*

I spread my arm across the bed, only to find that part of the bed empty and cold. I longed for Nidal's return. *What is so important that the king keeps the prince away from me for so long?* My thoughts went back to the way Nidal had kissed me a few hours ago, and my mind was spinning out of control.

A few moments later, the door opened and closed softly. I heard Nidal's distinctive light footsteps in the dark. He came to me at last. I pretended to be sleeping as I heard him walk toward the bathroom. Minutes later, he slipped quietly into bed besides me, and gently pulled me close to him. I had never felt more at home than at this transcendent moment. Peace settled in my heart. I knew that I could not live without him. He was my whole world, and I knew without a doubt that the feeling was mutual.

With his arms around me, Nidal snuggled close to me and whispered, "I love you." That made a hundred and one times that he had said it to me today. I smiled happily and surrendered to every whisper I ever heard from him. *I am so in love with this man. Nidal's love has affected me to a point where I am addicted, and I cannot survive without him.*

I wanted to tell him that I also loved him, but he would not—could not—believe me yet. But as I dozed off, I promised myself that I would make it my life's mission to do what it took to show Nidal that I too loved him as deeply as he loved me.

When I woke up the next day, my sleeping prince held me tightly. It was my turn to lie in bed and stare at him. All night, I kept waking up as his fingers softly and lightly touched my skin. He knew every inch of my body better than I did. He searched all night trying to find a spot he had not claimed yet. He was marking his territory.

Sleeping now, he looked powerless. He was breathing softly without a single wrinkle creasing his beautiful face. A slight smile was on his face as he lay there peacefully in bliss. I stole a quick glance under the covers and saw his shaft. It was huge and ready. *Is he dreaming of me or some Arabian princess?*

Jealousy ate at me as I snuggled closer to him, holding on to him and staking my claim on this beautiful man. *He is mine. All mine.*

I could not help myself, and I peeked one more time under the covers and groaned at the delightful sight. As I looked up, I found Nidal glaring down at me with an amused smile on his face. My face turned beet red with embarrassment. *Why did I allow my eyes to travel so much? What was I thinking?*

I did not want to get my prince mad again, but as I looked at his face again, I saw raw lust there. His eyes looked as if they turned a darker shade of blue. His hands tightened around my waist, and he pulled me up on top his hot, already aroused body. I felt his shaft pushing against my thigh, his hands squeezing me closer, and his mouth reached hungrily and trailed kisses down my neck.

Nidal pulled the nightgown off my body and flipped me on my back. His lips were demanding, his embrace was possessive and strong, and when he leaned his hips against mine, desire shuddered through me so intensely that a moan escaped through my lips. Nidal grabbed my breasts, stroking them gently and playfully in his hands. His lips worked their way to them as his tongue skillfully worked magic, teasing my nipples until they were hard as a rock. I heard him take a sharp inhalation of breath as he hungrily buried his face in my breast. His hands glided up my thigh and ignited a liquid fire within me so intense that it exploded inside me and traveled throughout my entire body, like hot lava escaping from a volcano. Losing all my senses and shaking uncontrollably, I called out his name in a voice I did not even recognize as my own.

Nidal made a strangled sound before his lips came crashing down on mine. His hands skillfully burned my skin with passion. With my hands, I also explored places I had never before touched. Nidal's sculpted, naked, warrior body trembled beside me as he whispered what he wanted to do to me, and finally he shifted his body on top of mine. His breathing sounded harsh, and I felt the thundering of his heartbeat against my breast. I was trembling with desire. He kissed me savagely. And with one plunge, he broke the barrier, claiming me his forever as he pushed deep within me. Nidal stopped for a brief second, waiting for the pain to subside. I could see in his eyes how it pleased him that he was the first to take my maidenhood. Then, unleashing all his emotions, Nidal lost all control and dug deeper and deeper until I trembled in his arms. He hoarsely called out my name as he rode me with wild passion to a point of no return. His husky voice mingled with my sweet cries. He spoke in his rich, husky Arabian tongue as he came, shuddering in my arms so intensely that it took my breath away.

I was totally and passionately in love with him. Wrapping my arms around Nidal, I never wanted to let him go. He was mine. I was his. We were now one. Complete. We were oblivious to anything outside of our lovemaking. We looked hungrily into each other's eyes, and at that moment, we both understood that we could never be without each other ever again. Together or nothing, that was what our eyes said. And that was how it shall be from this moment forward.

I traced the soft skin of his solid, muscled back. Nidal held me in his strong embrace as he lovingly stared deep into my soul. I was lost for words. He fell sideways on the bed, still holding me closely, and softly whispered words of endearment. And then suddenly he asked with a tortured and trembling voice, "Do you love me?"

Love him?

I answered simply yes.

How can he question my love for him after what we had just shared?

I saw adoration in his eyes at that moment, and he looked as if he were about to say something but changed his mind. Words were not needed anymore as he yanked me against his body and his lips once again claimed mine hungrily and sweetly took what had always belonged to him. I wrapped my hand around his shaft and immediately desire slammed through him, and I heard a husky sound rumble deep in his throat as he slid his knee between my legs, opened them apart, and savagely plunged into me, unleashing all his male strength inside me once again.

We moved together in the same rhythm. Hot passion swept us to a place either of us had ever gone to before, a new place of understanding each other's body as we do our own. I rode with him. It even felt like a new adventure this time around. I dug my nails in his back as I cried with passion.

At that moment, I thought I heard something, but I was so involved in our lovemaking that I hardly noticed the queen open the bedroom door and stare at us wide-eyed with embarrassment. She quickly closed the door as she went running down the hallway in astonishment. Nidal's eyes opened wide, and he asked, bewildered, if someone had just entered our room, but judging from my facial expression, he guessed the truth and mouthed the word "fuck." I, of course, thought it was funny because I had never heard him swear before while I was naked in his arms and having the queen walk in on us like that. I wondered why Nidal never locked the door and why people just entered private rooms without waiting for permission.

This was just too hilarious. My laughter got a little out of control, and Nidal joined the fun. And there we both were, laying on the bed, naked and spent, and laughing to tears, until I heard the big *boom, bang, kaboom*. I froze and stared questionably at Nidal, who looked at me, and then looked away and buried his face in his pillow.

What is all that noise? It sounded like someone had thrown a bomb. Terrified, I snuggled in Nidal's arms, trembling as the rippling noise turned louder and louder. I glanced at Nidal, and he quickly explained, "The servants fired the cannons. They are letting the people of Arabia know that we have consummated our union." He said this as if it were a normal thing to say. I stared wide-eyed in astonishment at him, not understanding a single word he had just muttered.

What in the world is he talking about? Letting his people know what? That we just had sex? Wide-eyed, I stared at him. *Is he crazy?*

While the rest of the world's history books wrote about the wars won and lost, the sacrifices, and the history of their countries, the Arabian world would have a section in their history books of our lovemaking.

"Loula, our union is a big deal to my people, and it is our custom and tradition to celebrate with a festive party out in the streets of Arabia. There will be food, wine, and dancing all night." He stopped for a brief second to see my reaction to all that he had told me before continuing. "They will also explode fireworks in the night sky. It is the way my people celebrate their future king's happiness, Loula," he said quietly, as he studied my face.

I stared at him wide-eyed, not knowing what to say. *All that just because the prince lost his virginity today?*

I wiggled out of his embrace and made a face in his direction, not understanding their customs or their traditions. Nidal's hand cupped my breast and softly caressed it. I tensed and slapped away his hand. I did not feel comfortable sharing my intimate relationship with the rest of the world.

It sure sucked being in love with a prince, I thought dryly.

Nidal must have noticed the hurtful expression on my face. "Don't worry. Just go with it, and all will be fine."

Well, that's what I should tell him next time his cousin kisses me. I will look at him sweetly and say innocently, "Oh, don't worry, honey. Just go with it."

But even the thought of his cousin anywhere near me sounded dreadful. Nidal would react wildly, so I had to quickly erase that thought.

As the day flew by, everyone was bustling about while getting ready for the party. The festivities had started a couple of hours ago. I could hear the music loud and clear from my open window, and I grew nervous wondering if at last the people of this country would accept me. I wondered what the queen's thoughts were about all this. *Is she secretly planning a way to get rid of me, or has she decided to welcome me into her family?*

As I dressed for the occasion, I felt humiliated and distressed and hoped my patience would be intact when the time came for me to step out of my comfort zone. It would not be easy walking around with a smile on my face knowing full well what the celebration was all about.

With shaky hands, I slipped into a gold-colored gown. It was a beautiful, shimmering, soft material with beaded lace trimmings, and it had a low neckline that showed off a little more cleavage than necessary. I checked myself in the mirror, and I had to admit that I looked absolutely beautiful.

My hair was in an updo with tiny little ringlets of soft curls falling delicately around my face. Earlier in the day, a servant had brought me a small tiara made of diamonds and said the queen had ordered that I wear it tonight. I wondered if it were sent as a peace offering. I hoped it was, because I really wanted the queen to like me. It would make my life a little less stressful if she did.

My personal maid was an expert with hair, as she finished the updo with expertise, and at last, she placed the diamond tiara on top of my head. She smiled at me, and I saw how pleased she was with the results. I thanked her as she bowed and happily headed out the door.

I slipped into my glass slippers and stood carefully, holding on to the chair, lest I fall flat on my face. The heels were a dab too high. Nidal was not around. He was dressing in another part of the palace, and I was glad. I wanted to surprise him with my appearance, knowing he would be pleased with the results.

I checked myself one more time in front of the mirror, and I really liked what I saw. I looked different with the tiara on my head. I almost looked like royalty. I smiled because I knew that material things could never change me into a different person. With or without the headpiece, I would always be Loula. *I do not seek the crown. I do not need to be living like royalty to be happy. All I need is Nidal. He is the only one who can make me feel complete.*

I swirled once around, and my gown wrapped around my legs. Then the shimmering material fell elegantly to the floor, covering my glass slippers. I loved this gown. It was one of my favorites, and my overall appearance was very satisfying, but I realized I was not wearing any jewelry to complement my wardrobe. I reached over to the dresser where my jewelry box lay on top, and I opened it. All my jewels sparkled like stars in the night sky. They were all gifts from Nidal. He had showered me with diamonds, emeralds, sapphires, and rubies. A king's ransom! I sighed sadly.

Nidal has not yet realized that these jewels mean nothing to me. They are just costly trinkets that are beautiful to look at. They are not what I crave. I never longed for such treasures. All I want is to be Nidal's bride. That is enough to make me happy in this lifetime, but I will wear the diamond necklace with its matching bracelet just to please Nidal.

I also clasped on the diamond earrings that Nidal had given me, saying they once belonged to his deceased grandmother. I had heard many stories of her and felt sad that I would never meet her. Nidal has told me that she was a philanthropist among many other great things, and it is with great joy that I am wearing something that had once belonged to her.

Now that my outfit was complete, I was ready to go to my prince. I walked toward the door, opened it, and stepped out into the hall. I was also in another part of the palace for the preparations. A large, bearded guard with broad shoulders was waiting for me outside the door. He had a glint in his eyes and a big smile on his face as he proudly took my hand in his and led me down the long, wide, circled staircase. I was nervous with each step that I took. Halfway down, I spotted Nidal. He looked dashing in his uniform, as he looked up at me with a huge smile on his face. I arrived on the last step, and the handsome man took my hand and placed it in Nidal's.

I froze in my tracks, I was so nervous that I thought my legs would turn to jelly and I would fall to the floor. I looked into Nidal's eyes. I tried to focus all my attention on him and pretend that all the other people who stood around the prince were not there. Nidal stared openmouthed at me. He looked stunned, and I heard whispering among the huge crowd as they also looked at me with approval. Nidal could not take his eyes off me. His eyes displayed so much love and passion. Tears of joy were in my eyes as Nidal took my hand and helped me down the last step.

My prince stared hungrily at the cleavage of my dress, and as he looked up at me, a twinkle in his eyes told me he was already thinking of later on tonight in our bed. I smiled, looked around the room at everyone, and bowed to them. The people of Arabia bowed back to me, and then they started clapping their approval. I looked quickly at the queen, and I thought I saw a smile on her face. I noticed that even the king looked pleasantly pleased, and Nidal, my handsome prince, looked dashing with his long, lean body clad in king's attire and all his medals hanging loose on his jacket. A crown was on his head, and truly, he looked like the next king of Arabia. He looked the role. Now he had to play the role.

His blue eyes were bright as ever on this festive day, and he was all mine. I could not wait for tonight. I just wanted to be in his arms. I sighed deeply, knowing it would be many hours before I could enjoy his naked body on mine. I loved him so much. As if Nidal read my thoughts, he winked at me, letting me know that he was also thinking the same thing as I was.

My prince led me through the crowd, as they all spread apart and opened a path for us to walk through. My prince and I stepped outside where there must have been thousands upon thousands patiently waiting for our appearance. Nidal took my hand in his and raised it in the air, showing everyone that I was his choice of a bride. Suddenly everyone was applauding and cheering loudly. Rose petals were thrown at us as we walked down the stairs outside the long stairway toward the people.

I was overwhelmed. Nidal noticed and held me tight. The cheering grew louder and louder. The fireworks started as everyone stared and cheered. *What a night this is going to be.*

Little, wide-eyed children walked up to me, reached over, and handed me flowers. Hundreds of children were forming a circle around us, and they started singing a song. Soon the huge crowd sang along with them, and I looked up at Nidal. He was staring down at me with such love, adoration to be exact. I swallowed, not knowing what to say.

This welcome and acceptance I was receiving from the people of Arabia, Nidal's people, touched me. It was easy to see that they loved their prince as he stood proudly and bowed to the crowd. The people clapped thunderously and cheered loudly with tears of joy that, at last, the prince had brought a wife to them: a princess, their future queen. Finally, they accepted me, and I was overwhelmed with joy.

The fun had begun. There was dancing in the streets, and fires were ablaze everywhere as the cooks roasted lambs on spits. The mouthwatering aroma traveled in the air, making everyone a victim of hunger. There was wine, and everyone was drinking to our health, or so they said. It was a merry night. I looked up and saw the stars twinkle in the dark sky, as if they also danced to the song of approval. It was an unforgettable night.

Nidal never let go of my hand as we walked around the streets greeting everyone. The people were so kind to me. Their acceptance touched my heart. Nidal stopped and talked with everyone we encountered. He was genuinely happy, and his smile made his face glow with the love he felt for his people. I was so proud of him. My heart swelled with happiness.

Sometime later into the night, after we were stuffed with delicious food and wine and had greeted about a million people, I felt exhausted, but Nidal asked me to dance with him. I could not deny him this. My handsome prince swirled me around the dance floor as all the onlookers applauded. I was getting a little dizzy, so I rested my head on his shoulders. Nidal pulled my body closer to his. The music slowed down. The song they were playing was slow and sensual, and we moved to the rhythm of the music, relaxing in each other's arms.

Nidal's lips touched my neck, kissing me softly, and I felt goose bumps go up and down my spine. I closed my eyes and lost myself in his arms.

Nidal squeezed me tight, and when I looked up at him, he leaned down and whispered hoarsely, "Loula, you are torturing me with that look. Let's disappear for a few hours. I need you now."

I kissed his lips in response, not caring who saw us. He pulled me closer to him, and I could feel his groin rubbing against my thigh. I closed my eyes, and his lips softly brushed mine.

"Please, Loula," he begged.

His hold tightened even more, and I completely lost my senses and almost fell to the ground. I was overwhelmed with love for this man, and I was not able to deny him a single thing. I wanted to disappear with my prince. I was also aching to lie next to him naked and feel his body touching mine. Just the thought of this made me crazy.

Just then, the king walked up to us and demanded I dance with him as he put out his hand for me to take it. I looked up at Nidal, and he nodded and released me from his grip. I walked over to the king, and he took me in his arms and whisked me away from my prince and onto the middle of the dance floor, giving the onlookers something to gossip about.

I could see Nidal from where I danced, and he did not look too happy that his father had taken me away from him. The king and I danced for a while before he passed me on to his men. They all took a turn with me on the dance floor, and I knew Nidal was upset. The cold look in his eyes gave him away. His eyes never once left mine. I knew he felt tortured watching me. He looked frozen as he stood there alone, watching and thinking with a moody expression on his face and hands stiff at his sides. He was ready at any moment to whisk me away from everyone.

If he could hide me away in a bottle and keep me to himself, that is exactly what he would do. He is that obsessed, and the funny part is that I would love every second of it.

The gentleman I was now dancing with, who was much shorter than I was, turned me around and was trying to keep up pace with the steps to the dance. My eyes traveled to where Nidal stood. I saw him sigh with distress as he motioned for me to come to him. So I smiled sweetly at the nice gentleman and pulled away.

I walked to Nidal, and I saw a sign of relief on his beautiful face. He exhaled as he pulled me into his arms and squeezed me hard. His lips tasted of wine. I could feel his heart beat rapidly. I looked up into his face, and the look he gave me said only one thing. We both knew what we had to do next as we hurriedly walked up the pavement away from all the people and noise and headed toward the palace.

Nidal lifted me up sideways and half-walked, half-ran up the stairs as bystanders stood there watching us with disbelief. He ignored all the greetings from his people as we passed them by, and finally when we reached the top of the stairs to the palace,

Nidal put me down and pulled me by the hand. The music seemed far away as we turned down the corridor and ran to our chamber. I was pulled into his arms and kissed so tenderly that I lost control of my senses.

The door flew open, and we entered our room. Nidal kicked the door shut. He threw me against the wall and kissed me with such passion. His hands were feeling my body up and down, reassuring himself that I still belonged to him. He moaned and groaned, and his passion leeched out, so violent and passionate, that I lost control as I was swept in this circle of lust with him.

With trembling hands, he unbuttoned my gown. As it fell to the floor, he was surprised to see that I wore no undergarments. I was stark naked. Nidal went crazy. He moaned as he pushed me hard against the wall, and at that moment, he lost all reason with reality. I could not keep up with him anymore. I was in total submission in his arms. All this passion inside me awakened and threatened to explode into a thousand pieces. I took control of myself and grabbed his pantaloons with trembling fingers, feeling for the strings. I pulled it, and it fell to the floor. I reached in his underpants and felt his shaft, huge and hot. I was ready for what was about to come next. At that moment, Nidal froze, grabbed my hand, and pushed it away from him.

With pleading in his eyes, he whispered painfully, "Don't."

I felt as if a ton of bricks had come crashing down on me. Nidal pulled back with a hurt look on his face. I was stunned. My chest felt tight. My hands were still trembling, and my lips still felt bruised from his lovemaking as I repeated his words that echoed from my lips.

"Don't? Don't what?"

His words baffled me. I looked up at him, questioning his behavior. He sat there helpless like a lovesick puppy, just looking at me with pleading eyes to understand what he was feeling. I could not—did not—understand. He looked tortured. *This man sucks the very life out of me.*

29

There was silence as I waited. He could not speak. He tried a few times and stopped. It was difficult for him to express himself at this very moment. He closed his eyes and squeezed them tightly. Minutes went by in utter silence, and then his eyes opened. He had that look again, the one that looked deep into my soul. His eyes watered up. I braced myself. I thought I knew what he was about to say, but my thoughts had been going a little crazy. I was standing here right in front of a man with no clothes on, a man with a hard-on that doesn't ever go away. I tried to take my eyes off it and look up into his face. He still had the same facial expression, a mixture of love and pain.

By this time, I was feeling cold standing naked, leaning against the stone wall, and waiting for Nidal to decide what he wanted to say.

Finally, he spoke, "Are you cold?"

I could tell he was concerned. I shook my head in answer, and he put both his hands on the wall, locking me in the middle. He was so tall.

He leaned his head closer to me and whispered softly, "I need to know the truth." Then he came a little closer, near enough that I could feel his warm breath on my face. "I need to know if you feel the same for me as I feel for you. It is very important to me to know the truth, Loula." He whispered in a soft voice, "I want to make love to you only if you feel the same way as I do. If you do not feel the same way, then I prefer to wait until you do." He spoke in a tortured voice.

He looked incredibly sexy at this very moment. It was hard for me to concentrate. *How could he think I feel anything less than he does? I am totally and crazy in love with him.*

"Loula," he said, frustrated now. "Tell me the truth," he whispered hoarsely. He put both his hands on my shoulders and pulled me closer to him. "I can't live this way. I need to know now," he said in a tortured voice as he waited again for my answer.

I looked into his eyes and felt the pain there. I knew that, no matter what I said to him, it would not be enough. He was totally insecure. *So where do I start? What do I say?*

"Nidal," I said softly. I looked at him tenderly as he waited for my response. I could tell he was getting nervous. *Is he afraid of my answer?*

I had to say reassuring words to him. I had to choose my words very carefully to make him feel secure with our relationship. Otherwise, he would suffer and act out, and I would have to pay the price. *I do not wish Nidal to be in pain. I want him to be happy. Love is a happy thing, not sad and hurtful.*

"Nidal," I said again, praying he would believe my next words. "I have been in love with you from the first time I saw you ten years ago. I just did not realize it." He was searching my eyes to see if I were telling him the truth. I took his hand and held it. "I feel strong feelings for you, Nidal."

He sighed with relief upon hearing this and waited for me to finish. I could see light in his eyes. They were shinier now. His face relaxed and loosened up, and he lightly put both hands on my waist.

"You are my life now, my heart and my soul. I cannot, even if I wanted to, live without you, Nidal. It is too late. I have reached a point of no return. I love you very much," I told him lovingly.

Nidal lost control, quickly lifted me up in the air, and placed me on his shaft. He took my breath away. He was making love to me standing up, right here by the wall. His hands on my waist were helping my body move up and down. My legs were wrapped around his waist, and I grabbed his hair, pulled his head back, and brought my lips down hard on his. It was an electrifying moment as our bodies trembled in the heat of passion. Instantly, we both reached our peak at the same time, and Nidal was beside himself with lust as he called out my name in his husky voice until he was spent.

I relaxed my chin on his head as he held me tightly, and whispered softly, "I love you."

If all this that we just shared did not confirm to him what we both felt for each other, then all hope was lost. Nidal lifted me gently and placed my feet back on the ground. He took me in his embrace and held me tight to his chest. I knew he was satisfied, and I smiled and relaxed in his arms. It was the most beautiful night of both our lives, a night full of promises and love, an unforgettable night where two souls became one.

Chapter Two
Loula

*D*ays later, I found myself looking out onto the terrace. The gardens were in full bloom, and there was a promise of summer approaching. I had never seen such beauty before. Lush green lawns with roses in all colors had bloomed everywhere. I ran outside joyfully to see all the beauty from a closer point of view. I saw paradise in front of me as a light breeze caressed my face. I closed my eyes, sucked in the fresh air, and just stood there listening to the wind chimes play their seducing music softly as my mind relaxed in meditation mode.

It did not take Nidal long to find me. He quickly hid the worried expression on his face and covered it with a smile. Even after all this time, all the lovemaking, and all the reassuring words we had shared, Nidal still felt insecure. So it was my job to constantly remind him that he was my whole world and there would never be another to take his place ever.

I reached over to him and kissed him tenderly. I saw that light in his eyes that appeared right before he wanted to make love to me. *Why is it never enough for him?* We had sex every night, every morning, and, many times, even in the late afternoons, and still, it was not enough. That worried me because I knew he still felt insecure and that could cause problems in this relationship.

He already had me locked up in his room all day, and when I had the chance to exit the room, he was right behind me within seconds. If I didn't love him so much and understand him the way I did, I would feel suffocated. Nidal pulled me into his grip and kissed me hungrily. Every time he did that, it felt like the very first time. The gardeners were busy watering the lawn, but that did not stop them from glancing over at us.

Nidal was in his own little world, oblivious to anyone or anything around him as he pressed his groin against my womanhood, sending ripples of sensation throughout my entire body. I saw one of the gardeners drop his bucket and stare at us with his mouth agape, and behind him walked a young servant girl holding a basket of vegetables staring bashfully at us. I realized that we had an audience. I quickly pulled away from Nidal, and he gave me a questioning look, just as one of the servants came running to us and announced a visitor.

Princess Shaeena elegantly made her way to us, looking as beautiful as ever. She was dressed in a maroon silk gown that showed off her tiny waist. Her hair was long and flowing. The cascading locks emanated a fragrance in the air. She wore diamond earrings with a matching diamond necklace that sported a teardrop going down her cleavage. With a wicked smile on her lips, she walked right up to Nidal and kissed him on his lips. Nidal tensed as he gently pulled away from her and took hold of my hand, a gesture that did not go unnoticed by the princess. Her smile faded quickly when she looked at me with jealousy written all over her face as she finally acknowledged my presence as well. I smiled sweetly at her, trying to hide my annoyance, but she saw right through me. My prince was unaware of the tension in the air.

The princess joined us for brunch on the queen's insistence, and even though the princess seemed pleasant and gracious, I could see behind her shield. She wanted my Nidal, and she was out to get him. She was waiting for a crack in our relationship for her to jump in, but I was not about to give her that opportunity. I smiled back at her, a grin that spoke a thousand words. She read my smile, and her eyes laughed at me. She was letting me know that she was on the prowl, and I knew she would strike if I turned my back.

After brunch, we went in the tea room. The princess sat between Nidal and the queen. She was smarter than I thought. *I have to really watch my back with this one.*

Conversation was going smoothly, but I was getting restless. I just wanted the princess to leave. She had overstayed her visit. Nidal was oblivious to anything around him. He was in his own little world.

The princess was telling us about the construction of her new sunroom in her palace when suddenly, without a care in the world, she laid her hand idly on Nidal's knee. Nidal tensed as she did this, and he quickly stood and walked over to the French doors, pretending he was observing the rose gardens. I, of course, knew better. He did not want her to touch him, and he knew not what else to do but remove himself without being rude. I sat in the chair across from them, and I did everything in my power not to scratch out her eyes. I contained myself, sporting a fake smile on my face. I knew she saw right through that smile, and she arrogantly smiled back. I was restraining myself out of respect for the queen; otherwise, Princess Shaeena would feel my fist down her throat. This woman brought out the worst in me, a side of me I never knew existed.

When the princess announced that her stay was ending, the queen and I rose from our chairs, and the three of us walked out in the hallway by the huge entranceway. Nidal followed closely behind us. Once again, the princess kissed him on the mouth, and Nidal's eyes swept over to mine. He searched my face, silently begging me for forgiveness. Princess Shaeena hugged the queen, glanced over, and looked at me with ice-cold eyes. A chill ran up and down my spine. I knew at that moment that I had an enemy.

She wanted what belonged to me, and I knew she would stop at nothing to get it. I was not about to let her take my man. I walked up to my prince and made myself cozy in his arms. Nidal automatically wrapped his arms around me and held me tight.

The expression on Princess Shaeena's face was priceless. I almost choked laughing at her. But I took control of myself and smiled good-bye to her with satisfaction. She turned her back and walked gracefully out of the palace. The queen followed after her. I turned and hungrily kissed a startled Nidal, reminding him that he was mine. His response reassured me that I had nothing to worry about.

It was almost time for dinner, and we were still in bed, unable to tear ourselves away from each other. Nidal was playing with my hair when the call from the other side of the door came and announced that dinner would be served in a half hour. Just then, Nidal rested his head on his elbow and looked at me with a smile on his face and a glint in his eyes. He was up to something. I could tell. His hand slid under his pillow, and he pulled out a diamond necklace. It was a magnificent piece, and I stared at it, speechless. Nidal pushed his body up in a sitting position and clasped the diamond necklace around my neck.

"Happy birthday, Loula," he said tenderly.

I looked at him, confused, but then I remembered. It was my birthday, and I had forgotten all about it. "How, pray tell, did you remember my birthday when it never once crossed my mind?" I asked him, surprised.

"I would never forget the day your mother brought such a treasure into the world," Nidal said hoarsely. He claimed my lips one more time.

I pulled away from his embrace. "Please, Nidal, do not tell anyone that today is my birthday. I prefer to share this special day only with you." I hoped he would abide by my wishes, but Nidal's response was another kiss, which took my breath away.

We walked into the dining area with flushed cheeks and sparkling eyes, which was not missed by anyone who sat there looking right at us, as if we had committed a crime. I felt a little uncomfortable, but Nidal never let go of my hand, and that gave me a little comfort. I stole a quick glance across the table at the queen, and she was once again giving me that look of disapproval. My heart sank. Without even realizing it, I tightened my hold on Nidal's hand, and he looked at me concerned, still unaware of his mother's real feelings toward me.

I plastered a fake smile on my face for his benefit, not wanting to upset him. He had other issues at hand here, like the fact that there were many guests tonight for dinner. I counted thirty in all, and that did not include Nidal and me. Besides the queen, I was the only other female at the table. All the men, with the exception of Nidal, were wearing their uniforms. *This must be an important dinner meeting. Something is happening right under my nose. I am sure Nidal knows what it is, but he has not shared the information with me.*

Next to the king, on his left side, sat Billal. Clearly, something was going on. I knew my bed would be cold tonight and Nidal would not be there to warm it. Just then, my thoughts of disappointment were interrupted when a servant walked in the room holding a birthday cake with a lit candle on it. Everybody started clapping and singing the birthday song to me. Embarrassed, I just sat there speechless.

The king stood and raised his glass of wine in the air and made a toast. "Happy birthday, Loula," he said joyfully.

Everyone, including the queen, who sat to the king's right, stood to toast me. Nidal pulled me close to him and kissed me on the mouth tenderly. I blew out the one candle that was on the cake, and the servants took away the pastry so they could slice it for dessert. All the attention I received touched me. Somehow they seemed warmer and kinder than they had been at other times. Conversation flowed throughout the room, and laughter filled the air.

The conversation wrapped around Nidal's childhood, as the queen and some of the guests remembered him as a little rascal always in mischief. I could only imagine him running in the palace's halls, trying to find a hiding place to avoid punishment. The queen's gaze occasionally went from Nidal to me. The fine lines on her face relaxed, and the tone of her voice sounded warmer than usual. *Dare I think that she is starting to accept me in her son's life?*

Dinner was served, but try as I might, I could not eat. I had lost my appetite. The thought of my lover going to another meeting tonight, and especially tonight of all nights, turned my stomach upside down. Nidal threw me a questioning glance, and I looked away, fearing the tears would roll down my face for all to see.

I could tell that he had guessed the reason for my sadness, and he whispered in my ear, "I will not be gone for long. Wait for me, and I will give you the second part of your gift."

And I looked up at him, and he winked at me, throwing me a smile to die for. My heart raced at the mention of my second gift. Just thinking about it set my heart on fire.

After dinner, the cake was brought out, all sliced up and ready to serve, but without even waiting for dessert, all the men, including Nidal, rose from the table and quickly disappeared. Nidal apologized as he hastily kissed my lips and followed the gentlemen out the door, leaving the queen and me alone at the table.

The queen, who was sitting at the end of the dinner table all the way on the other side, stood, picked up her teacup and the plate with her slice of cake on it, walked over, and sat in the empty chair opposite me. A young servant scrambled over to her and handed her a silver fork. The queen drank her tea and ate her cake in silence. I just sat there waiting for the queen to dismiss me, but she did not. Instead, she spoke to me for the first time since I had come to the palace.

"I think," she said, as her eyes turned to me, "you should try a piece of this chocolate cake. It is pure heaven." She smiled and dropped two sugar cubes in her tea while she waited for my response.

I was taken by surprise that the queen had decided to take this moment to talk to me, and I got excited and did not know what to say. So I just smiled and reached for my fork and started eating my slice of the cake, keeping myself busy while I devoured the pastry.

"I see you too approve of the chocolate cake." The queen laughed softly as she put the napkin she wiped her mouth with on the table and rose to her feet.

"Yes, thank you. It was delicious," I quickly responded.

Then I also rose and waited for the queen to exit the room before I did. The queen threw me a half smile as she elegantly strode out of the dining area and disappeared to her room. As I walked down the corridor to my room, I caught myself smiling, and I wondered if this were the beginning of a new relationship between the queen and me. It would sure be nice to have her on my side.

Closing the door to my room, my mind once again was troubled with the thought of what the gentlemen in the meeting were discussing with their king. I could only speculate what they were talking about behind closed doors.

I do not like the idea of Nidal keeping secrets from me, I thought dryly as I undressed.

I climbed into bed naked, feeling a little sleepy. In the middle of the night as I was still awake, I heard the door open and softly close. Nidal tiptoed to the bathroom, and minutes later, he walked to our bed and slipped under the covers as gently as he could.

I could feel his sweet breath on my face as he lay in bed next to my warm body. A full moon was outside, and the curtains were open so Nidal could easily see my face. I pretended to be asleep. As much as I wanted to throw myself into his embrace, I dared not. I wanted to make him feel my body heat and know what he could have had if he had come sooner to bed, but he made no sound, and he did not move at all. He lay still. I waited what seemed like an eternity. Finally not able to stand it anymore, I opened my eyes and saw him staring into my face. The moonbeams cast its light upon his face, and I saw him smiling right at me.

He quickly pulled me into his arms. I stared at his lips as he parted them to whisper something to me, but I could not wait any longer. With an impatient pull of his head, I brought his lips to mine and kissed him hungrily. Nidal pulled away from me.

"Did you miss me?" he asked me passionately.

"No," I lied.

He drew his head back and looked at me amused. "Liar."

He playfully tickled me until I cried from laughter.

So we spent our night blissfully in each other's arms as our entangled bodies passionately tasted the fruits of love.

When I awoke the next morning, I noticed that Nidal was missing from the bed. I looked around the room, but he was nowhere to be seen. I sighed and closed my eyes, thinking of last night. My body burned with desire thinking of my lover's naked body on top of mine. My hand automatically went to my throat as I remembered the beautiful necklace Nidal had showered me with. It was very thoughtful of Nidal to remember my birthday and share it with everyone. I smiled, thinking I could not be happier than I was at this very moment.

I got out of bed and dressed into a simple pink gown with yellow trimmings at the bottom, thinking this gown was befitting my mood right now. I was in love, and that was enough to make me swirl around with happiness. I was in my own happy little world and did not even hear the light tapping on the door as I danced around the room. I stopped dead in my tracks when I saw the door open gently and Billal's head peek inside, staring right at me with a smile on his handsome face. Embarrassed, I looked at him and opened my mouth. *Why did he open my door without asking first?*

Annoyed, I waved at him to enter, knowing I could not stay mad at him for long. He was a good man, and I enjoyed his company. Billal came inside quickly and shut the door behind him. He walked up to me, wrapped his arms around me, and kissed me softly on the cheek.

"Good morning, beautiful," he said cheerfully. He stepped back. "I am sorry to intrude on you like this, but I know that Nidal has gone to the village for some business, and I took a chance and came here to give you this." He pulled a gold bracelet out of his pocket. A charm, a gold heart, was hanging on it, and it was absolutely beautiful.

I was surprised that he would even think to give me a gift. I knew I could not accept a gift from Billal without some kind of retaliation from Nidal, but Billal took my right hand and clasped the bracelet on my wrist. The heart dangled elegantly as I raised my arm in the air and admired the bracelet.

"Happy birthday, Loula," he said softly.

What am I to do? Keeping this lovely gift means starting a war with Nidal. He would never allow me to keep it and would demand I give it back.

Billal must have noticed my change of heart. "Loula, please keep it as a token of our friendship. We are friends, are we not?" he asked, hopeful.

I sighed, knowing I would regret my decision one day. I hugged him. "Thank you, 'tis a lovely gift, and I will treasure it."

Pleased with my response, Billal smiled from ear to ear.

"I must get back to work. I have a million and one things to do today. Enjoy your day, my lady," he said, with a twinkle in his eyes as he turned gracefully and exited the room.

I lifted my hand and admired the bracelet, knowing I had to take it off and hide it before Nidal came back, for I knew that he would be enraged if he saw it. I walked over to the bed, sat on it, and unclasped the bracelet. I examined the beautiful item as it shined in my hands. At that moment, I heard footsteps outside my door, and I quickly hid the bracelet underneath my pillow, afraid that someone might see it.

Nidal walked into the room, and I was pleasantly pleased to see him. I ran to his arms and threw myself at him. The bracelet was quickly forgotten. My prince wrapped his arms around me and held on to me for dear life. When our lips met, no words were needed. It was magical as always. Nidal swept me up in his arms and took my breath away as he laid me tenderly on the bed and took my clothes off my heated body. Recklessly, I pulled his shirt over his head and untied the strings to his pantaloons as Nidal kicked off his boots. His hands skillfully caressed my entire body, igniting a fire within me that threatened to explode. I felt him hard and ready and held my breath, knowing he would enter me and take me to heights of passion that would have me screaming his name for mercy.

Nidal pushed hard inside me, breathing heavily as he called out my name hoarsely. "Loula!" he cried passionately.

He pushed harder and faster and moaned and groaned, and everything inside me exploded. Liquid fire coursed throughout my entire body as I trembled in ecstasy. I felt Nidal's hold on me tighten as he also reached his peak. As he slowed down and relaxed his body on top of mine, our eyes met and locked, and his lips came crashing down on mine.

Afterward when we cooled off, Nidal looked tenderly at me, and I noticed a shiny glint in his eyes. He was up to something.

I looked at him curiously. "What is on your mind?"

He straightened up next to me and took my hands in his, and I held my breath waiting for him to speak. My heart was pounding so loud that I thought it would burst.

Nidal looked deep into my eyes and spoke in a serious, loving tone, "Loula, you know how I feel. You know I cannot exist in a world without you. You are the very reason for my existence. I love you with all my heart and soul. I waited patiently for you all these years until you were ready for me." He took my hand, brought it to his lips, and kissed it. My heart pounded rapidly. "Loula, you know how much I love you," he whispered with deep emotion. "I want to make you my wife, and I want to spend the rest of my life with you. I want you to have my children. I want to grow old with you. Loula, will you do me the honor of becoming my wife?" he asked hopefully as he waited patiently for me to answer.

He took my breath away, my prince, the love of my life. He looked at me now as if his life depended on my answer. He stopped breathing, not wanting to disrupt my response.

"Nidal," I whispered his name softly as tears of joy sprang to my eyes, "I love you so much, and I could love no other. It is you to whom I lost my heart to, and it has always been you," I cried. "Yes, I will marry you. I want desperately to be your wife."

I threw myself in his arms and sealed our love with a passionate kiss. It was a moment that neither of us would ever forget, a beautiful moment full of love and promises. I treasured every second I had with Nidal. My heart burst with joy. My prince had asked to marry me, and I felt blessed.

After sharing this beautiful morning with my lover, I was reluctant to get out of bed. I wanted his warm body next to mine forever, but he announced that he had a meeting with his men. He slid out of bed and picked up his clothes. I stared at his lean, muscled body as he dressed, and for the life of me, I could not tear away my gaze. He looked so sexy that the butterflies in my stomach started dancing again. Nidal noticed and gave me a wolfish smile, and my eyes begged him to come back to bed, but in that instant, I noticed that Nidal was staring at something other than me. I followed his gaze and saw that his eyes had rested on the bracelet that Billal had given me. It had somehow made its way to the other side of the bed. My heart stopped beating as Nidal leaned over and grabbed it.

He held it in his hand and examined the expensive trinket. He lifted his gaze to me and asked in a low, dangerous tone, "Where did this come from?" I froze, knowing not what to say. "Where did this come from?" he barked again and shook the bracelet in my face.

Fearing the worst, I jumped out of bed and searched for my clothes, ignoring his question. I slipped into my gown, and with shaky fingers, I fastened the clasps to the front of the gown and frantically looked around for my slippers. Nidal's patience ran out.

He marched up to me and asked again a third time, "Where did this come from?"

Again, I ignored him because I was afraid to tell him the truth. Just that second, I saw Nidal's face tighten as he finally realized on his own. I waited for the explosion that was for sure going to follow.

"This is from Billal, isn't it?" He took a step closer to me. "You dare to accept a gift from the traitor as soon as my back is turned? Like a fool, I trusted you and asked you to be my wife! You are not loyal to the love that I thought we shared for one another! I will never marry a tramp like you!" he roared.

If he had stuck a knife in my heart and twisted it, the pain would have been less than what I felt at this very moment. With trembling lips, I said simply, "Then don't, but I tell you this. You are making a mistake talking to me in this manner. I shall never forgive you!"

Nidal threw his head back and laughed wholeheartedly. "Madam, the only mistake I have made was falling in love with you."

Those words cut deeply into my wounded heart and killed everything I held dear in this life. "No, Nidal, it was I that made the mistake, not you." I was unable to stop the tears that flowed down my face.

Nidal's jaw clenched, and his eyes turned a darker shade of blue. I turned and walked away, not knowing what else to do. Nidal grabbed my arm and turned me around to face him. Then he grabbed my hair with his two hands, twisted it, and pulled me forward. Our foreheads touched, and I cried out in pain, but he did not loosen his grip. He held me in this position. His hands were still holding my twisted hair tightly. I could feel his heavy breathing on my face. A single tear escaped and rolled down his face as he looked deep inside my eyes, searching for answers that would stop the agony in his heart. My head went numb as I stared into his beautiful eyes. My heart already regretted accepting the gift from Billal. *What was I thinking?*

A few minutes later, Nidal let go of my hair and dropped his hands to his sides. I saw the muscles on his face relax. He silently walked over to the bathroom and entered it, thrusting the door shut behind him. I bolted for the door. Blinded by tears, I ran down the long corridor, exited through the back doors, and went around to the stables.

A beautiful black stallion had his head in a bucket and was drinking water. I approached him slowly. His head bobbed up, and he took a few steps backward. Not wanting to scare him, I reached over and caressed his neck, whispering softly to him. When I saw that he accepted my friendship, I slowly grabbed his reins and pulled him gently toward me. I kicked over the bucket, and the remaining water spilled. I turned the bucket upside down and placed it next to the horse. I stepped on it, climbed on top of the horse, and pulled his reins. And off we went. *It's a good thing I know how to ride a horse.*

The horse galloped away from the palace. The warm breeze brushed against my skin, and I closed my eyes, allowing the tears to travel down my face, another reminder of the pain that tortured my heart.

After riding for a while, I had no idea where I was headed to, and as I looked around, I realized I was lost. I did not know which way would lead me to a safe haven. I wiped the tears from my eyes and tried to focus and see where I had come from, but as I looked around, I saw nothing but grass, trees, and hills. A new set of tears spilled forth, and I was tired of riding, so I decided to stop and rest a bit instead of moving forward. I jumped off the stallion and found a nice spot under a tree that offered some shade and a decent resting spot, but to my dismay, the stallion did not want to be a part of my adventure anymore, and he ran away. I panicked and called out to him, but it was of no use. The beautiful stallion had quickly disappeared from my view.

Now what? A new set of tears were threatening to spill forth, but I knew that crying would not help the situation. After much thought, I decided not to waste any more time, and I started walking down a dirt path, hoping it would take me to the village I had once visited with Nidal. I walked the whole entire day with only a few rests along the way. It was almost sundown, and from a distance, I saw many lit torches, which indicated a village was down that road. I picked up my pace, and I was relieved when I finally reached the village.

Almost immediately, I noticed this was not the same village I had visited before. Nothing here looked familiar as I walked down the empty, cobbled streets. The shops were closed, and the streets were deserted. I looked around, and a lump formed in my throat. Teary-eyed, I continued walking through the neighborhood and realized I had made a mistake in coming here.

I gazed along the path that led to another part of the village. I was getting a little nervous now. This part of the neighborhood did not look as inviting as the other side. The homes looked run-down and unkempt. A bad stench was coming from the side of the street that looked like an alley. Garbage was everywhere, and the torches were few. I slowly turned and walked the other way, hoping to find refuge before bedtime. As I walked closer to the nicer homes, the smell of fresh-baked bread filled my nostrils, and I wavered with hunger as my stomach growled, reminding me that I had not eaten a single thing today.

I debated if I should knock on someone's door, and I realized I might be recognized and taken back to the palace. My shoulders slumped as I walked away from the village and headed back on the dirt road from which I had come. The moon was full tonight, and that gave me a little guidance. Feeling hungry, thirsty, and tired,

I pulled off the dirt road, found a tree, and dropped beneath it. This would make a good sleeping ground until morning.

Not that I had another choice, I thought dryly as my eyelids closed and I fell into a deep sleep.

Chapter Three
Loula

In the morning, I felt something nibbling at my nose, and I immediately opened my eyes and screamed. I stared at my attacker. The little lamb looked at me with big, black eyes, startled as much as I was. Relieved that it was not someone or something that threatened my life, I slowly stood up and looked around for its owner. And sure enough in a distance, I saw him. The shepherd, a thin, young lad, was coming my way, and behind him followed a small herd of sheep.

The young man, who did not look a day older than twenty years of age, walked up to me, smiled, and asked, "What is your name, my lady?"

"Nadia." I quickly answered. I could not tell him my real name.

The young man bowed before me, allowing his hair that was pulled back in a ponytail to sway forward as he introduced himself.

"My name is Abdul," he said.

"What are you doing out here by yourself? Where is your chaperone?" He looked around suspiciously with his big, black eyes.

"I do not have one. I am all alone," I said too quickly without thinking. *What if he alerted the villagers and they seized me and took me as a prisoner?* I feared the worst.

"My lady, I will tell no one you are here. Please do not fear," he said innocently enough.

"Can you please help me, lad? I am lost and hungry, and I am scared." I hoped he would come to my aid.

It only took Abdul a few minutes of thinking before he announced cheerfully, "Well, you can come home with me. My mother and I hardly ever have visitors, and I know my mother would be delighted to meet you."

I believed him. His proposal sounded very inviting. *They have no idea who I am, so they will not alert the palace.*

So I eagerly accepted his invitation. Besides, had I not accepted, there was nowhere else for me to go. I followed Abdul as he herded the sheep toward his home. From a distance, I saw the little shack they called home. It was very small but looked warm and inviting. I waited patiently for Abdul to bring all the sheep to the stable, and then we went inside his home.

His mother greeted us at the door with a welcoming smile, exposing crooked, decayed teeth as she stepped aside for us to enter. Her gray eyes sparkled with curiosity as she closed the door and walked up to me. Her long, thick braid that hung low beneath her waist swayed as she tipped her head to the right and checked me out from head to toe.

Nervously, I threw her a smile and said, "Hello, my name is Nadia."

Abdul's mother wiped her hands on her worn-out apron, took my hands in hers, and held on to them. She seemed pleased that I was in their home.

"Please sit and break bread with us. We do not have much, but what the good Lord has given us, we will share with you." She gently pulled me to the wooden table in the middle of the tiny room and motioned for me to sit.

Not wanting to offend her in any way, I pulled out the wooden chair and sat on it. I looked around the small room and noticed it was almost bare of furnishings. There was a table with three chairs and two beds, one on each side of the room. There was a woodstove to cook on and a sink with the only window in the room above it, which was decorated with an old, cotton curtain. They did not have much, but they seemed like good people.

After washing his hands, Abdul helped his mother set the table. A hot bowl of potato soup and a slice of freshly baked bread was placed in front of me, and there was a slice of cheese and a glass of milk too. I devoured everything. I was starving. I sat quietly at their table while mother and son ate their food in silence, and when they were done, Abdul's mother removed the dishes from the table and dumped them in the sink. Abdul sat proudly in his chair, smiling at me.

The day wore on with the three of us sipping tea and listening to Abdul's mother telling us tales from long ago. Her words fascinated me. Clearly, she enjoyed telling her colorful stories, and she had us captivated as we gave her our undivided attention. I did not even notice that the sun had gone down and that it was almost time for dinner until Abdul announced that he was going to the stable to check on the livestock while his mother quickly busied herself with dinner preparations.

The table was set once again with the leftover potato soup and a repeat of everything else we had had for lunch, and it really did not matter to me because, by this time, I was starving again. Anything that was edible was just fine with me. We ate our dinner, and though it wasn't much, it was tasty. I was grateful for everything that Abdul and his mother offered me.

When we were done and everything was washed and put away, Abdul's mother smiled at me. "You look tired, my child. Would you like to rest now?" she asked politely.

I was very tired, and I nodded my head. "Thank you kindly. Yes, I am tired, and I would like to rest."

Immediately, Abdul stood. "Nadia, you can sleep on my bed. I can sleep on the floor by the fireplace," he chimed happily.

His mother quickly added, "Son, get the pillow from my bed and give it to Nadia. I do not need it tonight." And she turned with a smile and looked at me sweetly. "We are happy you have come to our humble home. Sleep now, my child. Rest your body, and God be with you," she said sincerely and hugged me. Then she turned, walked to the other corner of the room, and lay in her bed.

Abdul gave me his mother's only pillow and bid me good night, and he walked over to the fireplace, dropped on the floor, and slept on some blankets. I was feeling uncomfortable that I had the only pillow of the house, but I had no other choice. I did not want to disrespect them by not accepting their hospitality. So I lay in the bed, and I fell asleep almost immediately.

Early in the morning, I awoke to find the brilliant sunlight shining its way through the window. I looked around the room and noticed I was all alone. I got out of bed, walked over to the door, and swung it open. I found Abdul and his mother doing the outdoor chores, and when they noticed that I was looking at them, they smiled and waved. These people didn't have much material stuff, but they were loaded with other things that were more important, like love and kindness.

The day wore on. I helped Abdul with the rest of the chores, and his mother went inside to prepare something for us to eat. I was happy and felt serenity here. My mind relaxed, and I was at peace with myself. Thoughts of Nidal crept into my mind, but I quickly pushed them away.

Today, we had fried eggs, fried potatoes, and fresh bread. I was famished and sat down eagerly to eat. Abdul placed a glass of milk in front of me, sat down with his mother, and joined us. The conversation went smoothly at the table, and I was beginning to feel at home. But I knew that I had to pull my weight if I stayed here another day. After much deliberation, they finally agreed with me and gave me a task that I thought was easy enough.

Abdul showed me the garden in the back of their home, and I was to fill up the basket I was given with vegetables. I plucked all the ripe veggies and skipped back inside the shack to show Abdul's mother. She told me to wash them and place them on the table, where she had placed a clean cloth napkin.

"This, my dear child, is our meal for tomorrow," she said cheerfully. And then her eyes filled with tears as she stared at me. "Nadia, forgive me. I do not mean to cry, but you remind me of my daughter. She died of the plague many years ago," she said sadly. "The same disease claimed my husband as well and left Abdul and me to fend for ourselves. We do not have much, but at least we have each other. Abdul is a good boy, and he provides for me. I just love him so much." She wiped her tears with her apron.

I walked up to her and gave her a bear hug. I felt sorry for her. She was a good person, and life was not fair to her. Thus, our relationship started and blossomed into a beautiful friendship.

❈ ❈ ❈

As the days flew by, thoughts of Nidal were torturing my heart. I missed him tremendously and knew not what to do. On the one hand, I felt comfortable around these people who already felt like family to me, but at night when I lay myself down to sleep, my mind wandered to Nidal, and my heart broke in two. I cried myself to sleep every night and prayed I would be in his arms again one day. But I knew it was too soon. Only time would heal our wounds and allow us to start over again.

Chapter Four
Loula

Many days later, early in the morning, Abdul and his mother were outside taking care of the chores. I was deep in thought as I was sweeping the kitchen floor and did not hear the commotion outside. Suddenly, the door burst open, and I looked up, startled to find Nidal standing in the doorway. My heart pounded loudly in my ears as I froze and stared back.

I saw the raw emotions that played on Nidal's face. First, there was surprise. Then relief. And then pure love was written all over his handsome face.

But quickly it changed to anger as his jaw clenched shut. He marched right up to me and barked, "Madam, have you any idea what you have put everyone through these last two weeks? Have you any idea the humility we have suffered because of your selfish acts?"

I looked at him with disbelief. *How dare he throw his words around as if I had done him wrong when he had tore down what we once shared!* His gaze swept the room as if he expected an answer. His face looked more mature with tiny fine lines on his forehead

I had not seen before, and it looked as if he had not shaved in the two weeks that I was gone.

"Well, are you going to talk, or are you going to stay silent and admit to treason?" he sneered.

He was so arrogant and sure of himself. My eyes were shiny with tears, but I pulled my back straight. With a firm and unwavering voice, I said, "How dare you march in here as if you own the place! How dare you try to scare me into submission! I will not yield to you, Nidal! Go back to where you came from!" I turned my back to him.

Immediately, I regretted everything I had said, but it was too late to take it back. In an instant, Nidal's hands grabbed me roughly and turned me around. His eyes searched my face. His beautiful lips were tightly closed, and a miserable silence followed.

"That was a very bold statement, my fair lady," he finally said. "Are you sure it is what you want?" he asked in a dangerously low tone and released me from his iron grip.

I struggled for a reply, but none came. I glanced up at him. My chest tightened. I wanted to kiss his lips so badly, but instead, with a hint of desperation in my voice, I called out his name. "Nidal."

Nidal was unsympathetic to my feelings. He raised his eyebrow and said coldly, "An answer of yes or no will suffice, Madam."

In that moment, Abdul's mother rushed in and fell to the floor at Nidal's feet and tearfully begged, "Have mercy on the young mistress, my lord. Please do not punish her. She is young and innocent. Punish me instead," she cried.

The prince immediately lifted the old woman from the floor and gently pushed her to the side. "Women, leave us be." The whole time, his eyes were not wavering from mine.

The woman left, and Nidal closed the door behind her. He turned his gaze back to me and said roughly, "Well, what will it be?"

I did not like the way he was treating me. He was so arrogant. I pushed past him. I was not about to surrender. But Nidal grabbed me tightly in his hold and pulled me to him. "I will have your answer, Madam!" he said with a rough edge to his voice.

"I will come with you on one condition!" I said angrily.

Nidal lowered his eyebrows and gritted his teeth. He tightened his hold on me and waited.

"You must promise me that you will not punish these good people for harboring me here. They were good to me, and I will feel responsible if your wrath were upon them."

Nidal threw his head back and roared with laughter. "Madam, you are in no position to be asking for promises. I will do as I see fit. Do not worry. The punishment will fit the crime." He looked amused.

"Nidal, I will do whatever you say. Please do not harm these good people," I pleaded.

Without saying another word, Nidal pulled me by the arm and opened the door to the place I had come to love as my home. We walked outside. About twenty guards had traveled with Nidal, and one of them held Abdul captive. His mother was in tears standing next to him. She was murmuring to herself, and my heart went out to her. *What crime had they committed to be treated in such a fashion? They are the most decent people I have ever met.*

I broke free of Nidal's grip, knowing that such display in front of his people had consequences. Nidal's dark gaze measured mine. His frown firmly in place, I knew he was calculating his next move. I had humiliated him, and I knew he would make me pay the price. He took a step closer and barked, "Do not take another step, or I will be forced to take you as my prisoner!"

And I knew he meant every word. It was now his turn to humiliate me. I closed my eyes. My heart betrayed me. Nidal was so close to me that I felt his sweet breath on my face. His scent flooded my senses, making my heart race. His scowl deepened, and he gripped my arm. The contact of his flesh on mine sent ripples of sensation that spilled forth throughout my entire body, and I trembled with desire. I looked at his face and saw a glint in his eyes. He knew the effect he was having on me. It was sweet revenge.

Time stood still. Nidal was contemplating what to do to me. For a moment, I saw lust in his eyes, and I knew he was feeling the same as I was, but I knew more action was required to save face in front of his people. I braced myself and turned my heart to stone to keep it from breaking while Nidal did his job as the crown prince of Arabia. At first he hesitated. His hold on me lightened, and he sighed. I saw many emotions play in his eyes. Then without warning, he thrust me aside and gave orders to his men.

"Take her back to the palace. She is to be locked up in my room without contact from anyone, including the queen. She is a prisoner and is to be treated as such! Do not strike conversation with her. She is conniving and not to be trusted!" he warned.

My heart broke in two at his harsh words. I knew he spoke as such because of his position. He had an audience, and he needed to prove to them that he was strong and that he befitted the role of the next king of Arabia. I looked at him and pleaded with my eyes for his forgiveness. He had to know that I loved him with all my being. He regarded me thoughtfully, but in the end, the crown prince of Arabia prevailed, not the lover who had once warmed my bed at night.

Nidal pushed me harshly toward his men, and a guard pulled me gently in his grip and tied my hands together like a prisoner who was captured while committing a huge crime. I dropped my head down to my chin, embarrassed by such treatment, and walked away with the young guard. Behind me Abdul's mother stifled a cry, to which the prince called out, "Silence, woman! I will not have any more tears! Do you hear me?" he barked.

In the distance, I heard Abdul and his mother beg for mercy, and I winced, knowing I had put them in this predicament. Anger set in my heart. Nidal was not being fair. I never knew this side of him. *Is this what I have to look forward to if I become his bride?* But then I realized that he might not want to make me his bride anymore. *Hadn't he told me that dreaded day that he regretted asking me to marry him? He even called me a tramp! How dare he!*

The guard pulled me next to his horse and motioned for me to get on it. With his help, I climbed the horse. He joined me, and we headed toward the palace. I never looked behind me, but I heard the other horses with the guards traveling behind us. In an hour's time, we reached the palace. I sighed, knowing that everyone would see my tied hands and know the reason behind it. I was helped off the horse and walked with the guards like a prisoner guilty of treason. Such I was to the eyes of this kingdom. But they judged me unfairly. They knew not what lay in my heart.

Everyone at court, including all the servants of the palace, was lined up outside. They were going to make an example of me. I was paraded in front of all the people like a dog. They all stared at me wide-eyed, and I saw pity in their eyes. At the end of the line that stopped in front of the huge palace doors were the king and queen. I dropped my head in shame, unable to look them in the eyes.

"Release her this instant!" cried the queen in a voice full of agony.

"But my queen, we have orders from the prince to treat her like a prisoner. She is to be locked up in her rooms." He bowed in front of her majesty.

"I demand you release her immediately before I throw you in the dungeon. Do you hear me, lad?" the queen roared.

The young guard scrambled to do as he was told. He untied my hands and released me to the queen. The king raised his eyebrows and looked at me with disdain as I walked up to the royals and bowed. Tears flowed down my cheeks, and the queen reached out and pulled me into her arms, giving me a warm hug. I heard the king sigh disgustedly as he witnessed this. In the background, I heard the rest of the horses and the men approach the grounds. Within seconds, I heard Nidal's voice.

"Mother, you dare to go against my wishes!" he barked, more of a statement than a question. "You know by law she has to be punished for what she did! She stole our black stallion. She is a thief! I will not have you breaking the law for the likes of her!" He walked up to us, grabbed my arm in a tight hold, and pulled me away from the queen.

I saw the king's smirk before he turned and walked inside the palace. The queen stood frozen, staring at her son in disbelief.

"No one is exempt from punishment if he or she commits a crime. Not even Loula!" he said arrogantly.

The queen opened her mouth to give him a piece of her mind, but her son silenced her by putting his hand up in the air. "Enough, Mother!" he warned.

And the queen heeded the warning and clamped her mouth shut.

The prince pulled me through the palace doors as the guards stepped aside, and he marched me down the corridor to our chamber. He threw the door open and pushed me inside, closing the door behind us. Standing in front of me, Nidal gave me the meanest, cold look I had ever witnessed on his beautiful face.

"If you ever do that again, Madam, you will not be so lucky. I will personally see to it that you end up in the dungeon," he growled.

"And if you ever humiliate me again, I will personally see to it that you will never see me again!" I was quick to yell back without thinking.

Nidal threw his head back and laughed aloud. "If I were you, I would check my manners because my patience is running thin with you, my dear. You have overstepped your boundaries quite a few times today. In case you haven't noticed, you are but a prisoner bound to me for life. I will have you at my will for the taking whenever I feel like it, and when I am done with you, I will pass you along to my guards, for that is your worth now, Madam!" he sneered.

Without thinking, I raised my hand and slapped his face, catching him off guard. Immediately, he seized me and raised his right hand to strike me. I closed my eyes and feared the blow to my head. But instead of his wrath upon me, he crushed his lips on mine and kissed me brutally.

My heart raced rapidly, and I lost all my senses. I wrapped my arms around him and kissed him hungrily. I could feel his beard stubble grazing my skin as he kissed me savagely. He took my breath away. Then almost immediately, Nidal stopped. His mouth was set in a tight, determined line, and his eyes were now blazing with anger. I could feel his hands tremble as he loosened his hold on me. He was wounded, and he needed time to heal. I wondered if I had killed his feelings for me. I would die a slow death if that were ever true, for I could not live a life without him.

Nidal walked away from me. With long, easy strides, he reached the door and opened it and walked out, swinging it closed behind him. I heard the key on the other side. He locked me in. I was his prisoner now, a prisoner of love, a toy to be used at his will and tossed aside until the next time he craved me. He was true to his word. He did punish me, for this was torture. I'd rather suffer a thousand deaths than feel the pain of being rejected from my one true love. That night, I lay alone in the bed. Nidal did not come to me. I tossed and turned all night.

Two weeks later, Nidal still had not come to me. I was brought three meals a day and then left alone to fend for myself. The window was my only escape to reality. I sat in the chair by the window all day, every day, and waited for a glimpse of Nidal. A few times, I saw him walk across the grounds to the stables and ride away on a black stallion.

Tonight, to my surprise, as I lay in bed aching for Nidal, I heard the door unlock, and I saw Nidal's silhouette enter the room. It was a full moon, and the moonbeams shined through the window, allowing me to make out Nidal's body. My heart stopped beating as I looked hungrily at him. Then I closed my eyes and pretended to be asleep. I could hear him undress, and then he slid into bed with me. I held my breath. But I could not stop the tears that escaped my eyes and slid down my face. They were tears of joy. He had come back to me at last.

After Nidal's head hit the pillow, I heard him sigh. A few minutes later, his hand lightly caressed my face.

"Don't cry, Loula," he whispered softly.

I did not respond. Instead, I continued to fake sleep. Nidal caressed my face, and then his hand roamed downward, and he grabbed my breasts. He played with them gently, sending tingling ripples of sensation up and down my body. It was getting harder for me to fake sleep. Nidal's lips kissed my neck slowly as he licked his way down to my breasts. My nipples hardened, and I wrapped my hands around his head, enjoying the sensation that was coursing throughout my entire body. My body betrayed me, and I trembled as Nidal's lips continued down a path to nether land.

Nidal parted my legs, and he cradled his face among my most private part and played me until I heard myself scream in ecstasy. He continued to rock my world until I lay breathless, as my tears once again spilled down my face. Nidal's lips traveled slowly back up my body, creating an electrifying sensation, traces of his lovemaking, all over my entire body. I lost myself again in this world of bliss.

When his lips came up my neck and found my lips, he kissed me with fierce possession. I wrapped my arms around him and held on to him tightly. I was in heaven, and I never wanted to leave this place ever. But almost immediately, Nidal pulled back and rolled over to his side of the bed, turning his back to me. I stared at him with disbelief. My heart was still pounding. I did not understand what was happening. I was blown away. He was punishing me. He had made love to me, and then he had pulled away from me without any regard to my state of mind. I lay still, hurt by his sudden change of mind. His withdrawal was like a knife in my heart.

Suddenly, Nidal jumped out of bed and dressed quickly, and before I knew it, he was out the door. I heard him lock me in. Even if I tried, I could not stop the flow of tears that made their way down my face. In a way, it was therapeutic for me to allow myself the luxury of crying my heart out. In the end, I just closed my eyes and pictured Nidal here beside me. I slept with that thought every night until he next came to me, two weeks later.

I was by the window staring out at the moonless night when I heard the lock turn on the door. Like a thief in the night, Nidal unlocked the door and entered. After he closed the door, he stood there without moving for a few minutes. The small flame that was left on the candle was about to be extinguished. He was naked from the waist up, I could see the muscles on his bare chest, and I felt my body heat rise.

I stood frozen, waiting for Nidal to make the first move. The excitement of his appearance was shooting throughout my entire body. It took every ounce of strength I had to control myself. The minutes ticked by slowly. Finally, Nidal stepped forward, and he grabbed me, lifted me, and thrust my body against the wall. His mouth came crashing down on mine, and his hands cupped my butt and pulled it toward his manhood. His breathing became heavy with lust, and my heart skipped a beat when I felt his enlarged shaft pressing against me. I untied the strings to his pantaloons, and they dropped to the floor. I reached inside his underpants, grabbed his shaft, and played with it. Nidal groaned as soon as I touched him, and he grabbed my nightgown and ripped it off my body.

Within seconds, Nidal had discarded his undergarment, and he pushed his body up against mine. He put his knee between my legs and parted them, allowing for his groin to enter me hard as he plunged deep inside me. Electricity coursed throughout my entire body, and I dug my nails into his skin. Almost immediately, my body trembled with desire. I came long and hard. I cried out his name passionately in the heat of the moment. That drove him mad with desire. He moaned out loud as he continued to savagely thrust himself inside me. He was out of control and did not realize the wild way that he was making love to me. His hands slid down to my butt just as he was about to spill his seed inside me. Nidal stopped kissing me. His eyes met mine passionately, and I could tell that he was about to reach his peak. He pulled my butt tightly up against his groin as he slammed into me one more time, and then I felt his body shudder. His lips parted as he moaned aloud.

I was still trembling from the aftershocks of Nidal's sexy lovemaking, and my hands slid inside his thick, long, black hair. I pulled his head toward my lips, and I kissed him fiercely. I was lost in this moment of heavenly bliss. It came as a shock to me when Nidal instantaneously pulled his lips away from mine. Confused, I looked at him, questioning his behavior. Nidal ignored me and stepped away. Standing naked up against the wall, I watched Nidal pick up his clothes from the floor and dress quietly without even a glance my way, and then he swiftly exited the room.

Chills ran up and down my spine. It was suddenly cold in this room. I bent over, retrieved my nightgown, and threw it over my head. I walked over to the bed and slipped under the covers. I felt numb, unable to feel anything at all. I realized that even the tears were absent this time around. Suddenly, the flame from the candle extinguished, and it was dark in the room. The pain from my heart was absent. My heart was frozen. I sighed. Sleep claimed my body instantly that night, not allowing any room for regrets.

Almost a month later, Nidal came to me again. I was sitting by the table reading a book late at night. Many candles were lit around my room, casting shadows of the furniture across the walls. Nidal walked in the room and locked the door. He hesitated for just a few seconds before he walked across the room and dropped to his knees in front of me. Nidal looked up at me, and I saw sorrow in his eyes. He looked unshaven and disheveled. I did not understand what he wanted. *Why he had come to me after all this time?*

Try as I might, I could not feel anything. I was completely empty, void of any life inside me. I looked away from him, unable to seize the moment. Nidal dropped his head on my lap and wrapped his arms around my legs tightly, weeping silently. I really do not know how long we stayed in this position, but it was quite a while. Finally, breaking the silence and without looking up, Nidal whispered my name. His voice sounded like a tortured animal. I remained silent, unable to respond.

Slowly, Nidal raised his head and looked up at me. I was unable to tear my gaze away from him this time. His tear-stained face looked tortured. And slowly the old feelings crept up out of nowhere. I could not help myself. My tears flowed freely down my face, unashamed of my feelings for this man who was the love of my life. I threw caution to the wind and whispered his name. I knew I was taking a chance that history might repeat itself and my heart would not be able to bear the pain, but living without him hurt even more.

Nidal's gaze never left mine as he stood slowly and pulled me into his embrace. He sighed with relief and then lifted me up in his arms and walked over to the bed. He gently put me down and flipped over the covers, and I lay down and waited until Nidal pulled off his pantaloons and joined me. We fit comfortably together. Nidal held me in his arms all night. I was overwhelmed with happiness. We did not talk, for words were not needed at this time. We did not make love either. It was just simple and sweet. Two hearts reuniting and connecting strongly with each other again in silence. I dared not think of the morning. I didn't know if I would find Nidal still in my bed. I just enjoyed what I had for now until sleep claimed me.

When the first hint of morning hit my room, I awoke and noticed immediately that I was alone in the bed. My heart sank as I realized that he had abandoned me yet again. Fresh tears threatened to spill forth, and then I turned and saw him. He was kneeling on the floor at the side of the bed, looking at me with adoration. Tears were in his eyes too, and my heart raced so fast that I was at a loss for words. *But are words needed at this precious moment?*

I reached out and caressed Nidal's face lovingly. He tenderly put his hand on mine, pulled it to his lips, and kissed it. All was forgiven. I looked at him and realized I was his to eternity. I knew without a doubt that I was not complete without him.

"Am I forgiven?" he asked in a husky tone.

And I answered simply, "Yes."

Nidal dropped his head and whispered, "Thank you." He stood up from his position and ran his hands through his hair with a sigh of relief. "I must leave now. Get dressed, Loula. I will be back for you in a little bit." He left so quickly that I had to ask myself if he was really here to begin with or if I was just daydreaming.

True to his word, Nidal was back, and he burst into the room, smiling from ear to ear. I wished I could share his enthusiasm, but I was still scared that my world would turn upside down again at any moment.

"You look beautiful, Loula," he said breathlessly and pulled me into his embrace.

I had put on a fuchsia gown and tied a matching ribbon to my hair. I slipped on my slippers, and I was ready to go. Nidal took my hand, and I followed him out the door. It was the first time in over two months that I had left my room. It felt good being outside. We walked along the hallway, and everyone stared at us. They were surprised to see me out and about. Nidal stopped and kissed me, and he stole my breath away. I heard murmuring behind us. Nidal gave them something to talk about. I couldn't help but smile after seeing the expressions on their faces when they witnessed our little escapade.

The guards opened the palace doors, and we stepped outside. Nidal gently pulled me with him toward the gardens, and right before entering it, from the corner of my eyes, I witnessed Abdul and his mother further up by the stables. I stopped in my tracks and looked to make sure it was them, and when I confirmed it, I let go of Nidal's hand and ran to them.

Abdul's mother started to cry when she saw me. She dropped the basket with all the vegetables that she was holding and stretched her arms out to receive me. I fell into her arms, and she squeezed me tightly. We were laughing and crying at the same time. Abdul hugged the both of us, and the three of us, teary-eyed, were happy to see each other.

"When, pray tell, did you come here?" I asked excitedly.

"As soon as they took you from us, Nidal brought us here right away," Abdul answered happily. "We have been here ever since. This is our new home. Nidal said we can stay as long as we like."

"I am your new cook, Loula. Nidal put me in charge of the kitchen and the garden, and my son was put in charge of the stables. Loula, we have you to thank. It is all because of you that our lives have changed," Abdul's mother said excitedly.

"Where do you sleep?" I asked curiously.

"We have been given our own room, Loula. Your prince has been very good to us. God bless him," Abdul's mother announced.

Suddenly, Abdul and his mother both bowed at the same time, and I turned and saw Nidal right behind me. Nidal stretched out his arm.

"Come, Loula. Walk with me to the gardens. I need to talk to you," he said in a serious, calm tone.

I hugged Abdul and his mother and walked over to Nidal, slipping my hand in his as we walked together to the gardens. "Nidal, that was very kind of you to bring them to the palace," I said to him, teary-eyed.

"What else would you have me do? They took you in, fed you, and gave you a home. One good deed deserves another, don't you think?" He smiled at me and made the butterflies in my stomach flap their wings.

I stopped in my tracks, turned to him, wrapped my arms around him, and kissed him sensually. The gardener dropped his tools and looked at me openmouthed. He was probably wondering how I dare display my feelings in public. Nidal kissed me back hungrily, and took my breath away. I was deeply and hopelessly in love with him.

"Thank you, Nidal. This means a lot to me," I said wholeheartedly.

Nidal pulled me around the rose bushes to the other side of the garden, where thousands of colorful flowers were in full bloom this time of year. This place looked magical. There were three wooden benches, and I made my way to one of them and sat on it while Nidal walked around and cut the prettiest flowers. He then proceeded to make a wreath. When he was done, I was impressed. It was very beautiful.

Nidal placed it on my head. "You look like a princess, Loula. "Your beauty takes my breath away," he said hoarsely. Then he kneeled down on one knee. I held my breath, knowing where this was leading to. "Loula." He paused a second. He looked deep into my eyes. "I love you so much. Marry me. I want to spend the rest of my life with you." Tears were in his eyes.

My mind slipped back to the last time he had asked me to marry him, and I closed my eyes. The tears started to roll down my face.

"I am sorry for the pain I have caused you, Loula," he said sincerely. "Forget the past, and let's start over fresh. A new beginning."

"And who's to say that history will not repeat itself? How can I be sure you will not go crazy with jealousy again? Your cousin is my friend. We will talk and laugh again, as friends do. How can you guarantee me that you will behave?" I knew that he would do it again.

Nidal lifted a brow, and I noticed his eyes turn a darker shade as he studied my face closely. I swallowed in disappointment. Things remained the same. He would never change. "You are mine whether you choose to marry me or not. I will not give you up!" he said with fierce possession.

"Then you will live a life of misery, Nidal. Why do you want to suffer in this way? I cannot be locked up in my room forever! I need to have friends and live my life as a free woman. I do not want to be punished every time I talk to a man!" I was angry at him for ruining such a beautiful moment.

Nidal grabbed my shoulders and shook me gently. "You are mine! I will personally kill any man who comes near you, cousin or not!" he warned.

That was the end of our beautiful moment in the garden. I stood and walked away from Nidal. I knew it was too good to be true. *Nothing lasts forever.*

"Loula, wait," Nidal said impatiently. "You walk away from me acting like you do not care when I know that you love me. In the end, I will win, and you know that. I know you love me. I know you cried every day you were away from me. Loula, I cried too. Do you want to go through all that again? Can you live without me? Because I know I cannot live a life without you," he said truthfully.

He was right. We were born to be with one another. We were soul mates. We completed each other. What was the use of fighting it anymore? I sighed, reached out, and caressed his face. "You are right, Nidal. I am yours, and you are mine." And he looked at me and waited for my answer. I lovingly looked up at him and said simply, "Yes."

Nidal's handsome face lit up, and he lifted me and swirled me around. He filled my face with butterfly kisses.

News traveled fast, and it was buzzing around the palace grounds that I was out and about. We walked back to the palace and saw the queen walk toward to us excitedly.

"Loula," she said excitedly and gave me a warm hug. "I am so glad to see you smile again. Come, I want to show you our new cook. She is wonderful. She can cook up a dream," she said happily, pulling me alongside her and totally ignoring Nidal.

"Mother!" Nidal was not too happy to be left alone.

"Oh, Nidal, put a sock in it!" She winked at me with a smile as she pulled me toward the kitchen.

Chapter Five
Loula

As the days went by, we told no one of the marriage proposal or acceptance. It was our secret for now until we decided when the right time would be to make the announcement. I was very happy and felt like I was living in a dream. Everything felt so perfect.

The queen and I formed a beautiful relationship. She included me in all her conversations during dinnertime and even insisted that I join her for a few strolls in the rose garden on the evenings the men went to their meetings. I was happy to comply. Our conversations were pleasant enough, and I looked forward to them. The queen turned out to be a very nice lady. I felt much respect for her, and I knew the feeling was mutual.

During one of our walks with Her Majesty, she told me about the children in the orphanage. She was very fond of them. She called them "my children," and she said they were absolutely adorable. I looked at the queen with admiration after I heard her talk so lovingly about "her children." Although I felt sad that the children were without parents, I was glad that they were here because I knew they were taken care of in the best possible way.

I could not get the children out of my mind after that. One day, I asked the queen if I could spend some time at the orphanage with the children and teach them English. The queen was so excited about my proposal that she immediately agreed, and I was so thankful because Nidal lately spent every morning in training with his trainer to use the sword with expertise. I was left to entertain myself. *What better way to kill time than to be around the blessed children?*

The orphanage was behind the palace to the east, about a hundred yards away. Many flowers surrounded the home, and trees and bushes of all shapes and sizes were planted everywhere. In the backyard, there was a huge playground, and I could not imagine the children not being happy here.

In the home, there were many rooms, including a few bathrooms to accommodate all the children. The queen went all out and decorated the rooms with only the best. No Persian rugs or crystal glasses were in this home, but everything here was of the finest quality to best fit the situation so the children could feel right at home. It was a warm environment, clean and cozy. I could tell that the children were very happy here.

The furniture was made just for them, and many servants cleaned, cooked, and took care of the children around the clock. They seemed well adapted here. They were nicely clothed and well fed, and they had many toys to keep them occupied throughout the day. They were like one big, happy family.

Each time I visited the children, their faces lit up with excitement. There were thirty-seven in all in this part of the country. Each child was more precious than the next. They were all adorable, but the youngest, Natalie, was a delight. She was about seven years old, and she had long, black hair that she wore parted in the middle with two ponytails. She had long eyelashes, and her eyes were the same color as Nidal's. Whenever I looked into them, they reminded me of him. Her lips were full, and a sad smile was always on her face. The few times she smiled, I thought

I caught a glimpse of Nidal. If I ever had a little girl with Nidal, she would probably look just like Natalie.

I started by teaching the children the ABCs. They were easy to teach. They were eager, and they learned really quickly. Then I taught them to write their names. Every day, they learned a few words. They looked forward to my teachings. Natalie always sat next to me, close enough where sometimes I pulled her into my arms and hugged her. She was missing a mother's touch, and I knew she substituted me for the mother she never knew.

That was how the queen found me one day as she was visiting the children. She sat there in silence, looking stunned at the way I had all the children's attention as they sat quietly listening to the lesson of the day while I held Natalie in my arms. I saw the expression on her face. It went from stunned to admiration. Tears were in her eyes as she covered her mouth with her hand. Natalie wiggled out of my arms and jumped to the floor as she hastily ran up to the queen and wrapped her chubby little arms around her.

Witnessing this, I knew the queen had a heart of gold. Clearly this was not the first time that Natalie had done this. The queen gave her a squeeze and then ruffled her hair, as the child ran back to me and snuggled onto my lap. Her Majesty apologized for the interruption, and I continued with the lesson. The queen stayed back and watched with a pleased smile on her lovely face. After a while, I gave the children a few minutes of recess. The queen walked up to me and said wholeheartedly, "Congratulations, Loula, on a job well done."

"Thank you, my queen," I said proudly. "It is a pleasure being around these adorable children," I said proudly.

When she left, I realized that I had come to understand her and her ways. We had reached a new level of friendship, and it was surely going in the right direction. Pleased with that progress, I focused my attention on the children and continued the lessons.

Chapter Six
Loula

As the days turned to weeks, Nidal and I still had not told anyone that we wished to marry. It was our secret, something to hold dear in our hearts until the right time came along. Our love was endless as we cherished each moment we spent together. Our relationship blossomed into a fairy tale.

Each day that passed, I noticed that my prince was a rare jewel. There were many sides to him, and each one was better than the next. He taught me the true meaning of love, life, and laughter. He made me a better person and brought only the best out of me. I cherished every moment that I spent with him. And I knew the feeling was mutual. Whenever he looked at me, his eyes glowed with love.

Prince Nidal was a prince of honor, and he loved his people very much. And all his people loved him back. They welcomed him in their homes, and he gracefully accepted each and every invitation. Nidal always brought me along with him as we entered the homes of the rich and the poor. But it was the poor people's homes we entered and spent the evenings with that revealed to me yet another side of Nidal I had not known. He was humble in their homes, ate whatever was served, and complimented the peasants' wives on their cooking, even if they served only bread and potatoes. He drank wine with them and laughed and played with their children. I loved to sit back and watch him interact with these people, who did not have many material things, but they had plenty of love and happiness. They were rich in other ways that mattered to me the most. Nidal fit well with them, as if they were a part of his family. Never once did he look down on them. As a matter of fact, he talked, laughed, and shared stories with them. He seemed very comfortable around them, and to me, he looked like the great man that I knew him to be.

When it was time to leave, he bowed, thanked them for their hospitality, and dropped several gold coins on their table. He walked away quickly before they discovered the treasures, for he was not one to brag. He did not want the poor to feel like beggars or to feel unworthy. So he always helped them without blowing the trumpets. I did not think it was possible to love him any more than I already did, but I could not help it as I was overwhelmed with this new feeling of respect and adoration that I felt for my prince. My love for him overflowed until I was drowning in thankfulness to God for all the treasures he had given to me. I was very grateful.

A few times a week, Nidal still went to the private meetings with the king and his men. I never asked what the meetings were about, and Nidal never offered the information, so I kept silent, thinking for sure he would tell me on his own one day.

One day after dinner, as we walked into our room, Nidal surprised me by letting me know that he would be gone all night again because another important meeting was to take place. I tried to hide my disappointment, but Nidal noticed immediately that I was upset. He pulled me into his arms and kissed me fervently. The kiss did not last long. Nidal stopped abruptly and pushed me gently away as I looked questioningly up at him.

Nidal sighed and whispered softly, "Don't do this to me, Loula, please. I have to go. It's a very important meeting. I would not leave you like this if it were not," he whispered. His eyes looked sadly into mine.

I pulled away from him, knowing that I would be miserable tonight without him. Nidal quickly followed behind me, reassuring me that he would be back as soon as he could, but as soon as he spoke those words, we both knew it was going to be a long night. I walked into the bathroom and slammed the door shut in Nidal's face, as he stood there, stunned. He pounded on the door a few times, begging me to let him in, but I ignored him. A few seconds later, I heard him walk away, closing the door behind him.

Desperate now, I wanted to know exactly what was being discussed in the meetings. *Is there reason for me to worry? And why is he in training every morning? Is he getting ready for a battle?* Cold sweat broke out all over my body at the thought of Nidal fighting and putting himself in danger. I knew Nidal would never tell me anything that would make me upset. *So how am I to find out?*

Billal popped into my mind. I was sure that he knew what was happening. *Maybe if I try hard enough, he will tell me what the secret is.* I had no other choice. *Tomorrow when Nidal leaves for his lessons, I will send for Billal.*

I tossed and turned all night in my cold and lonely bed. I cried and called out Nidal's name, but no one answered. This was going to be a long night. Finally, at some point into the night, I drifted off to sleep, and it seemed like a million hours had passed when I opened my eyes and saw Nidal's silhouette by the window. It was a moonless night. The room was dark, but I saw my lover looking out the window into the black night. I held my breath, not wanting to let on that I had awakened. I watched him for a while, and I heard him sigh a few times. Something was deeply troubling him, and I had a feeling it had nothing to do with me. It must be the meeting. Something terrible was going to happen. I trembled as that realization hit me like a ton of bricks. I was desperate for answers, and I knew Nidal would say nothing to me, which made me even more desperate to get answers from Billal.

Finally, Nidal came to bed. I braced myself as I waited hungrily for Nidal to take me into his arms. But my prince lay quietly next to me and did not make a move to come closer to me. This was the first time something like this had ever happened. I did not know how to handle this, so I reached out to him and wiggled closer to his body.

He responded immediately by squeezing me tight into his embrace. "I thought you were sleeping, and I did not want to wake you." He sighed deeply. "I miss you." His arms squeezed me even tighter. "I barely heard a word in the meeting. I kept thinking of you, Loula."

My arms went around his waist. At this moment, I could not be angry anymore with him. I missed him too much. I found his warm lips and kissed him hungrily as my tears came without warning. I knew he was tired and needed to sleep, but I could not stop. I needed him at this moment, and my body was begging for him to touch me. *To be loved by this man is all I would ever need in this lifetime.*

As I trembled in his arms, I knew without a doubt that, for me, there was no life without him. He was the very air that I breathed. I was sure of this.

As Nidal took me to heights of passion, he kept asking me to tell him if I loved him. "Tell me now, Loula!" he demanded passionately, even though all night I told him over and over again how much I loved him.

He still insisted I say it one more time. He held himself back, withholding his pleasures from me and knowing full well that, by doing so, I was tortured to the point of no return.

"Tell me, Loula," he begged. "Do you love me?" he asked again.

He stood still as if to punish me. I let out a scream of passion, and I told him wildly that I loved him so much. Only then did he share what he so selfishly withheld from me. He took me to his place of heaven, a place only I had gone, a place where no other woman had ever visited. There, I melted and exploded into a million pieces of liquid fire. Whoever said sex was a sin was a big fat liar!

I woke up in the morning with Nidal's touch. His hands were roaming again. And I smiled, thinking that, if we keep this up, we would never get anything done.

"Nidal, how did you wake up? I thought you would sleep all day. You did not get any sleep last night."

But Nidal was never one to admit how tired he might be. He only smiled and said without a care in the world, "I slept enough, I feel great, and I'm late for my lessons." He kissed my nose, flipped the covers back, and jumped out of bed.

His tall, lean, and tanned body drove me crazy as I watched him get dressed. He turned his back on me and reached for his clothes. He knew I was watching, and he took pleasure in torturing me as he said, "You like?"

I ignored him, and he slowly turned around, revealing his manhood, which was aroused as always. I swallowed hard and looked into his eyes with raw lust. Then he dived in the bed and forgot about everything else. It was just simply beautiful.

As the day wore on, I was keeping busy at the orphanage. The children and I were having a splendid afternoon. And when I asked the children if they wanted to go out and play, they all screamed at the same time with excitement. They loved it outside. The queen had made a playground for them that had everything a child could possibly dream of. It was there, as I was watching the children and pushing Natalie on the swing, that I noticed Billal walking toward the playground. He had a big smile on his face, and he looked dashing in his uniform. His eyes were gleaming as he walked up to me and greeted me with a kiss on my cheek.

"If only you were my wife and these were all our children and you loved me and not my cousin," he teased, smiling from ear to ear, "I would be the happiest man alive." He took over pushing Natalie's swing.

Natalie turned her head and looked up at the prince with an adorable smile. I could not help but think how handsome he was.

If I saw Billal first before I fell in love with Nidal, I could have easily fallen in love with him.

"I received your message this morning, and I was thrilled to find out that you had asked for me. So to what do I owe this pleasure to?" he asked with a twinkle in his eyes.

I was not sure how to approach the subject without alarming him in any way. I did not even know if he were loyal to me.

"Billal," I said softly. I did not want the children to hear what I was about to say. "Are you loyal to me? Can I trust you?" My voice held no conviction.

Billal stopped the swing in midair, and he took Natalie off the swing and placed her gently down. "Natalie, go play with your little friends, and in a little while, I will come and join you." He smiled down at her as he ruffled her hair.

Natalie did not even hear a single word he said. As soon as her feet touched the ground, she was halfway across the playground running to the slides. The prince turned to me, and our eyes locked.

"Am I loyal, you ask?" He looked taken aback from what I just asked him. "Have I ever given you reason to think I was not loyal to you?" he asked, clearly distressed.

I looked at him quietly for a few seconds before responding. I needed to catch my breath. He looked so good, standing there looking at me with a straight face. He was right. Billal was always a gentleman where I was concerned. But still, you could never be too careful.

"Have you ever given me reason to believe that you are loyal?" I replied.

Billal sighed. He put his hands on my shoulders, and I could tell he was clearly upset as he said hoarsely, "Loula, you can trust me, for I would lay down my life for you."

"Billal," I whispered in a choked voice, "I know you to be a decent man, but before I tell you anything, I need you to swear your oath to me."

Billal made an agonizing sound. There was a shuddering tension about him, as if he were a hairbreadth from exploding. Then his grip relaxed, and he dropped his arms down to his sides. I could see how my words hurt him.

His voice sounded bitter when he delivered his next words. "I would have made your life happier had you chosen me instead of him," he said bitterly. "I am a better man than he is, Loula." Billal closed his eyes for a second, and when he opened them, he looked as if he were in pain. "I am loyal to you, Loula. Never ask me that again. Never doubt me again. It hurts." This time, his voice sounded cool, sharp as crystal. "Trust me. I am a man of my word."

"Billal, you are so melodramatic!" I accused him angrily. "I only wanted to make sure. That's all."

He drew his head back. His eyes were somber and held supreme confidence. "One day, you will regret choosing him over me. I am the real man that you need to quench your thirst. Nidal can never satisfy you! Give me a chance, and I can prove it to you," he pleaded.

I already regretted this meeting. I had made a mistake asking him to come here. Billal looked very upset, and this was not my intention. "Billal, please forgive me," I added quickly. "I need you to be my friend, but I think I messed up. Can you forgive me?" I begged sincerely.

"I can forgive you. What other choice do I have? I am in love with you. Tell me what you need to say. I promise that I will never betray you. Never," he said adamantly.

"I trust you. From now on, you will be my confidant. I don't know why, but I feel safe with you. I need you to be my friend." I looked into his eyes and knew instantly that I had whatever my heart desired from him. Pleased, I wrapped my arms around his waist and laid my head on his chest. In response, Billal embraced me with his strong arms, and it felt good to be in this place at this time.

Billal pulled back first and looked at me, waiting to hear what I needed to tell him. So I asked him straight out, "I know something is going on, something that is being kept a secret from the queen and me. It must be huge this secret that all of you are keeping from us. Nidal will not tell me. He does not want me to get scared. But you, my friend, who has sworn loyalty to me, you must tell me," I demanded softly.

Billal let out a big sigh. He must have thought I would tell him something else. He looked disappointed as he looked away. "Loula, I pledge my loyalty to you now and forever, but I still, first and foremost, am loyal to the king, my uncle. The meetings we go to are confidential. I cannot speak of them. Please understand my position. I beg of you." When he saw disappointment on my face, he moaned painfully, not knowing what to do. "Loula, you will know soon enough. No need to rush and find out something that will cause pain. Be patient, and Nidal will tell you when he thinks the time is right. It is not my place to tell you such things. Remember, you chose this, not I. Now you must wait until Nidal is ready to tell you."

I felt defeated. With a shrug, I walked away from the prince, upset that he chose not to tell me and implying that I chose Nidal over him. It wasn't even a choice. From the beginning, it was Nidal. *It will always be Nidal, for he is the love of my life, my one true love.*

Billal followed close behind, calling my name softly, not to alarm the children, who, from time to time, glanced our way and clearly looked uncomfortable with the talk that Billal and I were having.

"Wait, Loula. 'Tis not fair. You put me on the spot," he said, aggravated now with the way things turned out.

But I just kept walking. This conversation wasn't going anywhere. *What was I even thinking? Bringing Billal here! Servants are everywhere, watching us, and ready to report if need be. What would happen if Nidal found out? How would he react? What have I gotten myself into?*

And then I stopped in my tracks. There in front of me, just a few feet away, stood Nidal. He was fuming. Trembling, I scrambled out of his view, knowing that he was following right behind me. I picked up my pace, but it was no use. Nidal caught up to me, grabbed my arm, and pulled me close to him. I felt him tremble as he tightened his grip on my arm. I could not look up in his face. I had nothing to say. I was at a loss for words.

Nidal just waited for me to say something, anything at all that would explain why Billal was here. When I offered no explanation, he looked at Billal, who had just walked up beside me, and barked, "What the fuck are you doing here?"

He took a step closer to Billal. His cousin tried to speak, but I quickly interrupted them.

"Calm down Nidal. The children are watching us, and they look upset," I told him angrily.

Nidal's tone dropped to a whisper. "What is this the two of you have here? A secret rendezvous in the middle of the afternoon?" he growled.

He grabbed a hold of me and shook me gently. I lost my balance, and I was about to fall, but Billal caught me just in time, which infuriated Nidal even more. "Get your paws off my woman!" He took a step forward.

Natalie ran up to me screaming as tears streamed down her face. The child had gotten scared with all this tension, and she started trembling.

"Stop!" I said loudly. "Have you no shame? How dare you come charging here and start throwing accusations at us!" I yelled, angry now. "How dare you raise your voice in front of innocent children! Go away. Let us be. This is no time for a jealous rage. You are not fifteen anymore, Nidal. You are a grown man. Start acting like one!" I said sharply as I gently grabbed Natalie and marched away from both men.

Billal spoke for the first time, and I could sense the hatred in his voice. "Are you proud of yourself? Just what is your problem anyway? What are you afraid of? That if I am alone with Loula, she would choose me over you? That she will realize that I'm the better man?"

I knew those words would have a huge impact on Nidal, and I turned just in time to witness Nidal swing a punch on Billal's jaw.

Immediately, I ordered all the children to run as fast as they could back inside the house, and they hurriedly followed my instructions to safety. When all the children had settled in their seats, I ran to the window to see what was happening. I saw Billal angrily walk away as Nidal stood there frozen in his boots. I asked Nuray, the oldest child in the room, who was twelve years of age, to read a story to the children, telling her that I would be right back.

I marched outside where Nidal stood and yelled, "Don't you ever do that again! What's the matter with you? First of all, the children heard and saw everything. They were scared. Second of all, the servants were all ears. And third of all, there is nothing between myself and Billal!" I took a breath. "How dare you throw your accusations around like that! What do you think I am? A whore?" I spat.

"You sure acted like one!" Nidal automatically answered without thinking.

I could not believe my ears. I was stunned at what he had just said. I lifted my hand and slapped Nidal hard across his face. My hand left a red imprint on his cheek. He opened his mouth to say something, but he was too angry to say anything.

I turned and marched away from him but not before noticing that the servants had witnessed our fight. And all the children were gathered at the door, and even sweet, little Natalie was staring wide-eyed at us. Humiliated, I ran to the palace. I threw myself on the bed and cried. I once heard a doctor say that crying was therapeutic, food for the soul. So I cried my heart out.

I laid there for many hours waiting for Nidal to come for me and sweep me into his arms and apologize to me with kisses. But he never did. I eventually fell asleep, dressed as I was, from exhaustion and a broken heart. He still did not come. I woke up in the middle of the night, and still he was not in my bed. *Where is Nidal? Where has he gone? Why did he not come to me? I should be the one mad at him, not vice versa!*

So I undressed and threw myself back in bed, thinking he would soon come home to me. But as morning came and went, he did not show up. I had never felt so alone in my whole entire life. *Where could he be? Where has my lover gone? Who is he with? Where did he spend the night?* There were no answers to all my questions. There was no shoulder to cry on. I was completely on my own. Exhausted from the sleepless night, I fell into a deep sleep in midafternoon.

I awoke a few hours later, feeling defeated, a raw, lonely feeling. It was the kind you feel when all life has gone from your spirit, when you feel depressed and depleted. I could not say when the feeling set in my heart. I did not know the answer to that. The only thing I knew for sure was that I could not move on without Nidal.

I cried all day. The servants came and went. I asked to be left alone. I was not hungry; nor did I want to be bothered. They respected my wishes and did not come back. I cried all evening and into the next night. Still no Nidal. I tossed and turned and lay awake yet one more night. I counted sheep. I counted cats. I counted cattle. But I could not sleep. I wept all through the night.

The next morning, I had a headache that did not want to go away. And still no Nidal! I walked over to the mirror, and I did not recognize myself anymore. My eyes were swollen, and my hair was unkempt. My lips trembled, and the tears came again. I cried a river, and still no Nidal! I felt a little dizzy. Holding on to the wall, I made my way back to the bed. I had not slept in days. I could not sleep. I was feeling miserable and lonely, and extreme sadness had overcome me. I lay in bed yet another day and night, and sleep still did not find me. When the sun came out on the third morning, I looked around the room, and it felt as if the room were spinning. I shut my eyes and tried to rest, but I could not get Nidal off my mind.

I was trying to figure out where I had gone wrong when the door swung open with a crash and slammed shut with a loud bang. I did not turn around. I just lay in bed. I knew who had just walked in, and I did not have the energy to say a word. I felt defeated, weak, and angry, all at the same time.

I heard him walk through the room and sigh a few times, and then I heard a loud bang. He must have punched the closet door again. I winced, knowing how painful that must be. *What was he mad about? Why was he upset? I did not do anything wrong! He did!* I was furious now. *How dare he!*

I tried to lift myself up, but my hands felt heavy, and they just dropped to my side. Slowly, I wiggled out of bed and turned to look at my Nidal. I needed to see his face. Just one look. Just a peek at his beautiful face. But the room started to spin, and my legs gave out. I swayed and fell to the floor.

"Loula!" Nidal ran to my side quickly and lifted me in his strong arms. "Loula, what's wrong?"

His voice was thick and hoarse as he called my name a third time, but I was too weak to answer. Nidal laid me gently on the bed and ran to the door, where he threw the door open and called out for help. The servants came scrambling in one by one as the prince barked orders. He demanded the doctor to come immediately, and then he wanted to know what had happened in his absence. The servants explained that I had not eaten a thing in three days.

Anger was in his voice when he told them to leave the room. They all scrambled out of there just as the queen walked in. Clearly upset, she asked how I was faring, and then she told Nidal that she had ordered the servants to leave me in peace, thinking I needed to be alone during his absence to sort things out. Nidal was about to yell something at his mother, but the doctor rushed in and told everyone to leave the room.

Nidal refused to leave my side, and the doctor shook his head in disapproval, walked up to the bed, and felt my forehead. Then he felt my pulse. I heard him tell Nidal that my pulse was low.

Alarmed, Nidal asked, "What is wrong with her?"

"Relax, Nidal, there is nothing to worry about. Loula just needs to eat and catch up on some sleep."

I could hear the relief in Nidal's voice as he thanked the doctor for his services and walked him out of the room. Then he called the servants and told them to bring some food. The thought of food made me wince. I was not hungry for food. I was hungry for Nidal's touch. I was thirsty for his kisses. Weak as I was, I still yearned for him to make love to me. I missed him so much.

Nidal sat on the bed next to me. I looked up into his eyes and saw in them what I hoped to see. I knew that look. He still loved me. My heart did somersaults. My prince leaned close to me, kissed my forehead, and whispered his love for me. The servants came into the room with three trays of food. Nidal told them to place the trays on the side table and to leave the room immediately and not bother us for the rest of the day.

My prince lifted me into a sitting position so he could feed me, but I told him there was no way I would eat anything. I wasn't hungry for food. I needed Nidal. I needed him now. And Nidal, as if he read my thoughts, climbed into bed with me, held me in his arms, and kissed me hungrily. *This is the kind of food I was starving for. This is what I lived for.*

I finally fell into a deep sleep. I slept for hours and into the next day. When I awoke, Nidal lay next to me. I was in his arms. He squeezed me tight into his embrace. We did not say anything. Right now, words were not needed. He was back, and that was all that mattered.

Nidal jumped out of bed quickly, naked in all his glory. *When had he taken off his clothes?* He stood beside the bed looking down at me, teasing me with his nakedness. I reached for him, but suddenly the smile was gone from his face.

"It is time for you to eat. The doctor said you must eat something. And I promise you, after you eat, I will jump back in bed and give you what you crave." He then put on his clothes, and he threw my nightgown over my head and said teasingly, "Sorry, but I have to. Otherwise, we will not be able to concentrate on the food."

When had my clothes come off my body?

Nidal pulled me up into a sitting position. He then placed a couple of feathered pillows behind my back and brought the tray of food to the bed. Nidal fed me chicken broth and crackers.

"Something light, I do not want you overeating and upsetting your stomach," he said lightly.

But I was famished. I asked for more food and ate everything he fed me. I even drank some wine. Nidal took the tray away when I had finished my lunch. Then he served me the fruit he had promised me if I ate all my food.

❈ ❈ ❈

As the days passed blissfully, I regained my strength, but I still had no answer from Nidal. *Where was he for three days and three nights? Who was he with?* I waited patiently for Nidal to feel comfortable enough to talk to me about it. My suspicions took over, and a million things came to my mind. So I tried to focus on things that were pleasant and brought me peace.

One afternoon a few days later, when I was coming back from the orphanage, I saw Princess Shaeena coming down my path. As she approached me, she had a wicked smile on her lips, a smile I wanted to slap off her lovely face. But instead, I smiled back at her sweetly, playing her game, as I waited for her to speak. I was sure she was here to serve me with poisonous words.

"Taking an afternoon walk all by yourself, I see." She looked around. "Where is Nidal? Tired of you already?" she asked sweetly.

I just continued walking, ignoring her snide remarks. *I will not allow myself to stoop to her level.* But she marched right next to me, matching every step I took with her own. I knew I was not going to be rid of her any time soon as her cold glare scanned me from head to toe. I braced myself for her next words that I knew were coming.

"What's the matter, Loula? I know something happened with the two of you. Otherwise, he would not come over to my palace for three nights in a row warming my bed," she purred, smiling with satisfaction.

Even if she tried, she could not hurt me any more this moment than when she revealed Nidal's whereabouts on the day he walked out on me. My blood froze. My heart pounded out of control, and my senses whirled like a spinning tornado as I turned and looked at her, stunned. But I was not about to give her the satisfaction she was craving. I smiled and thanked her for taking good care of my Nidal. I simply walked away from her with my head held high.

"Yes, keep walking, bitch!" she hissed, as if trying to scare me, as if she were in total control of herself.

I heard her huffing and puffing and stomping her feet. I would have laughed my head off, but for the fact that now I knew and it was confirmed that my prince had spent three nights with her. *How could he do this to me?* I thought I knew him better than that. But Nidal was full of surprises. *Back home, they say, "If it's too good to be true, it's not true."*

Warm tears escaped my eyes as they made their way down my cheeks. I choked back a cry, plastered a smile on my face, and entered the palace. A smiling and welcoming queen greeted Shaeena, who followed behind me. They entered the tea room, but not before the queen threw me a worried look. Embarrassed, I ran as fast as my feet could take me to my chambers.

I could not believe it. A tight knot was forming in the pit of my stomach. *He had betrayed me! He had run off to her bed. How could he do this to me?* I believed every word he ever told me. *How naïve of me!*

Now what do I do? How could I accept his kisses without feeling betrayed? How could I make a life with him knowing what I now know? Maybe she was just lying. Maybe she made it all up. I have to ask Nidal. He needs to tell me the truth. I sat frozen on my bed, thinking of everything. I was trying to make sense of it all. I knew that things would never be the same now. Everything had changed.

About an hour passed, and Nidal still had not come home. I walked over to the window to see if he were anywhere in sight. Just as Nidal was making his way up the stairs to the palace, by coincidence, Princess Shaeena was walking out of the palace. They greeted each other with a hug and a kiss on the lips, which made my stomach turn as I witnessed this. The princess held on to Nidal's arm and whispered something in his ear, and Nidal smiled at her. Sick to my stomach, I saw the princess pull Nidal toward the rose garden. Nidal hesitated at first, but then he walked with her. She was still holding on to his arm as they disappeared into the gardens.

Now I know how Nidal had felt when Billal kissed me. If it were anywhere near the pain that I was feeling at this moment, then the punch he threw Billal was somehow justifiable. I leaned against the wall and prayed that this was a misunderstanding, hoping she was the one who kissed him just now on the lips. But I was witness to it. I saw him kiss her back.

I heard laughter, and I braced myself as I took another peek outside the window. The princess kissed him again, but it was on his cheek this time, as she laughingly said her good-bye and walked gracefully away. Nidal stood there looking at her until she disappeared from his view. The look on his face as he watched the princess leave was warm and pleasant.

I cannot believe it. I don't understand it. He had better do some good explaining when he comes to me, or else I will never forgive him. Never!

So I waited, thinking Nidal would come to me at any moment and make the pain go away. But he never did. Instead, he headed straight for the stables and rode away on his black stallion, taking the same road that Princess Shaeena's carriage had taken.

He is going to her, I thought miserably, holding back a stifled cry as my mind raced to remember again the conversation I had had with the princess earlier in the day.

She won, and I lost. I suddenly realized it. Exhausted now, I undressed, lay on my bed under the covers, and closed my eyes. I knew it was impossible for me to sleep right now, but maybe a nap was necessary. *Maybe when I wake up I will realize that it is all just a bad dream.*

Chapter Seven
Loula

*M*any hours had passed because, when I opened my eyes, it was almost dark in the room. I quickly got up and dressed, wondering where Nidal was. I opened the door, and the huge hallway was lit up with candles everywhere. I heard laughter coming from the dining room as I made my way toward it. I was very angry.

When I reached the doorway, a smiling, young guard with a glint in his eyes opened the door to let me enter. I swished past him angrily and stepped into the dining room, and my eyes found and locked with Nidal's. All the laughter stopped, and everyone stared at me. The men immediately stood. I walked over to where Nidal was sitting. He had a surprised look on his face when he saw me. The seat next to him, the one that belonged to me, was occupied with her. She was back, sitting in my chair next to my prince with a smug look on her face. I froze, not knowing what to do or say. It was an awkward moment for everyone except Shaeena. Her eyes gleamed with laughter.

Nidal stood up, smiled at me, and planted a warm kiss on my cheek. "Loula, my love, you finally awoke," he said teasingly with laughter in his eyes.

But at that moment he knew. He froze. The color drained from his face as he looked at me and saw the hurt and disappointment in my eyes.

The princess did not offer my seat to me. She just sat there, not budging and staking her claim to my chair and my prince. Nidal, the gentleman that he was, could not tell her to move. I looked around the table at all the guests and held my breath. I was not going to embarrass myself in front of everyone, especially Shaeena.

I walked around the table to an empty chair that was conveniently next to Billal and sat in it. All the gentlemen sat back in their chairs. Except Nidal. He stood frozen in his boots as his piercing gaze stared down at me and I stared right back at him, letting him know silently that two could play this game.

Slowly, he sat back in his chair like a lion, cautiously and ready at any given time to pounce on the enemy. Tension was in the air as everyone guessed what was happening. The queen looked with disapproval at her son, and to me, she gave a sympathetic look.

Throughout dinner, Billal and I had great conversation. Billal seemed surprised at the way I conducted myself. He played along just for amusement. Across the table, Nidal stared at the both of us, and I could tell he was dying a thousand deaths at this very moment. *Good! Suffer!* I had more surprises in store for him. Nidal needed to be taught a lesson. He could easily have asked for another chair to be brought to the table and placed on the other side of him, where I could have also sat next to him. Instead, he did not make an effort to do just that. He preferred Shaeena to sit there next to him, to please her and not me. Well, those actions deserved retaliation. I wasn't about to let him get away with that. This was war! He started it, and I was going to finish it, even though I knew I was playing with fire.

I smiled sweetly at Nidal from across the table and stole a quick glance at Shaeena. She looked angry. Hatred was written all over her lovely face as she witnessed Nidal's display of jealousy toward me. She tried everything she could to remove Nidal's attention away from me but could not succeed in accomplishing it.

I, on the other hand, was having a ball. This was fun. Torturing Nidal was on the top of my list at this moment. I talked and laughed playfully, and I even placed my hand on Billal's hand briefly. I saw Nidal ready to jump up from his chair, but the king, who also noticed, quickly called out to his son and asked him a question concerning the matters of the palace. For a second, Nidal's mind was occupied. I looked at the queen and saw her wink at me in approval with a smile on her lips. The queen approved of the way I was teaching her son a lesson. I guess she and I were the same when it came to our men.

Billal knew the game I was playing, and he took the opportunity to hold my hand in his. He looked at me and was about to whisper something in my ear, but just at that moment, Nidal pounded his fist forcefully on the table and startled everyone, including myself.

"That's enough!" he roared. "Get your dirty hands off my woman before I rip you to pieces." He leaped across the table and broke a few crystal wineglasses and fine china as he tried to reach Billal.

Billal was just as angry as Nidal was, and he stood and roared back, "What's the matter, cousin? Your woman doesn't warm your bed anymore, and you lost your cool?" he spat. "She prefers my attention to yours, and that makes you crazy, you jealous son of a bitch. You don't know how to treat a woman, and now you've lost her!" he said with satisfaction.

Rage exploded from every part of Nidal's body as he jumped on the table and flew at Billal, knocking him to the floor. He punched him over and over again, not realizing the strength he had. He unleashed his anger on Billal's bloody face. I tried to tear him away from Billal and lost my balance, and I went flying over a couple of chairs.

A gentleman reached over, grabbed my hand, and pulled me up. I heard the queen's cries as she ran over to me and tried to give me some comfort. By this time, chaos was everywhere. By the king's orders, the gentlemen pulled Nidal off Billal and held him steady, but Nidal was in such a rage that he tugged and pulled like a caged animal.

Billal finally stood and punched Nidal square in the face. "You don't deserve her. She is a rare jewel, and she should be with me! Watch your back, Nidal, for soon I will be warming her bed," he lashed out, pleased with himself, even though his face was all broken up and full of blood.

Nidal tried to free himself from the men who were still holding on to him, but he was not successful.

The queen walked up to her son. Looking humiliated, she said softly, "I am so ashamed of your behavior tonight, Nidal. How could you? You know not what you've done!" she said angrily. Then she turned to Billal and pointed a finger to her nephew. "And you of all people, Nidal's cousin and best friend forever, you know better than to provoke your cousin! You are like brothers! This is his future wife, possibly the next queen of Arabia! You cannot touch her, and you know it!" she said in a harsh tone. Then she turned to me and took my hand. "Come with me, my dear." She pulled my arm for me to follow her.

I did not want to leave the room with Princess Shaeena still occupying it. Nidal would be with her when I left, and she would seek that opportunity to comfort my Nidal. But I had no choice as the queen dragged me out of the dining area. I followed silently. I did not look at Nidal when I passed him by, but I knew his eyes were shooting daggers on my back.

The queen pulled me out in the hallway where she stopped in her tracks and said with a hint of anger in her voice, "Child, you misbehaved too. But I know why, and I think I would have done the same in your situation." She sighed, and continued in a lighter tone, "I know you love my son. And I know without a doubt that he loves you too, but I do not understand his behavior. Please be patient with him. He will come around. I promise you, dear." She gave me a warm hug. "Now run along to your chamber and wait for Nidal. I will send him to you shortly." And with those few words, she marched back into the dining room, and the guard closed the door.

I was left alone to deal with my pain by myself. I could not bear it if Nidal stopped loving me. Fear gripped my heart at the thought of that. *What am I to do now?* I hurried along the corridor and opened the door to my chambers. I felt cold in there as I stepped inside. Cold and empty! I will have to play the waiting game again. *But what if he chooses to visit Shaeena again tonight?* I could not bear the thought of that. I sadly undressed and crawled inside the covers. I closed my eyes and prayed for a miracle.

A few seconds later, the door swung open with a loud bang as it hit the other side of the wall. The picture frame that hung on the wall next to the door dropped to the floor and shattered. Nidal ignored it, and in two long strides, he came to the bed and dragged me out of it. His hold on my arm hurt as he pulled me to him. With his foot, he kicked the door, and it banged once again as it closed. Nidal turned his blazing gaze at me, and I thought for sure he was going to kill me.

When he opened his mouth to speak, it wasn't with a loud, vicious voice. It was in a low threatening tone. "If you ever do that again, I swear by all that is holy that I will kill you with my bare hands. I will rip your head off!" he warned. His hold on me tightened, and his voice started to tremble as he continued with his threats. "I will hang you outside the window!" Then he stopped abruptly, and he just stared at me relentless.

My blood boiled with conviction. He was the one who was deceitful, yet he wanted to punish me for his wrongdoings. *It must be a bad joke!* I was speechless. No words could justify the wrongful accusations. No one could take back what was already said. It was too late. I let out a sigh and pulled myself away from his firm grip. Everything that had transpired this evening had hurt me deeply.

We both looked at each other with sadness, for this was a mournful day. What was done could never be undone. We would have to live with this for the rest of our lives. I did not know if we even had the strength to overcome it. My feelings were playing tug-of-war with me. On the one hand, I was angry that he cheated on me. I had never wanted him to touch me again. On the other hand, there was no life for me without Nidal. *So what am I to do?*

I could tell Nidal was getting impatient as the seconds passed, and finally he burst out, "Are you not even going to apologize for what you have done to me today? Your wanton behavior destroyed us!" He ran his fingers through his hair. "You betrayed me to no avail! It was a slap in the face, a knife in my heart," he accused.

"How dare you judge me!" I yelled. "You of all people, you are the traitor who at first chance ran to Shaeena's house to sleep in her bed for three nights!" I spat. "I did not betray you. It was you who betrayed me!"

Nidal's face changed a few shades as he tried to grasp what I just revealed to him. "Loula," he said cautiously, "who fed you such poison?"

I laughed recklessly. "Can you deny it ever happened?" I asked hopeful. I desperately wanted him to tell me that Shaeena had lied and he was not at her palace during the three days he was missing. "Can you honestly say that you did not sleep in her bed? Can you look me in the face and swear to me that you did not touch her? Or are you guilty that you committed a crime against our love?"

"I did not do anything wrong!" Nidal yelled. "I am innocent of all your accusations!" he roared. "I did not do anything to jeopardize our love. How can you think that I have?" he asked, stunned.

"I don't believe a single word you say to me. Your precious princess told me you were in her bed for three days and three nights!" I cried.

"I swear by all that is holy that I did not do anything wrong!" he pleaded. "You automatically assume the worst in me. You do not trust me. You do not know me at all, Loula. Otherwise, you would never have said all these ugly things," he said sadly, turning his back and walking to the window.

Mixed feelings were swimming around in my head. I never stopped to think about that. If I had, I would know that Nidal would never do that to me. Shaeena had lied to me to split us up. That realization hit me like a ton of bricks. She lied to me, and I believed her. Nidal would never betray me. He loved me. I knew this to be true. My tears streamed down my face, and my sobs got louder as I cried.

"I trust you, Nidal," I whispered. "How could I be so stupid? She lied to break us apart, and I believed everything she said to me! Can you forgive me? Can you overlook my stupidity?" I begged. "My love for you has blinded me from the truth." Fresh tears streamed down my face.

Nidal gave me that look as he took a step closer to me, the look that spoke a thousand words of love, the kind of look that ignites flames that cannot be stopped, the one that melts your heart with liquid fire, the kind of fire that reaches deep into the soul and liquefies everything it touches, torching everything in its way until it reaches its destination and two souls unite and become one. I held my breath as he leaned closer and touched my lips with his. He kissed me softly, and his hands wrapped around my waist and pulled me closer to him.

"Loula," he said huskily, "to whom does your heart belong to? To whom does your mind wander to?" he asked hoarsely. "Tell me, Loula. Is it me you crave? Is it my name you call out in your dreams?"

"You're a fool if you think otherwise," I whispered as I caressed what belonged to me. Nidal closed his eyes. Desire slammed through him so savagely that he shuddered. "It is you, Nidal. It has always been you," I said truthfully.

"Loula," he groaned. His eyes were fierce and wild, and he yanked me against his body savagely. His lips were demanding, and his embrace was possessive and strong. And when his hips pressed against mine, I felt his bulge and moaned with desire.

Nidal pulled my gown off my body, and I stood naked before him as he feasted his eyes upon me. Within seconds, he had undressed and stood before me. His bronzed body glistened in the candlelight as my eyes roamed across his broad, muscled chest and down his stomach, gliding all the way down to his manhood. A soft moan escaped my lips, and I heard a husky sound rumble deep in his throat as he lifted me and threw me on the bed and jumped on top of me. He was wild with desire as he took me to heights of passion that burned so intense that it would make an erupting volcano jealous.

The next day, we both woke up at the same time. It was a happy day. The sunshine poured in through the windows and sparkled its light everywhere as we dressed for breakfast. Behind me, Nidal buttoned my gown and allowed his hands to roam over my breasts as he caressed them gently. He pushed his groin against my thighs, and I purred in response. I turned my head around, allowing his lips to brush down on mine, and I struggled to tame the emotions that threatened to course through me. He kissed me more deeply. His tongue explored my mouth and drove me insane. If we kept this up, we would end up in bed again, and everyone in the dining room would wonder where we were. I pushed him gently away, and he looked in my eyes, questioning my abrupt behavior. He sighed in understanding and gave me another quick kiss, pinching my breast playfully, before he finally pulled away.

We were both famished as we walked briskly down the hall, hand in hand, to the dining room. We were the first ones there, and we took advantage of the opportunity and kissed each other passionately once again. When we heard voices outside the doorway, we pulled apart quickly and sat down in our seats.

As the queen walked in first, she immediately noticed the sparkle in our eyes and smiled joyfully with understanding. The king followed and gave a nod in our direction. Slowly after that, all the other guests came in, one by one, until the table was full with hungry people. We had a delightful time, chattering away, gossiping to no accord, and acting as if the last time we all sat together nothing dramatic had happened, as if it were all wiped under the table and we started fresh.

Billal was sitting in his usual seat. He was still sporting a few bruises on his face, but he had his head held high. To me, that was a blessing. I did not want him to feel threatened by Nidal. They both needed to work on their relationship. They were, after all, cousins.

Nidal did not even bother to look at his cousin, not once. In fact, he ignored him totally. At least they were not fighting today. All wounds heal over time, and I was sure that their relationship would survive this downfall someday.

After breakfast, Nidal and I took a stroll out in the rose garden. Nidal held me close to him as we walked and inhaled the fresh air. I looked around at the little wonders of the world. A butterfly flapping its colorful wings as it flew over a pink rose. A bunny hopping into the bushes chased its little friend joyously. Flowers bloomed in all their glory, showing off their colorful coat as they intertwined with each other, reminding me of Nidal and me, embraced by love. Little birds chirped as they flew playfully around us, and my gaze followed them around the garden. They stopped at the bay windows of the palace, and that was when I noticed Billal gazing out the window at us.

He did not look too happy. My heart went out to him. I looked up at Nidal and saw he was looking in the same direction I was. I felt him tense, and I immediately reached up and kissed his lips to reassure him that he had nothing to worry about. When I threw a quick glance back at the bay window, Billal had disappeared. *Why is life so complicated?* Sometimes, I wondered what lessons are being taught to us when we suffer. I hated to see Billal hurting so. I wished I could take his pain away. It did not seem fair to me that some people had all the luck in this world and some suffered throughout their miserable lives.

We walked throughout the rose gardens and then wandered off away from the palace. It was such a lovely day. Nidal pulled me gently off the road, and we ended up in a meadow. It was so beautiful that it took my breath away. It was full of trees of all shapes and sizes and flowers in full bloom in all shades of bright colors. We continued to walk across the green grass until we stopped under a willow tree.

This tree, I was told, was three hundred years old. It held a lot of secrets throughout the decades. *How many lovers had kissed here? How many duels had been exercised under this tree? How many friends had revealed their innermost feelings here? How many maidens had given up their reputations here?* There must have been a thousand and one stories to tell if the willow spoke a thousand words. But it just stood here, straight and proud, allowing it to be a stepping-stone for anyone who wished to use it, a quiet friend that spoke not of all it has heard over the years but loaned its bark to lean on to any passerby who wished to rest under it.

Nidal pulled out a carving knife from his pocket and carved a heart with our initials inside of it on the tree. He was so romantic, this prince of mine. He made me feel like a schoolgirl all over again. It was such a beautiful feeling. Our lips met once again as a drop of rain splattered on my face. We both looked up just in time to see the rain come pouring down. It was all so sudden. We stood under the willow and tried to stay dry, but we were soon dripping wet. The rain smelled so good. I looked up at the tree and spotted a few birds taking refuge on some branches. Looking around, no one was in sight except for the endless green pastures. We were the only ones within miles from here.

Nidal reached below my waist, grabbed my wet gown, pulled it over my head, and took it off. It happened so fast that I did not have time to dispute it. I was not wearing a single thing underneath, much to Nidal's delight. Then he took off his clothes, and we were both under the willow tree, stark naked.

Nidal's hands worked their magic as they slid down and caressed me lightly. He dropped down on the wet grass and pulled me to him. I lay on top of him, feeling his groin ready to take what belonged to him. We made love out here in the meadow, under the willow tree. The warm raindrops splashed on our heated bodies as we enjoyed the fruits of love. It was such an experience as nothing we ever had before. Wet, spent, and exhausted, we lay in each other's arms and allowed the rain to dance on our skins. It was a nice hot day, and we welcomed the rain as it splattered all over us. *It cannot get any better than this*, I thought with a satisfied feeling.

After a while, the rain eased up, and the sun came out, shining its way through the sky and on to our bodies. We dried quickly and put on our damp clothes. We just lay under the willow tree, admiring the beauty in front of us.

I leaned my head against Nidal's chest and closed my eyes. I pictured mine and Nidal's children running across the meadow playfully. Maybe a little boy who had Nidal's charms and good looks and a little girl who looked like me. That would be all I would ever ask for in this lifetime. I had everything else.

"What is on your mind, Loula? You are so quiet. Is something bothering you?" Nidal asked, patiently waiting for a response.

He always wanted to know everything. I sighed. I did not like to share everything on my mind. I felt like a child when I was always told to say everything that I was thinking and not allowed to keep some treasures for myself.

So I lied. "I was just admiring the view and enjoying being here with you, Nidal."

There. That was easy.

"You are keeping your thoughts to yourself, Loula." Nidal was frustrated. "It must be something you don't want me to find out about," he accused as he pulled up his body and leaned against the willow tree.

"Will there ever be a day that I don't get accused of something from you, Nidal?" I was hurt. "You seem to always want to say hurtful things. You must accept what I say as the truth and stop trying to figure me out, Nidal, because it will hurt our relationship if you continue this way." I tried to make him see reason.

But Nidal was Nidal, and he was one of a kind. I knew he would not change. I had to accept him for who he was because I loved him so much. "Nidal, stop stressing when there is no need for it. Just live your life with me and be happy. Always think positive, and you will see how that can change your life," I said simply.

Nidal tried to analyze my words of wisdom, but he had trouble understanding them. I looked up into his face, and he seemed troubled with thought as he sat there quietly. "Nidal, I love you so much. I need you to understand this," I pleaded.

"Loula," Nidal moaned my name as if he were in pain, "whether I understand it or not isn't the issue here. What's at stake here is bigger than understanding your logic. I think I love you more than you love me, and that hurts," he whispered painfully. "I am always feeling this when I am around you lately. I know I cannot exist in a world without you. I'd rather kill myself than live without you," he moaned and ran his fingers through his hair.

He shifted his gaze toward the sky. I looked up, and far away over the rolling meadows was a rainbow. Its colors were brilliantly displayed for all to see. I rolled over from my sitting position and stood. I looked down at Nidal, square in the face.

"Nidal, I too love you more than life itself, and I know you know this. You just want to hear me say it again and again," I laughingly accused.

Nidal pushed his body up and stood in front of me. His face got serious as he reached over and pushed the falling strands of hair away from my face. "Maybe it is what I need to hear to feel satisfied, Loula," he said softly.

"Nidal, you will never be satisfied! You need me to constantly remind you," I said laughingly. "So here I go. I love you, I love you, I love you, I love you, and I love you! There. Do you feel better now?" I teased.

Nidal just stood there staring at me, and suddenly he grabbed my shoulders, pulled me closer, and kissed me with such passion that he almost bit my lips. I matched him, a kiss for a kiss, as our passion reached the heights of the blue sky. No matter what, I knew that I loved him so much that I too knew there was no life for me outside his embrace.

Life is good, I thought as we strolled back to the palace. The sun was about to set. We had been gone for most of the day. From a distance, I noticed the queen was sitting outside with the king and a few of his men. As we got closer to the palace, Nidal's steps quickened, and his hand tightened around mine when he saw the king's facial expression. The king himself looked mad, but the queen had a satisfied grin on her lovely face. She looked happy to see us together and in love.

As we approached them, the king did not waste a second. "Where have you been?" he asked furiously. "I called a meeting hours ago. Nidal, you know how important the meetings are!" he barked. He shook his finger in his son's face. "Have you no respect for your king, your soldiers, and your country?" He turned flamboyantly and marched into the palace. All his men quickly followed him, including Nidal, but not before kissing me and whispering for my ears alone his love for me.

I watched him leave my side with sadness, knowing he would not return to me until early morning. I turned and looked at the queen apologetically, and she smiled at me with understanding.

"I have not forgotten what it feels like to be in love, Loula," she said sweetly. "The king will get over it, and as for your prince, he will be back before you know it." She took my hand and pulled me toward the rose gardens. "Have you ever visited the gardens at night?" she asked sweetly as I followed her quickly along the brick path.

Torches were lit along the garden's path, and as we walked, I saw the fountains, magnificent structural gems, that graced the gardens with beauty. Roses of all colors sprayed their perfume in the air, and all this beauty took my breath away. The queen turned to look at me, and I smiled in approval of all I saw.

The queen tugged my hand to follow her, and she led me to a place behind a big rose bush. "This is where Nidal hid from me when he was a little boy and knew he was in some kind of trouble," the queen said sadly. "Now he is all grown up, and his attention is elsewhere," she said helplessly. "It's not easy being a mom and watching your beloved child grow up and replace you with someone else." She turned and faced me. A tear slowly rolled down her face, and then she smiled. "I'm so glad he brought you to us. The king and I love you so much. You are a beautiful addition to this family." She gave me a warm, sincere hug.

Her words touched me. I felt welcomed in the palace, and it was good to know that the queen mother liked me. I hugged her too. I was glad that Nidal's parents finally approved of me. We strolled in the gardens awhile longer before we decided to call it a night.

Chapter Eight
Loula

There was silence in the room when I woke up in the morning. Nidal was not in bed with me, and I looked around the room for him and saw him standing by the window. He kept running his fingers through his hair. I heard him sigh a couple of times as he stood rigid, staring out into the gardens.

I kept silent, knowing he had a lot on his mind. Something was bothering him, and I needed to know what it was. But knowing Nidal, he did not share stressful information with me, saying he loved me too much to upset me with stuff like that. But I had to know. I wanted to know everything that occupied Nidal's mind. I guess I was turning into him, needing to know and understand him fully and in every way.

As I was getting out of bed, Nidal turned, and I saw the pain in his eyes before he quickly covered it up by throwing me a loving smile. We both walked toward each other and hugged. I felt loved and safe in his embrace. Our lips met, and he quickly scooped me up in his arms. We both landed back in bed, but I needed to talk to him and not get distracted by his kisses, so I pushed him away from me gently.

With a serious tone, I said, "Nidal, stop it! I know you are trying to distract me. I see you suffering, and I can't stand it anymore. Have I caused this pain that I see in your eyes? Have I disappointed you in any way?"

Nidal's expression on his face was full of love and concern as he grabbed me by the waist, pulled me close, and locked me in his arms. "No, my love," he whispered softly. "It has nothing to do with you. I was just thinking about the meeting last night."

His strong arms tightened his hold on me, and he brought his lips down on mine. This was his way of avoiding answering direct questions, and this angered me. He shared only the information that suited him and withheld the rest. I wiggled out of his embrace, tipped my head back, and looked him square in his eyes.

"Don't you think, Nidal, that I should know what wanders in your mind? Isn't it about time you share your thoughts with me?" I asked, frustrated. He was protecting me from something, and I needed to know what that was.

"I can't tell you without hurting you. Don't you understand how much I love you? Do you know me so little? Don't you know that I would give my life for you? I would protect you from anything and anyone with my life! Telling you everything would make you scared and hopeless. Why would I want to do that to you, Loula?" he pleaded for me to understand.

"You are a hypocrite!" I accused. "You say all this, yet you want to know everything that's on my mind! I love you, and if you are going through a rough time, I want to know. It affects me too, when you are suffering. I suffer when you suffer! Please try to understand my feelings too. Don't be selfish!" I tried to reason with him.

"Selfish?" My accusations had hurt him. "You call me selfish and a hypocrite! The only reason I don't want to tell you is because I want to protect you. It's my job to make you feel safe."

But he needed to understand that we were equal partners in this. He could not pick and choose only what suited him. "I insist that you tell me!" I yelled. "You say you love me, but you are not willing to share. I do not understand this love you say you have for me that only serves your purpose and not mine!" I said angrily.

"Fine, Loula. Ask me what you want to know, and I will try to answer the best way I can," he sounded defeated.

I turned to him and went straight to the point. "I want to know everything about the meetings. I know something horrible is about to happen. I can feel it." I knew as I waited for Nidal's response that what he revealed to me might be more than I could handle.

Nida considered my statement and, without hesitation, asked, "Then why do you insist to know? It will only upset you." He tried reasoning with me. "The less you know the better." He was obviously genuinely concerned now for my welfare.

"No, Nidal, that's where you are wrong. Not knowing, no matter how bad it is, will only make me sick with worry." I tried to make him understand my logic.

Nidal knew he had lost the argument, and when he spoke, it was with great sadness. "Loula, in a few months, my beloved country will go to war."

"War?" I was terrified. "Who will lead them to war?" I already knew the answer to that before he even responded.

Nidal just sat there staring at me without answering my question. But his silence confirmed to me what I needed to know. I threw myself on him, crying.

"No, Nidal! You cannot go!" I begged. "I won't let you. Why do you have to even be there? Please, Nidal, don't go!" I cried.

Nidal tried to calm me down, but I was hysterical. "That is the reason I chose not to tell you. I knew you would be upset, Loula. Tell me you understand that, please," Nidal begged.

I looked into Nidal's beautiful face. He was so handsome, and he was mine. The thought that he was going to put his life in danger drove me wild with worry. I did not know how to deal with such news. I hugged him, never wanting to let him go. I held him in my arms so tight. I wanted this moment to last forever.

Tears rolled down my face, sobs tore from my throat, and I was trembling. I felt Nidal's hold tighten.

"Now do you know why I did not tell you before this, Loula?" Nidal gently asked. "I knew how you would react. I do not want you to feel this way."

"So what were you going to do? Run off to war without saying a single word? Did you want me to wake up one morning and realize you had gone to war?" I let out all my anger and frustration.

Nidal just sat there, not saying a word, which angered me even more. I started pounding on his chest. He didn't even wince at the pain. He knew I was right.

"So tell me, Nidal. How am I supposed to live without you now that I have lived with you for so long? What if something happens to you and I never see you again? I will kill myself! I will jump in the river and drown myself," I told him frantically.

In that instant, Nidal saw in my eyes the truth that I would do just that. He pulled me close to him and yelled hoarsely, "Stop it! Loula, stop it! Don't say such things! I will lead my men to war, we will destroy the enemy, and then we will come home. You have nothing to fear," he lied miserably.

I almost choked on my next words. "When are you leaving?" I stared him in the face without blinking. "Were you even going to tell me? Or were you going to leave without saying good-bye?" I knew what the answer to that was. "I am deeply hurt." I sobbed and felt the pain in my chest squeezing me tight.

Nidal's face flushed with shame. I pulled back and looked into his eyes, searching for answers. Nidal knew how to hide them well. He wanted to protect me from the truth. "Tell me, Nidal," I demanded. "I want to know everything, every single little thing!" I cried.

And Nidal settled himself uncomfortably on the bed and looked serene, like he was almost relieved that the truth was about to come out. "I will tell you everything, and I know later I will regret this," he said grimly. "But since you persist in knowing the truth, I will tell you all, but don't interfere until I am done talking." He sighed. "Every meeting I have gone to has been about the preparations for the war. I did not tell you. I wanted to spare you the awful details. I knew it would scare you to pieces, but you must know that I intended to tell you right before I left. Knowing before that would get you stressed out much sooner than necessary. I know you love me, and you would tell me to stay here with you, but Loula ..." He paused for a second and wiped the tears from my face. "I have to go. I have my honor and my love for my country. I cannot let my men go without me. I am not a coward! I am their leader. They look up to me. They love me, Loula, and I will not let them down!" He averted his eyes as he said this because he could not look me in the face. He knew I would say that he would be letting me down if he went.

My shoulders dropped, and my head swayed back and forth as the tears rolled down my face. The sobs ripped through my throat as I cried out his name in fear for his life.

"Oh, Nidal," I cried. "Nidal, please don't go. What if something happens to you and I don't ever see you again? What if you die in battle and they bring your body home in a bag? I cannot live without you! I won't live without you!" I screamed.

Nidal tried to calm me down, promising he would return from the war. He wiped away my tears and held me in his arms until my sobs stopped and I went limp in his arms. I was exhausted. I did not move from this position; nor did Nidal ask me to. Within minutes, I fell into a deep sleep, as if I were drugged. I passed out in his arms. I was emotionally disturbed, and it was easier to sleep away the pain.

When I awoke, I was still wrapped in Nidal's strong arms. The room was almost dark, except for a candle that was on the table. The flame, about to be extinguished,was casting shadows across the room. Nidal slept peacefully. I stared at him for hours. I could not get enough of him. I saw a wet tear on his lashes and knew he had been crying too. I knew I had no choice but to let him go. I would pray from the moment he left until the moment he returned back into my arms. I would beg God to spare his life. I would count the days, the hours, the minutes, and the seconds. I would light a candle every day until his return.

❧ ❧ ❧

Excitement was in the air as the days were getting closer. The palace was getting ready for the prince and his men to leave. Everyone was bustling about, preparing for departure. I only saw Nidal at night in our bed. He was too busy during the day to be with me. He was still doing last-minute training, and the meetings were still going on. In the night when he came to me, he was exhausted from the day's work, and my prince fell asleep as soon as his head hit the pillow. I was too numb to say anything, and in the middle of the night, I awakened to quiet kisses and caresses and murmured words of love and promises that only God could make come true.

The day before Nidal was supposed to leave, I was sitting alone on the bench in the rose garden, meditating and praying to God when I heard a familiar voice behind me.

"'Tis a beautiful day for a stroll in the gardens. Would you do me the honor and walk with me?" Billal asked charmingly as he stretched out his arm and waited for me to take his hand.

I sat there staring at him with a smile on my face, excited that he chose at this time to visit with me, a time when my heart was about to break. I felt lonely, and I accepted his invitation without skipping a heartbeat. I wrapped my arm around his arm, and we walked quietly, just enjoying the view.

Billal broke the silence. "So how are you holding up?" he asked, curious. "Have you prepared yourself for the departure of your prince? We will be gone awhile, you know," he chimed, as if he had not a care in the world, as if going to war were not a threat to his life.

I looked at him suspiciously, trying to figure him out, but Billal was a hard man to read. We walked through the gardens slowly. Billal was chattering with excitement when he suddenly stopped in his tracks, turned, and looked into my face. A very uncomfortable feeling was forming in the pit of my stomach. And then he leaned over and kissed me. It was so sudden that there was no time to react. He just kissed me without my permission. By the time I realized that I was kissing him back, he had already tasted my lips on his.

I tried pushing him away from me as hard as I could, but I was no match for him. He weighed two hundred pounds, and he grasped on to me with the strength of a lion. His strong thighs pressed against my body, and I could feel his manhood rubbing against me. Alarmed, I tried to free myself from him but could not.

Finally, he stopped and took a step back. "I'm sorry, Loula," he said, apologetic. "I could not help myself. You are a very beautiful woman, and I think I have fallen in love with you," he admitted as I stared at him wide-eyed in disbelief with what he just confessed.

I was about to slap him hard across his face, but I sensed someone was looking at us. I turned and looked up at the palace. I saw Nidal. He was staring coldly down at us from the window. He had witnessed everything. I saw him turn and walk away. My heart started pounding a thousand times a minute. He had seen us! He would assume that I had invited the kiss. He had no way of knowing that I did nothing wrong.

I pushed Billal out of my way and ran up the path to the palace. I had to find Nidal and explain that what he saw was not what he thought. I heard Billal run after me as he called my name. He was much stronger than I was, but I was faster than he was. By the time he caught up to me, I had entered the palace, and I was racing down the corridor, looking for Nidal.

I checked in our bedroom, but he was not there. I opened every door down the hall, but nothing. He was nowhere. I stepped into one of the rooms and ran to the window, thinking he was outside and I could catch a glimpse of him, but he was not outside either. I heard Billal enter the room and walk up beside me. I could feel his hard breathing on my neck as he tried to catch his breath.

He put his hands on my shoulders and turned me around. "Loula, why do you run from me? Why do you rebuke my kisses? I love you. Please give me a chance to prove to you that I am the better man." He leaned over and kissed me again.

"I hope your choice was a wise one, Loula," Nidal said with a cold, calm voice while leaning against the doorway of the guest room. I staggered backward with a scream.

Billal looked at Nidal, amused, and said with a laugh, "Well, you came just in time."

I closed my eyes, begging God not to allow Billal to bait my prince.

Nidal's face tightened, but he stood there with calm superiority. He was looking at the both of us with burning fire in his eyes. It was a dangerous look, and then, with a sudden sharp edge of anger in his voice, he said, "I'm done!" He turned and stepped out of the room.

I stared in disbelief at his stiff back as he walked away. His voice had sounded final. I ran to the door to see where he might be, but he had vanished through an archway that led to the east corridor. Somewhere in the distance, a door clicked shut. I stopped in my tracks, frozen where I stood. I tried to gather my wits. Billal came behind me and placed his hand on my arm. It felt like fire burned me when he touched me. I pulled away from him angrily and started running down the corridor. I needed to find Nidal and explain myself.

There were so many doors. I opened the door to most of the rooms, but Nidal was not anywhere. I ran to our bedroom, thinking he would eventually come to me. I heard Billal's voice somewhere behind me call my name, but I ignored him. I closed the door, walked over to our bed, and threw myself on it, crying hysterically. The pain in my chest tightened even more as I called out Nidal's name. I knew this time was different. I had seen the look in Nidal's face. It was cold and heartless. Fear struck me because I knew I might have lost him forever this time. He really was done with me. I saw it in his eyes and heard it in his voice.

At that second, the door to our room went flying and crashed against the stone wall. I turned and saw Nidal walk in. He did not even look at me as he headed straight for his jacket that lay on the chair by the window. He put it on, and he was heading for the door.

I ran up to him and pulled his arm. "Nidal, please, hear me out. Please," I begged tearfully. "Nidal," I called out his name. But he tugged his arm out of my grip, looked at me with a disgusted look, and strode toward the door without saying another word.

I was desperate for him to listen to reason. I grabbed the tail of his jacket and tried to pull it. He stopped, turned, and looked right at me.

With a snarl, he said, "Let go of my jacket, woman! We are done. I told you! Don't ever touch me again." He tugged at his jacket and headed straight for the door.

I could not let him go. It would finalize everything if I allowed him to walk out the door. Desperate now, I wrapped my arms around his waist and begged for him to stop. Nidal tried to pull my hands apart. He wanted to loosen my grip so he could escape. I dropped to my knees, grabbed a hold of his pantaloons, and begged him not to leave me.

With a cold stare, annoyed at me now, he pulled me up and pushed me aside. I quickly ran back to him, hugged him close to me, and kissed his lips. Nidal kept his mouth closed tight. I caressed his chest, I tried to pull the strings that held up his pantaloons, but Nidal slapped my hands away. He walked past me to the doorway, and I begged, "Nidal, please, don't go."

Nidal stopped, slowly turned around, and looked at me. His cold stare sent shivers up and down my back. This was a side of him I had never seen before. Nidal kicked the door closed with his left foot, and in two long strides, he was standing next to me.

"What is it you want, Loula?" Nidal asked coldly. "Do you want me to fuck you?" He grabbed me roughly and threw me to the floor.

My body was full of pain as it crashed on the cold, marble floor. Nidal kneeled down next to me, and with his bare hands, he ripped my dress to pieces. I lay there shocked as Nidal continued to rip all my undergarments off my body and left me stark naked.

Nidal's eyes raked over my naked body coldly, and he snarled, "Is this what you want?" He grabbed my breast and squeezed it roughly in his hands.

This was a huge mistake. I had pushed him too far. I knew it now. Nidal pulled the strings on his pantaloons, and it dropped to his knees. Then he pulled out his shaft from his underpants. I was shocked as he tried to enter me. He pushed and probed, and once inside me, Nidal was not gentle. He made love to me harshly, like an animal. His hands poked and pinched my skin roughly, and he grabbed my hair and pulled on it as he pumped his shaft hard inside me. He climaxed seconds later, without even a hint of satisfaction on his face. I lay there, numb and in pain beyond reason, feeling used and abused.

Nothing prepared me for his cruel actions. I did not recognize this man who destroyed everything we ever had together. I looked into his eyes, and they were cold as ice, empty of emotion, void of life. Spent, he got up, pulled up his pantaloons, and tied the strings. He combed his hair with his fingers, grabbed his jacket, and walked out of the room, slamming the door behind him.

It felt as if the room was spinning. I tried to get up, but the pain was unbearable. My body was bruised all over. Minutes later, as I tried to gather my wits, I heard voices outside. I pushed myself slowly up and stumbled to the window just in time to witness Nidal walking away from the palace with Princess Shaeena holding on to his arm.

Anger immediately gripped me as I watched them casually walk toward the stables. Minutes later, they exited the stables on a black stallion, heading in the direction of her palace. I heard their laughter as they rode away. It ripped my heart out seeing them together like that. Hearing Nidal's laughter as he rode away with another woman was extremely painful.

I threw myself on the bed and cried for hours. The servants came and went all evening. I sent them all away. Night came, but sleep eluded me as I lay in my empty, cold bed. I knew Nidal would not come home to me tonight. I played over and over again in my mind the scene with Nidal. His actions had left marks on my body and my heart. I remembered the pain I was feeling when he took me without my consent.

His lips never touched mine. His hands did not caress my body. His eyes were stone-cold as he stared at me with fury. I had lost him, and it hurt to admit this. I cried all night for the love I had lost today. I cried for what we could have had. I cried until the tears dried out and all my hopes disappeared.

By morning, I was still awake, sleepless, and still hurting. He did not come home to me, just as I expected he would not. He was at Shaeena's still. I placed my hand where my heart was, and my heart was pounding rapidly. He would come home today because this was the day that the army would be leaving for war. Cold sweat overcame me at the thought of Nidal going to war. I was at a loss for words.

There was a knock on the door, and my heart thumped loudly, thinking it was Nidal coming to ask for my forgiveness, I braced myself as the door opened, and the queen mother walked in. She had a worried look on her face as she walked over and sat on the bed next to me.

"Loula, dear child, what happened yesterday?" she asked softly. "The servants told me they heard a lot of commotion in your room. They saw Nidal stalk out of here and take off with Princess Shaeena, and they said he did not come back last night. Is this true, Loula?" She wanted me to prove her wrong.

"Mother," I said, using that word for the first time since I had met her. It just rolled off my tongue without me realizing it, but the word felt good as I said it. I could tell she was pleased with my word choice. She was tearful as she waited for me to speak. "Mother," I repeated again sadly, "there was a terrible misunderstanding yesterday, and Nidal and I had a huge fight. He said he was done with me, and he left!" I said with trembling lips.

"Oh, no, Loula. Don't say that," the queen mother pleaded. "Nidal will never stop loving you. I am sure of it. I know my son. He will love you forever. He is angry now for whatever reason, and he is behaving like a child. He will get over it soon. You shall see. Princess Shaeena told me yesterday that she heard gossip that you kissed Prince Billal. Is this true, Loula?" the queen asked. I knew she hoped against hope that it was not true.

But when I stayed quiet and did not respond right away, she had her answer. Clearly disappointed, she said, "I know it was not your fault, but my nephew's. I know you well enough by now, just as I know my son. You would never willingly kiss Prince Billal. Just as my son would never willingly kiss Shaeena! It is too bad Nidal doesn't know you the way I do." The queen sighed and stood from the bed, but before she left my side, she said, "Child, do not worry. Be strong. I will box my son's ears off when I see him. You, my dear," she said softly, "stay calm. He will return today, and you must ignore him. We must teach him a lesson he will never forget. He needs to learn to trust the woman he loves," she said proudly, "and not treat you this way. Loula, I stand by you. You are my child also, and I will not allow my son to treat you in this manner." She marched out of the room and closed the door softly behind her.

I was speechless, frozen. I was hurt beyond anything I had ever felt before. The queen was right. I had to teach her son a lesson. *How dare he treat me this way!* I got out of bed with a new perspective on things. I had to find a way to make him see the truth without compromising my pride. I knew it would not be easy, but there had to be a way to accomplish that.

I walked over to the mirror and looked at myself. I saw how terrible and pathetic I looked. My hair was tangled. Circles were underneath my eyes from a sleepless night. I pulled my nightgown off my shoulders and saw the bruises that were visible all over my arms. I was very emotional and distraught, but this time, I felt much stronger than before. *What doesn't kill you makes you stronger!* The queen raised my spirits, and I was going to show Nidal that he made a big mistake treating me so.

🕸 🕸 🕸

I got busy the next few hours. I bathed softly, not wanting to be rough where the bruises were. They were tender to the touch. I dressed in a beautiful red wine-colored gown that showed off my tiny waist. The cleavage was just perfect, inviting to the eyes of any onlooker. I slipped on my slippers and sat on the bed to comb my hair. I was thinking to let my hair loose today. My hair had grown another inch since the ball, and it was now well below the waist.

A sob escaped my lips as my mind wandered to yesterday when I watched my prince riding the black Arabian stallion with Shaeena holding onto his waist tightly as they laughed and rode away. It had been the worst day of my entire life. Nothing could ever hurt me more than that.

I walked back to the mirror to take another look at myself and make sure I looked perfect. The woman who stared back at me looked somehow older than her years. I smiled coldly, knowing that today started a new era. I erased the past, wanting to start fresh from this point on. The woman who looked back at me in the mirror was a stranger. I did not recognize her. I let out a cold laugh as my head tipped back and I took a deep breath. This day marked the beginning of a woman who was fighting for recognition as a woman scorned!

Let Nidal feast his eyes on me today. He will regret the day he ever left me with bruises. I walked over to the dresser and pulled out a gray silk shawl. The gown I wore had no sleeves, and I needed to cover my bruises. I wrapped the shawl around my shoulders, and as I walked back to the mirror to admire myself, I heard commotion outside.

I braced myself, walked to the window, and looked out. I saw Nidal helping Shaeena off the stallion. My heart skipped a beat. *Why had he brought her here today of all days? To rub her in my face?* Anger ripped throughout my entire body. *How dare he think he can treat me in such a fashion! He took me from the only people I knew as family and the only place I knew as home and brought me to this country. He locked me up against my will in this room for months until I fell in love with him. He taught me the ways of love, and I now live just to love him, but never once did he teach me how to live without him. How dare he!*

I marched out of my room and down the hallway, but I stopped in my tracks. I heard the princess laugh. It came from down the hall and around the corner. Frantically, I looked for a room to hide in.

The first door I found, I turned the knob, opened the door, and entered the room, closing the door softly behind me before anyone saw me. I heard their voices closer now as they walked down the hall and came to a halt right outside the door that I was behind.

"My prince," Shaeena purred, "thanks for yesterday. You made me so happy, Nidal," she said softly. I froze. Hatred burned deep inside me. I placed my ear closer to the door, expecting Nidal to say something, but she continued talking, "I am glad you finally came to your senses. I told you she was not good for you!" she said convincingly.

"Don't bring up her name. I told you I never want to speak of her again!" Nidal was clearly annoyed.

And then I heard their footsteps walk away, and their laughter echoed down the corridor as they fled to privacy. I opened the door to the room and stepped out. I needed some fresh air. I could not breathe. I had chest pain. I pulled the shawl from around my shoulders and held it in my hands to wipe away my tears. I ran as fast as I could to my room. Tears blinded me, and I did not notice

Nidal standing there in front of the doorway to our room staring at me. He stood frozen, all alone. I stopped running and came to a halt about a yard in front of him. His eyes dropped to my shoulders as he stared in horror at my bruises. I quickly wrapped myself with the shawl and ran past him into our room and locked the door. I leaned against the stone-cold wall, feeling upset at myself for allowing him to view my bruises. I did not want him to get the satisfaction that he had hurt me so much.

Nidal tried to open the door but found it locked. He pounded on the door, yelling, "Unlock this door right now, Loula!" he demanded. "I need to speak to you. Unlock the door!" he howled.

I was terrified, not knowing what he might do if I dared open the door. Last time he was this angry with me, he left me with bruises. So I ignored his calls as he continued to pound on the door. I crouched in the corner of the room, terrified, as the door burst open, and an angry Nidal marched inside.

I was trembling with fear, holding my hands up in front of my face for protection, not knowing how Nidal would react now that he was a few inches from me. "Please don't hurt me, Nidal," I begged. "Please, I'm sorry for whatever it is you think I did to you. Please don't hurt me again," I pleaded.

I saw Nidal's puzzled face display many emotions as he played with his feelings. I saw the old Nidal in his eyes for just a second. And within a split second, the angry Nidal came back. He reached for me, but I screamed, "No, please, Nidal. Don't." I was terrified now that he would hurt me.

Just that instant, the king rushed in with his queen and started yelling at Nidal to leave the room. The queen made true to her word and boxed his ear as he walked angrily past her. Nidal stopped. He was about to say something but changed his mind. Instantly with long, angry strides, he left the room. The king followed angrily after his son, giving him a piece of his mind, and the queen stayed behind to comfort me. The queen mother's eyes rested on my shoulders with horror as she witnessed my bruises firsthand.

Her hand automatically went to her mouth, and she looked horrified, not able to believe what she saw. She stared at me speechless. My body was in shock, and I started shaking uncontrollably as the tears came and I started to cry hysterically. The queen mother frantically came to me and wrapped her arms around me. She pulled me to the bed and held me in her embrace for a while until she saw that my body started to relax.

Neither of us spoke, for words were not necessary at this time. We were both at the same understanding. I was thankful that she did not probe for answers. She was an aristocrat, and she handled herself with grace. I appreciated her at this very moment. She was very comforting and helped me to relax. She soothed my soul with her gentleness. Before she left me, she told me that she knew in her heart that all would be fine. I smiled at her and prayed to God that she was right.

Soon after the queen left my side, I heard the trumpets outside blasting away. I knew the time had come. They were preparing to leave for the war. A cold shiver ran up and down my spine. I automatically ran to the window just in time to witness Shaeena kiss Nidal on the lips. It was a good-bye kiss. It looked as if he did not kiss her back, but it was hard to see for sure from where I stood. The queen was standing next to the princess, wiping her tears as her son kissed her too.

Then Nidal walked toward his horse, and I held my breath. He was about to leave without saying good-bye to me. *Had he stopped loving me so soon? Did I mean nothing to him anymore?* I asked myself these questions, but nevertheless, my heart knew what I had to do. I started to run as fast as I could. I ran from my room, down the corridor, and out the huge double doors. I stopped. I was too late. My prince was already riding away with his horse to join the rest of the warriors.

The tears came pouring down, my heart tightened, and I had never felt as alone as I did at this very moment. I kept staring, hoping against hope that he would turn his head my direction, but he just kept riding away. Shaeena turned and looked at me with contempt, but I ignored her and focused on Nidal.

Just when he was about to join the thousands of the warriors, who were patiently waiting for him on the outskirts of the palace grounds on their horses, he turned his horse around. His eyes searched the grounds until he found me, and his eyes locked with mine. My heart skipped a beat. He looked at me for a few minutes. Then he turned and rode away. I was beside myself with happiness. He turned! He thought of me. He cared.

I knew at that instant that he would return to me. I knew I still had a special place in his heart. I smiled for the first time in a long while. The queen, with tears in her eyes, walked up to me and gave me a reassuring hug. She too thought as I did. I sighed, turned to the queen mother, and hugged her back. From a distance, I saw Shaeena eyes shoot daggers at me, and I just smiled at her sweetly. She had won the battle, but I had won the war, and she knew it. The princess marched to her carriage and jumped in, and off she went without even a good-bye.

The next few days were quiet, thoughtful ones. I took my meals in the privacy of my quarters. Not able to eat much, I just nibbled on enough to keep me alive. I had lost my appetite the day Nidal rode off.

Billal came to my room a few times, and I was astounded to see that he had been left behind. *Isn't he going to help his country win the war? Is he a coward? What is he doing here?*

"My lady," he said as I opened the door for him to enter.

He bowed and walked inside. I saw the servants down the hall scramble away, like a pack of rats. *Great*, I thought. *Now they will gossip about my new lover.*

"My lady, how have you been faring?" He was smiling from ear to ear. "You look well." He pulled his chair next to mine and sat in it.

I looked at him in silence, trying to figure him out, and finally, I blurted out, "Why are you here, Billal? Why are you not joining the rest of them to fight for your country?" I asked with disapproval in my voice.

Billal looked at me. He did not understand what I was asking. Clearly, he was measuring my words and took his time responding. "My lady, I was left behind to wait until the king was ready. My men and I will escort him to the waiting place. That might take a day or two." He waited now for my response. "I was hoping to visit with you until it is time to leave," he said with hope in his voice.

Well, that answered my question. I wish it had been Nidal who had been left behind instead. Billal noticed my disappointment and tried to comfort me. "I know I'm not Nidal, but I hope you will allow me to entertain you until I leave." He looked at me for approval. His eyes were wide and glowing.

I sighed once again. "I don't mind if you visit. It's just that I will not be good company for you," I said softly.

Billal just looked at me for a few minutes. "Loula, first I would like to ask for your forgiveness for my most recent behavior," he begged. "Second, I know you love Nidal and not me. I would like to at least be your friend, your confidant. Please, Loula. Say you will forgive me and allow me your friendship," he begged desperately.

I considered what he had to offer, and I knew he was sincere. Based upon that conclusion, I accepted his apology and his friendship. And for the next couple of days, Prince Billal came and visited me, and we talked as friends do. He made me laugh. I had no time to feel sorry for myself.

We took strolls in the rose gardens, we went riding to the village and admired the shops, and we even walked all the way to the willow tree where Nidal and I had made love. Billal saw the names that Nidal had carved on the bark of the tree and stood silently for a few minutes just staring down at the green grass. His hands were in his pockets, and he was in deep thought.

When he looked at me, he smiled bitterly. "I envy Nidal. He has everything I want." He sighed and kicked a pebble, watching it roll away. I kind of felt sorry for him. Billal continued sadly,

"I was always jealous of the fact that Nidal is the crown prince, next in line for the throne. Growing up, he was always better than I was. He ran faster than me, and he fought better than me. He even beat me at chess, each and every time," he said dryly. "I wanted to be him. He was handsomer, and all the ladies of the court preferred him over me! But I never hated him. I loved him. We were always best of friends. We were raised together as brothers," he admitted, "but all that changed the moment I saw you. It was like love at first sight. I fell deeply in love with you, Loula. I don't care anymore about anything else. All I want and need is your love." He looked at me as he said this, making me feel a little uncomfortable.

I saw something in his eyes that I never noticed before. I saw the love he was feeling for me. It was written all over his handsome face. My heart went out to him. I knew firsthand what it felt like when the person you love rejects you, how it could tear you up inside. I felt pity for him. I did not know what to say. I stayed quiet and listened to Billal pour his heart out.

"Your prince can never make you happy. He is a selfish man. He wants you all to himself. That's not love. That's obsession! He is obsessed with you. Tell me, Loula. What kind of a life will that be for you? You will be miserable with a man like that!" He tried to convince me that he was right.

He did not know that he was wasting his time with all that he said. I could never stop loving Nidal. No matter what, he was and always would be the man I would love until the day I died. I could never be with another. But somehow I knew that, even if I told this to Billal, he would not listen to me. In a way, he was like Nidal. Once he made up his mind, there was no changing it.

I knew he would not give up trying to win my heart. He was a good man, but my heart belonged to Nidal. I suddenly missed Nidal. Pain tugged at my heart. I wanted Nidal to return home. I placed my face in my hands and sobbed. I cried my heart out.

Billal took me in his arms and stroked my hair. "Loula, I hate seeing you like this. You are crying for the wrong man! Nidal does not deserve you! He says he loves you, yet he slept in Shaeena's bed!" he spat. "Nidal wants it all! Why do you allow him to treat you so? He goes from your bed to hers! He does not deserve you!" He tried to prove his point. "He does not believe you. He accuses you of sleeping around on him, yet he is the one who is a whore! He is not worthy of your love!" Billal said angrily.

It was true, all of it. I desperately wanted to run away somewhere where I did not have to hear the truth. It hurt to acknowledge everything that Billal said, and to admit that he was right would mean that I would have to admit that Nidal did not love me. It was easier for me to believe otherwise. A pounding headache was forming inside my head.

Billal realized he had gone too far and immediately apologized. "I'm so sorry. I did not mean to hurt you. Please forgive me," he said sincerely as he reached out and pulled me into his arms.

I allowed him to hold me close to him. I needed a hug desperately. I needed it like the fish needed the water.

We walked back to the palace quietly, each in our own thoughts. The sun had set, and the torches were lit and lightened up the pathway to the palace. It was a beautiful, peaceful night. When we reached the stairs that led to the doorway, Billal took my hand to help me up the stairs. We said our good nights, and I went to my room and closed the door. The tears came rolling down. I undressed, washed up, slipped into my nightgown, and crawled into bed. The tears still had not stopped. I cried myself to sleep. It wasn't the first time, and somehow I knew it would not be the last time either.

Chapter Nine
Loula

A full week had passed since Nidal's departure, and this morning would be the day the king and Billal, with the rest of the soldiers who had been left behind, would ride out to meet up with Nidal and his army. My heart was pounding as I dressed quickly and raced out of the bedroom. I had to see Billal before he left. I did not want him to leave without a proper good-bye.

Billal saw me run to him. Smiling, he opened his arms, and I fell into his embrace. He wrapped his arms around me. Everyone watched, including the king and queen. Only the queen understood my actions. The others just stood there openmouthed. But I did not care. Billal and I shared a special friendship. I wanted him to go in peace and return to me healthy and happy. It would be hard for me to step aside and watch him go. He was the second man that I cared about who was leaving for war. I was afraid for his life. I did not know if he would return to me, so I wanted him to go to war peacefully with a clean mind. It would be safer that way. So I stood on my tiptoes and gave him a good-bye kiss. Surprised, Billal took this opportunity and kissed me back passionately, as all the onlookers watched with amusement.

The king rode away and led his men who followed him toward the war. Billal turned and waved wholeheartedly to us. I waved back with tears in my eyes, not knowing if I would ever see him again. After all, they were going to war. When they disappeared from our view, I looked at the queen and noticed she was staring at me. I tensed. She had witnessed everything, and I hoped she did not get the wrong idea.

She smiled at me. "Well, that was very noble of you, sending a man to war with a lot of unspoken promises. It is a good way to bring him home safely. If he has something to look forward to, chances are, he will come running home when all this is over." She smiled. "But tell me, my dear. What will you tell him when he does come home?" She arched her eyebrow while she waited patiently for me to reply.

"I just want him to have a clear head when he is fighting. I want him to come back to us. He is a fine man, and if he went to fight with a cloudy mind, then it would be very dangerous for him. I'm sorry if I was misunderstood. I am sorry if you are displeased with my actions. But I meant well." I hoped she believed me.

The queen smiled at me. "I know exactly what you were doing, my dear, and I would have done exactly the same thing if I were you. I know your heart was in the right place," she assured me. She gave me a warm hug, and together we walked into the palace for brunch.

We ate in silence. Neither one of us was very hungry. We nibbled our food and drank our tea, and when we finished, the queen asked if I would like to accompany her to the rose garden. I politely declined faking a headache and asked to be excused. When I reached my room, I ran inside, tore my clothes off, put on my nightgown, and slipped into bed. Even though it was the middle of the afternoon, I was sleepy. Not having had any real sleep for days, fatigue finally caught up with me, and I fell asleep instantly.

✸ ✸ ✸

As the days flew by, the queen and I started to worry for our men at war. We did not get any letters stating their whereabouts. It was nearly a month since they had left, and still not one word of their journey had reached us. Every night I went to bed, I cried myself to sleep.

Every day, the queen and I took our meals together. We pretended all was fine as we chatted about things we did not even care about just to take our minds off the war. Every morning and every night, together the queen and I prayed for the well-being of our men and for peace. We wiped away each other's tears and comforted each other during the really bad days when we felt scared.

One afternoon, I was walking with the queen to the tearoom, and I felt a little light-headed. I placed my hand on the stone wall for support, but I could not hold myself up. The room was spinning, and I fainted. Next thing I knew, I was in my bed with a hovering queen mother above me. She looked concerned as she sat on my bed, not saying a word. Someone had placed a wet cloth on my forehead.

"What happened?" I asked, worried, trying to find answers in the queen's eyes. She simply smiled. "Nothing, my dear. You will be fine. You fainted. That's all." Again, that smile on her face was there.

I looked at her suspiciously. I knew she was hiding something from me. "Your Majesty," I croaked, "is there something you are not telling me? A secret perhaps that you should be sharing with me?"

The queen wiped the smile off her face and sighed. She pushed my hair strands away from my face and asked softly, "I have noticed that you scarcely touch your meals and you nap many times throughout the day. Loula dear, have you fainted any other time before today?" she asked sweetly, eagerly waiting for my reply.

I needed time to process her questions before I answered her. I had never given it any thought. But now that the queen had brought it to my attention, I did remember feeling dizzy a few times. There were days when I threw up, and I had just forgotten to mention it to her. My eyes widened in realization. I looked at the queen, and she smiled at me from ear to ear. *Oh my Lord! Could I be pregnant?*

I tried to get out of bed, but the queen gently pushed me back down. "Now, now, child, lie still. You need your rest. It is my grandchild you may be carrying, and I will not have you bouncing about the palace," she chimed happily.

I placed my hand on my belly, still unable to comprehend the realization that I could be pregnant. *Could it be true? Could I be pregnant with Nidal's child?* I was overwhelmed with happiness. Happy tears rolled down my cheeks, and it must have been contagious. The queen was crying too. She bent down and gave me a warm hug.

"Congratulations," she said excitedly.

"Your Majesty," I said, wide-eyed, "don't you think that it's premature to congratulate me now? I have not gotten a confirmation yet from the doctor." The possibility of being pregnant with my lover's child already excited me.

"Loula, call me Mother, please, from now on," she said sweetly. "I know enough about pregnancy to know when someone is with child. I don't need a doctor to tell me something I already know!" she said proudly. "But that doesn't mean that I will not call for a doctor. As a matter of fact, he is on his way as we speak." She took the wet cloth off my forehead and gave it to the servant to refresh it.

The doctor came right after that and asked a thousand questions. Finally, he confirmed the pregnancy. I was overjoyed. It was one of the happiest days of my life. My hand automatically went back to my stomach, and I cried a river of happy tears. The doctor told the queen that I needed lots of rest. The queen assured him that she would make sure of that, and they walked out of the room, closing the door behind them. I could hear their voices echoing throughout the halls as they walked away until finally it was quiet.

That was when I allowed myself the luxury of crying my heart out. They were happy tears. I laughed and cried at the same time. *Nidal's baby!* I was pregnant with his child. I desperately wanted to share the news with him. I wanted to feel his arms around my stomach. I wanted him to feel the love I already felt for this love child. I cried out his name as the tears flowed down my face.

The proud grandma-to-be pampered me, saying it was her duty to see to it that I was comfortable while I carried her grandchild in my womb. She personally fed me, clothed me, and held my hand as we walked outdoors to the gardens. She was so attentive, and it was a delight to be around her. Every chance she got, the queen placed her hand on my stomach and sang lullabies. She had the finest seamstress in the country come to the palace and design maternity clothes for me, and she even ordered some designed clothing for the baby. I was so happy.

Chapter Ten
Loula

hree months had passed since the day Nidal and his army had left for the war. The queen and I were sipping our tea in the tearoom by the huge windows that overlooked the water fountain. The rain pelted on the glass hard as the lighting flashed everywhere across the dark sky. I looked out and saw a man on a horse riding toward the palace. My heart pounded rapidly. *Could it be Nidal?* The queen turned and looked in the direction I was looking, and we both stood and ran to the window at the same time.

The rider got closer. We noticed it was not Nidal. It was a soldier from Nidal's army. We raced down the hall and ordered the servants to open the palace doors. The man entered, dripping water everywhere on the multicolored marble stone floor. The servants quickly took off the man's boots, and the queen, after greeting him, told him to follow the servants to the other room where he would find dry clothes to change into.

The wet man thankfully followed the servants. Minutes later, he came out of the room escorted by the servants and was brought to the tea room, where we sat patiently for him to tell us some news of the war. He started by telling us that, thus far, there were no casualties. Upon hearing those words, I was so thankful to God for taking care of the king, Billal, all the men, and, above all else, my Nidal, the love of my life. The queen and I hugged each other and cried happy tears, and then we started asking a million and one questions at the same time.

The man, Jafar, said he was sent back to us to let us know that they were safe and not to worry. He then told us that the war was dragging out across Persia, and it would be months before they returned. My heart sank at the news of this. *How am I supposed to live without Nidal for so long?* I wanted to share the news of our baby with him. I wanted Nidal to hold me in his strong arms again. I wanted to lie in bed with him and make love to him. Feeling emotional, I cried out loud, not caring who witnessed it. I was heartbroken. I wanted Nidal to come back now.

The man looked uncomfortable. His finger combed his short, black beard thoughtfully as he sat quietly in his chair. He did not know how to respond as he looked down at his cup and added a few more sugar cubes into his tea. When he finally looked up, I saw him look at me with respect and adoration as he sat there without saying a word, allowing me to cry my heart out. His eyes looked sad. I wondered if he too had someone for whom his heart ached for.

The queen was concerned for my welfare and came and sat next to me, trying to comfort me. Neither one of us told the man that I was expecting. Except for the doctor, the seamstress, the queen, and me, no one else knew. I wanted Nidal to find out first before we told anyone else. When the time came that I could not hide my pregnancy anymore, the servants would be sworn to secrecy.

The man hesitated for a few minutes, and then said, "Nidal has led his countrymen to the other side of the border, where they met their allies. There they rested, and then they joined forces with the Turks, and continued on their way to fight the Persians. That was weeks ago," Jafar said carefully, as he tried without success not to alarm us. "By now they are probably in the midst of war." He sighed and his shoulders slumped, and my heart went out to him. "Your Majesty, I have to leave first thing in the morning. It will take me about three weeks to catch up to them. If you will excuse me now, I will go and get some much-needed rest." He rose and walked over to where the queen sat and bowed before her.

The queen smiled smiled up at him. "Jafar, go get your rest. We will see you in the morning."

Jafar followed the servant to the guest room. As he walked away, I noticed that his posture was terrible. His shoulders were slouched, and he walked with a limp. Clearly this man had seen better days in his life. My heart went out to him. I wondered if he had a wife and children. *Does someone cry for him to come home, as I cried for Nidal's return?*

I looked at the queen with a worried face. "Mother, do you think they are fine?" I asked when we were alone again, hesitating only a few seconds while I searched her face for reassurance. But I found none, for she too was just as worried as I was.

"I can't stand it anymore, Mother," I cried. "I want Nidal to come home now. I miss him terribly!" I choked back a sob.

"Now, now, don't get too emotional. It is not good for the baby," said the queen with concern as she raced up to me and hugged me. "Our men are just fine, Loula. Soon they will come home, and we will celebrate their return!"

She was a miserable liar.

We comforted each other a while longer until we got tired, and then we said our good nights. It was a long night. I was tossing and turning and thinking and crying. The last words Nidal had said to me right before he left were playing in my mind over and over again.

When morning finally arrived, the queen and I had breakfast with Jafar. He ate with a huge appetite, but the queen and I picked at our food with our forks. We did not feel hungry. The queen told the servants to pack up food and wine for Jafar's trip back. When it was time for the man to leave, we walked our guest outside to his horse and said our good-byes. He rode away, but not before reassuring us that our country would find victory in this war and they would return soon. But even as he spoke those words, we all knew, including Jafar, that the outcome was in God's hands alone. I stood there watching a stranger ride away, not knowing if we would ever meet again.

The queen and I walked back inside the palace, and I noticed that the servants were bustling about, cleaning the marble floors, and sneaking peeks at me with curiosity. They knew I was keeping a secret. They just did not know what it was.

Today during brunch, I thought of the children at the orphanage, and I asked the queen if I could resume my teachings there. She smiled and agreed that it would be a good distraction. The children were so excited to see me again. They all came running to me and hugged me. The queen, worried about the baby, pulled the children away from me, but I reassured her that it was all right. I needed their hugs because I missed them greatly. Little Natalie was sitting by herself in the corner. She was the only child who did not come and hug me. When I looked her way, she put her head down and cried softly.

I walked up to her and asked her if she had missed me, and Natalie nodded her head sadly without looking up. She swung her legs back and forth. Natalie was by far the most adorable child I had ever laid eyes on. My heart went out to her. I reached for her, and she slid off her seat and jumped in my arms. Her Majesty immediately put a protected hand between Natalie and my stomach. I smiled and told her that was not necessary. It was only a hug.

Five ladies attended to the children day in and day out. They cleaned, cooked, and dressed the children. They were nice, and they did their job well. But it was just a job to them. They lacked the mother's touch that these children desperately needed. I was glad to be back. I would give them what they craved. The queen made it her duty to come with me every day to the children and keep an eye on me. She wanted to make sure I was not overdoing it.

I noticed that the queen had taken a special liking to Natalie, as I had. *What is it about that child that draws us to her? Could it be that she reminds the both of us of Nidal?* Those blue eyes were captivating. The queen loved all the children, as I did, but we both shared a special interest in Natalie that was different from the way we felt about the rest of the children. They were all special to us, but little Natalie stole our hearts.

The queen made sure I did not exhaust myself with the children at the orphanage. She made sure I had enough rest, ate all my vegetables, and exercised every day. She drove me nuts, but I loved every minute of it. I knew she would lay down her life for my baby and me. It made her very happy to occupy her time with me, so I allowed her to spoil me rotten. I needed the distraction, and I also desperately needed a mother figure in my life.

The days turned to months, and the baby bump was showing. The queen rounded up all the servants and told them that I was pregnant with her grandchild. I heard all the gasps, and then they all congratulated me, one by one. The queen told them that no one was to leak out the information. It was to remain confidential. No one outside the palace should know. They were all sworn to secrecy, and then they went about their daily chores.

One day as the queen and I were sipping our tea, I felt a little flutter inside my stomach. I quickly put my hand on my stomach and sat in silence, not breathing. The queen's eyes popped open, and she ran to my side.

She too put her hands on my stomach and asked excitedly, "Loula, did you feel the baby move inside you?"

"Yes, I did, Mother," I cried happily.

As I said that, the baby fluttered again. The queen could not feel the fluttering, and she stepped back, disappointed. "I can't wait for my grandchild to start kicking. Loula, you have brought me so much joy. Thank you, dear." She smiled.

That night, I could not sleep. I waited all night for the fluttering, but I did not feel the baby move again until about a week later.

The days came and went, and the queen and I were busy with the children and the preparations for a separate room. I told the queen that I expected the baby to sleep in our room the first year and not in the baby's room. She hesitantly agreed, not wanting to upset me, but I could tell she wanted the baby in its own room, where she could cater to him day and night and spoil him rotten. I knew she would make a wonderful grandmother, and I loved her so much for that.

❀ ❀ ❀

I felt huge now that I was almost seven months pregnant. I wobbled around the palace like a duck. The queen said I was glowing. But glowing or not, I still looked fat. The maternity dresses were being let out every couple of weeks. I was growing at a fast pace. The doctor's last visit had been a week ago. He told us all was good and not to worry. He said the weight I was gaining was normal, and for the last trimester, he said I should expect more weight gain. I was horrified. I did not want to look too fat. *What would Nidal say when he saw me?*

The baby kicked so much that I thought he was playing ball in there. The queen laughed with excitement, saying her grandson was an athlete. We focused all our thoughts and energy on my precious baby and decorating the baby's room. The queen ordered the most expensive baby furniture I had ever seen. A gold crib, silk sheets, and satin blue ribbons, for it was a boy she assured me. The painter finished with the blue walls, and the servants hung the satin blue curtains on the windows. There was a solid black cherry dresser with gold knobs, and it was filled to the max with baby clothes. There was every kind of wooden toy a child's heart desired. The queen went overboard.

The children at the orphanage were also getting excited about the baby's birth, all but Natalie, who feared the baby would take her new mommy away from her. I made it my business to explain to Natalie that no one would take her place. She was my little girl and always would be. My heart went out to her. I loved her so much. I loved all the children, and I wanted to make them feel like we were all one big happy family. I included all of them with news of my pregnancy. Every day we talked about the baby, and I noticed that even Natalie was getting excited about the baby's arrival.

One morning, I woke up, dressed, and went to have breakfast with the queen. I did not have much of an appetite anymore, but the queen insisted I eat with her at every mealtime. I abided by her wishes just to make her happy. She was good to me, and I wanted to please her any way I could. So I ate eggs and bacon and drank my freshly squeezed orange juice, and we discussed the agenda for the day.

After breakfast, I went to my room. I was given a different bedroom now. This one was upstairs. The queen said we should sleep next door to the baby's room. It had a connecting door to our room. I did not mind at all. The new room did not have any memories of mine and Nidal's lovemaking in it, and it felt like I was starting fresh. It took my mind off many things that were better left alone for the baby's sake.

I changed into another gown and slipped into comfortable slippers when I heard commotion outside my door at that moment. I opened it and saw the servants scrambling about, happily singing, "The king is back!"

My heart pounded fast in my chest as I ran to the window, and I could not believe what I saw. They were back. Nidal was back! Tears rolled down my face as I watched Nidal on his black stallion lead his men to the palace. Excitedly, I raced to the side of the room, swung open the doors that led to the balcony, and stepped outside.

And there was Nidal and thousands of his men behind him. I saw the queen crying down below and waiting patiently for her husband and son to come to her. At that moment, I looked at Nidal, and he turned and looked up at me. We stared at each other for a few minutes. It was as if time stood still. I could not take it anymore. I turned around and ran inside. I wanted to go downstairs and greet him, throw myself in his arms, and tell him how much I loved and missed him.

But when I reached the stairs, my body was overwhelmed, and it slowed me down. A few servants came to me and asked if I needed help. I shook my head and held on to the banister. When I stepped off the last step, I hurriedly walked to the double wooden doors that stood open and stepped outside just in time to see Nidal turn with his horse and ride away. I ran fast down the palace stairs that led to the cobblestone street, yelling his name as loud as I could. Nidal did not hear me as he continued to ride away. I called his name a few times, and by now, his men saw me and were trying to get his attention to tell him I was out there for him.

There was too much noise for Nidal to hear what anyone was telling him. Finally everyone was pointing my way and chanting my name. Nidal turned and saw me. I stopped to breathe a second because I was out of breath, and I saw Nidal's face light up when his eyes rested on my face. Then his eyes roamed to my stomach, and he looked confused. When realization struck him, his eyes widened with surprise. Then everyone was quiet, waiting to see what would happen next.

Nidal jumped off his horse and walked slowly toward me. He looked like a mighty warrior. His tall, lean, powerful body was even browner than I remembered it to be. He was not wearing a shirt, and his muscles flexed with every step he took. His black hair hung loose over his shoulder, and he had a short beard growing on his handsome face. I drew in a deep breath, and my heart pounded rapidly as he approached me. When he was a few feet away from me, his glance lowered to my stomach, and he paused and looked overwhelmed. He opened his mouth to say something, but at that moment, I felt a pain in my side and passed out.

Next thing I knew, I was in Nidal's arms, and he was carrying me to our old room. He placed me on the bed and asked if I were feeling better. I could not speak. I was at a loss for words. The queen came bustling in, followed by the king and Billal. The servants stood outside the entrance waiting for the prince's orders. Nidal yelled for someone to get the doctor and then ordered a wet cloth to be placed on my forehead.

Nidal searched my face for answers. He placed his hand on my stomach and swallowed. The baby kicked at that very moment. Nidal's eyes popped open, and he asked with excitement, "Was that our baby I just felt?"

Before I could even answer his question, he placed his lips on mine and kissed me tenderly. I thought I would die from all the love I was feeling at this very moment. The words "our baby" sent a warm feeling to my heart.

The king and queen hugged and kissed each other and quietly left the room, closing the door behind them. I looked at Nidal. He was staring at me quietly. He looked so handsome. I choked back a sob. I had missed him terribly. Nidal looked at me from head to toe and then rested his eyes on my face.

Tears were in his eyes as he spoke. "Loula," he said hoarsely, "why did you not tell me you were carrying my child?" He placed kisses on my stomach. Our baby was kicking wildly. Nidal's hands were around my stomach now, waiting to feel his child. He laughed, he cried, and he kissed my stomach until he was worn out.

At that moment, the doctor burst open the door and ordered Nidal to step aside. Nidal jumped quickly out of the way, and the doctor asked me a hundred questions. I assured him I was fine, and he relaxed. He told Nidal that I needed a lot of rest and I should always eat a healthy diet. He concluded that under no circumstances was I to be stressed out, saying it was not good for the baby. Nidal thanked the doctor and rushed him out of the room. He locked the door, came back to the bed, and sat next to me.

He looked tired, hungry, and dirty, and my heart went out to him. "Nidal," I said softly, taking his hands in mine, "you need to take a bath, eat something, and go straight to sleep. You look exhausted," I told him, concerned.

Nidal ignored my remark, took me in his arms, and kissed me hungrily. Immediately, my body responded to his touch. Then he let go of me abruptly and went to the bathroom where the servants had the tub with hot, steaming water waiting for him. When he was done, he came back and stopped near the bed naked, except for a towel wrapped around his waist.

He stood before me, legs spread apart, with his warrior body, and I struggled to tame the emotions coursing through me. Nidal flexed his muscles. He was teasing me. His nostrils flared, and his eyes darkened as his gaze searched mine. My eyes roamed across his bronzed, broad, muscled chest. His body looked toned and sexy. Then with one swift movement, he pulled the towel, and it dropped to the floor. I stared at his beautiful, naked body hungrily. His manhood was rock solid. Desire surged through my veins. Desperately, I reached for him and waited with a thundering heart.

His eyes were fierce and wild as he jumped on the bed and pulled me into his embrace. His hips leaned against my body, and I felt his manhood piercing my skin. Desire shuddered through me so intensely that a moan escaped my lips.

His hands were burning my skin with his every touch. He leaned his head, and his lips brushed mine, sending ripples of sensation throughout my entire body. I was drowning in ecstasy. Nidal's hands softly caressed my breasts, and they were tender to his touch. I felt shy and embarrassed of my new body, a body Nidal was not used to. I wondered if he could enjoy making love to me even though I was big with child.

"Loula, don't shy away from me. I want to know every inch of your new body," he said huskily.

My heart raced as his lips trailed kisses over my entire body. His slow, sensual movement of his skin against mine was intoxicating. I grabbed his shaft and stroked it gently, and a husky sound rumbled deep in his throat. His strong arms held me possessively as he pulled me over his body, wanting me to ride him. Placing both hands on my hips, Nidal pushed deep inside me, and a moan escaped my lips as I trembled with desire. I could no longer control my feelings as my body betrayed me and I cried out with lust. Nidal thrust himself deeper inside me, again and again, until my body shook with ecstasy. He tightened his hold on my thighs, and his eyes burned with desire beneath his hooded lids as he came inside me. His husky groan echoed throughout the walls of the room as his body shook savagely.

He is the sexiest man alive! A gasp of pleasure escaped my lips as I lay atop my skilled lover. I had never seen a more handsome man than Nidal in my whole entire life. My eyes roamed over his handsome, chiseled face, and his eyes were wild with lust. His hands cupped my breasts as he gently stroked them. I leaned down and brushed my lips on his. Nidal slowly swayed his hips from left to right, and I closed my eyes and allowed the sweet feeling to penetrate my being. A moan escaped my lips, and I felt Nidal's hands tighten around my breasts as he pushed his groin deeper inside me. The sensation was too much for me as the electricity coursed throughout my body once again. I opened my eyes and looked deep into Nidal's as I came. A cry of pleasure escaped my lips. Nidal cupped my face, brought my head down to his, and kissed me brutally.

We could go on like this all night, and it still would not be enough. It was never enough. Finally, I pulled away from him and lay beside him. I was so emotional that I started to cry. Nidal cradled me in his arms and whispered words of endearments. I wanted to tell him that I had missed him so much and I suffered without him. I wanted to tell him that thoughts of him during his absence played through my mind like a symphony. I wanted to tell him so many things, but Nidal rested his forehead against mine and smiled a slow, seductive smile. I trembled.

A whirl of emotions flared inside me, and I ached for his lips to claim mine again, but I knew that my prince had not slept in days. I closed my eyes tightly, and my hands scrunched the fabric of the silk sheets between my fingers, trying to control the ache in my body that was yearning for his touch again. Finally, when Nidal surrendered to sleep, I lay next to him and admired his handsome face. He had been without sleep for days at a time. Exhaustion caught up with him. Nidal slept for two days and two nights. I was glad he got the rest he needed.

The queen mother came to our room on the second day of Nidal's arrival, and I told her he was sleeping like a log. She left and had not come back since. The servants brought food and wine, and I nibbled just enough to feed the baby. I was not hungry for this kind of food. I was hungry for Nidal. I stayed in bed, snuggling next to him and waiting patiently until he woke up.

A million thoughts troubled my mind, and this was a great time to put everything into perspective. While Nidal slept peacefully, I had the chance to think things through. The fact that Nidal and I were together again as if nothing happened prior to him leaving for war did not make sense. Things had been drastically wrong the day he left. He came back, and we acted as if everything was perfect. *Which can only mean one thing. Sooner or later, everything will explode in the air.*

Early on the third day, Nidal's hot kisses that trailed across my breasts awoke me. His strong hands palmed my hips and lifted my bottom as his lips traveled downward and nestled between my thighs. His tongue glided softly, stroking me and causing my entire body to go up in flames. My fingers worked their way through his hair and twisted into a fist as I pressed his head, and his tongue glided even deeper inside me. I was trembling with passion, reaching a point of no return, and I cried out loud in ecstasy as I came with such a force that my body shook violently.

"Fuck me! Now, Nidal! Fuck me!" I cried feverently.

Nidal growled savagely, and he pulled his body upward and entered me, slamming into me wildly. Unleashing his passion inside me as he thrust himself deeper and deeper until his body jerked with spasms of electricity. I wondered how he could still have cravings for me, even though I was so huge. He did not seem to mind. In fact, he told me he was aroused even more this time around because he had missed me so much. All the months he was away from me left him aching for my body. Nidal told me that he did not care what I looked like. He loved me no matter what. To him, I was still the most beautiful woman in the world.

Nidal's appetite was huge, and he ate so much food. I watched him gobble down beef, baked potatoes, freshly baked bread, and hot apple pie, and he washed it down with red wine. I was not hungry at all. I nibbled on some bread and drank orange juice. We ate in our room, not wanting anyone to bother us. I waited patiently for Nidal to finish. I wanted to ask him a thousand questions about the war. I wanted to share my experience of this pregnancy with him. I was simply overjoyed that he was home.

When Nidal finished eating, he gulped down the rest of his wine, and then without hesitation, he pulled me close, and I eagerly slid into his arms and closed my eyes, trying to take it all in. Life was beautiful. Nidal was beautiful, and I was happy. But I did not know how long this mood would last. There were many issues to be resolved. And I dreaded each and every one of them. The baby kicked all day long, and Nidal took every opportunity to rest his hand on my stomach and feel his child kick. I felt very blessed, but I knew it would not last. *Nothing lasts forever.*

The next day, I went looking to find the queen. Nidal was busy with the king, going over political things. With some free time on my hands, I thought to visit Her Majesty and ask if she wanted to take a stroll with me in the gardens.

I was almost at the glass doors that overlooked the gardens when I heard voices coming from the outside. I stopped in my tracks. One voice was the queen's; the other sounded like Princess

Shaeena's. Immediately, I felt dizzy as I swooned on my feet. I stepped over to the stone wall and leaned on it for support. I could feel my heart pound at a fast pace as sweat formed on my forehead. I was angry at myself that she had this effect on me. I had not seen her since Nidal left for the war. And now she reappeared conveniently, just a few days after Nidal's arrival. Angry with myself for getting upset, I walked over to the glass doors and peeked outside.

She was there, sitting down with the queen, sipping tea, and looking comfortable as if it were her right to be there, as if she had not overstepped her boundaries the last time she was here. I pulled the doors open abruptly, and stiff as a board, walked over to them. The queen looked uncomfortable when I looked at her, and then I turned to Shaeena's direction. The ice-cold stare that she gave me sent shivers up and down my spine, but that was nothing in comparison to what I felt when my eyes rested on her lap.

I froze. My voice failed me. I could not believe what I saw. There in front of me was Shaeena, staring coldly at me with a bleak smile and looking 100 percent pregnant. The blood drained from my face, and I felt like I was going to pass out. The queen immediately stood and grabbed me, preventing me from falling to the ground.

"Loula dear, are you feeling under the weather?" the queen asked with sincere concern in her voice.

I looked at her, and she immediately understood. Shaeena looked pleased that she had this effect on me. A smug grin was on her face. My baby was kicking in my stomach so hard, as if he too knew the effect this woman was having on me. I studied her face right before I spoke. She really did a good job hiding her misery. But I knew better. I had what she wanted, and it killed her.

The pregnancy was a huge surprise to me, and even if I tried to ignore it, the fact still remained that she was pregnant and she would probably claim that Nidal was the father. She looked about seven months pregnant, which would have placed conception at the same time that Nidal had spent three nights in her bed. So

Nidal had lied to me. *He had slept with her! And this was the result! How would he deny this?*

"Hello, Shaeena," I said sweetly, trying hard not to slap her hard across the face. "It is very nice to see you again," I lied.

But Shaeena was sly as a fox. She knew I was suffering at this moment. The queen sat back in her chair and stared at us cautiously. I pulled an empty chair closer to Shaeena and sat in it, thinking my feet could not support my weight anymore. "So, what brings you by? We haven't seen you since before the war. How are you faring?" I asked with trembling lips, ignoring the fact that she was pregnant.

"Well, Loula, as you can see, I am pregnant, and Nidal is the father," she said straightforward, as if that were not a bomb she just dropped casually in my lap.

The queen was sipping her tea, and when Shaeena made her announcement, she almost choked.

"Why are the both of you acting as if it is a surprise?" Shaeena asked innocently. "I told you then, Loula, that Nidal spent three nights in my room before he went to war. You were a fool not to believe me," she said smugly. "And you, my queen, are sitting here with me all this time, and not once did you care to ask if I were pregnant and whose child I was carrying!" she said boldly. "Your son slept with me, and now I am pregnant." She looked at the queen as if daring her to deny the baby's paternity.

The queen looked as if the cat had her tongue. All color had vanished from her face as she looked at me apologetically. By this time, I was fuming. *How dare Princess Shaeena come here and tell us all these lies! How dare she try to pin this on Nidal!*

I got up from my chair and said coldly, "How dare you throw your accusations around and expect us to believe them! I insist you leave us and never come back! We all have had enough of your wanton behavior!" I yelled, not caring who heard me.

The queen sat in her chair, stunned, not saying a single word. I was beside myself with anger. Life was not fair. I knew not what to do. I wanted to strangle Shaeena with my bare hands.

"Get out of here!" I yelled at Shaeena.

Shaeena rose from her chair. Her stomach was huge as she stepped aside and marched toward the palace without saying a word. *She is going to find Nidal!*

I marched beside her. "I said you are to remove yourself from this property before I throw you out, whore!" I yelled.

But Shaeena kept walking toward the palace without an ounce of embarrassment. She was full of arrogance.

As the princess reached the first step, the queen ran along beside her and begged, "Please, Shaeena, don't make a spectacle of yourself. Go home, child."

The princess angrily turned toward the queen and pointed a finger at her. "Shame on you. I just told you I'm pregnant with your grandchild, and you disrespect me in this way! The both of you will regret this day! My father will hear about your behavior, and I promise you that he will be livid!"

She turned away, and we scrambled after her.

I came to the queen's defense. "How dare you speak to the queen like that! Who do you think you are?" I spat. I climbed the stairs, trying to maintain my balance, as I reached the step that Shaeena stood on.

In that instant, Nidal heard all the commotion and came running out. "Ladies, please, you are making spectacles of yourselves out here in front of the servants. Behave yourselves!" He looked at the three of us, oblivious to the real problem at hand.

We all stopped and looked at him angrily. He looked from me to his mother and then rested his eyes on Shaeena. "What pray tell is your problem, Shaeena—" He paused when his eyes landed on her stomach.

He stared at her wide-eyed and speechless. The princess looked at him with satisfaction. She let him swallow the revelation before she announced to him sweetly, "Nidal, I'm pregnant, and you are the father of my baby!" She eagerly waited for his reply.

It was as if time stood still for all of us. Nidal just stood there, stunned. He was at a loss for words. I saw the different emotions that played on Nidal's face. *Why is he even hesitating to deny her accusations? Could it be true? Could Nidal be the father of Shaeena's baby?* I felt dizzy, but I held my ground, desperately waiting for a denial. But it never came.

Shaeena sat there, pleased with the results. "It's your baby, Nidal," she said convincingly enough.

Again, Nidal did not deny or accept her words. He turned slowly and looked at me confused. I knew that look. He was trying to think back on those three days he had spent with Shaeena almost seven months ago.

"Shaeena, that's a lie! Nidal would never betray me for a tramp like you!" I screamed.

The princess spoke without thinking. "Shut up, bitch!"

Nidal immediately came to my defense, saying furiously in his rich Arabian accent, "Madam, contain yourself. Do you know who you are talking to? Loula will be the next queen of Arabia. How dare you speak to her in such a manner!"

Shaeena turned toward me, and in slow motion, she reached over and pushed me. I lost my balance, tumbled down the stairs, and rolled onto my stomach. I felt numb as all three of them came running down the stairs to where I lay. Nidal lifted me cautiously into his arms and cried out to the servants who had popped out of nowhere to get the doctor.

I blacked out for a second, and when I came to, I felt excruciating pain in my stomach. I lay in a fetal position trying to deal with the pain. Nidal was crying as he held me close to him, whispering his love for me. Shaeena was behind him, afraid she had gone too far, and the queen went running to the palace to look for the king.

As I lay there in Nidal's arms, I felt something wet underneath my gown. I shut my eyes as the tears rolled down my face. The pain was pulling on my stomach. "Nidal! I think I am bleeding!

Please save our baby, Nidal! Please, don't let my baby die," I pleaded.

Nidal cried out when he saw the blood seep through the gown. "Oh, God, no! Please, God. Save Loula and my baby, please," he begged. "Please, God, do not let anything happen to Loula and my baby, please," he begged, crying his heart out.

The doctor, having moved into the guest quarters awaiting the birth of our baby, came running and yelled for everyone to step aside. He examined me, right there on the lawn in broad daylight, and after a few minutes, he shook his head sadly. I held my breath for the next words that came out of his mouth, and I was sure they would strike like a knife through my heart.

"Call for help, Nidal. I need to do surgery on Loula immediately," he said without any hope in his voice.

There was silence in the air, as we all tried to come to terms with the outcome. The pain was shooting up my back, and I screamed aloud. I could not think clearly at this time. The baby was not kicking anymore. I was petrified, and I did not know if the baby were still alive.

Nidal lifted me in his strong arms and took me inside the palace, in a room that was set aside for medical emergencies only. The doctor ordered everyone out, but Nidal insisted on staying, saying he was not going anywhere. The doctor eventually gave in, not having enough time to argue with him. The queen had ordered the servants to bring hot towels and clean sheets to the room, and a few servants stayed in the room to assist the doctor. The last thing I remember was Nidal's hands holding mine as he cried a river. Then I passed out.

There was hardly any light in the room when I opened my eyes slowly. The first thing I saw was Nidal right by my side. His eyes were red and swollen. He looked down at me with the saddest expression on his face. The tears started again as he sobbed like a child. He brought my hand to his lips and cried his heart out. That could only mean one thing. My baby had not made it. I tried speaking, but no words came out of my mouth. I was frozen.

Then tears welled up in my eyes, but that was about it. My tears dried up quickly. I lay there staring up at Nidal hopeless. I slowly pulled my hand away from his grip. Nidal stood still. He had noticed my withdrawal. Alarmed, he pulled my hand back in his. At this moment, I felt numb. I blamed Nidal for everything. It was his fault! He was the one who did this to me. He was the one who allowed that bitch to act as if she had a hold on him. He was the one who got her pregnant, and because of him, I had lost my baby. I felt empty, like my world had come crumbling down and shattered everything that mattered to me. I felt all alone, like I had no one I could trust anymore.

I stared coldly at Nidal and said in a clipped tone, "Leave this room."

"No Loula, I am not leaving you." He said softly.

But when I looked at him with cold eyes he cringed and took a step backward. His eyes pleaded for me to understand that he loved me. But my eyes pleaded for him to leave me alone. I could not accept his apology at this time. I just wanted to be left alone. I closed my eyes and pretended to sleep, but he would not budge. Eventually, I slept from exhaustion.

The next time I woke up, the sun had disappeared, and it was almost dark in the room. Sitting next to me was Nidal, and he was still holding on to my hand. He stood immediately when he saw I had awakened and told me how much he loved me. I ignored him and closed my eyes again, praying for sleep once again. I did not want to deal with Nidal now. I had nothing to say to him.

The next couple of days, I was in and out of sleep. Nidal was always sitting next to me, waiting for me to wake up and speak to him. I refused. I was still not ready to say anything to him. My innocent, little baby was dead. Gone just like that. From one second to the next.

When I opened my eyes on the third day, the sun was shining in the room, and Nidal was still sitting next to me, looking at me with sadness. "Please, Loula, talk to me. Allow me in your thoughts. Let me soothe your pain," he begged. "Please, I need you now. Don't shut me out," he cried.

I looked at him, but the feelings I once felt were not there anymore. I did not want him to touch me. I did not want him around. I needed some alone time. "Nidal, please, let me be. I need to be alone right now. Please go. I'm in mourning. Don't you understand? My baby died!" I cried.

"Our baby died, Loula. He was mine too!" he said in a tortured voice. "Please, Loula, don't shut me out. I love you and need you so much now! Please talk to me," he pleaded.

I looked at him, and I did not feel that he deserved anything from me now. "Please, leave me alone, Nidal," I said coldly.

I looked around and saw that flowers—carnations, daisies, and roses of all colors of the rainbow—were filling the room. On the table next to the flowers were notes with get-well wishes. A lot of food was laid out: chicken, beef, potatoes, fruits, wine, and chocolates fit for royalty. I wasn't hungry, but it was nice to know that they cared enough to pamper me.

I smiled at Nidal, and he smiled warmly back. But in that instant, I was reminded of my baby, and my smile quickly faded. Nidal noticed my reaction and took me in his arms. Then the tears started again. We both cried until our tears dried out. I had lost my zest for life.

Nidal looked at me through his tears and said softly, "We have to bury him soon, Loula," he said as a sob tore from his throat. "We can't hold him for long. He is in a wooden box, and he needs to be buried immediately. Do you think you can handle it?"

I knew it would be one of the hardest things I would probably have to do in my lifetime. The only reason I knew I would be able to handle it was because my baby needed to be laid to rest. So I agreed, and Nidal went hastily and gave the orders for the burial. When he came back, it was with a heavy heart that he announced the burial would take place in an hour.

I wore a black gown and a veil to cover my head and face. When Nidal scooped me up in his arms and took me outside, way back behind the gardens where the cemetery was, everyone was already there, and they were all wearing black. This was the first royal grandchild, and everyone was mourning his death.

Nidal had put a chair for me to sit on, and I sat on it and stared at the small box with my baby in it. It was placed next to the hole that was dug. I heard my cries. They were loud, heart-wrenching sobs that tore from my heart, made their way out of my mouth, and ripped through the air. It sounded like a tortured animal was wailing in pain. I heard the rest of the crowd cry too. The queen was the loudest. The king cried silently as his tears rolled down his cheek. And Nidal, he looked the worst of all. He had not shaved since our baby's death, and the black circles under his eyes were proof to all that he had not slept for days.

I dropped to my knees and threw my body across the wooden box that my baby lay in. I let out a scream and cried my heart out. The crowd screamed with pain when they saw me do this, and Nidal dropped next to me and held me close to him. I cried, screamed, wailed, and prayed, and in the end, I went limp on the box. Nidal tried to pull me away from the box, but I held on to it for dear life. I talked to my baby and told him that I would always love him. I told him that I would be with him in heaven one day. I heard the crowd's cries as I said this. I pulled my hair, I pulled my clothes, and I pounded on the dirty ground. I turned and pounded on Nidal's chest, pleading for my baby's life, but nothing. No answer. It was finished. Done. He was gone forever.

There was silence now. The crowd watched in tears as I said my peace. When I was drained of everything I had, Nidal lifted me up in his arms and took me back to the palace. Behind me, I heard the people cry. I shut my eyes and prayed one more time for God to allow my baby into his kingdom and to watch over him until I was with him again.

I was exhausted, and I held on to Nidal for dear life. My prince carried me inside the palace and walked down the hall to our chambers. The door was open, and he walked in and placed me on our bed. I lay my head down on the pillow and wept.

The next day, I woke up and looked at Nidal. All these days, I was thinking only about myself and not once of Nidal. I knew he was hurting as well. I looked at his face. The beard made him look older in a way. I cuddled closer to him, and he awoke immediately and took me in his arms instantly. We kissed, touched, and cried. It was our way of comforting each other. It was therapeutic. I forgave him. It was the only way I knew to release my pain.

The days came and went, and except for the three meals that the servants brought us, no one else bothered us. We just ate enough to live, and then we grieved together the loss of our child, a child who we never got the chance to name, hug, or raise. He was our firstborn, and he was gone to us forever.

We had not talked about the incident on the day of the tragedy. We both avoided it like the plague. We knew that, if one word was said, it would be like opening a can of worms. So for now, we thought it best to stay silent. Neither one of us wanted to spoil the moment.

Nothing lasts forever!

Chapter Eleven
Loula

A week later, I had regained my strength, and my appetite had come back. I ate enough food to last a lifetime. Nidal laughed at me saying that, if I kept this up, the palace would be an economic failure from all the money spent to feed me. His laughter sounded good, like music to my ears.

I don't really know how everything started. We were simply talking about how I needed to lose the few pounds I had gained during the pregnancy, but that really hit a chord. I started to think of my baby, and the tears started. Nidal raced to my side to comfort me, and then one thing led to another. I realized that, all this time, Nidal had been trying to run from the truth. He did not want to assume responsibility for all the heartache he had caused. It was all Nidal's fault, and he knew it. The realization of what he was doing hit me like a ton of bricks.

Nidal noticed my mood change and froze. He knew I was about to start a fight, a fight I was going to win. He quietly waited for the inevitable. I was getting ready for the biggest fight of my life.

And so it started.

"Why did you go to Shaeena's palace seven months ago? Why did you spend three nights there?" I asked angrily.

Nidal looked defeated. He said not one word. His beautiful blue eyes were clouded with tears. He said nothing.

That made me even angrier. "Why is our baby dead, Nidal, but Shaeena's baby lives safely in her womb!" I yelled.

Silence is golden an old wise man once told me.

I looked him in the eyes, and in a cold and dangerous tone I asked, "Does she carry your child, Nidal?"

Nidal pulled me into his arms and passionately whispered, "I'm sorry. I never meant to hurt you. You are my life, the very reason I exist! I would never hurt you intentionally, Loula," he moaned.

I knew he meant what he said, but I needed to hear more. The princess was claiming Nidal as the father of her baby. I needed to know the truth. I pulled away from Nidal and motioned for him to sit in the chair by the window as I pulled the other chair close to his and sat down.

"Nidal, I need to know why you went running to Shaeena's palace on the night of our disagreement." I patiently waited for his reply.

Nidal sighed and stared at me without replying. This wasn't going to be as easy as I thought, so I moved on to the next question. "Nidal, you stayed three days and three nights in Shaeena's palace! What did you do there? Where did you sleep?" I asked in a dangerous tone, getting tired of playing the waiting game. But Nidal continued with his silence.

Aggravated now, I raised my voice just a notch. "Tell me then, Nidal. Do you plead innocent?" I waited in silence for his reply, but again, he did not say a single word.

He kept silent. I could tell he was trying to think his way out of answering me. This angered me even more. "Nidal, if you do not talk now, I will automatically assume you are guilty! I have given you many chances to respond, but you just refuse to share your thoughts with me!" I said a little louder now. I was losing my patience, and he knew it.

Nidal fell down to his knees in front of me and took my hands in his. He looked up at me, and I could see the tears starting to well up in his eyes. "Loula," he whispered hoarsely, "I am not able to tell you what happened when I stayed at Shaeena's palace because I do not remember. The whole three days are a blur to me! I barely remember anything at all!" he said. "Please believe me, Loula. I love you and would never deliberately do anything to hurt you," he cried fervently.

A typical man, I thought. *Never wants to admit to fault! Or take responsibility for his actions!*

"Tell me, Nidal. Is there anything you do claim responsibility for?" I asked sarcastically, anxious to hear his reply, but it seemed the cat had his tongue.

The silence was unbearable. He was trying to figure out what to say to get him out of the trouble he knew he was in. "Please, Loula," Nidal begged. "I honestly do not remember anything! You must believe me! I'm telling you the truth!" he cried.

I pulled my hands out of his grip, stood abruptly, walked to the middle of the room, and gave Nidal a menacing look. Nidal stopped breathing and braced himself for my outburst that he was sure would follow. And it did. I was crazy out of my mind. He was holding back the truth. He was hiding something from me. He was guilty. I just knew it.

"You went to Shaeena! You slept in her bed. Just as she told me! And now she is pregnant with your child! Our child is dead! Dead, Nidal!" I screamed. "Our child is dead!" A sob tore from my throat.

Nidal raced to my side and took me in his arms, and he tried to comfort me, apologizing and crying with me for the loss of our child. "Please, Loula, forgive me. I too am suffering in my heart for our child. He was my son too, Loula, and I loved him just as much as you did! I died a million deaths when our son died! I will never get over it, just like you never will. We need to come together and comfort each other; otherwise, we will destroy our love if we suffer separately. Please, Loula, try to understand what I am telling you." He tried desperately to convince me, but I was getting sick and tired of hearing about his feelings. He was the one who had done all of this. Everything was his fault.

I pushed him away from me, but Nidal grabbed me again in his arms and held on tight. I tried to break free from his embrace, but he was stronger than I was. Defeated, I stopped trying and just went limp in his arms. His strong arms lifted me while he whispered words of endearment and placed me gently on the bed. He sat next to me and cradled me in his arms, and I cried myself to sleep.

A few hours later, I awoke to find Nidal's head resting on my stomach, and his hands were around my waist. I loved this man so much, but he had done me wrong, and he needed to acknowledge his mistakes. I ran my fingers lightly through his hair, and I caressed his cheek. I was madly in love with him. He was my whole world, but I was still angry. I knew if we did not resolve it quickly, it would turn into something really ugly.

The sun had gone down, and night settled. I sent the servants away when they came in with our dinner. I had lost my appetite, and I was sure Nidal would not eat anything either. Nidal still slept. I wish I could sleep so peacefully, but I could not. We had ignored Shaeena's accusations for too long. We needed to get to the bottom of this. We could not just sweep it under the carpet and expect it to go away. It was there, and I was determined to get the truth out of Nidal, even if it meant that the truth would kill our love.

I thought back to the last time we had made love. It had been powerful. We fit perfectly together. Like the yin and the yang. We belonged only to each other. *No matter what, no matter where we are, our hearts are united in such a way that, with just a simple thought, it will reach the other across oceans and even mountains. Nothing could keep us apart. Eventually, we will find our way back to each other. I am sure of it.*

Sadly, I was also sure of something else. If Nidal had somehow fathered Shaeena's baby, our relationship did not stand a chance. But in the end, I knew we would find each other again, with a love as strong as ours, but there would be suffering in between. The thought of Nidal with another woman ate at my heart little by little, and now my heart was bleeding. I would not stop until I found out the truth. Sooner or later, Nidal would spill the beans. I would find a way to make it happen.

Chapter Twelve
Loula

Early the next morning, I awoke to find my lover gone from our room. The servants filled my tub with warm water, and I bathed and quickly dressed into my lime-green gown. I pulled my hair up in a ponytail. I pinched my cheeks to bring a pink color to them, and satisfied with my appearance, I left the room hurriedly to search for Nidal's whereabouts.

I wanted to tell him that I knew he loved me and I believed he would never betray me. I wanted to tell him that I believed him when he said he loved me. Shaeena was lying just to take him from me. Nidal would never betray me. I would tell him I believed in our love, and I knew it would make him really happy.

After checking in the dining area and finding it empty, a servant directed me to the tearoom, saying we had a visitor and Nidal was in there. I walked happily over to the tearoom, and as I was going to push the door open, I heard Shaeena's voice saying something about the baby. My heart pounded faster as I pushed the door open and stepped inside.

Everyone turned and stopped talking instantaneously when they saw me. I could tell Nidal was stressed out. His face was ashen, and his hands were shaking. He walked up to me and kissed me with trembling lips. I tensed, realizing I was about to hear something terrible. I looked around. The queen was in tears, the king was standing quietly with his back turned to everyone, and Shaeena stood triumphantly alone, holding on to her abdomen.

I braced myself for what was about to be told to me. I was sure it would be a bombshell. I knew it would destroy everything I had come to love. It would change my life as I knew it. The color drained from my face as I thought of what I stood to lose. *Wasn't losing my baby enough punishment? Why am I going to be subjected to more pain?*

Nidal sensed my feelings and took me in his arms. He whispered his love for me. His hands held on tight to my waist as he placed me in a nearby chair. My prince knelt down on his knees and looked at me. He looked ill. I opened my mouth to say something, and Nidal stopped me with a brutal kiss. I felt it. It was the kiss of Judas. He was about to tell me about his betrayal.

With trembling lips, Nidal confessed, "Loula, I am the father of her baby," he said simply as his tears rolled down his face.

The queen stifled a cry, the king hit his fists on the table, but Shaeena, when I looked in her direction, had a huge smile on her face from ear to ear. My body temperature dropped immediately. The room spun round and round. The king and queen ran to me, panicked by my appearance. I heard Nidal and his parents calling my name from somewhere far away, but I had not the energy to respond. I passed out in Nidal's arms.

The smelling salts brought me back to the hard reality. I tried to collect my senses. I looked at every person in this room. Each was in his or her own hell, as was I. All except Shaeena. She sat there with a smug expression on her face. She claimed victory today. But I did not care about her. She was not my concern. Nidal was, and his parents would suffer for his thoughtless mistakes. But no one would suffer more than me. I would never be able to get over it.

I looked coldly at Nidal. He cringed at the look I gave him. I was not about to make it easy for him. He had just torn down my world. He betrayed me to no avail. I was speechless for the first time in my life. I knew not what to say or do. Nidal dropped his head on my lap and cried like a baby. I sat frozen, not able to give him the comfort he craved. He had done this. He had destroyed both our lives. It was done. There was no going back. I pushed Nidal's head off my lap and stood.

I looked over at Shaeena and gave her a cold smile. She grinned wickedly. She may have won the battle, but I knew I would win the war. Remember the yin and the yang? The mountains and the oceans that couldn't keep us apart? Well, it might take a long time to recover from this disaster, but I knew deep in my heart that, in the end, I would be in Nidal's arms again. But in the meantime, my pride told me to run as fast as I could out of here.

I turned around, held my head up high, and walked to the door, and I knew there was no turning back once I walked out that door. *Maybe one day. A long time from now but not anytime soon.* My bleeding heart had to heal first, if that were even possible.

"Loula! Loula, please! Please, Loula, we could get through this if we try, please," Nidal cried aloud.

He ran to my side and grabbed me roughly to him. He was begging. I remembered a day a long time ago when I cried, begged, and tried to stop him from leaving me. I remembered how he had sex with me. He was cold, heartless, and mean. I remembered when he walked away from me and left me full of bruises.

That was the day he had come back from Shaeena's arms. He had jumped into her bed. I remembered. It had come full circle. The tables had turned. I pushed Nidal away from me. He grabbed me again. He tried to kiss me. I felt his salty tears on my lips. I did not kiss him back. Nidal pulled his head back and looked deep into my eyes. He took a step backward. *Did my eyes look empty and cold, the way his had all those month ago?* They must have because his hands dropped to his sides.

I knew he remembered that day. He looked at me defeated. *Good*, I thought. *Suffer like I did! Cry your heart out like I did! Men are fools!* I stepped around Nidal and walked out of the room. I heard the queen's soft cries behind me, and my heart went out to her. She was a good woman, a good queen, and I hated what this was doing to her. But I had no other choice. The one person who had sworn to love me until his last dying breath had betrayed me. He had lied.

Out in the hallway, I saw all the servants scramble away from the doorway like a pack of rats. *They heard*, I thought sadly as the tears escaped my eyes. I told myself that I would be all right. *I do not know where I am going to go, but anywhere else in the world is better than here!* I had a lot to think about now. A rough road was ahead of me, but I was a survivor, and I would manage somehow.

I walked to the end of the hallway and looked out the glass doors. The sun was shining, and the garden looked fresh and inviting. Teary-eyed, I pushed open the doors and walked outside. I took a deep breath, and the aroma from the roses filled my nostrils with perfume that was still lingering in the air. I smiled sadly. I never took the time to smell the roses because I was always busy with life's trials. Always walking past them and admiring their beauty, but not once had I stopped to smell them. I took another deep breath and allowed the aroma to hypnotize me.

I did not notice when Billal had walked up behind me, but his hand felt warm against my skin when he caressed my cheek and wiped away the single tear that had rolled down my cheek. I slowly turned to him and fell into his arms. He held me silently and allowed me to feel what I was feeling without passing judgment.

A few minutes later, I pulled away. "Billal, I am hurting so much, and I do not know what to do. Please help me," I begged.

"I will help you, Loula. I will help you get over your pain. Soon you will be smiling again. I promise." He pulled me into his embrace to comfort me. It felt good to be in his strong arms. I knew he cared for me. Billal gently pulled me away. "Loula, I know what happened. I spoke with Shaeena early this morning. It must have been devastating for you," he said sympathetically. "I wish I could make it all go away, but it's the harsh reality." I just cried all over again.

Just then, I heard Nidal call out as he ran toward us, "Get your hands off her! I will kill you for this!"

I pulled away from Billal immediately and came to Billal's defense. "Go away, Nidal!" I held up my hand to stop him from getting any closer. "Nidal, stop! Go away! You have no business being here! We're done. Finished," I told him coldly.

Nidal froze in his steps, trying to read my face. But I was not going to make it easy for him. Nidal turned his cold glare to Billal and said in a cold and suspiciously calm voice, "You don't miss an opportunity, do you? Like a cobra waits patiently until the right time to strike. You are a backstabber, you son of a bitch! You want what's mine!" He squeezed his hands into tight fists at his sides.

"Well, you weren't man enough to hold on to her! And this time, I did not take her from you. She left you and came to me willingly! And Nidal, I'm going to hold on to her, and I will never let her go. She is mine now," he said victoriously. "You were a fool to let her go! But your loss is my gain." He smiled wickedly, showing off his even, white teeth.

This enraged Nidal. He charged and swung his fists into Billal's jaw. I was surprised to see so much hate in Nidal's eyes. Billal's head snapped backward, and he lost his balance. Quickly, he regained his footing and threw himself on Nidal like a lion. Both men fell to the ground. I was worried sick for the both of them. Backing away from the fight, I heard the queen yelling as she came running toward us. The king followed behind her. Nidal and Billal fought to the end. A lot of anger was unleashing in this fight. Some of the king's men came and tried to pull them apart, but to no avail. They were bent on ripping each other to pieces.

Finally, the king himself stepped in and roared, "Stop it this instance! Or I'll throw the both of you in the dungeon!" They both stopped immediately and got up on their feet. They were both out of breath and looked like a mess. "How dare you fight on palace grounds! The both of you are fools!" the king barked, disgusted, as he walked away with his men.

The queen walked over to me and asked, concerned, "Are you all right, child?" She gave me a warm hug. "It seems like the boys are back to being five years old again. They have not grown up. They act like little children," she said angrily. She turned to her son. "Nidal, your concern should be to try to bring Loula back to your bed. Instead with your actions, you are pushing her further away from you. Jealousy blinds you, and you do not realize the truth!"

"Mother, stay out of this!" Nidal said coldly. And then he turned his gaze on me. "Loula, come back to the palace with me. Please, I beg of you."

A stern look was on his face as he waited for my reply. He thought it was simple to forgive and forget, as if everything that happened earlier did not exist. It was very typical manly behavior. Well, I was not about to forgive and forget that easily. I wanted revenge. Someone had to pay for all the heartache.

"Nidal, go away. I am not going anywhere with you," I said coldly.

I could clearly see cold sweat break out on Nidal's face. Nidal was hurting. He looked tired as he spoke now, "Please, don't be so quick to speak." He stepped closer to me.

I took a few steps backward and fell into Billal's arms, and he wrapped his arms tightly around me. Nidal reached out and tried to pull me away from Billal's grip, but I held on for dear life. Nidal noticed and backed away. I could tell my actions hurt him.

Nidal's eyes never left mine. I saw fear in his eyes as he continued to look at me. I had never seen fear in his eyes before. *He must think I don't love him anymore.* I wanted to tell him that I would never stop loving him, but my ego did not let me. He had betrayed me in the worst possible way. He had made love to another woman. The hands that caressed my body had touched another woman. I closed my eyes. The stabbing in my heart was very painful. He had gotten another woman pregnant. *She carries his child. My baby is dead! No! I will not go with him!*

My prince looked like he was about to cry. He held out his hand to me one more time. "Take my hand, Loula. Come with me, please. I beg you. I am deeply sorry for all the pain I have caused you. I will never stop trying to make it up to you. Please, Loula, come with me," he begged.

"No! I will not come to you! I will never come to you again! You have killed whatever feelings I ever had for you, Nidal! Go away. I do not want you anymore! I do not love you anymore, Nidal," I lied through my teeth.

Nidal stood where he was, staring at me and not believing the words I had just mouthed. His eyes were wide as he tried to figure out what to say next. The queen, who stood silently all this time, gasped at the mention that I didn't love her son anymore.

Billal tightened his hold on me, and he whispered for my ears alone, "Come with me, Loula. I will keep you safe."

"I am going with Billal!" I lifted my head up high. "He treats me with respect."

"Why Billal?" Nidal asked with a deadly calmness.

"Because I have come to realize that it is him that I love, Nidal, not you." I lied again, but this time, I felt my heart twisting with pain.

"Stop it!" Nidal ran his hands through his hair. "You do not love him! You're lying! Your heart belongs to me!" he said tightly.

"You are wrong, Nidal. I do not love you, and I never have. I love Billal! It was his baby I carried in my womb, not yours. I have loved Billal from the beginning, but I stayed with you because you were the crown prince. I used you!" I lied.

Nidal's face changed many shades of color before anger set in. I saw his jawline tense, and he roared like a lion ready to attack. "No, you love me! The baby was mine! I know it was!"

The queen ran to her son to comfort him. I knew I had gone too far this time. But like the fool I was, I continued pouring out the poison that finalized the end of our relationship. "No, Nidal, you are wrong about that. I'm sorry, but I do not love you. Never have, and the baby was Billal's," I said calmly.

The trembling of my lips was the only thing that gave me away, and to hide that fact, I turned around and kissed an unsuspecting Billal on the mouth. Billal wrapped his arms around me and eagerly returned the kiss. He knew I only did it to irritate Nidal. He was playing my game, and he allowed me to use him.

That did it. Nidal looked devastated. His shoulders slumped as he turned and walked away. His mother followed him for moral support. They walked to the palace and disappeared inside. This was all too much for me. I fell into Billal's embrace. I cried until there were no more tears left. He was so gentle with me, so understanding and so supportive. Billal was a kind man, and I knew he would take care of me.

Chapter Thirteen
Nidal

I was never a passionate person about any one particular thing. I was self-centered and spoiled rotten. I cared only about drinking and gambling, and sex was always on my mind. I tried my best to live my life as a young prince, abiding by my father's rules, but I was my own person.

I had no siblings. I was raised with my cousin Billal from infancy. We were like brothers. Billal's father was my uncle, my father's brother. The Persians kidnapped and executed my uncle and his wife. My parents raised Billal as their own. Billal and I, growing up, were very adventurous. We sailed across the globe and visited many countries.

One year when we were nineteen years old, we went to the Americas. It took a little over two months to reach the New World. Fascinated with America, my cousin and I extended our stay and traveled by horse to different parts of the country. There in a little town, I saw Loula.

It was hard for me to even explain what I felt when I first laid eyes on her. She was the most beautiful girl I had ever seen. She had big black eyes; thick eyelashes; long, thick, wavy, black hair;

olive-toned skin, and a body to die for. She was Greek. Some people called her a Greek goddess. I could not disagree.

That was not the only reason I was crazy about her. A long time ago, the night before I was to turn fifteen years of age, I had a strange dream. It was the day before I was going to lose my virginity. My father, the king, wanted me to sleep with a lot of women. He wanted me to lose my virginity and become a man, but the night before I was to lose my innocence, I saw the dream that would change my life forever.

I saw a woman who looked like Loula. She was stunningly beautiful. I fell in love with her, and she fell in love with me. I saw the two of us making love, and the feeling was magical. It was an unforgettable experience. In my dream, I was a lot older, and so was Loula. The love we had for one another was powerful. Our lovemaking was deep. I told her that I would never betray her and make love to another woman. At fifteen, I did not understand the dream and thought nothing of it.

In the morning when I woke up, I could not shake the feeling away. The dream felt so real. All day long, it was on my mind. I told myself that it was just a wet dream because I was going to lose my virginity today, so my mind conjured this dream together to get me ready for the big night.

I remember when this beautiful-looking woman my father had sent to my room walked in. I did not want to touch her. I could not explain it. I just knew that I could not go near her. My father was puzzled. He said maybe I was too young. I should wait another year. But I knew that, even a year later, I would not want to have sex with another woman. I only wanted the woman in my dreams.

Every single night thereafter when I slept, she came into my dreams, and we made love. It felt so real, as if we lived that life somewhere, at some other time, in another dimension.

As the days turned to months, the dreams continued. I was madly in love with the woman in my dreams. I was afraid to tell anyone, for fear they might think I had gone mad.

One night in my dream, Loula told me that I needed to be patient and we would be together one day. She told me to never stop looking for her. She said I would find her if I kept searching.

So I searched for four years with no success. And then one night, she told me that we were soul mates. She said that, in another lifetime, we were deeply in love with each other. She said we were so happy, and we both promised each other that we would always be together. She said I had to find her before I turned thirty. If I failed to do so, I would never find her in this lifetime.

I did not know why, but I really believed what she told me in the dream. I begged her one night to reveal her whereabouts to me. She told me to go to the New World and she would be waiting for me there. I was beside myself with excitement. The New World had to be this place I read about, this place called America.

America was so far away. I did not know how I was going to go there, but I knew I would find a way. I asked my father to allow me to sail his ship and go to America. He laughed in my face. He told me that I was now nineteen years of age and it was time I found a bride. He said that Princess Shaeena was a good match for me and I should make her my wife. The king said I was old enough to get married and I should take a bride soon. Or else he threatened to choose one for me. After much arguing back and forth, I lied to him and said that, if he allowed me to sail to America, I would take a bride upon my return. Pleased, my father agreed, and I sailed away with my cousin and thirty-six of my most trusted men.

Two months later, we reached America. I was thrilled to start my search, but I had no idea where to start looking for Loula. As the weeks flew by and we went from town to town, I had no success. Exhausted and feeling like I would never find her, I was ready to give up, but a week before our ship was to set sail, in this little town miles from shore, to my delight, I found her.

I felt overwhelmed with joy that I found my soul mate. I did not know how I would convince her to believe what I was about to tell her, but I knew in my heart that I would find a way and we would be together. My men thought I was crazy, but that did not stop me from following my dreams.

She was running the corner bakery shop for the people she lived with. I sat outside the little coffee shop down the street, where I had a perfect view of the bakery and sipped the unsavory coffee until she was done with work. Then I followed her discreetly, just to see her walk home. Her beauty mesmerized me. I was madly in love with her.

I tried to get as much information about her as I could from the people who lived in town. Loula was only fifteen years old. She had been an orphan from a very young age. The people she lived with opened up their home to her and raised her like their own. They had a son who was my age, a young, good-looking lad who worshipped the ground Loula walked on. He was her second shadow. Wherever she was, he was right behind her, guarding her as if his life depended on it. She didn't look too interested in him. I could tell because, when she spoke to him, her eyes never looked into his. I could not contain my excitement.

One day, I followed her after she left work. I noticed that her bodyguard was not with her. She did not take the same route as she usually did. Instead of going straight down the wide cobblestone street, she turned down the corner and headed down the opposite side. I quickened my pace, not wanting to lose her, and I saw that she headed toward a dirt road that led to a prairie. I was glad the shadow man was not around. I had her all to myself.

Loula walked into the prairie and stopped at a place where there were wildflowers in full bloom everywhere. Loula found a spot and sat herself down. I saw this as my opportunity to announce myself. My heart pounded in my chest as I walked up to her. I startled her when I said hello and apologized for intruding during her private moment. At first, she was cautious, not saying much and eyeing me suspiciously. But as we spoke, I saw her relax, and she even threw me a smile. I melted. I knew at that moment that I was totally in love with her.

"What is your name?" She asked.

"Nidal." I said, withholding the part that I was a prince. She did not need to know I was the crown prince of Arabia.

She padded the dirt floor next to her and asked politely, "Would you like to sit down?"

I sat down next to her, and we talked until sunset. Our conversation was very pleasant. She smiled at me the whole time I was with her. My heart pounded loudly in my ears. This felt like my dream was turning into reality. When I looked into her eyes, I remembered our lovemaking in the dreams, and I just wanted to take her in my arms and make love to her right here in the prairie.

I found out many things about her that day. She was lovely on the inside as well as the outside. My heart burst with love. She told me about her life with the family she lived with. She said that Angelo, the young man, the only child of the couple she lived with, was a nice person. She said he had declared his love to her, but she was not sure if she felt anything for him. Loula said he had asked for her hand in marriage, but she refused him, saying she was not ready for marriage yet.

I was holding my breath, and when I heard her answer to Angelo's marriage proposal, I let out a big sigh. I was so glad she had turned him down. I was having the best time of my life until Loula stood and announced that she had to return home because it was getting late. I asked her if I could see her again, and she threw me the most beautiful smile I had ever seen and said she would meet me here in this spot on the morrow.

We walked back in silence, each in our own thoughts. I was overjoyed. This was the happiest moment of my life. Tomorrow, I would tell her everything. I would pour my heart out, and then I would beg her to come with me to Arabia.

Right before we reached the town square, Loula turned, looked me in my eyes, and said. "Thank you, I had a lovely time.

I feel like I have known you for years. Have you visited our town before, because you look very familiar?"

My heart skipped a beat. She was remembering me from another time, another dimension. I just knew it! But I could not tell her the truth yet. I did not want to scare her.

Loula said softly, "Nidal, I'm sorry but you cannot walk with me after this point because someone might see us together, and that would create major gossip, which isn't good for my reputation." I immediately withdrew from asking if I could walk her all the way home.

I bid her good night, but not before asking, "Can I meet you at the prairie again tomorrow?"

She smiled at me, and my heart stopped.

I whistled all the way to the ship. This was one of the happiest days of my life. Being in love was one of the nicest feelings in the world. When I reached the ship, I found Billal drinking whisky on the deck with his mates. Billal was surprised when he saw me, and he followed me to our cabin. He wanted to know where I had been all day, and I told him. He thought I was a nut. But that did not bother me. I was in love, and that was all that mattered.

I went to meet Loula in the prairie every day after the day I first saw her. It was the best time of my life. I was dancing to the tune of my heart. Our time together was so special, so beautiful, and so real. Two days before my ship was to set sail, Loula and I were walking away from the prairie.

"Loula, there is something I need to tell you," I said. I wanted to tell her everything, including how much she meant to me. "Please come to the prarie tomorrow," I begged.

In response, she leaned over and kissed my lips. It was a simple kiss, but I almost lost control of my legs. I stood there frozen like a lovesick puppy. I lost my voice, and terrified, I turned and ran away, leaving Loula behind just staring after me. My private part was rock solid the rest of the night, and I masturbated with her on my mind to release all the tension.

I could not sleep that night. I tossed and turned and argued with myself.

"Will you please stop acting like a nut!" Billal yelled, "She is just an American and we will never see her again. Get over it!"

I knew he would never understand, so I just dropped it. The ship was going to sail the day after tomorrow. I had to tell Loula my feelings before then and beg her to come with me.

On the last day at the prairie, I listened to her chattering away about the different kind of loaves of bread that the bakery offered, while my mind wandered to the kiss she had given me the day before. It was almost sunset, and just as I mustered up the guts to tell her my most inner thoughts, we heard someone calling her name. We both turned at the same time and saw Angelo running to us, angry as could be.

"Loula, where have you been? I have been looking all over for you!" he scolded. Then he threw me a mean look and said, "If you go near her again, I will kill you."

Angelo took her by her arm and dragged her home, while I just stood there openmouthed. I wanted to rip her out of his grip. She was mine. She belonged to me! *Soon*, I thought, *she will be in my arms.*

I followed them from a distance until they disappeared inside their home. I was overwhelmed with sadness. The day had not turn out as I had hoped. I never got the chance to tell Loula how I felt. I thought to visit Loula early in the morning, right before we set sail, and declare my love for her.

I went back to the ship and drank a bottle of vodka. I got drunk and passed out in my cabin. The next day in the afternoon, I awoke with a pounding headache to the sunshine that had made its way inside my room through the small portal. I slowly looked around the room and tried to adjust my eyes to the brightness of the room. That was when I felt the ship moving, and I jumped quickly to my feet and ran out of the cabin and onto the deck.

My suspicions were real. We were in the middle of the ocean, miles from shore. I got sick to my stomach and ran to the side of the ship and barfed. My men came running to my aid, and I pushed them away from me.

"Why have we sailed away without my permission?" I angrily yelled at my men.

The only answer I got was that the tide had set in earlier than expected and we had to leave immediately. Besides, they chimed, the king had warned them to return on time, or else he would behead them. So they wanted to make good time reaching Arabia. I was devastated. My whole world came tumbling down.

I was a tormented soul thereafter. By the time we reached Arabia, I was a mess. I had lost my appetite, and I cried myself to sleep every night in my cabin. I, the crown prince of Arabia, who had not cried ever, cried now for Loula like a little baby. Billal told the crew what I was suffering from, and I was the laughing stock on the ship. But I did not care. I loved Loula, and one day, I would be back to claim her as mine.

When we reached Arabia, the king was told of our adventures, including the part about Loula. He was not pleased with that specific information, but I pleaded my love for her, and he just shrugged it off as if it did not matter. I was devastated that he would not even hear me out. He laughed at me every time I mentioned her name.

One day, he brought a harem to the palace as a gift to me, saying these women would make me forget I had ever met Loula. I rebuked his gift, locked myself in my room, and cried all night

❀ ❀ ❀

The years passed by quickly, and I still could not get Loula out of my mind. I loved her even more now. I was twenty-five years old. Six years had passed, and Loula was still fresh on my mind. I did not want any other woman, only her. The people of Arabia could not believe that I was twenty-five and still not married. They could not believe that their prince was still a virgin, and they could not get over the fact that I still refused every girl they brought me to marry.

I lost my zest for life. I had lost my appetite and had no desire to drink and get drunk like most men did. The king, my father, was losing his patience with me.

"Nidal, I demand you marry the lovely Princess Shaeena," he said gruffly.

"Impossible, Father, I see her only as a brother sees a sister!" I declared.

My father laughed in my face. "Son, do you have eye trouble? Have you taken a second and third look at her? Maybe you have missed something! She is one of the most beautiful maidens in the country, not to mention the fact that she is a princess."

I simply ignored him and walked away.

Every night when I closed my eyes, I thought of Loula, her lovely face, her big, black eyes, and soft, full lips. I imagined running my fingers through her thick hair and bringing her head closer to mine, and our lips touching as I caressed her lovely breasts. I whispered my love for her in her ear, and she whispered it back to me. I entered her with a passion above and beyond anything I had ever felt in my whole entire life.

I had masturbated every night since I had seen her, and it was only the memory of her on my mind that I shared these moments with. I told no one because I knew no one would understand the love I felt for her. They were precious moments, and I treasured them.

I was a prince obsessed with a girl who was a world away. I begged the king every day to allow me to sail back to America and bring her here to Arabia. He only laughed in my face. My mother begged me to stop thinking of her. I told them that they need to understand the depth of my feelings for her. I would never love another. They did not believe that. Even Billal, instead of siding with me, laughed too. So I kept to myself, and I accepted all the criticism from everyone. I did not care that they laughed. What was that to me? They were fools! They did not know what love meant. I continued to bring her memory into the bedroom every night. It was there that I felt her in my arms. It was there that I shared my thoughts and feelings with her. It was there that I made love to her every night thereafter. It was during my dreams that I lived the happiest.

Another four years passed, and I was really feeling the pressure to marry the princess, my best friend. I held my ground and told them that I would not even consider her or any other woman. I wanted Loula and no one else. By now, the people of Arabia were crying for me to get married. The pressure was tremendous.

One day, my mother took me aside and cried in my arms.

"Nidal, you do not smile anymore. You have lost your zest for life! All you do is obsess over this American woman! You are getting older and you must choose a bride soon! Reconsider Princess Shaeena. She is a perfect match for you!"

"I would never marry anyone but Loula, Mother. It has to be her or no one," I told her.

"I want grandchildren! You are depriving me of a happy life. You are selfish, Nidal! she said, and she ran out of the room crying.

I went back to the king, begging him to reconsider.

"Father, you will be waiting for years, because I will not change my mind! I am not going to marry Princess Shaeena! I want Loula and no other!" I told him sternly.

"You are an obsessive, self-centered fool!" the king growled, but in the end, after much deliberation, he gave up and finally agreed.

I sailed away a week later, and I could not contain my excitement. My mother begged me not to go, but I refused to listen to her, telling her that I was going to bring her back a daughter-in-law. She gave up the argument and stalked off to her room, but not without saying first that I had broken her heart.

My father, the king, laughed at me and told me, "It has been ten years since you last saw Loula. She is most likely married with ten children." I flinched at this possibility.

"If you come back without her, I will have you marry Princess Shaeena," he said without blinking an eyelash.

And I agreed, knowing deep in my heart that I would not come back without Loula. I would move heaven and earth if I had to. I would cross mountains and oceans and kill anyone who stood in my way. I would do all that, but I would not come back without her.

Every day on the ship, I stayed in my cabin and tried to figure out ways to tell Loula that I was back and wanted her to marry me. There was a good chance she was married, as my father had said, and even if she weren't, she might be in love with another. It had been ten years. Anything was possible. My nights were the same as always. I lay in bed, closed my eyes, and thought of her. My excitement was released in masturbation, and I would fall asleep with her on my mind.

The dreams never came back. Ever since I saw her ten years ago, the dreams had stopped. I did not know what that meant. It worried me. *Am I chasing a dream that was never going to become real?* I would die if that happened. There was no life for me without Loula. I could not explain it any better. It was just simply Loula or no one. I would not yield. I had to find her and make her mine.

The weather was perfect, and that allowed our ship to make good time reaching America. Almost two months later, we docked at port, and I could hardly contain myself. I jumped off the ship and ran to town to the little bakery to find Loula. To my dismay, she was not inside, and when I asked the young girl who worked there if she knew where I could find her, she stood silent, not saying a word.

I went to the house where I knew she had lived the last time I was here. I knocked on the wooden door, but there was no answer. My heart pounded drastically as I walked around to the side of the house and peeked inside through the window. The house was empty. No one was home. The reality was that I had taken too long to come for her. Ten whole years had passed, and she probably did not remember me after all this time.

Sick to my stomach, I roamed the town like a chicken without a head. I knew not what to do. So I went to the corner cafeteria to have a cup of coffee and gather my wits. It was there that I overheard the conversation between two older men that tore my heart out.

They were discussing the wedding that was to take place an hour from now. I heard them say the names Angelo and Loula. I jumped off my seat, ran up to them, and demanded they tell me where the wedding was to take place. The two men looked skeptical about telling me a single thing. I pulled five gold coins out of my pocket, and I got all the information I needed from them.

Loula and Angelo were getting married in a little chapel about a mile from here. The wedding party and all the guests were on their way there now. My heart pounded in my ears as I ran to find a horse and try to get to the chapel to stop the wedding. But first I needed the help of my men.

I bought a horse, rode back to the ship, and told my men what was happening. They all wanted a piece of the action. Even Billal was excited to steal the bride from the groom. I could hardly contain myself as we all rode as fast as possible to the chapel. We had a plan. We were going to kidnap my woman. It was a little risky, but I had no other choice. I wanted her, and I would go to any lengths to get her.

Some men stayed behind to prepare the ship to sail away as soon as we returned. We couldn't waste any time on our way back. The law would probably be after us when we kidnapped the bride. Our plan was set in action, and we were on our way to the chapel to steal the bride.

When we got there, the plan was set into motion. My men very quietly surrounded the little chapel, just as we had planned, and we waited for the best opportunity to grab the bride. I peeked through the little side window, and my heart tightened. The chapel was full of people, the groom stood proudly by the side of the altar alongside the minister, and they all waited for Loula to walk down the aisle.

Loula was taking little steps as she walked toward her groom. She was wearing a simple white gown with short sleeves that were trimmed with lace, and she was holding a single white lily in her hands. Her hair was pinned up in a simple updo that showed off her beautiful facial features. She was breathtakingly beautiful, but no sparkle was in her eyes. No smile on her face. In fact, she looked very sad.

I caught my breath as I watched her walk closer to the altar. The love I felt for her at this moment overwhelmed me. It had been ten long years. Ten years of torture! Frantic now, I acted quickly. I just wanted to get this over with and put this day behind me. My men were all in position. All was set. Nothing could stop me now. This was my fate, and Loula was my destiny. I took a deep breath and opened the side door to the chapel, the one closest to the bride, and walked in.

Everyone's head turned, including the groom's. I ran to Loula, swept her up in my arms, and started running as fast as I could out of the chapel. Behind me, everyone was screaming and yelling, and the groom chased after me. As soon as I stepped outside, my men barred the chapel's door from opening. That would give us ample time to ride away.

My men were outside with the horses they had stolen from the guests who were inside the chapel. They held on to Loula as she was kicking and screaming for help. I jumped on my horse, Loula was handed to me, and off we rode. All my men rode behind me, and we raced toward the ship. Loula was holding on to my waist for dear life. I had never felt a bigger rush than what I felt at that very moment. I closed my eyes for a second and allowed the wind to blow in my face. It felt so good. I took a deep breath and smiled. *Life is good*, I thought.

The horses behind me galloped at a very fast pace. We had to reach the ship within the next few minutes. At exactly four thirty, the ship would sail away, according to plan. Loula's hold on my waist tightened as we raced up some small hills and down the other side. I could see the ship from where we were, and I was thrilled that we had almost accomplished our goal. I heard some of my men riding behind me, while most of them raced ahead, and finally we were there.

I jumped off the horse, grabbed a hold of Loula's waist, and pulled her off the horse hastily. The ship was just about to sail away as we rushed up the plank. Loula resisted and tried to break free of my hold, so I lifted her, threw her over my shoulders, and ran up the plank. My men pulled up the plank, and we sailed away just in time. Angelo and about twenty of his men raced up to the dock, but they got there too late.

Everyone on the ship cheered with excitement. They were glad to be going back home. I took Loula to my cabin and threw her on the bed. She was enraged, raving, panting, and throwing a fit. I smiled down at her, and I was just so glad to finally have my prize. She was my life now. I knew at that moment that I could not live without her.

I locked Loula in the cabin and went to thank my men. We ate bread and cheese and drank wine in celebration. Some were singing, some were dancing, and everyone was drunk. This was a happy day for them. Their prince was finally bringing home a bride!

I left them to go visit my girl, thinking they were right. I finally was bringing home a bride, but would she have me? She did not look too happy to be here. I slowly opened the door and peeked inside. Loula was lying on the bed fast asleep. Tears were on her eyelashes, and I knew she had cried herself to sleep. That hurt my ego, but, most importantly, my heart. I loved her so much, and I only prayed that she would feel the same way for me one day.

I lay down on the bed next to her and looked into her beautiful face. This woman was mine. And I was never going to let her go. Never! I slowly took her in my arms and held my breath. I was bursting with happiness. My dream had come true. Eventually, I fell into blissful sleep.

The next morning, I had to explain to Loula why I kidnapped her on her wedding day. She patiently waited for my explanation. I was not sure she would understand what I was about to tell her, but I had to say something because I could tell by the way her eyes looked around the room that she was searching for something to throw at me. I took a chance and told her the simple truth. Even as it came out of my mouth, I knew she was not going to believe me. The whole thing sounded ridiculous.

I bent forward as the oil lamp came flying out of nowhere and crashed on the wall behind me. This wasn't going to be as easy as I thought, but I would try my best every day to make her understand my feelings for her. Only then would she see what I saw, that we were meant to be together forever. It was our fate. It was our destiny.

I made many attempts to speak to her, but she would not listen to reason.

"It is not fair to Angelo that I was taken from him in such a way. He is a good man and does not deserve what he got," she said angrily.

My heart twisted with jealousy at the mere mention of Angelo. I hated him with a passion.

Loula cried many times in our cabin, and I tried comforting her, but she pushed me away, saying she wanted to be left alone. One day, I asked her flat out, "Do you love Angelo? If you swear to me that you are in love with him, we will sail back to the Americas and hand you back to him." I held my breath for her answer, but to my delight, she clamped her mouth shut and spoke not. My heart swelled with love. I now knew that my chances were greater to win her love. I would take it slowly, one day at a time. I knew one day she would understand my motives, but until then, I respected her wishes and did not push her in any way.

The months passed quickly, and we reached Arabia in no time. There was excitement in the air as we docked. Thousands of people were waiting to greet us. They cheered and sang as we walked down the plank. I was so proud of my country and so thankful that they finally understood my feelings for the woman I loved.

When my feet touched Arabian soil, I felt a rush in my body from head to toe. I was blown away with this feeling that had consumed my entire being. I gently pulled Loula next to me. Everyone was pushing and shoving to get a glimpse of her. I bowed and waved to my people, and the huge crowd went crazy.

The royal carriage was waiting for us at the end of the walkway. I took Loula's hand and helped her into the carriage, and then I too climbed in and sat next to her. I stole a quick glance toward the love of my life, and I caught her looking at me nervously. Taking her hand, I gave her a reassuring squeeze, hoping it would ease her tension. Finally, my cousin Billal climbed in, and the driver closed the door, climbed on the front of the carriage, and pulled the reins. The six stallions galloped away. Everyone was cheering wildly behind us. But we had a good day's ride to the palace, and I did not want to waste any more time getting there. I was eager to get home and claim Loula as my bride.

Loula rode with me in silence. Just like the whole two months on the ship, she hardly said a word to me. She ate very little, and I started to get concerned, but I knew she would eventually come to terms with her new life. I knew in my heart that she would fall in love with me. In fact, I had no doubt. I believed what Loula had told me in my dreams. She was my fate, my destiny. She was my sweet obsession!

We reached the palace by nightfall, and everyone was excitedly waiting for our arrival. My mother was the first to greet us. She hugged and kissed me. She was so glad to have me back. But Loula did not receive the same welcome from the queen as I did. My mother had a cold stare for her as she scanned her eyes up and down Loula and shook her head in disapproval. I saw Loula shrink back when my mother scrutinized her in such a cold way.

The king was more gracious. He looked at my future wife and flashed her a warm smile. "You are a rare jewel," he said with a twinkle in his eyes. My father then winked at me before he stalked off after the queen.

⊠ ⊠ ⊠

From that day forward, I was in heaven. There was so much love inside me to give Loula. She was the only reason for my existence. It was like a sickness in me. I could not live without her. I had slept in the same bed with her since the day I brought her home. I held her in my arms and even stole some kisses from her whenever I got the chance. But I never overstepped my boundaries. I could not make love to her without her consent. Not only did I want her consent, I wanted her to love me back and crave my lovemaking. I knew it would happen one day. In the meantime, I waited patiently until she was ready.

I was jealous of everyone around her. I was even jealous of the bedsheets that were wrapped around her body as she slept. I wanted to be the only one who touched her. I wanted to be the center of her world. I wanted to be her world. I would have it no other way. I'd rather be dead than live and see her with another man.

I could tell that, as the days went by, she softened up to me. My groin was hard as a rock. I needed to spill my seed. But I was controlling my every emotion and waiting patiently for her to come around. A few times, I went in private and masturbated, but I held off as much as I could. I preferred her touch on me only.

As the days turned to months, I could not contain my excitement. We became closer. She was warming up to me, and I think she was now in love with me, but I was afraid to ask her. I wanted her to say it on her own. I would wait until the end of the world if I had to. This was how much I loved her.

The first time I kissed her, I lost my senses. I almost blacked out. That was how powerful her love was to me. I dared not share my feelings with anyone. They would all make fun of me. They did not understand the love I felt for her. Every fiber in my body answered only to her. I didn't even understand it myself. I'd rather kill myself than make love to another.

No one understood something like that. I didn't either. I remember all the years I had waited until I kidnapped her. I had wasted practically my entire life just waiting for her. I was twenty-nine years old, and I had not been with a woman. I was laughed at, ridiculed, and joked about, but I did not care. Before I ever set eyes on Loula, I had had a hard-on for every female I laid eyes on. But when I started having the dreams of Loula and I saw her in America for the first time, I lost all appetite for sex with other women unless it was Loula herself who was in my bed. I knew that she was my soul mate, and we had lived together in some other life. That was the only explanation I could find.

Finally, the time came, and we made love. Not only was it the best day of my life, it was my life. Our bodies united, and both of us became one. That was how I felt. Nothing in the world could affect me more than Loula. When I looked into her eyes, I saw the missing puzzle piece from my life. I was not complete without her. Only she could complete me.

When I was inside her and making love to her, no human words could describe what I felt. Humans had not invented that word yet. The feeling was above and beyond anything you could possibly imagine. Everyone said I was obsessed. Maybe I was, but I was also deeply in love with her. She fulfilled my every desire!

I knew Billal was in love with my woman. He always wanted what was mine: my parents, my crown, my palace, and now my heart, Loula. He could have it all, but he couldn't have Loula. I would never let him or any other man take her. She was mine, as I was hers. If he took her, if anyone succeeded in taking her from me, I would finish my life, for I could not live in my world if she did not exist in it.

Billal tried many times to take her from me, but her heart belonged only to me. When I left for the war, I took only my mind and body with me. I left my heart behind for Loula. We fought right before I left. I went to Shaeena's palace for three nights. I can't remember what happened while I was there. She claimed her baby was mine. I could not believe that. I would never betray Loula like that. I was innocent of any wrongdoing!

I saw Loula with Billal so many times. I didn't know why she kissed him. I still couldn't believe it. Maybe my eyes were playing tricks on me. Maybe she really did not kiss him. When our baby died, I was devastated, and so was Loula. I thought that maybe somehow that would unite us, but as always, Billal got in the way again. It was hard to get over such a tragedy. But now that Loula was with Billal, to me, it was just as tragic. I could not live without her. I did not know what to do.

In the meantime, Shaeena was staying at the palace, and she was still claiming that the child she carried was mine. I could not deny that it was my baby because I didn't remember what had happened the three nights I stayed at Shaeena's palace. I didn't think I had sex with her. But she claimed I did. I didn't remember a single thing.

I knew I could not possibly have slept with her. I would not—could not—sleep with any other woman. My body ached only for Loula. She was my universe, my soul mate. I would die for her.

This baby in Shaeena's stomach could not be mine. But if it were, I would not know what to do. In my country, the law said that, if the crown prince got a woman pregnant, he must marry her so the child would not be born a bastard, especially if it were the firstborn. I had to find a way to prove that Shaeena's child was not mine. I had to hurry before it was too late because I stood to lose Loula every second that went by. I thought I still had a chance to win Loula's heart back. She was very angry with me. She thought I had betrayed her in the worst possible way. But I knew that I could not do that. I'd rather stick a knife in my heart and kill myself than be with another.

Shaeena was sharing my room. She slept in my bed; I slept on the floor on some blankets and wrapped myself with the blanket that Loula and I had shared. The blanket brought me comfort. It had touched Loula's body; it had covered us when we made love. It had caressed Loula's body, and her scent was still on it. I could smell it as I lay myself down to sleep each night.

I missed her touch so much. When I closed my eyes in the dark room, I saw her. I felt her. Her face was full of passion as her lips claimed mine. I could not stand it. My hand gripped my shaft, and I played with it wildly until I was spent. If this was the closest I could get to Loula, then so be it for now. My memory would have to do. But soon, I would once again enjoy Loula's body next to mine. I would claim her heart again. I knew I would, even if it was the last thing I did!

Loula spent her nights in Billal's room. She made it her home for now. I would not believe that she shared his bed. I could not believe that! He didn't love her like I did. No one loved her like this. I would give my life for her. She was my life. Every breath I took, it was for her. I decided that today I would go to her and take her back. She belonged to me. She was mine.

I got up early before Shaeena awoke. I dressed and tiptoed out of the room. Billal's chamber was upstairs on the second floor. I knew that Billal had gone hunting today with his friends. I had not wanted to sleep last night. I knew Billal would leave before dawn. I wanted to be awake when I heard the men leave the palace.

I tiptoed up the stairs barefoot and ran to the room where my beloved slept inside. My heart was racing so fast that I thought it would burst. I took a deep breath and slowly and quietly opened the door. Thankfully, it was not locked. As I stepped inside, I slowly closed and locked the door. I barely saw Loula's sleepy form. I tiptoed slowly toward the bed, and my eyes watered up at the sight of her. I could not resist, so I undressed quickly, got in the bed, and lay right next to her. I held my breath as my heart pounded in my ears. If she woke up now, she would be startled, and she might scream. Then I would be in big trouble.

I slipped my arm slowly around her waist and pulled her close to my naked body. Loula purred and wiggled closer to me. I could tell she was still sleeping by the way she was breathing. I caressed her body lightly, and she arched her body backward, accepting my caresses, as she always had in the past. My hold tightened around her waist, and my lips pressed on hers. Heat raced through my entire body, and I was on fire. I lifted her nightgown and pulled down her underwear. I rolled on top of her, and she parted her legs and allowed my shaft to enter her.

I pounded into her with such force that I almost exploded immediately. I heard her moan with delight, and she lifted her bottom in rhythm with mine. It was a moment of pleasure that was beyond any words. A few minutes later, we both exploded at the same time. Her fingers tightened around my bottom as her nails dug deep into my skin. Electricity hit me from the top of my head all the way down to my feet as I continued to pump my shaft inside her. She called out my name in the dark. The passion between us was powerful. I could not stop moving inside her. She did not want me to stop. She begged me not to stop. I lost all my senses.

As I rode her, we both climaxed together. My body shook violently as the spasms spread throughout my entire body. We could not stop. We did not know how to. I missed her so much. I loved her so much it hurt. Loula's fingers traced my body as if she were making sure that it was me she just made love to. I confirmed her suspicions with the seal of a kiss. And she hungrily kissed me back, bruising my lips with hers. The sun slowly allowed its rays to enter through the window, and I saw Loula's lovely face. She greeted me with a smile.

Spent, I lay sideways, my shaft still inside her. I looked into her beautiful eyes and cried. I cried for all the nights I had lain alone without her. I whispered my love for her, and she cried a river. I told her I missed her so much, and she swore her love for me. I trembled in her arms. She took my breath away.

I told her I was sorry, and she forgave me. She forgave all my mistakes and clung to me for dear life. Her hips started to sway back and forth, and my manhood prepared itself for another round of lovemaking. This time, it was different than all the other times. I knew she was mine. She would always be mine, now and forever until death do us part. My lovemaking branded her to me. My seed spilled inside her, claiming her soul. I wanted her to carry my baby. And I would stop at nothing to make that happen.

We lay quietly next to each other, each in our own thoughts. We were tired, exhausted, and happy.

Loula looked into my eyes and asked passionately, "What took you so long to come to me?"

My heart burst with joy. I did not want to tell her that I wanted to come sooner, but that I feared she might reject me. I could not mouth those words. They were horrible words. I closed my eyes shut and took a long deep breath before I answered her.

"I am here now. That is all that matters, my love."

I squeezed her tightly into my arms, and I heard her cry softly. Her tears dripped onto my chest. Each teardrop that touched my skin burned my skin. I was being tortured for the damage I had done. I cried with her. I wanted to take her suffering away. But she cried even more and clung to me for dear life. I regretted the day I had hurt her. I would protect her from anguish. I would guide her to happiness, a place she so richly deserved.

It is told that some souls are linked across space and time, connected by an ancient calling that echoes through the ages of ages. If you listen to the language of lovers, you will hear the echoes of that infantile bliss that whispers softly in the air, across the universe into other dimensions as two souls unite again and again, satisfying their thirst for love. They feel complete only when their hearts are united in harmony.

If that harmony is broken, the links that connect the souls break, and they get lost into an eternity of torture until they call out for mercy and the gods set them free. And then they search into infinity until they reunite and become one once again.

I held her close to my heart. Breathlessly, I boldly declared my love for her and demanded she love me back in return. She answered recklessly without a second thought that she would kill me if I left her again. Then she demanded that I take her once again to heights of passion, and she thrust her body onto mine and kissed me wildly. I lost myself inside her as she rode with me to places of the heart.

By now, the sun's rays extended beyond the universe. Daylight entered the room, and it was time to part. I kissed her lips, not wanting to let go, but I knew I had to leave for now. I quickly jumped out of bed and dressed hastily, but as I leaned over to kiss her one more time, it suddenly occurred to me that no blankets were anywhere on the floor. I looked around the room and did not see any sign of Billal's sleeping blankets. And then I realized the truth. It hit me like a ton of bricks. My knees buckled, and I almost dropped to the floor. I held on to the bedpost for support and gritted my teeth furiously.

Already knowing what her response would be, I asked in a dangerously low tone, "Where does Billal sleep at night?" I held my breath, preparing myself for the answer that was coming.

She did not answer right away. Unconsciously, Loula pulled the blanket up to her chin. Her lips trembled. "In the bed with me, but it's not what you think. I can explain," she said quickly and reached out for my hand.

I staggered backward as a loud roar rumbled out of my throat. The room started to spin. *This isn't happening*, I thought wildly.

Loula choked back a sob. I was unsympathetic to her pain. She cried hysterically.

"Don't even try to fake a cry. You destroyed everything I believed in," I ruthlessly spat at her. "While I suffered and died a thousand deaths, you were sleeping in the same bed with the enemy!"

I wanted to hurt her, like she had hurt me, but I could not. I loved her still, but her betrayal was worse than death. I searched her face for a trace of regret. There was none. I looked deep into her eyes, deceiving eyes. They fooled me into believing in love. I searched her face for the truth, but I saw no truth there, only deceit. I took one last look of her face and turned and walked away. She jumped out of bed and raced after me, just as I opened the door to leave. She closed the door and pressed her naked body against it so I could not leave.

"Nidal, please," she pleaded. "Let me explain." She tried to catch her breath. "I have not slept with Billal! I have never slept with him!" she cried. I tried to push past her, and her hand came up quick and stopped me. "No, Nidal, stop. Listen to me. I swear I have not slept with him ever!" she cried. "I would never betray you in that way. You must believe me!" she said in an agonizing voice.

I drew my head back and allowed fresh air to enter my lungs. There was a tightness in my chest. I staggered backward and fell helplessly onto a chair that leaned against the wall. Loula dropped to her knees by my side and fell onto my lap in total submission.

I could not breathe. It felt like the air had been sucked out of the room. I took a deep breath and inhaled. I felt much better. I clasped my hands around her hands tightly. In my heart of hearts, I knew I could not live without her, even if she had slept with Billal. She was still mine, and somehow I had to find a way to forgive and forget and look past all this. I pulled her up on my lap and held her close to my heart. She was my heart. I loved her more than I loved my own life.

I had to think of a plan, a rock-solid one. We could not keep breaking up and making up and torturing ourselves even more, wasting our lives in turmoil, when we could live in bliss. Loula wrapped her arms around me and allowed her head to rest on my chest. I pushed the strands of hair away from her face and caressed her cheek. Her eyes were wet from the tears that were still rolling down her cheek. I wondered when the tears would stop, when the pain would go away, and we could live our lives to the fullest. The past fourteen years of my life I had suffered a tremendous amount. *Are we destined to be together, or is our destiny to be apart?* But the thought of a life without her seemed unbearable.

There is hope for a new beginning. I am sure of it. I know in my heart that we will prevail. Our love is strong. It is real, and I will stop at nothing to accomplish my goal. Gently, I pulled Loula up, looked into her eyes, and smiled. *How long has it been since the last time I smiled at her?* Her eyes looked into mine. Hope filled them. I could see all the love and trust that was there. I never set out deliberately to hurt her. All of it was unavoidable.

I would do anything for her. I would give up my crown, my family, and even my life for her. I never wanted to be a king. I just wanted to live a normal life. I envied the commoners. They did not have much, but they were rich in places of the heart. They were happier than I ever was. I would trade lives with them in a heartbeat if I had the chance.

I brought her hands to my lips and kissed them. Her eyes searched mine for answers. Clearly distressed, she asked, "My prince, what ails you?"

I spoke with conviction. "You know I love you deeply, and I cannot and will not live a life without you by my side. We have to figure out what to do and fast. Shaeena's baby is to arrive soon, and I am under pressure to marry her." The last words rolled off my tongue without thinking the effect it might have on Loula. Immediately, she gasped for air and choked back sobs that were threatening to rip from her throat.

"If you marry her, Nidal, I promise I will throw myself off a cliff. Do not think for one moment that I will not," she threatened with a deadly calm.

Fear gripped me at the thought of that. I grabbed Loula's shoulders and shook her, and with a sharp edge of anger in my voice, I yelled, "You will do no such thing. We will be together, and I will do everything in my power to claim you as my wife. I promise you. You must be patient, Loula," I begged.

Loula kept her eyes averted from mine. I could tell she was hurting. A miserable silence followed, and it was agony for me to try to figure out what she was thinking.

I broke the silence by calmly asking, "Loula, do you think you could wait until I figure out what to do? I promise you I will not take too long. I know you want things to change now, but it's not that easy. This is real stuff. People can get hurt, lives could get destroyed, the country could suffer, and I need time to accomplish our goals without hurting anyone more than necessary." I hoped she understood what I was trying to tell her.

"I need time. Please be patient with me. I love you. You know that to be true. I need to think of a good plan. In the meantime, my love, we will pretend that we are not talking. Our affair will be a secret for now." I knew my words were killing her slowly. But I continued, "We have no choice, Loula. It must be kept a secret until we figure out what to do. I will come to you when Billal is away hunting." I hoped my words brought her some comfort.

She dropped her head in her hands and started to weep. My heart went out to her. I knew her pain. It was like a knife twisting in the gut, and it hurt so much. But we had no other choice. It had to be done as I said. There was no other way around it, and she knew this to be true.

In that instant, we heard the horses outside. They were back from their hunting trip. We quickly jumped to our feet and kissed each other hastily, and before I reached for the door, I turned and whispered my love to her. I opened the door, stepped quietly outside, and closed the door behind me. I had to get to my room before they entered the palace. I flew down the stairs and ran to my room just in time. As I softly closed my bedroom door, I heard the commotion of the men down the hall. I turned and looked at Shaeena, and she was still asleep. I went into the bathroom to gather my wits.

I could still feel Loula's scent on my skin. I took a deep breath and recalled her soft body next to mine, her lips, soft and sweet, kissing me tenderly across my chest, and her hands traveling up and down my body. I could not take it anymore. I was on fire. I grabbed my shaft and masturbated until I came. Immediately my body trembled. I called out her name and groaned when there was no answer. My body was still shaking from the aftermath.

Spent, I looked into the mirror and saw myself. I felt no shame. *Is it shameful to make love to the memory of the woman you love? When fate cast me this burden of living a life without her, I ran, but I cannot hide from her memory! When she is within reach but I cannot touch her, I was dealt with unfairly! The gods cursed me with a life of misery! I defy them!*

I sighed, knowing we were dealt a life of pain. *But I am master of my life, aren't I? I could turn things around. I must, for I cannot go on like this.* I walked out of the bathroom smiling. A light had to be at the end of the tunnel. *Things will work out. I'm sure of it.* I tiptoed to my blankets on the floor and dropped down, and as soon as my head hit the pillow, I fell asleep instantly. When I woke up a few hours later, I looked up and saw Shaeena looking down at me from the bed. I blinked a few times, trying to focus. *If I blink hard enough, the nightmare will go away.*

She smiled down at me, and I tried with all my power to smile back. My eyes slowly eased down to her stomach. She was huge. I swallowed. *Is that my baby she carries, or is this all an act? How can I find out the truth? There must be a way!* The days were closing in on me. In a few weeks, she would have the baby, and then by law, I would have to marry her unless, by some miracle, the baby was proven not to be mine.

I had to go to my father and ask him if there were a way around the law. He was, after all, the king. *Couldn't he change the law if he chose to?* I quickly got up and dressed. I knew that Shaeena's eyes were on me, making me feel uncomfortable. I walked over to the bathroom and closed the door. I threw cold water on my face, and I looked in the mirror and remembered last night. Right here in this spot, I had touched myself. My woman was upstairs with another man, and I had touched myself! I braced my hands on the porcelain sink and leaned closer to the mirror. A jack-off stared back at me. *This is what I have become!* But I felt no shame. All was fair in love and war. I ran my fingers through my hair, combing them into place, and then I raced out of there. I had to find my father. If anyone could help me, he could. I ignored Shaeena's questioning glance and walked right past her to the door, where I exited.

The servants scrambled to their duties when they saw me coming, and if I weren't in such a hurry, I would have laughed my head off. Even though they didn't realize it, I envied them. Their lives were so simple. They cleaned the palace. I served the crown for a lifetime. I couldn't run like the wind and live a life of pleasure and happiness. Instead, I was committed to serving a life of duties to the throne. I was told who to love and who to marry, and my whole life was planned out for me. That was no life at all. I would rather be a servant, a peasant. Servants had a much richer life full of happiness. *True happiness is not measured in the amount of fame or money you have; true happiness is measured by all the love you have and feel. I am rich in money and power, but I am poor in love and happiness! I would trade places with the peasants any time.*

I found my father in the tearoom drinking tea with Mother. They did not look too happy to see me, which made me hesitate a bit before I spoke. "Father, I come to you begging for mercy. I know you have been disappointed in me lately." I stole a glance at Mother. She looked as if she wanted to box my ears off my head. "Father, I come to you not as the prince of Arabia, but as your son. Please may I ask you for a huge favor?"

The king put down the teacup and looked curiously at me. I could tell his patience was running thin with me. "I can't wait to hear what you have to say, son, for lately you have been full of surprises," he said sarcastically.

I took a deep breath and dropped the bomb. "Father, I can't marry Shaeena! I know the law says I have to, but I cannot marry her in good conscience for I am in love with Loula! I want her to be my wife. She is the one I love."

The king looked angry upon hearing my words, but my mother looked as if she were pleased with what I had just confessed.

My father was about to say something, but I quickly spoke, "Father, please, hear me out. I beg you." I kneeled down next to him and looked up into his face, begging for mercy. "Father, I know you are angry with me. I messed up. I know. But I meant no harm. I promise you. You know how I feel about Loula. You also know that I cannot live without her. Please, have mercy on me, Father. Change the law. I do not wish to marry Shaeena. In fact, I despise her! And I do not even know if it is my baby she carries!"

"Enough!" the king roared. "You made your bed. Now lie in it! Even from a young age, you disobeyed me! You ran like a bull and chased the wind! There are consequences, Son! You chose this, not I. Now you must live with it!"

He hit the table with his fists. The servants jumped out of fear, ran out the door, and disappeared. Mother put down her teacup and grabbed her neck. I could see fear in her eyes as she stared at me sympathetically. I stood my ground. My father did not intimidate me; nor was I about to run scared from him. He could rule his country, but he could not rule me.

"I will not marry Shaeena! I do not love her, Father," I raised my voice to another level, knowing how that would infuriate the king even more.

In a very calm voice, the king smiled coldly. "Oh, yes, you will. Prepare for the wedding. It will be in two weeks," he said with a finality in his voice.

I knew I could not say anything to change his mind. I felt defeated. Loula's face came to my mind, and I thought about the promise I made her, how I would fix everything. I had lied. Deep in my heart, I knew my father would stick to the law. He was the law. He was hardheaded. I suddenly felt sorry for my mother, who had put up with him all these years. I looked into her eyes, and I saw tears there. I had won her favor, but I could not win my father's. I stood, bowed, and walked away in silence.

As I stepped into the empty hallway, I felt deeply depressed. Knowing not what to do, I slumped against the stone wall and allowed my head to roll from left to right in agony. Upstairs was my lover, for whom I would give up my life, and I could not claim her as my wife. There had to be a way around all this. I would find a way.

I started walking past my room and down the corridor to the glass doors. I pulled them open and stepped outside. The fresh air hit my face, and I took a deep breath, swallowing the fresh air as it traveled down my lungs. I walked to the rose garden, knowing that my mother would meet me here in a few minutes.

I looked at all the beautiful roses, and a lump formed in my throat. I saw the roses for the first time through the eyes of Loula. She always spoke of their beauty. I saw the bright colors, and I smelled their perfume. I felt awful that I had never taken the time to appreciate them before this.

I bet the commoners took the time to smell the roses. They planted them in their backyards with their own two hands, and they took special care of them. I was always on the run, too busy for such pleasures. I never once took the time to smell them. I walked up to one of the rose bushes, grabbed a single rose, pulled it gently to my nose, and inhaled.

At that moment, I heard my mother walk up to me and sigh. She bent forward and smelled the roses too. Then she turned to me. "I'm so sorry things turned out this way for you, Son. I wish things were different. I know how much you care for Loula. I too want you to be with her, but your father insists you do the lawful thing," she said regretfully. "You know your father always abides by the rules, and there are no exceptions. Not even for you, Nidal," she said sadly.

"Mother, I will not marry Shaeena! I don't care what Father wants! I am going to marry Loula. She is the one I love." I hoped she would understand me. I paused for a minute, allowing her to grasp what I had just said to her.

"Mother, you have lived a loveless life your whole existence." Before she even had the chance to reply, I told her, "Don't even try denying it. I am a man in love, and I know what love is. You never had that with Father! Your whole life has been empty. Father is not in love with you, and I know you are not in love with him! Is that what you want for me, to live a life without love?" I looked straight into her eyes.

I could feel her pain. Maybe I had gone too far. But I needed to get my point across, and I did not know any other way. "I am not saying this to hurt you. I love you, Mother, but I know it is the truth when I say you do not love Father."

"Nidal, you are wrong. I do love your father, and he loves me back!" she argued, but she wasn't convincing enough.

"Yes, Mother, I believe you and Father love each other, but you are not in love with each other. There is a difference between loving someone and being in love with someone. You and Father love each other as friends, spouses, and a family unit. But you are not in love with each other. Your eyes don't shine when Father walks in the room. Your heart doesn't beat faster when he looks at you, and you don't even sleep in the same room as he does! You have not had a sex life with Father in years!" I yelled.

My mother's eyes were wide open with disbelief. Now I knew I had gone too far and I had hit a nerve. She opened her mouth to say something but closed it shut, unable to say a thing. Tears were in her eyes. I hoped she understood my feelings for Loula now.

"Mother, when Loula walks in the room, I feel butterflies dancing in the pit of my stomach. My heart rate doubles, and I lose my thoughts. I know without a doubt that there is no life for me without Loula. She is my whole life. When I make love to her, our bodies unite and become one. I love her, Mother. She is my soul mate, and I will not choose another." I hoped I was getting through to her.

My mother's head lowered as she stared at the ground. When her head came up, she had fresh tears in her eyes, and she reached inside her pocket and pulled out something. "My dear son, you and Loula are truly soul mates. I know her heart. I do believe she is the one for you. Therefore, you have my blessings." She stretched out her arm and placed something in my hand. I looked down and saw the most beautiful ring I had ever seen. It was my grandmother's, which had been passed down to my mother.

I looked at her, questioning her actions.

"I want you to give it to Loula. She must wear this ring, not Shaeena. She must be the wife you choose. I want you to live a life filled with passion, not cold and empty like mine is!" She allowed the tears to roll down her face.

My heart went out to her. I took my mother in my arms and hugged her tightly. I loved her so much, and I knew I had said too much and it was very selfish of me, but I had to make her see the truth. I needed her to side with me.

She pulled away from me and quietly walked toward the palace without saying another word. I heard her sniffles, and it broke my heart. My mother deserved a better life, but instead, all she got was misery. I looked down at the ring, and it sparkled so elegantly. The pink diamond must be at least a total of ten karats. It felt very heavy in my hand. My mother wished for me to give it to Loula, and I would do just that. The ring belonged to the woman I loved. It belonged to Loula. I closed my hand and dropped the ring in my pocket. I had to find Loula alone and give the ring to her. She would be my wife. My heart sang with happiness at the thought of Loula and me getting married.

I stayed in the garden for the next half hour, just dreaming of the day when Loula and I would get married. It would be a joyous day. I would make it a national holiday. My heart swelled with joy. I was overwhelmed with delight. Walking back to the palace, I knew the king would stand in the way of my happiness, but I would overcome all the obstacles, and I would prevail in the end.

As I walked down the long hallway, I remembered when Loula and I were running on this marble floor, trying to get to our rooms hastily to make sweet, passionate love. I could almost hear her laughter echoing around the walls. I closed my eyes, and for a brief second, I swear I thought I felt her fingers caressing me. I opened my eyes, and I was standing alone, aroused and full of lust because that was what the thought of my love did to me. I quickly ran to my room and headed straight for the bathroom. Thankful that Shaeena was not there, I slammed the door shut, locked it, and pulled the strings to my pantaloons. They dropped to the floor, and I reached inside my underwear and grabbed my shaft. I enjoyed the sensation that it brought me. My eyes were closed as I thought of her. Every cell in my body was responding to her memory. I pulled hard and fast. I thought of her kissing me and playing with my shaft. I thought of her silky skin touching mine; her breasts, round and soft; and her legs, long and slender. I thought of my shaft entering her and Loula moving to the rhythm with me. I could hear her moans as she called out my name. I bent down and kissed her lips, and she screamed in sweet ecstasy as I pumped my seed into her. Wild now with memories of her, my body reached its peak, and the spasms I was feeling electrified my whole being. A moan escaped my lips as I called out her name just as I climaxed.

Exhausted and spent, I still felt the tingling sensation up and down my body as I tried to slow down my heart rate. I washed up and ran my fingers through my hair. As I looked into the mirror, the face looking back at me looked at peace with himself. After tying the strings to my pantaloons, I reached inside my pocket and pulled out the ring. It sparkled in all its glory. I had to find Loula today and give this ring to her. I needed to find her alone. I would pour my heart out to her and present her with this ring. I would ask her to marry me, and when she accepted my proposal, I would announce my feelings for her to the whole world.

I happily exited the bathroom and stopped immediately in my tracks. Sitting in the chair by the window, staring at me with a menacing look on her face, was Shaeena. She was tightly clutching both sides of the arms of the chair that she was sitting in. Her piercing gaze alarmed me. *Had she heard my moans in the bathroom? Did she know I was masturbating? Had I called out Loula's name in the heat of the moment? If the answer to all these questions is yes, then too bad!* She knew from the beginning that my heart belonged to Loula. And up until my last dying breath, that would not change.

I walked right past her, opened the door, and stepped out. She could pant and rave all she wanted. Nothing was going to change. My feelings for Loula would always remain the same. I would find her and stake my claim on her. I would ask her to marry me, promising her my undying love. My hand tightened around the ring. This was not an ordinary ring. This ring held a promise of a bright future, a future between Loula and me.

A smile was on my face. There was always a smile on my face when I thought of her. I felt complete and whole knowing she loved me too. The servants were staring at me as I walked right past them. I knew they didn't understand me. No one understood me. Only Loula knew the deep feelings in my heart. I whistled a happy tune, a love song. The echo bounced off the walls and got louder. I heard the servants whispering behind my back. I whistled even louder.

My father's voice interrupted my thoughts. His loud roar scared the servants as they scrambled hastily to their tasks. I looked at the king, and for the life of me, I couldn't remember the last time I had seen him smile. *He was, is, and will always be a miserable man.*

"Son, where have you been hiding? I have been looking for you!" he roared. "You keep running away from your responsibilities. Lately, I am wondering if you are worthy of the throne or if I should have to pass you up and hand it to Billal! I think he would make a better king than you. He would never abandon his responsibilities like you have!" He spat angrily.

I looked at my father calmly and sighed. He ran this country with a fierce passion, without mercy, ruthlessly, and with great superiority. He was a good king for this country, but he just needed to soften up a bit. He ran his marriage the same way. *Poor Mother.*

"I really don't care, Father, if I do not become king. I do not want to become like you, a miserable old man, a man without a life of his own and all the responsibilities of the world on his shoulders. No time to be a husband to my wife and a father to my children! So, Father, please do pass the crown to Billal. He is ruthless, just like you!" I knew he would rip my head off in less than thirty seconds.

But the king threw his head back and laughed so hard that the echo from his laughter rumbled through the walls of the palace. I stared at him, speechless. A few minutes later, the king, sober now, looked at me and, in a cool voice that was sharp as crystal, said, "Tomorrow I am throwing a ball with you and Princess Shaeena as the guests of honor. I will announce your marriage to her, which will take place in two weeks," he said as if he were daring me to disagree with him. There was a shuddering tension about him, as if he was a hairbreadth from exploding, as he continued in a deadly whisper, "And Nidal, if I were you, I would shape up and not do a single thing to agitate your king, for he has had enough of your bullshit to last a lifetime!" The king walked away arrogantly without a care in the world, and I stood there speechless.

A ball? Marriage to Shaeena? Pain tugged at my heart as I leaned against the stone wall for support. It was the first time in my lifetime that I did not know what to do. Father had control of my life. He had me by the balls. My happiness was in his hands, and he did not care if he destroyed it. I could not breathe. I felt as if I were suffocating. The walls were closing in on me. I quickly ran down the hall and back to the glass doors that led to the gardens. I opened them and quickly stepped outside. The fresh air hit my face, and I swallowed the welcoming air. I ran as fast as I could down the stairs and through the gardens to the spot I went to when I was a child. I fell to the ground in a fetal position and sobbed.

I cried and cried until I had no more tears to spill. The ache in my heart was painful. I knew not what to do. The world around me went still as I thought of Loula. I reached in my pocket for the ring. I felt it as I tightened my hold around it. This ring belonged to Loula. And Loula belonged to me. I felt powerless, knowing that, when the king made up his mind, no one could change it.

Suddenly, my mother appeared out of nowhere. She sat herself down and took me in her arms, just like she had when I was a little boy. She caressed my back, trying to soothe my pain. My mother's comfort saved me from going crazy.

The sun was going down, and soon it would be time to go back to my room. My mother and I had already missed dinner, and everyone in the palace was probably looking for us. I did not want to go to my room. I had no desire to look upon Shaeena's face. I wanted to stay here all night in my mother's arms. She was the only one who knew how to comfort me, but I knew that the king was fuming by now, and I did not want my mother to get punished because of me.

I straightened up. With a fake smile, I looked at my mother. "Just like old times, thank you. I needed your hugs. I feel much better now." I stood up now and gently pulled my mother to her feet. "We need to get back now. We do not want to make Father angrier than he already is," I said sarcastically.

My mother gracefully stood up and gave me another quick hug. "Nidal, I pray that everything will work out the way you want it to. I want to see you happy. Please don't blame your father. He is just trying to follow the law. Being king is not an easy thing. He has a duty to his crown. He is a slave to it. He wants you to be happy too, but the law requires you to marry the princess because she claims to be pregnant with your child. It is out of his hands. We have no choice in this matter. We must do what is the right thing for this country. Otherwise, the people will question our judgment. They will say, if the prince doesn't follow the law, then we too don't have to. Imagine what that will do to our beloved country! Nidal, being the royal family, we have certain responsibilities. We have to set examples. Along with all the glory, we are obligated to serve the crown. It is the law. You must marry Princess Shaeena to keep the peace in this country. Maybe we can talk to your father to allow you to take Loula as your second wife," she said hopefully.

It was hard for me to be angry at my mother, but I could not understand how she had changed her mind so fast. "Mother, why have you turned against me? What lies has Father fed you? I am loyal only to Loula. I will not marry Shaeena!"

I pushed away her hands that were about to hug me. I started to walk away from her, angry now. I felt betrayed. She followed silently behind me. I could tell she was crying, but at this moment, I knew not what to say to her.

I climbed the stairs two at a time as rage consumed my mind. I opened the glass doors, walked in the palace, and marched through the hallways, thinking that, if they wanted me to marry the princess, I would. But I would make her life a living hell. I would make all their lives a living hell. I heard my mother running after me as she called out my name. I did not want to talk to her anymore tonight. I felt betrayed by her. I marched to my room, opened the door, and slammed it behind me with a force that shook the walls of the palace.

The princess was still sitting in the same chair as before. She looked at me as I raced past her to the bathroom. I slammed the door shut and fell against the wall. I knew not what to do. My life had been one heartache after another. When I was younger, I had been so sure of myself that I had never cried. I had not cared about anyone but myself. But for the past fifteen years, I had cried every day. I played with myself. I loved a woman more than I loved myself. I had lost my firstborn, and now I was being forced to marry a woman I despised. My hands trembled as I pulled my hair away from my face. I pulled the ring out from my pocket and cried. This ring was my symbol of love to Loula. I had not seen her today, and my heart hurt from missing her.

Jealousy ate at me as the thought of Billal and Loula together ripped my heart to pieces. I panicked at the thought of Loula finding out about the ball and the marriage. I had to find a way to tell her immediately before she found out from someone else and assumed the worst. I put the ring on the sink and washed my face. I was going to sleep early today. I was going to get a good night's sleep and wake up early tomorrow so I could find Loula and explain everything to her.

I walked out of the bathroom, already feeling a little better. Shaeena had gotten herself in bed, and I spread my blankets on the floor and blew out the candles. It was pitch dark in the room, but I could tell Shaeena was still awake from the way she was breathing. I wondered why she wanted to marry me. *Has she no pride at all? She knows I don't love her. Why would she want to spend the rest of her life with a man who does not care for her?*

I got down on my uncomfortable bed. Thoughts of Loula came to mind. I missed her terribly. I wondered what she was doing at this moment. I was tortured with the thought of her in bed with Billal. I wondered if his paws ever reached out in the night and touched her. My heart tugged with pain at the thought of that. I could not bear the thought of anyone touching her. She was mine, and only I had the right to touch her.

I awoke in the morning with the sun directly on my face. I turned and looked up at the bed. I saw the princess looking down at me with a smile on her face. She had many reasons to be happy today, or so she thought! There was nothing for me to be excited about. My heart was bleeding. I closed my eyes and pretended to sleep again. A few minutes later, Shaeena got out of bed and went to the bathroom.

Minutes later, Shaeena opened the bathroom door and walked to the window. Her stomach was huge. She was due to have the baby soon. My father wanted me to marry her before she gave birth. I had to quickly find a way to avoid marriage to her at all costs. But right now, I needed to find Loula and have a talk with her. I needed to explain everything right away. Things had gotten complicated, and I would have a hard time explaining the truth to her. I quickly got up, raced to the bathroom, and cleaned up. I dressed and ran out of the room. Shaeena was left behind in her misery. She was quickly forgotten and replaced with the image of Loula.

Excitement was everywhere in the palace. Everyone was bustling about preparing for the ball tonight. I raced up the stairs two at a time, heading straight for Loula's room. I did not care if Billal were still there. I needed to talk to her, and nothing and no one was going to stop me. I reached the door to their chamber and opened it without knocking. I stepped inside and saw only the servants. They were busy tidying up the room. Startled, they looked at me puzzled. I asked them where Loula was, and they said that she and Billal had gone to the village.

I was too late. She knew of the ball and who knew exactly what Billal told her. She was probably angry with me. Not knowing what to do, I went flying down the stairs, through the hallway, and to my chambers. I slammed the door closed and walked up to Shaeena, still sitting in exactly the same spot I had left her in. I grabbed her by the arm and pulled her up from her sitting position.

"Why do you insist on marring me when you know that I am in love with Loula?" I yelled.

She looked into my eyes and said calmly without batting an eyelash, "I am pregnant with your child. You are the father, and it is your responsibility as the father to ensure that he is not born a bastard!" she said coldly. "It is time you forgot about Loula. She is a commoner, and I am a princess! I carry your child, not her!" she hissed. She placed her hands on my chest and said in a softer tone, "Please, darling, give us a chance, and you may be surprised to find that I am the better choice."

I slapped her hands off me and took a step backward. "You crazy bitch! You can never replace the woman I love! If I am forced to marry you, I will make sure that your life will be a living hell! Every night, I will be in Loula's bed, enjoying her pleasures, while you sleep all alone in your cold bed! I will never yield to you. Never!" I yelled at her, trying to make her see that it would be a mistake marrying me.

But to my dismay, she smiled coldly. "We shall see about that, Nidal. Two can play this game. You will not succeed in getting rid of me. I was born a princess and promised marriage to you from birth. I was trained from an early age to prepare for our wedding. I stood by you all these years. I gave you my loyalty and my love. You gave me nothing but disrespect! I will not allow a commoner, a whore, to steal you away!" she spat.

I didn't know what I was thinking. It just happened, a reflex of my arm when I heard her call Loula a whore. I slapped her so hard that I thought I heard her head snap. I did not regret slapping her.

She stumbled backward and bumped into the wall. Fuming, she straightened up and took a step toward me. "You will pay for this, Nidal. I will bring you to your knees, begging me for mercy!" She stormed out of the room, slamming the door shut behind her.

She was a drama queen. I would hate to turn my back on her. Shaeena was not to be trusted.

Everyone was getting ready for the big night. I was desperately trying to figure out what I was going to do. A servant came in the room and announced that the king and queen asked for my audience for lunch, but I declined the invitation, saying I was not hungry. As the servant walked away and closed the door behind her, I heard commotion outside, and I ran quickly to the window and saw Billal helping Loula step down from the royal carriage. They were engaged in conversation as they walked up the stairs and into the palace. I heard Loula's laughter, and my heart sank. *What is she trying to do? Kill me little by little with her actions? I* opened the door slightly, just in time to see her run up the stairs as Billal playfully chased after her, pulling on the folds of her gown.

I was beside myself with jealousy. The knife twisted in my heart as I doubled up in pain. I leaned against the wall for support.

At that moment, Shaeena entered the room. She walked up to me and smiled coldly. "What's the matter, dear? Are you feeling sick at the pit of your stomach? Did Loula crush all your hopes and dreams?" she said sarcastically as she walked to the bed and sat on it.

I could not bear the sight of her. I would not give her what she craved. My heart belonged to Loula. She was the only one for me. I didn't even know if Loula would still have me. She was really mad at me now, but I would find a way to show her that she was my whole world. If I couldn't talk to her before the ball, then I would talk to her during the ball. I would dance with her and whisper my love for her in her ear. In a few hours, I would see her and make her mine once again. I let out a big sigh. Shaeena looked at me suspiciously

The princess waddled over to me. She stuck her finger in my face. "I am going to take a bath, and then I am going to get all dolled up for the ball because, whether you like it or not, your father is going to announce our wedding today. You, my dear, are going to take me as your wife in two weeks." She pushed past me briskly and laughed all the way to the bathroom as she stepped inside, leaving the door open while she bathed. I did everything in my power to resist the urge to strangle her.

Shaeena took her time bathing. She taunted me by singing a love song. The servants came and helped her out of the tub, wrapping her in a huge towel. The other servants emptied out the old water and filled it up with fresh water for me to take my bath.

As I dipped into the hot water, the last servant walked out of the bathroom and closed the door behind her. Alone at last, I closed my eyes, hoping I could release all the tension I was feeling, but heartache consumed me once again. My life was a mess, and I didn't know if I could ever fix it. If my father didn't stop this nonsense, then I might just kidnap Loula and run away with her. I would live my life my way, not the king's way. I would not yield to him. *Never!*

Today at the ball, I would tell Loula my plans, and I hoped she would agree with me. I jumped out of the tub, hyped up now. I was excited about the thought of running away with her. It was my turn to sing a love song. I walked over to the door and tried to listen to what was happening on the other side. I heard the servants say that her gown was down the hall in the pink dressing room and they would dress her and do her hair in there.

It was time for me also to get dressed. I put on my attire with all its trimmings and looked in the mirror, feeling pleased with what I saw. I would try to swoon Loula off her feet tonight. When she took one look at me, she would come running back into my arms.

I combed my hair, tucked my shirt in my pantaloons, and put on my jacket, and as I leaned over to put on my boots, my medals that were pinned on my jacket swung back and forth as if they were announcing proudly that I was a worthy prince.

I could hear the music down the hall. It was time for me to go to the ball. I walked swiftly to the door and opened it. I saw in the distance the guests arriving as they walked into the palace and the servants guided them to the ballroom. I took a deep breath, and I too walked to the ballroom. I wanted to be there when Loula walked in. I wanted to be the first one to greet her. She was mine, and this evening, I was going to take her back.

The orchestra was playing a famous tune, and some guests were already dancing. The ladies sparkled in their gowns as the gentlemen twirled them around on the dance floor. As I entered, everyone turned and looked at me. I threw them my famous smile, even though I was hurting deep in my heart.

The king spotted me and was making his way to me with a stern expression on his face. I braced myself as my father approached me.

"Where is Princess Shaeena?" he asked gruffly.

Like I care about her whereabouts!

"She's getting ready, and she will be here shortly. She told me she needed some alone time," I lied.

That answer seemed to please my father, and he strode away with a half smile on his old face.

As the evening wore on, I searched everywhere and could not find Loula or my cousin anywhere, but just at this moment, a very pregnant Princess Shaeena stood at the doorway. Everyone turned and acknowledged her appearance with a curtsy, and she bowed back and walked elegantly through the crowd and made her way to me.

When she got close to me, her smile faded, and she whispered for my ears alone, "One day, Nidal," her lips trembled as she continued, "you will love me as I love you, and you shall regret everything you have done to me, and I will forgive you." She hooked her arm inside mine and stood proudly next to me.

I quickly pulled out of her grip and hurriedly walked to the other side of the room, engaging in conversation with some men who were arguing about politics, but my eyes never left the doorway where I was expecting Loula to walk in at any moment.

She was fashionably late as she entered through the doorway on Billal's arm. My heart raced at a rate of one hundred and fifty times faster than its normal rate. She looked glamorous. She captivated every man who looked her way. I feasted my eyes on her. A whirl of emotions flared inside me. I inhaled sharply.

She was wearing a beautiful, strapless, white satin gazer gown. It had silver diamante embellishment at the waist. It was like a second skin on her body, and I had never known that gowns like this existed. She clearly had her own style, and the skirt was circled with the same silver diamante at the bottom of it. Only she could wear such a daring dress and get away with it.

Her hair was let down. Her long brunette locks cascaded down her back with soft curls and gave it a more relaxed look. She was the only one tonight at the ball who dared to wear her hair down. This time tomorrow, her look would be the next style of the century. She looked beautiful. She took my breath away.

I saw her scan the room quickly until she found where I was and rested her eyes on me. The chemistry was powerful between the two of us. Automatically, we walked slowly toward each other, not once taking our eyes off the other. It was an electrifying moment. She threw me a dazzling smile. Immediately, I got a huge hard-on. She had a powerful effect on me, as if she had cast a spell on me. I was mesmerized. Billal walked tensely besides her, clearly not pleased with the direction that she was headed. His eyes were blazing fire.

As Loula walked to me, everyone in the room had his or her eyes on us. The music stopped, and there was dead silence. From the corner of my eyes, I saw Shaeena push people aside as she tried to make her way to us. My beautiful Loula came to a stop right in front of me and bowed elegantly. I bowed back, took her hand, and brought it to my lips, and I kissed it. I saw my cousin's hands turn to fists at his sides as he stood there witnessing the exchange between Loula and I.

Loula's eyes were watery, and she immediately looked down to the floor. At that moment, Shaeena walked up to us, placed her arm inside mine, and tried to pry me away, but I would not budge. This was where I belonged, right here next to Loula, the love of my life.

There was a peculiar atmosphere in the air, a mixture of tension and anticipation. I could hear the people around us murmuring. They were waiting to see what we were going to do. I could not help myself. I leaned over and kissed Loula on the mouth. It was a quick, sensual kiss. Loula kissed me back without hesitation, and it was magical.

The crowd went wild. My cousin took a step closer, and he was ready to throw me a punch. I pulled back from Loula, and I was ready to pounce on Billal, but just then my father waved to the orchestra to start playing again and then he angrily barked to the crowd, "Dance, now!"

The king made his way to us and I could tell that I was about to get the scolding of a lifetime. Even Princess Shaeena looked ready to claw my eyes out, but my mother came to the rescue just in time and whisked Loula away from us. She took her to the other side of the ballroom.

My fuming father raised his finger in my face and in a low dangerous tone said. "Now I have tolerated the two of you much longer than you both deserve! Start acting like grown men or I will throw the both of you in the dungeon, and don't think for a minute that I won't. Do not test me, my boys, for you will soon see another side of me that you have never seen before!" Having said that, he marched away and disappeared into the crowd.

Shaeena looked extremely mad. I could tell that she was about to do something that we would all regret later. Her jaw set firmly and her head held high, she marched over to Loula. I ran quickly after her to stop her from more embarrassment, and at that moment, Shaeena lifted her right hand, and I saw my mother's pink diamond sparkling on her finger. I froze in my tracks. *How had she come to possess the ring?* I placed my hands in my pockets and confirmed that it was not there. Wide-eyed now, I remembered placing the ring on the sink yesterday when I was washing my hands, and I had forgotten to retrieve it.

Loula looked as if she were about to faint as she stared at the ring.

With a half smile playing on Shaeena lips, she said, "I'm engaged to the prince of Arabia. We are to get married in two weeks, right before our baby is due to arrive," she said with satisfaction. Loula stood frozen in place. She said not one word as Shaeena continued her taunts. "The king will make the announcement tonight to confirm our union." She caressed her stomach playfully, rubbing the pregnancy in Loula's face.

Loula swayed and almost fell off her feet. Billal had just reached her side and grabbed her before she fell. I could tell that Loula's heart was bleeding, as was mine. The same knife that tore at her heart also tore at mine, as it twisted in pain and killed me. Billal wrapped his arms around Loula and whisked her away from me, as I stood there rigid, not able to move.

"What's the matter, dear? The cat got your tongue?" Shaeena laughed with pleasure. "I told you that you would lose, didn't I?" she purred, pleased that the outcome had gone her way.

I felt like slapping her face, but I did not want to give her the satisfaction that her words hurt me. I smiled coldly at her, and that was enough to wipe the smile off her face. I could tell that she was holding back the tears that were threatening to spill down her lovely face. She was proud and did not want to show the pain she was feeling, so she simply walked away and headed toward the king.

My mother stepped next to me and gave me a much-needed hug. I knew she needed a hug just as much as I did, so I hugged her back, letting her know with my actions that I loved her too. She was my hero. Anyone who can put up with father for so many years deserved a medal. She pulled away from me and motioned for me to follow after Loula, and I was more than happy to comply with her wishes.

I spotted Loula with Billal on the other side of the room. I quickly walked up to them and begged Loula for her audience. Loula said nothing as she looked sadly at me, and Billal tightened his fists at his side, preparing for a fight, which struck a cord of fury inside me. *When would he realize that she is mine? I would never give her up!*

I quickly looked at Loula. "I have some explaining to do. There has been a misunderstanding, and I need to clarify a few things." I looked at Loula and waited for an approval. But none came. She looked away from me. I stepped in front of her and pleaded one more time, "Please allow me to explain. I did not give her the ring. She took it without my knowledge. The ring was for you. I was going to give it to you today, here at the ball, but she took it without me knowing it." I hoped she would accept my words to be the truth.

Billal looked amused as I begged for mercy. He knew as well as I did that Loula would never forgive me. I wanted to wipe the lazy grin off his handsome face. But I had more pressing matters now. I had to convince Loula that I spoke the truth. I searched her face for some kind of acceptance but found none. She did not seem inclined to argue. She looked tired, weakened by the turn of events.

I took advantage of her silence and begged again for mercy. "Please, Loula, I beg of you. Forgive me for causing you pain. I love you and only wish for you to be my bride. Loula, I want to marry you. Please believe me," I cried.

The tears rolled down her eyes as she continued her silence. I was desperate now. I got down on one knee, not caring who saw me, and looked up at her with pleading eyes as I once again asked for forgiveness. Everyone around me stood back as they watched in amazement while I, the prince of Arabia, begged a commoner. All the ladies were staring in disbelief as they placed their hands on their heart and waited for Loula to give me her answer. The gentlemen looked envious that I had the love of two of the best-looking women in this country, as they too were waiting with anticipation to hear Loula's answer. But the answer never came.

At that moment, the music stopped once again, and the onlookers gasped. I looked around me to see what was happening, just in time to see Shaeena walk up behind me.

"Ladies and gentlemen, may I have your attention please," the king said. "It is with great pleasure that I announce the engagement of my son, the crown prince of Arabia, to the beautiful Princess Shaeena." Everyone cheered and applauded with excitement.

Loula leaned against Billal, and he grabbed her before her feet gave way and dropped her to the floor. Billal took this opportunity to whisk Loula away from me, lead her through the crowd, and disappear from my sight. The people around me were staring at me suspiciously as I fought to keep my anger under control. I would not let Billal win Loula away from me. *She is mine, and she will always be mine!*

I pushed past the crowd and ran after them, but as I looked ahead of me, they had disappeared. I heard Shaeena call after me, but I slipped through the crowd and sneaked out of the ballroom. I looked up and down the great hall and did not see them. I asked the guards who were placed outside the ballroom which way they had gone, and one of them motioned up the stairs. I ran up those stairs two at a time. I had to get to her before Billal brainwashed her and took advantage of her vulnerability, and then I would have to kill him with my bare hands. Reaching their door, I did not even knock. I kicked the door open and walked right in. They looked stunned to see me. They were sitting on the bed, and Loula's head was resting on his lap as she cried her heart out.

Billal gently lifted Loula from his lap, jumped up, and charged right at me. I swung my fist and punched him square in the face. He fell a few steps backward, but he immediately balanced out and sprung forward and swung back, catching me by surprise. We both swung our fists into each other's face until blood was everywhere. I could hear Loula's cries as she demanded that we stop the fighting. But we were both enraged with madness, and we would not stop until we ripped each other's throat out.

Loula somehow threw herself in the middle of us, and we immediately stopped, not wanting to hurt her. "Stop this now! You are both acting like children. What's the matter with the two of you? You should be ashamed of yourselves!" she yelled. "Nidal, leave this room immediately! Why have you come here?" My appearance clearly upset her.

"I came for you! And I am not leaving here until I say my peace." I fought to keep the anger out of my voice.

Loula looked at me, and for a moment, she looked as if she would give me the chance to speak, but clearly distressed, she ordered, "Nidal, leave this room!"

"No, Loula!" I said angrily. I was not about to leave here and allow Billal to stake his claim on her. "I will not leave until I say what I came here to say!" I wiped the blood that slid down my lips with my sleeve.

Loula sighed, and Billal took a step toward me, but Loula quickly put out her arm and stopped him. "Don't, Billal. Please, no more fighting! This has to come to a stop!" she cried. Then in a lower tone, she announced, "I will hear what you have to say, Nidal, and then I want you to leave."

So this was my last chance. I had to make it sound good. Maybe she would forgive me and we could be together again. So I mustered up all my energy and poured out my feelings.

"Loula, please. I love you. You know that! Shaeena found the ring and just took it, assuming it was for her. The ring was intended for you. My mother gave it to me to give to you. My father wants me to wed Shaeena, but I cannot. I do not love her! It is you that my heart aches for. It has always been you. Please, Loula, come with me. Let's run away, you and me. We can cross the border and be free of the crown." My heart was pounding in my ears loudly.

Even before Loula spoke to me, I knew her answer would hurt me. I saw it in her eyes.

"No, Nidal, we cannot do that. You have a responsibility to the crown! To your people! I will not let you abandon everything for me! I could not live with myself knowing I took you away from what belongs to you by birth." Her lips were trembling as she continued sticking the knife deeper into my heart. "You will do the right thing. You will marry the princess and give the people of Arabia an heir to the throne. You cannot allow your child to be born a bastard. How can you live with that? I know I cannot. I would feel endless guilt. Your child is innocent. You must protect the baby at all costs!" She knew how to play with my feelings.

I felt tortured. "The child is not mine! I did not sleep with Shaeena. She lies! I did not betray you! I am not the father of the baby she carries in her womb!" I said firmly, trying to make her see reason.

But it was to no avail. Her mind was made up. "Please, Nidal, go away. I have not the strength to keep pushing you away. I will give in to your request, and then you will be exiled. I love you too much to ever allow that to happen to you."

That was all I needed to hear. She loved me. She said it. The words slipped off her tongue before she realized what she had just said. She quickly realized her mistake and tried to rephrase her words, but I was too fast for her. I pulled her into my arms before she even realized what had happened. Our bodies slammed into each other as we tightened our hold and our mouths locked together with fierce passion.

Suddenly, I felt strong arms tear us apart as Billal ripped me from her embrace. He pushed me hard, and I went flying and crashed into the wall. Billal ran to me before I had a chance to gather my wits and punched me in the gut. I doubled up in pain and spit up blood. Before I was able to catch my breath, Billal threw me one blow after another until I fell to the floor.

He caught me off guard, but I was the stronger of the two. Enraged now, I grabbed his leg and pulled him down to the marble floor with me. I jumped on him and beat the living fuck out of him. I could hear Loula's cries behind me, but my anger was unleashed, and I knew not my strength as I slammed blow after blow on Billal's body. He had passed out, but I was unable to stop hitting him. I was angry. My fists automatically kept slamming into his face. Blood was everywhere, and Billal lay there motionless. Finally, I stopped hitting him. My breathing was heavy as I tried to get up from Billal's body.

Loula ran to me and threw herself at me. I cradled her in my arms. It felt like old times. She felt so good in my arms. I squeezed her tight, knowing it could be the last time I held her this way.

There was commotion outside the door, and then the door burst open. Plenty of my father's men came running in, picked up Billal's body, and removed him from the room. My father was standing by the doorway. Loula averted her eyes, unable to look the king in the face because she was full of embarrassment. But she had no reason to be. I loved her, and I knew she still loved me. There was no shame in love. As for Billal, he got what he deserved.

I raised my head up high and stared at my father, letting him know by my actions that I would not yield to him. This infuriated the king even more, and I knew I should not bait him, but I could not help it.

Recklessly, I opened my mouth and announced calmly, "No matter what you say, no matter what you want, I will do as I want, not as you wish, Father. I love Loula, and I will make her my wife, whether you want me to or not. It is not your decision. It is up to me whom I choose to wed!" I said boldly.

A shiny glint was in the king's eyes as he threw his head back and laughed aloud. "Son, you sound so compelling, I almost forgot who was in charge here," the king said sarcastically. "You will do as I say, Son, for I rule this country, not you! I will hang you for treason if you dare to speak to me like that again!" the king declared. "Or better yet, I will hang Loula and throw you in the dungeon until you learn your lesson," he threatened.

At that moment, I knew he would make good on his threat. "Now clean yourself up and come downstairs. Bid Loula farewell, for it's the last time you will see her single. I will order her hand in marriage to your cousin Billal! He will make a great husband for her. Son, do not look at me with contempt. Have you forgotten you are my son, the crown prince of Arabia, and she is but a commoner?" Then he arrogantly walked out of the room without looking back.

I looked at Loula, and I saw raw pain in her eyes. Tears were streaming down her lovely face, and she was unconsciously pulling her hair. I took her in my arms and held her tight. I never wanted to let her go. I kissed her tenderly on her soft lips. I loved her so much, a bold, breathless, never-ending love. This was, by far, the greatest love story that will ever be told. She was my soul mate in every way possible. If I lost her, I would kill myself, for there was no life for me without her.

"Loula, I promise you that, no matter what, I will remain faithful to you." I meant every word that I said to her. I pulled her closer to me as I continued professing my love. "I have never willingly betrayed you, and I never will! I promise you on this day that I will love you and only you forever until my last dying breath! All I ask in return is that you never betray me either." I waited for her confirmation on this.

Without hesitatation, Loula said, "I have never betrayed you, and I never will. You are the love of my life and I will love you till my last dying breath. I promise this to be true, Nidal." And she sealed it with a kiss.

At that moment, there was a hard knock on the door, and a voice said that the king was requesting my presence in the ballroom immediately. I froze, knowing exactly why the king wanted me. I did not know what to do. I was afraid not to abide by the king's orders. He had threatened us, and even though I did not care what happened to me, I was afraid for Loula.

Reluctantly, I pulled away from Loula and looked down at my clothes. They were soiled with blood. I found some clothes in Billal's closet. Since we wore the same size, they fit perfect on my body.

I pulled Loula into my arms and said, "I want to make an oath to you, a binding oath, the kind that will seal our love forever, Loula. I know that our souls will be together to eternity. I also know that the dreams I had all those years ago were real. We have lived in other lifetimes as lovers, and even after this lifetime, Loula, we will find each other again, I am sure of it!"

I looked into her beautiful eyes. "Loula, please, I need you to be patient. I will find a way for us to be together. I promise. Do not be bothered with what the king says tonight. I will never marry Shaeena! But we must play along until we come up with a plan," I whispered. "I love you, and I promise I will love you until death do us part," I told her passionately, holding her tight in my arms and unable to let her go.

Loula looked up at me, and with love shining in her eyes, she said, "I love you too, and I too promise you my love and loyalty until death do us part." We sealed our promises with a loving kiss one more time, but somehow I felt as if it were the kiss of Judas. My heart tightened, but I pushed the feeling aside. I wanted to focus on this moment.

I was beside myself with happiness at this moment as we walked down the long staircase that led us to the main floor. Back to the ball! Back to hell! I gave her one last kiss, not caring who saw us. Then I let go of her hand, and we walked into the ballroom together. I allowed Loula to walk in front of me. Everyone was staring at us. Loula held her head up high as she gracefully walked through the guests and all the way to the other end of the ballroom, where Billal waited and took her hand in his. The knife twisted again in my gut. I could not stand the sight of him touching Loula. The bastard's face looked broken. His clothes were stained with blood, and he probably had not changed them so he could remind Loula what I was capable of. *Sneaky bastard! I need to watch my back.*

Billal leaned close to Loula and kissed her on the cheek. One day, I was going to rip out his throat.

At that moment, my father, the king of Arabia, started his speech. "Ladies and gentlemen, I have an announcement to make, one that is long overdue. As you all know, Shaeena will give birth to my grandchild in a couple of weeks."

There were cheers in the ballroom at this announcement, but there were also people confused and disappointed.

"My son, the crown prince, your future king …" The crowd cheered. The king smiled. "Prince Nidal will wed Princess Shaeena in two weeks, hopefully before the arrival of his child, and you are all invited to the wedding. It will be an event that will go down in history!"

There were loud cheers and applause, and at that moment, the king walked over to Shaeena, took her hand, and pulled her to where I stood. He placed her hand in mine and raised both our hands up in the air.

The guests went wild. They clapped, cheered, and sang our national anthem. I looked around to find Loula, and my eyes rested on hers. We both had tears in our eyes. Life was not fair, but I was the captain of my life, and I would steer my ship in the direction that I chose and not in the direction my father dictated for me. I smiled coldly at the crowd. They could cheer all they wanted, but I didn't care. I didn't want the crown. I wanted Loula. And I was going to have her. She was mine, and I would not give her up. I would rather die than live a life without her.

I looked at Shaeena. *What the hell is she smiling about? She knows I do not love her. She knows what my feelings for Loula are! Her baby is not mine, and she still insists to marry me. I will play her game. I will play everyone's game until the right opportunity comes along. And then bam!*

As night wore on, it was unbearable for me. I felt sick to my stomach. My father and mother, along with Shaeena, seemed oblivious to what was at stake here. No one asked me how I felt, what I wanted. No one cared. I looked over at Loula. Her head rested on Billal's shoulders as they danced on the dance floor.

I swallowed a double shot of arak, one of many tonight. Drinking made life's blows more bearable. I almost stumbled to the floor as I walked over to the table where the liquor was and grabbed another bottle of arak. I cradled the bottle in my arms. I knew I had too much to drink, but my heart was full of pain, and I knew not how to make it go away. Arak helped to temporarily ease my pain. I lifted the bottle to my lips and drank. I felt the sting of the liquid as it made its way down my throat, burning my insides. I kept drinking until I felt the room spinning. I leaned against the table for support. *This is going to be a long night*, I thought wearily.

My father walked up to me, and his smile faded as he whispered for my ears alone, "Son, I have been very patient with you tonight. In fact, I have tolerated too much from you, and I tell you now, Son, that, if you do not stop your childish behavior, I will punish Loula. She will have to suffer for your mistakes. And do not think for one minute that I won't carry out my threat!" he said in a threatening tone. "Now go get Shaeena, your betrothed, and dance with her. It is your duty to bring a smile to her face. Go do the right thing, Nidal. Now!" he growled.

And so the king had spoken, and I marched to his tune. I clumsily walked over to Shaeena, took her in my arms, and danced the night away. She happily complied and settled comfortably in my arms with the biggest smile on her face. I almost felt sorry for her. I could feel her pain. She loved me, and I did not return her affections. She must be in a lot of pain herself. I pulled her closer. I was not in love with her, but I did not want her to suffer. I did not want anyone to agonize, especially on my account. Her huge stomach prevented us from getting too close, but she still tried to push as close to me as possible. I closed my eyes and pretended it was Loula I held. I was so drunk that it almost seemed real that it was her in my arms and not Shaeena.

I caressed her back lightly, loving the feeling of her skin. She snuggled closer to me, and my lips kissed her neck. She smelled different. I quickly opened my eyes surprised at who I held in my arms. I searched around the room and could not find Loula anywhere. I gently pushed Shaeena away from me and stumbled over to the table to grab another drink. I drank a river and got very drunk. The king ordered his men to take me to my chambers before I made a fool of myself again. Shaeena followed behind us. A smile was on her face. My vision blurred, and then I passed out.

Next thing I knew, I was thrown in bed. Not on the floor, on my blankets, but on the bed. I heard the men's laughter as they left, and then Shaeena walked up to me, sat on the bed, and removed my boots and socks. She then started to take off my clothes. I resisted, but I was so drunk that I had not enough strength to push her away, so she won. My pantaloons came off, and she was working on taking my shirt off. Just then, I saw Loula's face. I blinked a couple of times, but Loula, my love, was here with me, undressing me and caressing me, and almost immediately, my shaft hardened at her touch.

My vision was blurry, but I could feel her playing with my shaft. I called out her name. Loula did not answer, but she pulled my shaft up and down aggressively. She missed me as much as I missed her, and she was the horniest I had ever seen her to be. Aroused by her aggressiveness, I called out her name and pulled her closer to me. I kissed her with passion, and she begged me to take her.

I flipped her over, got on top of her, and entered her with force, plunging deep inside her. I was crazy with lust as I lowered my mouth to hers and kissed her passionately. She moved her body along with mine and cried out like a wildcat as her nails dug into my skin. I felt the electricity course throughout my body as I shuddered in ecstasy. I was wild with passion, blinded by reality, and then my world came to a halt. The door opened to our room, and I turned to see Loula staring at me with a horrified expression on her face.

"Nidal, no!" she cried out. "How could you betray me like this?"

Loula put her hands on her heart and fell backward into Billal's arms. Confused, I looked down at the woman in bed with me, and I saw Shaeena's face for the first time, smiling right up at me. The blood drained from my face as I realized that I had just betrayed the woman I had promised to love forever.

I quickly jumped up from the position I was in and called out, "Loula, please, let me explain. I thought it was you! I thought I was making love to you, please," I cried.

But it was too late. Billal had whisked her away, slamming the door behind them. I could not believe what I had just done.

Mortified, I tried to get away from Shaeena, but she pulled me back to her.

"Let go of me!" I demanded. "You tricked me into having sex with you!"

"And you enjoyed every minute of it, Nidal! I know you were pleased with my lovemaking." She dared me to deny her words.

I was at a loss for words because she was right. I had enjoyed her lovemaking, but I thought I was having sex with Loula, not her. Suddenly, I was disgusted with myself. I did the one thing I had promised Loula that I would not do. I had betrayed her. I grabbed my chest. The pain was unbearable. I dropped my head onto the pillow and cried out in pain. That was the last thing I remembered that night before I passed out.

Chapter Fourteen
Loula

*T*was having a terrible day today as it was, and to top it off, Billal told me that today there would be a ball in honor of Nidal and Shaeena's engagement and the wedding date would be announced. My heart could not hurt any more than it hurt already. I didn't understand what exactly was happening. Nidal promised me his love and loyalty, and I believed him. He would not betray me, especially for Shaeena. He did not love her. He wasn't even attracted to her, according to him. The king was probably forcing this upon him. Nidal would correct it at the ball. He would tell everyone the truth that I was his one and only love. He would announce to everyone that he wanted to marry me, not Shaeena.

Today, Billal had brought me to an ancient, old village because he had ordered a gown to be made for me to wear to the ball. I hoped it would be appealing to the eye. I wanted to look beautiful so Nidal would not be able to take his eyes off me.

Walking alongside Billal in this beautiful village, I could not help but admire the surrounding beauty. The hundreds of trees and banks of colorful flowers that surrounded the village captivated me.

The homes were made of stone and they were painted white all around. Flowers were displayed on their window ledges and on the steps of their front doors. The women proudly swept the street surrounding their home and chatted with their neighbors as they glanced curiously in our direction. As we walked along the pavement, Billal greeted them with a smile, which made them blush with excitement, and I could hear them whispering behind us. This would be the highlight of their day. I could envision them drinking their tea and chattering away happily to their friends about the handsome prince who threw them a smile to die for.

As we approached the village square, the merchants happily displayed their merchandise outside their shops. And many shops there were, lined up next to each other all the way down to the very end of the village. I looked excitedly about and admired the way everyone was smiling at each other, as if they were happy and without a care in the world. I envied them. I thirsted for such peace and tranquility in my heart.

Children were playing in the cobbled streets as their laughter filled the air. Mothers held their wee ones in their arms while taking a walk, admiring the displays in the shops as the owners bustled about, preparing for yet another day of work.

"I remember when I was but a child and my father brought me to the village with him," Billal chirped happily. "My friends and I played in the outskirts of the village, until Father announced our departure."

I could only imagine Billal as a little boy, running up and down the cobbled streets of this enchanting village with his little friends. I stole a sideways glance up at Billal, admiring his handsome, chiseled looks. Billal's head turned, and his eyes gazed down at my lips hungrily. I quickly averted my gaze, embarrassed that he had caught me staring at him. Billal grabbed my hand and held it in his as he gently pulled me alongside him.

That was when I saw her, a little old lady dressed in black from head to toe. Even her head was covered with a black scarf that was wrapped around her head and face, leaving only her eyes exposed.

Her dark, piercing eyes were gazing right at me. I shivered as goose bumps ran up and down my spine.

"Do not fear her, Loula. She is harmless," Billal whispered.

"Who is she? Why does she stare at me so?" I tried to shake away the eerie feeling unsuccessfully.

"It is rumored that she is a witch. She claims to have visions, and she sells spells and enchantments. Do not mind her, Loula," he added quickly. "She is old and senile. Come, the shop with the gowns is around the corner. I am sure you will love what the headmistress has made for you," he said excitedly as he pulled me alongside him.

As we turned the corner, I could not help but glance one more time at the old woman. I saw her eyes open wide and her hand reach out to me. I quickly turned around and held tighter on to Billal's hand, trying to forget the woman, but I felt her stabbing stare on my back. It was all too creepy for me. I climbed the two steps to the shop with Billal and did everything I could to relax my shaken mind that was running all over the place with fear.

Walking into the parlor, I saw a huge room full of glamour. Lavender curtains trimmed the windows all around the store. Candle chandeliers hung from the ceiling, tapestries decorated the walls, and lavish carpeting was throughout the entire parlor. The French couches and cherrywood side tables were of exquisite taste. Fine crystal decorated the tables, and there was even a crystal bowl full of chocolates. Rumor had it that chocolates were of aphrodisial quality. I stole a glance at Billal and caught him eyeing them with interest. God only knew what was going through his mind.

Billal leaned his head near my ear and whispered, "Relax, Loula. I don't need chocolates to get a fix! I can prove it if you like," he said with a wolfish grin.

I rolled my eyes and quickly looked away, lest he got any more smart ideas.

The head seamstress eyes lit up when she saw us. She was a dainty mistress, with a touch of class, and she threw Billal a smile to die for. I raised an eyebrow. Clearly she wanted Billal and wasted no time showing her affection for him as she walked up to us.

"Welcome to my parlor." She swept her gaze from me to Billal. "I was expecting you today." Billal took her hand and kissed it. "It is good to see you again," she purred batting her eyelashes flirtatiously.

I rolled my eyes and waited to be introduced.

"Please allow me to introduce to you our lady of the court, Loula." Billal stepped aside and pulled me closer to him, a gesture that the mistress did not miss.

I could tell that she was not happy to see me as her eyes scanned me from head to toe, regarding me thoughtfully. I tried my hardest to resist the urge to slap her face. I needed that gown she had for me, so I smiled and curtsied in her direction.

"We are here for the gown, my lady, and I hope you have finished it as you had promised," Billal said, hopeful.

"Have I ever let you down?" she purred.

I sensed that Billal was getting uncomfortable and I thought to come to his rescue. "Can you please bring out the gown, mistress? I have been waiting all week to see it." I said, flashing her an innocent smile.

I detected a hint of anger in her eyes as she marched off into the next room. Seconds later, she came back with the gown in her hands. She walked over to the dressing room, hung it up, and told me to try it on to see if the fit was good. I complied with her wishes, and I followed her into the dressing room, closing the door behind us. I undressed, took the fashionable gown, and slipped into it without really paying attention to its details. The mistress buttoned all the buttons behind me, stood back, and appraised me from head to toe. She looked pleased and asked me to step out of the room, opening the door and walking out as I followed after her.

As soon as Billal's eyes rested on me, he drew in a sharp inhalation of breath. I knew he was immensely pleased at what he saw. His eyes feasted upon me, and I blushed, not knowing why he was overreacting until I turned around and looked in the huge mirrors. Then I understood.

I looked absolutely beautiful. The gown was one of a kind. This gown was made to perfection. I must say that the mistress had plenty of talent. I turned slowly around, and the soft white material wrapped around my legs and then cascaded down to the carpet.

Just then, the door flew open, and two couples walked in. The mistress went to greet them, allowing us a few minutes alone. Billal could not tear his gaze away from mine as he stared hungrily at me. His eyes were blazing with desire.

"Loula, you look very beautiful. You take my breath away," he said hoarsely. And without meaning to, I dropped my gaze to his groin. His bulge was huge and pressing against his pantaloons. Embarrassed, I quickly looked away.

Billal leaned in closer to me and whispered, "I wish you would reconsider your choice in choosing a lover, Loula. You know very well only I am capable of making you happy. Nidal has his duties to the crown. I am a free man to love and to choose any woman I desire. And I am pledging my love to you, Loula," he said convincingly, trying to reassure me that he spoke the truth. "I can love you way more than he can. Please reconsider. Nidal will only break your heart," he pleaded.

I looked at him in silence. I had not a thing to say.

Billal took me by the shoulders and pulled me close to him. His eyes were blazing passion. His voice was hoarse as he continued, "I can give you a life of happiness. I can love you like you deserve to be loved! I can protect you from harm. Nidal cannot! Has not! He says he loves you, but he does not show it." Billal softly shook me. "Loula, tonight he will break your heart again. He will follow orders and marry Shaeena! He will break your heart, and I will be there to pick up the pieces!" he said softly. And he dropped his hands, walked over to the window, and looked out on to the cobblestone street, leaving me staring after him, speechless.

Deep down inside, I knew that Billal believed he spoke the truth. I knew without a doubt that tonight was going to be a difficult night. But I had hope, and I believed in Nidal. He would stand up for our love. I knew in his heart of hearts that he wanted me and not Princess Shaeena.

Billal had been by my side through thick and thin. He was my protector, my friend. He was my everything. Everything except my lover! I wished I could tell him that I loved him too. I wanted nothing more than to make him happy. But I could not say this to him. I loved Nidal, and that would never ever change. Tonight, Nidal would tell the world how much I meant to him and how he and I would be together forever.

The mistress walked to Billal's side, leaned close to him, and whispered something for his ears alone. Billal searched the room for me, and his eyes rested on mine. A longing was in his eyes as he silently pleaded for me to reconsider my decision. The mistress pulled back and followed his gaze to mine, and I saw her pretty facial features twist with hate.

Billal was oblivious to anything around him except me. He stared hopelessly at me as if his life depended on my next words. I walked over to him and placed a soft kiss on his lips. I knew that display would be an eyeful for everyone in the parlor, including the mistress, who I was sure wanted to gouge my eyes out by now.

Billal said not one word. He just closed his eyes and let out a sigh full of anguish. He paid handsomely for my gown and asked the mistress to send the garment to the royal carriage. Then he grabbed my hand and pulled me out of the shop while everyone, including the mistress, watched the display with interest.

Once outside, Billal turned to me and demanded, "Why did you kiss me, Loula?"

I knew not how to answer that, as I stared silently at him. His full lips pressed together angrily as he waited for my reply. His beautiful eyes sparkled with anger.

"How dare you play with my feelings!" His dark gaze measured mine. Then his scowl deepened, and he pulled me to him, close enough where I felt his heart pounding rapidly through his shirt. "You have bewitched me, and I am suffering!" He pounded his hand on his chest. "Release me of this pain, Loula," he begged in a tortured voice.

Can it be possible for someone to love two people at the same time? I wanted desperately to love this man. I wanted him to hold me in his arms forever, and I wanted to wipe away the tears that were threatening to spill forth from his eyes. He was beautiful. He was every woman's dream come true. I loved him to no end. But I did not love him more than I did Nidal. I lowered my gaze to my feet, ashamed I could not give him what he so richly deserved.

Billal regarded me thoughtfully. "I know you care for me. I can see it in your eyes. I have seen desire there too. If you allow your mind just for a second to be free of Nidal, I know you could fall in love with me," he said passionately.

I looked up at him, and the trail of tears now flowed freely down my face. I placed my hands on his chest and felt it tighten as he braced himself for my next words. "This is not by choice, Billal, that I hurt you. You are very important to me. You must know that by now." I cried, and Billal drew a sharp breath and closed his eyes.

I saw tears on his long eyelashes that slowly glided down his cheeks unashamedly. Billal's hands gently pulled me into his embrace and held me tight.

"Can you at least answer me this, Loula?" he asked softly. The life was already gone from his voice. "Is there even a small hint of a possibility that maybe you can feel for me anything at all one day? Because if there is, I shall wait until the end of time for you."

The sudden realization blew me away. In truth, I loved him very much, dangerously enough. I wanted to tell him this but could not. Revealing such to him would be a disaster. Nothing good could come out of it. My heart belonged to Nidal, but a part of me wanted Billal as well. A small part of me wished that things could have been different. Had I met him first, I could have easily loved him the way he deserved to be loved. Now as I stood here in his arms, I knew I could never tell him of my feelings because he would fight tooth and nail to make me his and I would lose Nidal forever. The decision to keep silent was easy for me. I wanted Nidal. I had always wanted Nidal, and I would let nothing stand in the way.

Billal read all the mixed feeling in my eyes and dropped his hands to his side. He walked away from me, and I silently followed behind him. I looked around and saw that we had had an audience during our little heartfelt moment. Embarrassed, I looked down at the pavement, trying not to bring more attention my way. Billal's long strides got him a few feet away from me, and as I tried to catch up with him, I noticed the old lady dressed in black come toward me.

I picked up my pace and tried to avoid confrontation with her, but she was quick to catch up to me, grabbing the back of my gown, and pulling it, chanting, "Death is in the air. I feel it! Change the course of your life, or you shall bring death upon yourself and your soul mate." She cried desperately, "The visions are clear. Both of you will suffer, for it is written. Your fates have been sealed even before the both of you were born."

This woman was mad. I tried to run from her, but she quickly grabbed my wrist tightly and held on to me for dear life. She looked at me with huge eyes, and I saw fear in them.

"Please, you must not go back to the prince!" she begged desperately. "Leave him be! Or both of you will suffer death! Save yourselves! You can change the course of your life if you do the right thing and walk away from him. Do not let death win!"

What is she saying? Could she know the future? Or is she mad? My head was spinning with pain. *What does she know of my fate?*

"My visions always come true! But you have the power to change your fate if you choose to. Destiny can be cheated if you play your cards well." Then she let go of my arm and walked away muttering to herself, leaving me staring after her, dumbfounded.

Billal raced to my side at that moment and anxiously asked, "What, pray tell, was that all about?"

I looked up at him and nervously asked him to take me home. I had had enough drama today to last me a lifetime. Everything that had transpired had blown me away.

We rode back in silence, each in our own thoughts. It was a bumpy ride, and our bodies were thrown together every time the carriage shook. Billal circled his arm around my shoulder and brought me close to him. I felt loved and protected. If things were different, I would have chosen Billal as my husband. He was a good man, and I loved him, but not enough to choose him over Nidal.

Finally, the carriage came to a halt in front of the palace. I looked out the little window, and looked straight ahead at the palace window, and caught Nidal looking right at us. Billal jumped out first and helped me get down from the carriage, and the driver whisked the horses and carriage away to the stables. Billal informed me that the servants would bring in the packages as he gently took my hand in his and pulled me up the stairs to the palace. I knew Nidal was watching, and I hoped he was not getting angry with me.

❂ ❂ ❂

The rest of the day went by very slowly. I was counting the minutes and seconds until it was time for me to start getting dressed for the ball. My personal maids were excited to help me dress. When they saw the gown I was to wear, they nearly fainted with approval. They helped me slip into it, and I stood back, admiring myself as I twirled around. The circle skirt opened up, and the cloth flew around me, wrapping me up in elegance. I looked like a princess, and I knew every woman tonight at the ball would envy me. But none of that mattered. All I wanted was for Nidal to take me in his arms and claim me as his bride. In this elegant, white gown,

I looked like a bride, Nidal's bride. I smiled to myself and sighed. *Nidal is mine, now and forever and into eternity.*

I decided to let my hair down. I knew it was daring, but I felt audacious. Tonight, I would dance with my Prince Charming. I would dance the night away in his arms and show the world how much we cared for one another. I slipped into my glass slippers and took one last look into the mirror.

Billal walked in the room looking dashing, just like the handsome prince that he was. He smiled from ear to ear as he stood staring at me. I could tell he was pleased with what he saw. His eyes were blazing with lust as his gaze swept me from head to toe. I smiled bashfully at him.

Billal gave me his arm, and I placed my arm inside his. We exited the room. We walked slowly down the stairs, and I was a little nervous. The guards at the door were staring at me. Their appreciating gaze swept me from head to toe. One of them winked at me, and I quickly looked away, embarrassed. I let go of Billal's arm and entered the ballroom. All eyes fell on me. I lifted my head up high and walked into the ballroom. Everyone moved aside and made a pathway for me to walk through.

I glanced around the room and spotted Nidal. He liked what he saw. I could tell by the expression on his face. Shaeena was next to him, and she looked angry. Nidal took a step toward me, and I walked right to him.

The whole night was full of surprises. When I saw the ring on Shaeena's finger, I lost all sense of reality. The universe was playing tricks on me. I could not believe it. Nidal had excuses for everything. When we danced and I was in his arms, I felt like a lost little sheep who had found its way home. I belonged in his arms, but Nidal messed everything up again.

Later when Nidal and I were alone, it was electrifying. I melted in his arms. I gave him my heart and soul. I thought that he too loved me the same way, only to find out later that it was all a lie. It was a horrible nightmare.

The only person who never lied, cheated, or disrespected me was Billal. He treasured every moment he spent with me. He made me feel truly loved. He did everything he could to win my affection, without betraying me, not once. I loved him dearly, but it was a different kind of love. I never gave him the love that he deserved. He did warn me, but love blinded me. Never once did it cross my mind that Nidal would betray me. Billal knew Nidal was deceptive, and I did not—could not—believe it.

Billal convinced me that Nidal was cheating on me. I was so stupid and did not believe him. I laughed in his face, saying that Nidal would never ever do that to me. Billal took me by the hand and dragged me down the flight of stairs, and we walked down the hall to Nidal's door. Billal opened it and gently pushed me inside. I could not believe what I saw. My Nidal was making love to Princess Shaeena!

My nightmare had come to a reality. My Prince Charming was all a lie. He had never loved me. He had never fought for our love. He gave in to lust. All my dreams came crashing down. Billal was there to help me pick up the pieces. He took me in his arms and carried me to our room, placing me on the bed and comforting me in my time of despair. He was gentle and caring. He was kind and understanding, even though I did not deserve his love. He was there for me. Because of him, I got through all of this. I owed him my loyalty and devotion. I owed him my life.

I did not sleep all night. How could I? Billal had me in his arms. I cried and cried until there were no more tears to shed. Billal whispered sweet nothings in my ear until he saw a smile on my face. I smiled because he was so sweet. He was my hero.

I did not know what I would do from here on. I had had other plans for my life's direction, but now things had changed. I had to accept what had happened and deal with it. I knew it would not be easy to just stop loving Nidal. I didn't know how to do that or even if that were an option. But I had to at least try or face a life of suffering.

I tipped my head back and looked up at Billal's face. He was so handsome. He cast a curious sideways glance at me and smiled. He stared at me in silence for several long moments before he took my hand in his and kissed it. His body was warm next to mine. Each night I spent in his bed, Billal, out of respect for me, wore his pajamas. Last night, however, even though I was under distress, I remembered him taking off his clothes, but I was in so much pain that I did not comment on the fact that he wore only his underpants. I felt his bare legs rub against mine, and I did not feel the need to move away. I just lay there in his arms and enjoyed the moment.

I did not miss the glint in Billal's eyes as he bent down and put his mouth on mine. His lips felt warm. I kissed him. It seemed like the right thing to do. I lost myself in the heat of the moment. He was a good kisser. I could honestly say that I enjoyed it. Billal sensed my thoughts, leaned down, and kissed me again. This time, the kiss was more passionate. I kissed him back too, feeling a stirring inside me.

When Billal kissed me, it was different than when Nidal did. Billal's kisses somehow seemed more genuine because Billal loved me and only me. When Nidal kissed me, Shaeena was always in the way of our happiness, making me feel like I was competing for his love. Billal, on the other hand, made me feel number one in his life, like no other woman existed in the world, like I was very special to him.

I gave into his passion and matched his kisses with my own. Billal's body moved closer to mine, and he tried to pry my legs open by gently sliding his right leg in the middle of my legs. I felt his huge groin piercing my thigh. He was undeniably male. His breathing got heavier as his body now shifted on top of mine. I allowed Billal to touch me. His hands traveled up and down my body with expertise. I could tell that he was more experienced in the ways of a woman's body than Nidal was. My body betrayed me. I was feeling the heat between my legs.

Billal lifted my nightgown over my head and exposed my breasts. Cupping my left breast in his hand, he brought his lips down and played with my nipples, making them hard as a rock. His other hand was caressing my body as it slipped downward to a place that only one other man had ever touched. My body betrayed me as lust overpowered my senses, and I found myself arching in total submission.

At that precise moment, I heard the door open to our room. I turned my head and saw Nidal standing there with his mouth open. He leaned back against the door frame for support. The sorrow I saw in his eyes made me want to hide under a rock and never crawl out of it. My body went rigid.

Billal stood frozen on top of me. He did not make a move to get off me. I was at a loss for words. Nothing I could say would get me out of this. I did what I did because I wanted to. It had felt right a few moments ago. But now I knew it was dreadfully wrong. I tried to push Billal off me, but he would not budge. I looked over at Nidal again, and he was still staring at me with such a sad expression. That was when I felt my heart break in two. I knew this was the end of his love for me. I knew he would not forgive me. It was written in his eyes, and the realization at this observation broke my heart. I could not blame him, but I could not forgive him either for what he had done to me. So I did nothing. I said nothing until Nidal stood up straight and quietly walked away, closing the door behind him.

I should have breathed a sigh of relief. I should have felt satisfaction that we were now even, an eye for an eye, a tooth for a tooth. *Isn't that what people say?* I should have been singing with joy that I had gotten even with him. But I was not happy at this very moment. I did not feel triumph. I felt pain, like a knife twisting deep in my heart. This was a sad day for me. I felt empty, alone. I felt the blood drain from my face as this realization sunk in. There was no life for me without Nidal. I pushed Billal off me, and I jumped out of bed, feeling disgusted with myself. *What have I done? Oh my God! What have I done?*

I knew deep in my heart that it was truly over this time. Nidal would never forgive me, just as I was not ready to forgive him. Billal called out my name, but I was not able to answer him as I ran over to the couch, threw myself on it, and cried my heart out. I cried a river until there were no more tears left to shed.

Billal sat on the edge of the bed, staring at me in silence. He had that knowing look in his eyes, as if he too were done with me. I felt all alone in a world made out of glass. My world had shattered into a million pieces that could never be put back together again. Life had given me many blows, but this was, by far, the worst.

In all reality, I had never really cheated on Nidal. I had not had sex with anyone but him. A kiss did not count in the same way. Nidal, on the other hand, had made love to Shaeena. That was the real betrayal. I suddenly had a pounding headache. I dropped my head in my hands. I heard Billal sigh. I could only imagine what was going through his mind. I had not been fair to him. He deserved better.

In two long strides, Billal was standing right beside me. Then he dropped to his knees and took my hands in his. The tingling sensation was there again. I felt confused. *Why is my body betraying me like this?*

"Tell me what you want, Loula," Billal asked in a husky voice.

My body trembled as his hands trailed down my legs. He pulled me to him, and we both fell back on the carpet. I landed on his bare chest. Billal's eyes were blazing fire. He rolled me over gently and trailed kisses along my neck. With his knee, he parted my legs and sexually rubbed his rock-solid shaft between my thighs. His lips came crashing down on mine brutally as he kissed me passionately. I did not resist. The tingling sensation had now gone up and down my spine. I could feel my heart beat faster.

I kissed him back hungrily, as if he were the one who my heart ached for, as if he were the one that I loved. I knew I was headed the wrong direction, yet I did nothing to stop it until Billal gently pushed me away from him.

"Loula, you are not in your right state of mind. I only want you to kiss me if and when you really want me to be kissing you. I will not have you in this way," he said in a tortured voice.

He pulled himself up and walked away with his head held up high. His pride would not let him enjoy my kisses because he knew he was second choice. My headache was still pounding, or else I would have told him that I chose him at this moment. At this moment, I was not faking it. I wanted him to kiss me, to touch me. I wanted to make love to him. But I kept silent. I knew my heart was hurting, so I was making desperate decisions. Because I was in love with Nidal, nothing and no one would ever be able to change that, not even me.

There were not many things for me to do under the circumstances. I could not have Nidal. He would never marry me. I would not have his firstborn child. Shaeena beat me to that. The king would never accept me in Nidal's life. So my only other alternative was to be with Billal. I knew he loved and cherished me. I knew he worshipped the ground I walked on. I knew I was attracted to him, and I knew his kisses had the ability to turn me on. So I thought I would take that route. I might as well accept my fate starting now, for it would save me from a lot of heartache later.

I turned sideways and caught a glimpse of Billal as he dressed into his uniform. His muscles flexed with every movement. He was so sexy. I swallowed nervously. He had a beautiful physique.

Without realizing it, I called out, "Billal!"

He turned my way, and in two seconds, he was next to me, sweeping me up into his arms. His lips came crashing down on mine. His hands were holding me tight. I kissed him back hungrily. He tasted good. He smelled delicious, and I was lost as my body betrayed me once again.

It was a crazy, long-lasting kiss that was long anticipated. I was thirsty for his touch, and I held on to him tight as I melted into his embrace. Just at that moment, I heard a knock on the door. Someone announced that the king and queen requested our audience in the dining room for brunch. We were told to go immediately, not to waste any time.

Billal looked at me apologetically, with hungry eyes, as he withdrew from my arms and finished dressing. We both knew that we needed to go. We were summoned, and there were consequences if we were late. I slipped into a comfortable light green dress with yellow fringe trimmings on the bottom. I pulled my hair back in a ponytail, adding a green ribbon to spice up my appearance. As I looked around for my slippers, my heart started to beat faster, knowing that Nidal and Shaeena would join us for brunch. I did not know if I were in the right state of mind to see them today, but clearly I did not have a choice. I was summoned.

When we were both ready to leave our room, Billal reached out his hand, and I slipped mine inside his, lacing my fingers with his. I needed it for comfort. We walked silently down the stairs and through the hallway to the dining area. The guards pulled open the doors, and I held my breath as we both walked in together with plastered smiles on our faces.

The room was full. All the gentlemen stood until I was seated, and then they all sat down, including Billal, who had a seat next to mine. I looked over at Nidal and Shaeena, and I knew today would be an interesting day. Billal's hand rested on mine. Nidal did not miss the gesture, and I saw him tense up. The princess was watching him like a hawk.

The conversation went smoothly for the first half of the brunch. Everyone was engaged in pleasant conversation. Nidal and I pretended we were happy with our mates. Shaeena and Billal acted as if all were normal, so we ate our meal and enjoyed our surroundings, or so I thought. There was no warning sign when the room started spinning. I held on tight to Billal's hand. I feared I would fall off my chair. Billal noticed something was wrong.

"Loula, is something wrong?" Billal leaned close to my ear and whispered with great concern, "Your face looks ashen. What ails you?"

Nidal overheard Billal's words and looked suspiciously at me. He was waiting for my reply. *As if he cared! As if he loved me and was concerned! I will not give him the satisfaction.* I whispered back in Billal's ear and for his ears alone that I was fine and he need not worry about me. Then I threw him a smile, and he relaxed. But that was farthest from the truth. The room was still spinning, and I was about to throw up. I quickly jumped up from my seat and walked around the dining table hastily. I could hear the commotion behind me as I exited the room, but I had no time to react. I ran as fast as I could to the guest bathroom, thankful it was nearby. As soon as I closed the door behind me, I threw up in the toilet.

I heard Billal's voice outside the door asking if I were all right. Before I could even respond, he started pounding on the door.

"Loula, open the door," he yelled, pounding harder now. "Open the door. Let me in," he said, reminding me of a time when Nidal had once pounded on the door and threatened to break it down if I did not open it.

Without hesitation, I opened the door, and Billal stepped inside just in time because Nidal's voice was heard down the hall. He was coming right at us. Billal closed the door and locked it just as Nidal stood outside.

"Loula, what is wrong? Are you feeling under the weather?" Nidal asked impatiently, pounding on the door.

Billal took me in his arms and held me close to him. I was still feeling a little dizzy, and I did not respond to Nidal.

"I know you are both in there. Open the door now!" Nidal demanded.

I could hear another voice now outside the door. It was the queen. She was asking Nidal what had happened, and he told her that I was inside with Billal and would not open the door.

"Dear, are you all right in there?" the queen mother asked with concern in her voice.

I hated to keep the queen waiting for an answer, and I responded out of respect, "Yes, Your Highness, I'm feeling better. Billal is here with me. Please, go back to your guests. We will come back to the dining room in a few minutes," I lied.

"Are you sure, child? Should I call the doctor?" she asked, waiting patiently for a reply.

But before I could answer, Nidal stepped closer to the door. "Loula, I demand to know what happened!" he asked, startling me with the tone of his voice.

I was annoyed with him. *Who does he think he is? How dare he act as though he is concerned for my welfare after everything he put me through!*

"Go away, Nidal. I'm fine. Do not worry about me. Billal is here with me, and he is taking good care of me," I said in a dismissive tone, trying to make him jealous.

I heard his footsteps walk away.

"Loula, we are going back to the dining room, and I will look forward to your return promptly," the queen said. Without waiting for a response, I heard her light steps walk away from the door.

Billal lifted my chin up, and our eyes locked. "You have a lot of explaining to do. After we drink our tea, we will excuse ourselves and go to our room. I want you to tell me everything that is on your mind," he said in a threatening tone.

Then he opened the door, and we both walked back to the dining area.

We sat in our chairs, and all eyes were upon us. Nidal's piercing gaze was so scary. I winced and looked away. Shaeena looked at me suspiciously. The king looked like he wanted to throttle me, and the guests looked embarrassed. Only the queen looked at me with some compassion. I suddenly missed my mother. I choked back the tears that threatened to spill, and I looked down at my empty plate. At this time, it was the safest place to look at. My mother, who had died from the whooping cough when I was but a child, had loved me unconditionally. I had felt safe in her arms. When God took her from me, I was devastated and felt all alone in this world. My father had died the previous year from a rattlesnake bite on the leg. My mother and I were left to fend for ourselves, and after my mother was taken from me, I was living in a world of make-believe.

Now here I was again, feeling all alone. The room started spinning again, but I just sat there, trying not to get anyone's attention. The last thing I needed was trouble again. I did not have an appetite anymore, and the tea only made me want to throw up, so I just played with my napkin until it hit me like a ton of bricks. The spinning room and the feeling like I wanted to throw up could only mean one thing. My eyes opened wide with the realization that I could be pregnant again with Nidal's child.

I do not know if I should laugh or cry. To be carrying Nidal's baby is a blessing, but if anyone found out, especially Shaeena, my baby's life would be in danger again. Especially since I have lost all favor with the king. I would have to lie if I am pregnant and say that Billal is the father. I know Billal would come to my rescue and save me from some horrible fate that might await me if the truth be known. Unconsciously, my hand was rubbing my stomach. The idea of carrying Nidal's child again was overwhelming.

I looked sideways and caught Billal curiously studying my face. His expression looked as if he knew my secret. We shared eye contact before I quickly looked away. This would not be the right time to explain my situation to him. He knew something was up, and he took hold of my hand and gently squeezed it. Nidal sensed something was going on as well, and he sat quietly staring at the both of us, trying to figure us out.

The servants cleared the table, brought out the pastries, and poured tea into our cups. Shaeena was engaged in conversation with Billal. They sat across from each other, and Nidal sat across from me. Most everyone at the table was listening to the king tell a tale. He had grabbed their attention with his clever words.

He loved being the center of the universe. The queen rolled her eyes as the king exaggerated the legendary saga. But as the king continued his story, I realized he had chosen this particular story for a reason. He was warning me in some way, for the story he told was of a forbidden love that ended badly. He stared at me as he ended his story about the mistress who was executed because she stood in the way of the future king. There was silence in the room. Even the servants stood still at the last words the king spoke. Not a movement in the room until the queen started to laugh nervously, saying, "Oh, hush. You are so melodramatic!" She waved her hand at him as she laughed some more.

But I knew the queen well. Her laugh was a cover-up. She too knew what the king was implying. At that moment, Billal stood up and announced we would be going to our room for a nap. He winked at the king, grabbed my hand, and pulled me to my feet. I followed behind him as we walked out of the dining area. Billal grabbed me by the waist and pulled me to his side. The guards by the door took notice of this and smiled at us. We took the stairs two at a time, and when we reached our room, Billal opened the door and gently pushed me inside. He quickly closed the door and led me to the bed. He motioned for me to sit on it, and then Billal kneeled down in front of me.

"Tell me what is wrong, Loula," he pleaded.

"I am pregnant with Nidal's baby," I said simply. "I need your help, Billal, or the baby does not stand a chance. Will you help me?" I hoped his answer was what I needed to hear.

Billal's face looked ashen. He stood abruptly and walked to the other side of the room. He started pacing back and forth. I knew my news came as a shock to him, but I too was shocked to realize that I was pregnant again with Nidal's baby. Finally, Billal walked back to the bed and sat down. He turned and looked at me steadily, and I saw the tiny fine lines on his face. When he started to speak, I heard the bitterness in his voice. I waited, anticipating the worst.

"Loula, I love you, and you know that. I have only told you about a million times." He laughed bitterly. "I have tried many times to warn you about Nidal, but to no avail. You still love him. You are carrying his child again! A child that will never be accepted as Nidal's by him or the king! You will put your unborn child in danger by your own admission! Once you announce that you carry Nidal's child, the baby is as good as dead!" he whispered ruthlessly. His brutal words took me aback. A miserable silence followed for a few minutes as I tried to gather my wits.

"Your baby will be in grave danger once the word is out! You must never reveal to anyone who the father is! The king does not favor you anymore! Once he learns your secret, he will find a way to kill the baby! Your baby is a threat to the crown! The king will see to it that you are hanged!" Billal grabbed my shoulders and shook me lightly. "Please, Loula, you cannot tell anyone who the real father is!"

I could tell that Billal was frightened. "So what am I to do then? Who should I say is the father?" I knew what his answer would be. Tears welled up in my eyes. My heart ached. I was in a bad situation, and I too believed that the king would lash out at me. He would let nothing stand in his way. He wanted Nidal to marry Shaeena.

"I will claim your baby as mine! I will tell the world I impregnated you," he said.

I did not feel inclined to argue. I knew it was my baby's only chance of survival. My hand automatically dropped to my stomach, and I rubbed it unconsciously.

"Thank you for the offer. I accept," I said quickly before he could overthink his decision and change his mind.

I was exhausted, and my heart was tortured, but under the circumstances, I was left with no choice but to go along with the deception. I dropped my head on his shoulders and wept. Billal wrapped his arms around me and tried to comfort me, but it was too late for comfort. The hard fact was that I was never going to be able to share my life with the man whom I loved more than life itself. I felt cheated out of happiness, but I was grateful for having such a friend as Billal. He was a blessing in my life, and I knew that he would protect me from harm.

Billal gently pushed me back and looked into my eyes. "Loula, we have to announce that we have been lovers all this time. Otherwise, they will not believe that I am the father of your baby," he said. I could tell that he was hoping I would agree with him on this. "We must announce it immediately. Otherwise, everyone will speculate the truth. Tonight at dinner, I can make the announcement. I will tell them that we fell in love, we have been having a secret affair for some time now, and you are carrying my child." He paused only for a second. "I will announce that we are going to be married as soon as possible. I will tell them how much I love you and that your feelings are mutual, and ask the king for his blessings." I could tell he was pleased with himself for figuring it all out.

I sighed. *What choice do I have? None!*

"Fine, Billal. Make me your wife. I promise you that I will not let you down. I will try to be a loving bride," I said, not sure if I would be able to keep that promise.

Billal scrambled to his feet. He smiled from ear to ear. "I'm so happy, Loula. You will not regret your decision. I will do everything in my power to make you happy. I know you still love Nidal. This will be very hard for me to deal with, but as God is my witness, I will do everything in my power to make you love me and only me!" he said excitedly. "Come on, Loula. Let us go find the king. He is probably in the tearoom drinking tea with the queen," he said happily as he pulled me up to my feet. I was exhausted, but I did not want to burst his bubble. He was, after all, helping me to a better life.

Billal opened the door to the tearoom and pulled me alongside him through the doorway. The king and queen were sitting by the table in the middle of the room, and Nidal and Shaeena were sitting on the couch on the other side of the room sipping their tea. They were startled to see us as we bustled in the room. Nidal looked totally surprised to see us. He put down his cup and waited for Billal to say something, as he looked from Billal to me for an explanation because we had entered the tearoom without announcing ourselves first, as was the custom. Even before Billal opened his mouth to speak, I witnessed Nidal tense, sensing Billal was about to announce something that would not sit well with him.

Billal bowed in front of the king and said, "Forgive us, Uncle, for barging in like this unannounced."

The king smiled. He favored Billal and motioned for us to sit down. "Please join us for a cup of tea," he said. There was a glint in his eyes that made me weak with worry

"Thank you, Uncle," Billal said, "But first, if I may, I have a couple of announcements to make." Billal turned, took my hand, and pulled me next to him. "Uncle, I want to let you know that I have asked Loula for her hand in marriage, and she accepted. Now all I need is your blessing." He moved closer to the king, waiting for his reply.

"Well, well, well!" The king licked his lips. "This is sudden news! When did the both of you become an item? I was under the impression that the lady was pining for someone else." He laughed, pulled the napkin from his lap, and wiped his mouth.

"Well, Uncle, we have found love. Loula and I have been together for a long period of time. As a matter of fact, Loula is going to have my baby." Billal glanced at Nidal with satisfaction.

My heart stopped beating. I looked around the room at everyone, and my eyes landed on Nidal's face. He looked stunned. His face turned white as the blood drained from his face. Shaeena's mouth dropped open, but she looked extremely pleased with Billal's confession. The queen stared at us suspiciously, surprised by the turn of events, and the king threw his head back and roared with laughter.

"You son of a bitch, you did not skip a beat, did you? You impregnated her! Boom! Just like that!" the king said with amusement. "Of course you have my blessing. See to it that the arrangements are made hastily before people start running their mouths. All we need is to have rumors flying around the palace questioning the baby's paternity," he said with a lazy grin.

"Thank you, Uncle. I will forever be thankful for your kindness," Billal said.

The king motioned for us to sit down and drink tea with them. And we did. It was the polite thing to do. The king looked at me, making me feel uneasy. He did not waste any time making me feel unwelcome as his gaze swept over me.

He shook his head. "Are you sure you want to marry her? She is but a commoner, you know," he said with calm superiority.

As if I were not in the room at all … as if his words did not take ten years of my life away. I squirmed in my seat, knowing the king had the power to crush me at any given moment if he chose to. He was very powerful, and he hated my guts.

"Uncle, please, we love each other. I want nothing more than for Loula to be my wife," Billal declared.

I looked over at Nidal and realized there was a shuddering tension about him as if he were a hairbreadth from exploding. Our eyes met and locked.

Nidal's voice held a dangerous softness as he asked me, "Is it true, Loula? You are pregnant with Billal's child?" He looked at me, as if daring me to deny Billal's words.

I swallowed, knowing I could not deny a single thing. My baby's life depended on it. "Yes, it is true. I am pregnant with Billal's baby." I knew what these words would do to him.

Nidal's eyes searched my face. I knew he was looking for the truth. An agonizing sound escaped from his lips as he stood and whipped the teacup and saucer to the floor, shattering it to pieces. Broken fragments scattered across the floor.

Shaeena jumped off the couch and snapped at him, "Why do you care so much about Loula and her baby? I have always told you that she is a tramp!" she spat viciously.

Nidal angrily turned and pointed a finger at the princess. "Don't! Mind your own business, woman! This is between Loula and me!" he yelled, quickly dismissing her as he turned toward me with accusing eyes.

The princess, embarrassed by Nidal's daring words, stalked out of the room angrily, slamming the door behind her. I glanced sideways at Billal and noticed that he stood there enraged, waiting for my response. The king and queen were taken aback by what they had just witnessed their only son say, and I stood my ground. I'd had enough of Nidal's childish behavior. I'd had enough of his broken promises, his betrayal, and his tantrums. Billal was the one who stood next to me and proudly announced his love for me. He was the one who always came to my rescue. He was the one who deserved my love and loyalty.

The king stood from his chair and said in a threatening tone, "You would do well, Son, leaving this alone. What is done is done. She is nothing! A commoner. A whore you brought back from the Americas! I warned you many times about bringing a foreigner here! But you did not listen! You never listen!" the king growled, and he marched out of the room, disgusted.

The queen ran to me and hugged me. "I am so sorry, child, for all that has transpired. Sweet child of heaven, you have endured too much pain these last few months," she said tearfully.

"Mother, she does not deserve your love. Father is right. She is a whore!" Nidal spat, stunning both the queen and me.

Rage filled Billal's face. In an instant, he flew next to Nidal, grabbed him by his jacket, and whipped him across the room. Nidal tripped over the Oriental rug that was lavishly displayed on the marble floor and went flying into a china display. The whole display crashed to the floor, smashing everything inside it. Fine crystal shattered across the floor.

Nidal turned abruptly and punched Billal square on his jaw. Then all hell broke loose. They fought until blood stains were everywhere. The queen and I ran to the other side of the room to protect ourselves. The two were fighting with the strength of lions. Finally, Nidal threw the last punch, and they both fell to the floor, depleted of their energy, and passed out. Like two schoolboys fighting over the prettiest girl in class. The room was a mess. Shattered glass was everywhere, as well as blood splattered on everything. The servants came rushing in, not daring to say anything, as they quietly cleaned up the mess.

The queen pulled me out of the room and dragged me to the next room, and when we stepped inside, she closed the door, put her fingers to her lips, and whispered, "Shhh, even the walls have ears." I waited curiously for her to speak. Her next words came as a shock to me.

"Do you take me for a fool, Loula? Do you not think I know that the baby you carry inside your womb is my grandchild? I might be an old woman, but I can tell a lie when one is spoken! You and Nidal are in love! Shaeena does not carry my grandson in her womb! My son would never sleep with her intentionally! He loves and wants only you! And you, my dear, want and love only him! What has gotten into you two? Both of you are destroying any chance you might have for happiness!" she hissed as I stood there openmouthed at her choice of words.

She was right, but I could not admit it as much as I wanted to, not even to her. Doing so would only put my baby in harm's way. So I pushed past her and ran to the door to get away, but not before saying, "No, Your Highness, you are wrong. This is Billal's baby I carry. It is him that I choose." I left, leaving behind a confused queen.

I ran down the hallway and took the stairs two at a time to get away from all this turmoil. I could not do this anymore. I had had enough. I walked into my room and locked the door. I did not want to be bothered by anyone anytime soon. I dropped on the bed and cried like a two-year-old. I cried for Nidal. I cried for the love lost. I cried for the baby I lost, and I cried for this poor baby who would never know the truth about his father. Life was just not fair to me.

I heard a loud pounding on the door. Billal was calling my name and ordering me to unlock the door. I quickly jumped out of bed and ran to open it. Billal entered and pulled me into his arms.

His clothes were covered in blood, and his face looked all broken up. A tinge of guilt tugged at my heart. All this had happened because of me. It was my fault that they fought. Everything was my fault. That realization was unbearable. I hurt the people I loved the most. I held on tighter to Billal, squeezing him closer to me. He responded by lifting my face to his and kissing me on the lips. I allowed him to kiss me, and it felt so good. I kissed him back passionately. I was hungry for love.

Billal lifted me up in his arms and walked over to the bed, where he gently dropped me and slid down beside me. Holding me in his arms once again, he kissed me fervently. My body was responding to his touch. I felt like a betrayer in the first degree. But at this moment, I did not care. I was lonely, and I welcomed his kisses.

I was a damsel in distress. Two men fancied me, one who deserved me and one who did not. My heart betrayed me and wanted the one who did not deserve me. My heart wanted the one who destroyed my life! The betrayer of love!

Billal's kisses relaxed me, and I eventually drifted off to sleep. I slept peacefully for the first time in many months. The next morning, I opened my eyes and saw Billal lying next to me, sleeping like an angel. He looked peaceful and very handsome. I could not decide which of the two, Billal or Nidal, was more handsome. Sometime in the night, Billal had taken off his shirt. His looked mighty sexy lying in bed next to me. I traced the muscles on his arms with my fingertips.

Billal opened his eyes and smiled. It was a beautiful smile. I snuggled closer to him, and he wrapped his arms around me. I knew I loved him, but it wasn't enough. I did not—could not—love him as much as I loved Nidal. But I wanted to. I forced myself, but to no avail. It was useless. Nidal was the reason for my existence. I dropped my hands and pulled away from Billal, but not before I felt him stiffen.

"Loula," he whispered. "Don't turn away from me now. I need you," he said hoarsely. "Please," he begged. He tried to pull me close to him again, but I pulled away from him and rolled out of bed.

It wasn't fair to lead Billal on like this. I was giving him false hopes. He deserved better than this. He deserved to be happy. Just because I wasn't happy, that didn't give me the right to mess with his life. I walked over to the other side of the room.

"Billal, I'm sorry. I don't know what to say," I apologized because I felt it was the right thing to do. "I did not mean to give you false hopes. I love Nidal, and that will never change," I said tenaciously.

I saw him wince and immediately regretted my choice of words. I did not want to hurt him. He had treated me with great respect. But I could not give him false hope either. Both of us were quiet for the next few moments. Billal was sizing up the situation at hand. When he spoke, my heart went out to him.

"You say you love Nidal, but he has caused you nothing but pain from the moment you met him. I have loved you and treated you with the respect that you deserve," he said without wavering. "I have been true to you from the beginning. You can never have Nidal. He belongs to the princess now. And I belong to you. Say you want me, Loula, and I will promise you the world." Billal begged me to accept his proposal. "I will ask nothing in return until you are ready to give me your love. I can wait until you are ready. I promise you that I will not force you in any way. Marry me, Loula," he begged. "Marry me, and give your baby a chance to grow up with a father. I will love the baby as my own. I will love you until death do us part. Loula, I promise you this!" Billal pleaded for me to say yes to his marriage proposal.

I leaned my head on the stone wall and tried to focus on what Billal was telling me. His offer sounded inviting. I was tempted to accept. What other choices did I have under the circumstances? I walked over to the French couch and dropped on it. My back was hurting. It was clearly a sign for me to slow down. I was fatigued. This pregnancy, even at this early stage, was putting a strain on me. For both of my pregnancies, I would not have Nidal next to me, comforting me and enjoying alongside me the beautiful memories of having a child inside me, a true miracle from God. I envied all the woman of the world who enjoyed their pregnancies alongside their lovers. Life was not fair to me. I felt cheated.

I looked up at Billal, and he looked stressed out. Was it fair to him that he was the one to pick up the broken pieces of my life? Would he one day resent me for all the heartache he would feel, knowing that my heart would always belong to Nidal? Even the child I carried belonged to Nidal. Wouldn't that one day create animosity between the two cousins? I was the one who had destroyed their relationship. I had come between them, and now they despised one another. It was my fault, yet Billal still wanted to marry me, despite the fact that my child and my heart did not belong to him and never would.

Billal held his breath as he looked hopefully at me. He was still waiting for my answer to his marriage proposal. I sighed once again. I was about to turn my life in a different direction as I opened my mouth.

"Fine," I said simply. "Let's do it. Let's get married." And once the words came out, I knew my life had changed forever at that moment.

Billal flew to my side and swept me up in his arms. He kissed me so passionately that I could not breathe. He squeezed me tight and looked so happy. At that moment, I knew I had made the right decision. I hugged him back. It felt good to be in his arms. I knew Billal would do everything in his power to make me happy.

But sometimes, happiness is not enough because, if you are living in a world full of fear, hate, and revenge, your happiness can come tumbling down so fast that you won't know what hit you. Late that night, I realized just how much truth there was to my words.

I was sleeping in Billal's arms when the bugles started blowing loud and clear in the middle of the night. Startled, Billal and I jumped out of bed at the same time and ran to the window to see what was happening. We saw people running toward the back of the gardens, screaming something about fire and the orphanage. My heart raced. Immediately the thought of the children came to mind. I threw on my robe and ran after Billal out the door. He was racing toward the stairway.

"How could she! Oh my God! How could she!" he cried frantically.

Fear gripped me as I raced after him. *The children? Were they in danger?*

"Billal, wait! How could who? What are you talking about?" His behavior puzzled me.

Billal stopped in his tracks right by the banister and turned to me. He reached out, grabbed me by my hand, and pulled me down the stairs with him.

Outside, behind the palace grounds, people were running frantically with pails of water in their hands. My heart raced at the speed of light, as I too ran in the direction they were headed. Panic gripped my heart as I looked ahead. Black clouds of smoke filled the night sky, and I saw the fire, brilliant orange, against the black sky. It was an inferno.

The hostile flames were devouring the orphanage. The children were burning alive. They were trapped inside. I could hear the loud screams of the children as they fought to get out of the building. The people were doing everything they could, but it was too late. They could not contain the fire. The flames had already engulfed the building.

I ran as fast as I could around all the people and went in the back of the orphanage. I heard Billal yelling at me to come back, but I could not, knowing the children were still inside. I had to help get them out. In that instant, I saw Nidal. His eyes popped when he saw me so close to the flames. He flew to my side and pulled me to him.

"What in God's name are you doing here? Go back inside the palace! It's not safe here!" he pleaded with me to do as he said.

But I wiggled out of his arms and dashed for the burning building. Smoke was billowing from the front of the building. I ran right through the flames inside the orphanage and toward the rooms where the children were. Everything was on fire, and the smoke was horrendous. I made my way to the room where Natalie's bed was, and I saw her through the flames, crouched against the wall and screaming at the top of her lungs. Behind me, I heard Nidal call my name frantically, but I needed to get Natalie out before it was too late, and I ignored him. When I got closer to Natalie, I saw the queen. She held Natalie in her arms. The fire was trapping them.

Shocked, I took off my robe and started to hit the fire, succeeding in only temporarily keeping the flames from burning them alive. The queen looked up at me, terrified, and she and Natalie were coughing from all the smoke they had inhaled. I stepped through the fire, pulled the queen up, grabbed Natalie, and pulled them both out of the room. My eyes stung from all the smoke, and I covered my mouth, not wanting to inhale the poisonous air.

I could still hear the cries of children being burned alive, and it tore my heart out. Nidal came up behind me and grabbed Natalie. She collapsed in his arms. The queen covered her mouth with one hand and grabbed Nidal's shirt with her other, not wanting to lose Nidal from her sight. Nidal yelled hysterically for me to follow him, but I could not, not when children were still trapped inside. I ran the opposite way, to another part of the building, and tried to help a child who was screaming for help. She was trapped under her burning bed, but I was too late. The flames swallowed her, and she was gone within seconds. Horrified, I took a step backward and froze in my tracks. I was trapped in this room with nowhere to go. Flames engulfed the entranceway.

I started coughing. I knew I had swallowed a lot of smoke, and my throat burned. It was time to exit this building before I put my unborn baby at risk. My vision was blurred, and I could not see where to go. At that moment, I heard glass break behind me, and I felt someone's arms wrap tightly around me and pull me out the window. Immediately, fresh air filled my lungs. I opened and closed my eyes a few times, trying to clear them from the sting of the smoke.

Nidal held me in his arms and brought me to a safe distance away from the fire. He placed a kiss on my lips and handed me over to a worried Billal. Relief flooded Billal's eyes as he cried my name over and over again until I saw tears roll down his face before he buried his face in my hair. He then gently placed me on a blanket that was on the grass right next to the queen and Natalie. The doctor was checking their pulse.

Billal left me and went to give orders to his men. He was their leader. He was in charge of catastrophic events like this one. He took control of the situation, and he directed the whole operation. I turned my attention to Nidal and saw him running back into the burning building. The raging fire swept across the building, and the flames had engulfed most of the orphanage, making it very dangerous to go inside. Nidal's life was threatened, and fear gripped my heart. I quickly jumped up and raced toward the building, and I heard everyone yelling for me to turn back, but I could not. Nidal was in there, and I could not just sit back and watch him get burned alive. At that moment, I heard Billal's voice behind me, yelling for me to stop. I kept running. I ignored everyone, and I ran even faster.

Billal caught up to me, and he lifted me up in his arms and ran the opposite direction from the fire. I kicked and screamed for him to put me down. He dropped me gently on the grass and held me down so I would not escape.

He yelled, "Stop it! Do not put your baby in harm's way. Stay put. Nidal will return. I promise you."

He was a terrible liar. I could see it in his eyes. He was just as afraid as I was.

At that moment, the whole roof caved into the flames, and I screamed out Nidal's name, terrified out of my mind. I sprung to my feet and started running as fast as I could toward the fire, but Billal once again caught me just in time and held me at bay. I cried and yelled, and I screamed and kicked at Billal, begging him to release me, but he held me even tighter. I looked into his eyes and saw raw fear there.

With trembling lips, he said, "Stay here. I will go for him. Promise me that you will stay here, Loula. Promise me now," he demanded. And without waiting for a response, he ran inside the burning house, and I ran after him.

The walls were falling down. The flames and the smoke had consumed the better part of the building, making it impossible for anyone to survive. Billal disappeared inside, and as I too followed behind him, I knew not where to go. I could not see a thing, but I knew I had to find Nidal. If anything happened to him, I would rather die right here with him than live a life without him. I forgot I was pregnant and that I was putting my child in harm's way. All I could think about at this moment was Nidal and his life. I loved him with all my heart, and I could not stay outside knowing he was in here.

At that moment, I heard Nidal call out my name. He sounded terrified. At the opposite direction, I heard Billal call out my name as well. They were both alive. But I could not answer their calls. My throat burned from too much smoke inhalation, making it impossible for me to talk.

The wall behind me collapsed. I scrambled out of the way just in time. Frantic now, I looked for the exit. But I knew not which way it was. I started to run, realizing I was trapped with nowhere to go. I stood in fear as the rest of the building started to cave in. A piece of wood came crashing on my head, and I passed out.

When I awoke, I saw Nidal. His face was black from the smoke. He was kneeling above me, pulling his hair, and crying aloud like a little baby. When he saw that I had opened my eyes, he grabbed me in his arms and held me tight, as if his life depended on it. I never felt happier as I did at this moment. He was alive, and that was all that mattered to me.

That instant, Billal grabbed Nidal by the shoulders and tried to push him out of his way, but Nidal would not budge. He held on to me, kissing me on my lips, and I melted with love. He was my life, and I knew I was his. I kissed him back with a force so passionate that I was oblivious to anything or anyone around us.

It was very selfish of me to be displaying my feelings like this. I saw Billal stand quietly next to us. In that instant, my hand automatically went to my stomach, and my eyes widened in disbelief. *The baby.* I had forgotten about its existence.

"Billal!" I cried. "My baby! Is my baby all right?" I asked, terrified of the answer.

Billal dropped to his knees next to me, and Nidal backed away. His face was stone cold as he disappeared into the crowd.

At that moment the doctor arrived, and after checking me twice he said, "You and the baby are going to be just fine, Loula."

"What about the queen and Natalie? How are they faring?" I asked, worried about their health.

"Thanks to you, Loula, for playing the hero, they are alive and well, but please don't you ever do that again!" he said sternly.

When the doctor walked away to check on all the other people who needed his help, Billal lifted me up in his arms and walked toward the palace, squeezing me tight.

The people cleared out a path for Billal to walk through, and I heard them praise my name for saving the queen and Natalie. They saw me as a hero, but I did not feel like one. I only did what I did in the name of love, not to be praised as a hero. As Billal raced up the stairs, I closed my eyes and took a deep breath of fresh air in my lungs. This was a horrible night that will never be forgotten, not by me or anyone else in the kingdom.

I lay awake in Billal's arms all night as he held me close to him. Tonight, we lost all the children from the orphanage except

Natalie. Her fate was not to die in this fire. Not tonight. Not here in this way. I cried for all the lives lost, all those little children who had had miserable lives from the moment they were born. Their fate was sealed. Natalie survived because the queen was with her. She was the real hero, not I. She kept the child alive until I got there. This queen of ours had a big heart. She was by far a better person than our king was.

At first glance of sunlight, I heard a light tap on the door and the queen's voice from the other side asking if she could enter. I quickly jumped out of bed, ran to the door, and opened it. The queen walked in, fell into my arms, and cried a river of tears. I cried along with her for all the little lives that were lost.

The queen straightened up and said, "Loula, you are a very brave lady. Last night, I saw another side of you that I did not know existed. You saved Natalie and me from being burned to death, and for this, I will be forever grateful," she said sincerely. "And I am so thrilled to know that your child is safe." The queen threw a quick glance at Billal, and then she returned her gaze to me. "I need to see you later alone, please. Maybe after lunch?"

"Yes, of course." Is anything wrong?" I asked worriedly.

The queen looked at me sadly. "We will talk later, all right?" She kissed me on the cheek, opened the door, and left the room.

Puzzled, I looked at Billal as he jumped out of bed, walked up to me, and gave me a big hug. "You feel so good in my arms, Loula. I am thankful to God for keeping you and the baby safe. I love you." There were tears in both our eyes as we hugged some more.

❋ ❋ ❋

During lunch, everyone ate in silence. Nidal, Billal, and I did not touch our food. We were not hungry. I looked around the table and saw that yesterday's fire had emotionally disturbed everybody who sat at the table. Only the king and Shaeena sat smugly. The rest of us were still feeling last night's pain. I knew not what caused the fire that killed all the innocent children and servants, but it was being whispered that it was arson. Who would do such a thing to innocent little children?

I stole a few glances at Nidal, and each time, I caught him looking straight at me. There was a different look about him, one I did not recognize. I knew he had enough heartache in his life to suffer a great deal. I felt I too had just as much. Shaeena noticed I was staring at Nidal, and she took that opportunity to hold his hand and throw me a smile that warned me of her stake on him. I sighed. Shaeena was a cold human being who only cared about getting what she wanted and nothing else. God help anyone who stood in her way. Nidal was not the right match for her. She and the king had so much in common. They complimented each other. They were both heartless.

Nidal's raw emotions were exposing his thoughts. I knew he loved me as I loved him, but the disharmony in our lives left us empty of life. I looked at the queen, and she too looked emotionally drained. Her attachment to all the children had been tight. Now she was left with only Natalie. The queen unconsciously played with her food on her plate. She did not have an appetite either.

The servants served tea and pastries afterward, and when all was said and done, we all rose at the same time and exited the room. The queen pulled me aside when I walked past her and asked if I would follow her up to her quarters. Immediately, I complied with her wishes, and I tagged along behind her. When she opened her door to her chambers, I was surprised to see little Natalie lying in her bed asleep. I threw the queen a questioning glance, and she put her finger to her lips and pulled me to another room that was connected to this one. Her quarters were huge with what looked like four other rooms attached to this one. The decorations were of French taste, and each item looked unique in itself. She had an eye for elegance, and I was sure she played a big hand in decorating her rooms.

The queen closed the door behind us when we entered the second room, and she walked over to the couch on the opposite side of the room, sat on it, and motioned for me to join her. All was quiet around us, and the queen leaned close to me and whispered, "Even the walls have ears. What I am about to tell you is only for your ears alone! Swear to me that you have loyalty to your queen." She waited patiently for my response.

"I swear by all that is holy that I will not reveal the secret that you are about to tell me without your permission, my queen, and yes, I am loyal to the crown. I am loyal to you," I promised, waiting eagerly to hear what was on her mind.

The queen took a deep breath. "What I am about to tell you could lead to treason if it is revealed. I trust you, Loula, because I have found a good person in you. The child you carry, it is my belief that it is Nidal's. You carry my first grandchild, not Shaeena. Her baby is not Nidal's. I know this without a doubt, just as I know without a doubt the child you carry is my son's! The king's infatuation with Shaeena is clouding his judgment, and he is going to ruin my son's life if I do not put a stop to it. I am in the process of finding out the truth. Shaeena is up to something, and I am not going to let her get away with it!" she said angrily. "I have suspected for some time now that Shaeena is scheming with someone. She is desperate to marry my son, but she does not love him. She only wants to marry him because she wants to be the next queen in line!" she said bitterly.

I did not feel inclined to say a word as I stared at her wide-eyed waiting for her to continue. "In my opinion, Shaeena started the fire intentionally to kill the children." She waited for my response, knowing I would have a thousand questions for her.

"Your Highness, why would the princess want to kill the children? They were just little angels living their lives. What threat could they have been to Shaeena?" I asked, not really believing her accusations. It was hard for me to imagine the princess a murderer.

The queen lowered her tone a notch before responding, afraid someone might hear her. "She wanted to kill Natalie, and to do that, she had to kill everyone in the process. She wanted Natalie out of the way." The queen was tearful now as the memories of the fire clouded her mind.

I looked at her, confused. I did not understand what the queen was trying to say. "Mother, why would Shaeena want Natalie dead? She is but a child. What threat can a child have on Shaeena?" All this information that I was trying really hard to process baffled me.

"About eight years ago, the king raped one of the servants. He got her with child. When he found out about the pregnancy, he ordered her death sentence to cover up his crime. I overheard her beg the king for mercy, swearing her silence to the identity of her baby, but the king wanted her out of his way, and he ordered her to be beheaded. The night before her death sentence, she went into labor, and she sent for me. She pleaded with me to save her child. My heart went out to her. I did not know what to do, so I sent a message to the doctor to come immediately. He is my good friend, and he is very loyal to me. When the young mother delivered her baby, the doctor took the baby and hid it in his home. He told the king that the baby was stillborn. He kept the baby for a full year, and then he brought her to me, and we put her in the orphanage with the other children. The king has no idea that she is his. The few who know have been sworn to secrecy. Natalie's mother went to her death knowing that her child was safe," the queen said tearfully.

My heart went out to the queen. She had endured quite a lot from her husband, the king. He should be feared, for he was a ruthless man. I leaned over to her hugged her. "My queen, you have a big heart. Should the king find out the identity of Natalie, he will hurt her." As soon as I mouthed those words, my eyes widened in surprise. "Does Shaeena know the truth?" I already suspected the answer to that question.

"I think she does. She is a very smart woman, and I think she figured it out somehow. I think she is the one who started the fire and killed the children," the queen said. "Natalie is Nidal's sibling, so she has royal blood in her. She is a threat to the princess.

Shaeena wants to secure her position to the crown, and she will stop at nothing to accomplish it. Shaeena does not love my son. She wants to be his wife only to wear the crown! She is not to be trusted," the queen said angrily.

I was at a loss for words. My mind was spinning. *If the princess were such a manipulator, then who's to say that the child she carries is Nidal's?*

"Mother, are you saying that we have to watch our backs where Shaeena is concerned? Shouldn't we warn Nidal?"

The queen smiled sadly. "Nidal does not accept the idea that Shaeena is so desperate. He thinks highly of her. Remember that he grew up with her, and he loves her as a sister. He knows she is not perfect, but he would never believe her capable of starting the fire." The queen looked down at her lap, where her hands rested. She sat silently as a teardrop escaped and rolled down her face. This was too much information for me to process so quickly. My thoughts were running wildly from one thing to another.

I thought back to the many times when I looked at Natalie's face and commented on her eyes. They were the same color as Nidal's. She resembled him, and he had a sister he did not even know about. My heart bled for Nidal. He was in for a rude awakening. *And Shaeena, what do we do about her? How can we protect Nidal and Natalie from such an evil woman?*

"Mother, if the king finds out that Natalie is his child, what will he do?" I asked, tired now of all the lemons that life was throwing at us.

"I'm afraid, my dear, that he would kill her, for he too will see her as a threat. As a matter of fact, I think the princess has already told the king of her suspicions. I think the both of them set the fire. We must hurry and figure a safe hiding place for Natalie before it's too late," the queen said nervously. "I promised Natalie's mother that I would keep her safe, and if it is the last thing I do, I will keep my promise!" the queen said stubbornly. And I believed that she would, for she was a loving and kind person.

"What about Nidal? Should he not know that he has a sister? And should we not tell him of Shaeena's evilness? He needs to be warned," I told her eagerly. "The baby is not his. Nidal would never betray me like that. Shaeena is a liar! Mother, we have to stop the wedding. Nidal cannot marry her. He is mine, and I love him with all my heart and my soul! And I know he loves me too." I was now crying hysterically.

Everything was a mess, and I knew not what to do. We had to find a way to fix everything before it was too late. It was the queen's turn to comfort me, and she did. She held me close to her and whispered words of endearment.

I pulled away from the queen's embrace. "What do we do now? We must find a way to prevent Shaeena from accomplishing her goals. Natalie is in grave danger. She is a helpless child who has been tormented from birth, and Nidal can't marry Shaeena, Mother. I love him, and I want him back!"

The queen said Shaeena was not as big a problem as the king was. The king was the one to fear the most. He was the one who held all the power.

I asked her, "Who do you think is the father of Shaeena's baby?"

The queen looked at me troubled, unable to speak. Finally, she whispered, "That remains a mystery to be solved. But my suspicions point to the king. I think he fathered her baby. I am not sure, but I believe this to be true because he is adamant about the marriage between Shaeena and Nidal. He wants the child to remain in the family, and what better way than to bring Shaeena into our family as Nidal's wife and claim the child as Nidal's. But this is all speculation, Loula. I am not certain of the truth. I cannot accuse the king of sleeping with Shaeena. How can I prove that?" She was clearly distressed.

I hesitated, not knowing how to answer that question. The queen was right. There was no way of proving it. My shoulders slumped. I felt defeated.

And just then, the queen surprised me by asking me the one question I dreaded answering. "Tell me, Loula. I trusted you with all I have told you, but you withhold from me the truth about who fathered your baby. I know it is not Billal's baby that you carry. It is Nidal's! You have my grandbaby in your womb, and you keep the truth from me! Why, Loula? Why are you hiding the truth?" She was eagerly waiting for my reply.

I did not know what to say. To reveal the truth could put my child in jeopardy. It was like the queen said. Even the walls had ears. I trusted no one with the information, not even the queen. My baby was my life now, and I had to protect it with my life.

"The baby is Billal's, Mother." I felt my heart race faster.

The queen's eyebrows arched. She knew my secret, and she smiled knowingly. "Loula, do not worry. Your secret is safe with me. I know it is hard to trust anyone at this point in your life, and after everything you have been through, it is safer for the baby to be Billal's than Nidal's. The king and Shaeena will come after it if they find out it is Nidal's." She smiled, and I stared at her, apologetic, knowing she understood my reason for keeping it a secret.

I knew I was in a tough situation, and I had to figure out what to do. The answer to my problems was Billal. He was the only one who could help me pull off the lie. In the meantime, we had to have the memorial service for all the lost souls who were innocent victims to the fire.

"Mother, when are the victims going to be buried?" I knew this question would bring tears to the queen's eyes.

The queen looked like she had aged ten years in the last hour. My heart went out to her. She had endured a lot in her lifetime. She wiped away the tears that threatened to spill from her eyes and answered softly, "Today. They are preparing as we speak. We must hurry and go back now before they start getting suspicious of our talk."

We both rose at the same time from the couch, and as we walked over to the connecting door, the queen opened it slowly, afraid she might awaken Natalie, who still slept peacefully in her bed. We walked past her, and as we entered the hallway, the queen told the servant who was standing outside not to leave Natalie's side. The queen took me by the hand and walked me over to my room.

"Loula, change into something more appropriate quickly and meet us by the cemetery as soon as possible, I think we will be summoned for the burial in a few minutes. I too have to hurry and change." She smiled sadly and hugged me. Then she hurried along to the king's chambers. Even as she walked away, I could hear her sobs, and my heart went out to her.

I opened the door to my room and found Billal sitting on the bed. He quickly jumped up when he saw me and walked over to where I was and took me in his arms. I felt really safe in his embrace. I surrendered to every whisper that came from his lips. Comforting words of love and adoration, words that spoke the truth, truth that defied reality, reality that provoked the soul, and the soul that burned with desire, and I became a slave to all that was whispered, for there was no place else for me to go.

I allowed Billal to touch me as he caressed my back. I closed my eyes and thought of Nidal. His hand lowered down my back, and his lips claimed mine. Nidal's arms pulled me closer to his body as I arched my back in total submission. But my tears spilled down my face, and my sobs tore from my throat as I cried aloud for everything I had lost in this lifetime. Reality stuck the knife deeper into my heart, and I was lost forever.

❁ ❁ ❁

Everyone was wearing black. It seemed as if all of Arabia were there. Everyone was crying, even the men. I looked over at Shaeena. She had her veil over her face, and it was hidden from us, but I knew a face full of evil was behind the veil. She was not mourning the dead. She was pretending, and Nidal believed her. But the queen and I knew better. Nidal was holding on to her, and she was leaning on him, pretending she was suffering like everyone else was.

I heard the wails from all the people, but the queen's voice was the loudest by far. Her cries were piercing my ears, and a few sobs tore from my throat. Billal instantly put his arms around me. Nidal was staring. His piercing gaze was making me feel uncomfortable, so I quickly looked away.

The coffins were all laid on the grass, one next to the other. There were thirty-five in all, five big ones and thirty smaller ones. It was a horrible scene, heart-wrenching. When it was all over, everyone started to walk away. The cries were unbearable. No one would forget the lives lost. This day marked a day of the year that would be remembered for ages to come.

The king looked indifferent to all the lives lost. He looked impatient to be done with the funeral. He was in a hurry to leave the premises, as he pushed everyone out of his way and marched back to the palace. I wondered if his guilty conscience had gotten the better of him and that he was looking for solace in the privacy of his chambers. But knowing his cold heart, he wasn't suffering the loss of all the humans who died in the fire without a cause. He was angry that Natalie was still alive. A cold chill ran up and down my spine at the thought of that. *Is he planning the next fate for Natalie? Does he want to finish the job himself?* The queen and I needed to protect Natalie as best we could. She was blameless, innocent of any wrongdoing, a helpless child of God.

We ended up in the tearoom with a select few. I drank my tea quietly, looked around the room, and noticed that Nidal was not sitting next to the princess. He was sitting at the other end of the room with a few gentlemen engaged in conversation. Shaeena was sipping her tea by herself, and she looked as if she were in deep thought, as if she were emotionally disturbed. *Good! Let her suffer for the rest of her life for what she has done!*

Billal was sitting next to me, and he gently rested his hand on my thigh. I quickly looked over at Nidal and saw him immediately tense up when he witnessed Billal touching me. I wondered why I still cared after what he had put me through. Billal, on the other hand, was so good to me. He wiped away my tears when Nidal punished me without reason. Billal's warm embrace brought serenity to my life. Without thinking, I placed my hand over his.

Nidal jumped up that instant and marched out of the room. Shaeena went running after him. I glanced at the queen, and she winked at me. We both knew the mind and heart of the princess. She was heartless, and she was someone to fear. Billal squeezed my hand, and I smiled at him. He was so kindhearted, and I wanted to make him happy. He deserved it. We both rose from our chairs at the same time and exited the tearoom. We climbed silently up the stairs to our room, and once inside, I fell into his arms and kissed him hungrily. No words were needed as he kissed me back. Billal lifted me up in his arms, walked over to the bed, and gently dropped me on it. He lay next to me and continued to kiss me passionately. His kisses were hot and sweet. I enjoyed his lips on mine, but they were not Nidal's kisses I tasted, and my heart sank into oblivion.

I closed my eyes and pretended Nidal was kissing me. I wrapped my arms around him and slid my body close to him. I fantasized Nidal's lips on mine, his shaft rubbing against me, as his hands undressed me in the heat of the moment. I lost my senses as I accepted this emotional encounter with Billal. He knew how I felt. He knew exactly what was going on here. Billal could not blame me for anything. He was taking advantage of me, not the other way around. I was the one who was vulnerable, not him. This was like a game to him. I had played this game before. I never won. I was never good at it, but I played anyway.

The kiss did not last long. Billal pulled back and just stared into my eyes. He knew. Billal was a very intelligent person. I wish I knew what he was thinking at this very moment. He looked very emotional as he stared at me, speechless. I sighed and looked away. I knew not how to comfort him. I was in dire need of someone comforting me at this time too. A miserable silence followed as Billal slipped out of my embrace.

"I am so sorry, Billal. Please, can you forgive me?" The bitterness of my own voice startled me.

Billal stared at me in silence for several long moments. Then he scrambled off the bed and glanced sideways. "Humor me and say it wasn't Nidal who was on your mind when you were kissing me!"

I was tired, exhausted to be exact, to feel or say much of anything at this moment as I looked up drowsily at him through my eyelashes.

"Loula, I can't play your game at this time," he said with a hint of sarcasm in it. "This is not a time to be playing games. This is real stuff, and I am hurting here! You can't play with people's lives like that!" His voice held a dangerous softness as he looked at me with a piercing gaze.

I knew a high color flooded my cheeks. I was temporarily frozen from embarrassment at his words. I dropped my face on the pillow to cover myself from his accusing stare. I heard his footsteps walk away from the bed as an agonizing sound rumbled from his throat. He was suffering. I could tell. Seconds later, the door opened, and he stepped out and slammed it shut behind him. I winced at the sound it made as the door closed, and I felt guilty about everything. I subconsciously rubbed my abdomen, and tears welled up in my eyes almost immediately. I was hurting the only person who ever cared about me, and I did not know how to stop. I was very emotional with this pregnancy. I had made a mess with everything. I knew I must apologize to Billal for my wrongdoing. He deserved a whole lot better than this. I was going to personally see to it that Billal had a smile on his face by tomorrow morning. Exhaustion took me into a deep sleep, and I passed out almost immediately.

The next morning when I awoke, I noticed that Billal was not in bed with me. Alarmed, I quickly jumped out of bed and made my way to the connecting room that was used as a reading room. I found Billal sleeping on the couch. He looked very uncomfortable lying there. His feet were hanging at the end of the sofa. He was too tall to be resting there. I walked over to him, kneeled down, and kissed his lips. Billal grabbed me by the waist and pulled me aggressively to him as he kissed me back hungrily. When the kiss ended, I was left speechless.

Billal looked at me, and his eyes sparkled. "What? You take me for a fool? I saw an opportunity to kiss you, and I took it," he said wolfishly, and he smiled from ear to ear.

I breathed a sigh of relief. *Billal is not mad at me anymore*, I thought happily.

"Loula, you drive me mad!" Billal playfully played with my hair. "Every time I try to stay mad at you, I cannot. You have an effect on me that makes me crazy. I do not know what tomorrow will bring, but as for today, I know without a doubt that you are my life. I love you, Loula, and I will stay by your side until you ask me to leave," he said without a trace of regret in his voice.

I recklessly threw myself at him once again, and we kissed, but this time, it was not a game. I wanted to kiss him. I wanted to taste his lips on mine, and as we kissed, I did not once think of Nidal. I knew exactly whose arms I was in and whose lips were on mine, and I treasured this moment with my heart. I was exactly where I needed to be, in Billal's sweet arms.

Chapter Fifteen
Nidal

It had not been easy living with me these last few days. I hated myself, and I hated everything I had become. Every morning when I looked in the mirror, I did not like what I saw. I was once innocent of wrongdoing, living my life like a child should. At fifteen, I fell in love, and my whole world turned upside down. I wasn't good at loving. I took another's life and destroyed it. I turned Loula's world upside down. I did not mean to. I loved her, and that love I felt tortured me every day of my life. Everywhere I turned, her memory was there. I could smell her in the air. Her perfume lingered everywhere she visited. I could see her in my heart, mind, and soul, for her image was stamped there forever. I could hear her laughter in the wind as she ran playfully in the garden and fell into my embrace. I could feel her at night when I lay down to sleep. She was there in bed with me and in my mind as I touched myself and made sweet passionate love to her.

I tried really hard to get her out of my mind. I rejected every thought of her. I tried over and over again to erase her existence, but to no avail. She was, is, and always would be my soul mate.

And I accepted that and came to terms with it. I would always love her as long as I lived, and even beyond that into infinity!

The day I found Billal sucking on Loula's breast was almost the end of my life. I almost killed myself, unable to handle the scene I witnessed. It was like the end of the world. The walls closed in on me, and I suffocated. During that time, I saw something else, the bigger picture. I looked on the brighter side for the first time. She was alive and well. She was in good hands. I knew Billal loved her too, and above all, she was not in any immediate danger from the king. Let everyone think that Billal was her lover. That would keep her safe until I came up with a plan to whisk her away from here and into a life with me, living happily ever after, together in bliss. So even though my heart hurt to know that she found solace in Billal's arms, I knew in my heart that it was only temporary and I soon would be the one to hold her and make sweet love to her for the rest of her life. She was mine and would always be mine. To death do us part. And even then, my soul would find her, and we would live together thereafter, wherever that may be.

When the fire happened, I was beside myself with grief. Those innocent children and servants did not deserve to die like that. When I saw Loula, my heart, running into the burning building, I almost died right there and then. My heart stopped, and I was left speechless. I did what I had to do to get Loula out, even when she went back in and almost caused me to have a heart attack. I pulled her out of the fire and stepped back as Billal came running to her and took her in his arms. I allowed it because it had to be that way for now. It guaranteed her safety.

At the funeral, I cried for all the victims who died in the fire. My heart went out to Loula. I knew she was in a lot of pain. She had loved those children as her own. I too felt pain in my heart for all the lives lost unnecessarily in the fire, a fire that my father likely started.

I hate him. He is evil. My mother is trapped in this marriage with nowhere else to go. I can't do anything about it. This is her fate. There is nowhere for her to run. But for me, it is different. I will run. I will take Loula and run like the wind out of here one day.

The king, my father, is a very ruthless man, and he has his eyes on Loula. He is waiting for a chance to strike against her. He sees Loula as a threat to the crown. The real threat is the king himself. He is the one who is the threat to his own crown. He is self-destructive. This country cannot and will not flourish with him in reign. One day, his kingdom will collapse. But I do not care. I will be long gone by then. I will take Loula and run the hell out of this land. We will live our lives without animosity. We will live in love.

Loula says she is pregnant, and she claims her child's father is Billal. I do not believe her. I know she has not slept with Billal yet. Therefore, the child she carries is mine. I allow her to think that I do not know. It ensures the child's safety. If my father knew or even suspected it is mine, he would destroy the pregnancy, and I would die a thousand deaths, knowing that two of my babies have died. So for now, I will watch Loula get big with child and adore her from afar.

At times, I cannot hold back, and my anger gets the better of me, like the times I fight with Billal. It feels so good when I punch him. He wants Loula, and he thinks he can take her just like that. I will never give her up, not to him or anyone else in the world. She is mine and mine alone! When Billal spoke to my father about taking Loula to be his wife, the king agreed and was relieved to see that things were going smoothly for him. What he doesn't know is that I will never ever allow Loula to be wife to Billal or anyone else either! She is mine, all mine now and forever until death do us part. This I swear by all that is holy. If I can't have a life with Loula, then I will kill myself, for there is no life for me without her.

Today as I lay in bed with Shaeena—yes, I now sleep in the bed with her—I am not afraid. I can control myself. I do not lust for the princess. I lust after Loula. As I lie here looking up at the ceiling, I wonder what the future has in store for us. Shaeena is sleeping restlessly. As she tosses and turns, I look at her and see a sleeping beauty. She is very beautiful, and she could have the whole world in the palm of her hands if she chose to. Instead, she insists on marrying me and claiming her child as mine. She is greedy and ruthless just like the king. I know the baby in her stomach is not mine, but I play along with her games for now. It is very crucial that she believe that I am getting comfortable with her, for that is the only way I can keep her from hurting Loula, but when I am ready, I will strike, and she will not know what hit her.

The princess moaned. As she turned toward me and opened her eyes wide, she let out an eerie scream and clutched her big stomach. "Nidal, our baby. I think it's time. Call for the doctor quick." She screamed again.

I quickly jumped out of bed and ran to the door. I opened it and called down the corridor for someone to hear me. Almost immediately, a few servants and a guard came running, and I told them to get the doctor hastily. I ran to the king's chamber, opened the door, and called my mother's name, hoping against hope that she had slept here last night.

The queen came running almost immediately to the door. "What happened, Nidal? Are you all right? Where is Loula? Is she all right?" she asked with a worried expression on her face.

"Mother, Loula and I are just fine, worry not. I came here to let you know that Shaeena's baby is on its way. Soon the child will be born, and I need you to come along with me to assist with the delivery."

The queen wasted no time, as she quickly dressed, and ran with me to Shaeena's side. She was in labor, and she was screaming with pain. I winced at her loud screams. Even though I did not like her, I did not want her or anyone to be in such pain. I pulled a chair next to the bed and sat there holding her hand until the doctor came.

Everyone was chased out of the room, with the exception of the servants who were given orders from the doctor to get warm, clean sheets and boiling water. Everyone scrambled to do their duty. My mother insisted she stay in the room to help with the delivery. The doctor looked at her with compassion in his eyes and something more. I could not put my finger on it, but he allowed her to stay and assist him. The door was closed in my face, and I paced the hallway back and forth, as if the child she were about to deliver was mine.

The screams inside the room became louder as Shaeena wailed and cried out in pain, a reminder that I was better off being a male instead of a female and having to suffer giving birth like that. Finally after what seemed like hours later, I heard the baby's cries, and my heart warmed. I opened the door and entered the room. The princess lay in bed, and she looked peaceful. I had never seen her look this way before.

The baby, a beautiful baby girl, lay on top of her, already suckling her mother's breast. It was really a touching sight. My mother was standing with the doctor next to the bed, smiling down at the mother and child, proud of themselves for helping bring an angel into this world.

I was at a loss for words. It was a beautiful sight. My eyes welled up in tears, and at that second, I thought of Loula and the baby she had lost. My baby, taken from us by this woman who held her baby in her arms. Loula was right. Shaeena had her baby, but our baby was dead. And it was all Shaeena's fault. I turned around and stalked out of there. I did not belong in there. This was not my child. My child slept peacefully in Loula's womb. And I would do everything I could to protect it, including allowing Loula and Billal to claim the baby as theirs. It would ensure its safety.

I raced down the corridor to the double wooden doors that led to the gardens. I stepped outside and breathed in fresh air. I walked down the stairs and headed straight for the rose bushes. It was time to smell the roses. I reached over, pulled a few flowers to my nose, and breathed in the heavenly smell. Its scent made me drunk with its perfume. I closed my eyes and imagined Loula here next to me. It was a good feeling.

A hand lightly touched my shoulders, and I turned abruptly, startled, and saw Loula standing behind me, smiling. She took my breath away. She was so beautiful. I had not seen her for a few days, and I grabbed her, pulled her in my arms, and kissed her passionately. She kissed me back, and I lost myself in sweet ecstasy.

Reluctantly, we pulled apart, looked in each other's eyes, and saw tears of happiness in them.

"I love you," I told her passionately and didn't wait for her to respond. I pulled her close to me again and claimed her lips one more time.

This time, Loula pulled away and asked sarcastically, "Are you the proud father of a baby girl or a little baby boy, Nidal?"

My heart twisted painfully at her choice of words. I grabbed her shoulders and shook her lightly. "I am not the father of her child. I told you before. I have not had sex with her. I did not get her pregnant! You must believe this, Loula. I am not the father!" I knew what her next words would be.

"Even if you are not the father of this baby, Nidal, you did have sex with her. I saw you, remember?" She dared me to deny her words.

I winced. I knew exactly what she meant. But that was not fair. I had been drunk, and I thought I was making love to her. "You know as well as I do that I was drunk that night. I would never have sex with anyone but you. What do I have to do to make you understand my feelings for you? You are my world, my life. You are the very air that I breathe! I cannot ... will not ... live a life without you! I will never marry Shaeena! You are my wife in every way that matters, and Loula, I am yours and yours alone." I prayed that she would understand and forgive me all my mistakes against her. "Please, Loula, say you forgive me, and tell me that I too am the love of your life. Please, release me of my suffering. I am tortured every day living without you. Please say you love me still, Loula, and I will die a happy man." I was unable to keep the tears from spilling down my face.

Loula looked at me speechless. I read all the emotions playing on her lovely face. Disharmony was in her life, and it was my fault. I did not mean to hurt her. I was deeply sorry for any pain I caused her.

Finally, she spoke, "Nidal, if you die, I will die too, for I too cannot live a life without you in it. You are my everything. I love you so much that I hurt just thinking about it. I will never stop loving you." She fell into my arms, and we kissed like there was no tomorrow.

"I need to make love to you. It's been so long, and I can't wait any longer." I looked into her eyes and saw the depth of her love for me in them.

Loula took me by the hand and pulled me further back in the gardens, to the place I hid when I was a child. I looked around, and it was secluded. Loula pulled the strings to my pantaloons, and I was beside myself with lust. I undid the ties on the back of her gown, and as it dropped to the floor, I saw Loula standing there stark naked. Her nipples were ripe and full, and there was a baby bump. My hands caressed her stomach lightly.

I closed my eyes and allowed my hands to feel every inch of her stomach, and I said hoarsely, "I know this is my child you are carrying. Don't even try to deny it. I know without a doubt that what I say is true! I am the father. This is my baby, Loula!" The tears slid down my face.

Loula was speechless. She did not say a single word. I could tell she was very emotional. She too had tears rolling down her cheek as well. I wanted to find comforting words to say to her, but I knew not what to tell her. These were troubling times. Loula was not in favor with the king; nor was I. We were on our own. My father was the most powerful man in Arabia. With a snap of his finger, he could destroy us. He had it out for Loula. She was in grave danger, but I would not tell her so. I did not wish to alarm her. She was with child, and I did not want to frighten her any more than she already was.

I focused on something positive, like the fact that my heart sang a happy song whenever she was in my arms and the fact that she carried my child in her womb. Right now, here in the garden on this glorious day, I held her, and I knew without a doubt that her heart belonged to me.

I quickly undressed, and we both fell down on the green grass. As I entered her, my name was on her lips as she gave herself to me. This woman was my life, and as I spilled my seed in her, I looked into her eyes. I knew she was in total submission at this very moment in my arms. Spent, I rolled off her and wiped the tears from her face. These were tears of joy. I knew this because I too had the very same kind of tears rolling down my face.

We only had a few minutes left to be together. Lingering in this garden, together like this, was putting ourselves and our baby in danger. If someone were to see us, my father would seek the death penalty for Loula. Who knew what kind of punishment he would bestow on me. I didn't care what he did to me, but I was afraid for Loula and my child.

Loula saw the fear in my eyes. "Nidal, what is wrong?" she asked, alarmed. "And do not say that nothing is wrong. I can see it in your eyes. You are worried. I can tell." She pulled herself up into a sitting position. "Tell me, please. I want to know what is troubling you," she begged.

I sighed and slumped my shoulders. I felt defeated. "Loula, my love for you has no end, but I am but a prince. I am not the king yet. My father, he has all the power, and I fear he has set out his anger on you. He has targeted you, and I know not what to do." I didn't know how to tell her the rest. "Loula, listen very carefully to what I tell you. It is very important that you do as I say. Your life depends on it." I hoped against hope that I didn't scare her too much. "It was smart of you to claim our baby as Billal's. That ensures its safety, even though it kills me not to be able to claim my own child. At least for the time being, our baby is safe. We must play this game until I figure out what to do. It is crucial that no one suspects our motives," I warned. "It kills me every time I see you with Billal. Just knowing that you share the same bed at night is enough for me to want to strangle him. But we have no choice. We must continue to do what we do to ensure the safety of you and our baby." I said what I needed to say to make her understand what was at stake here.

Loula stared at me wide-eyed. She tried to talk, but I quickly sealed her lips with mine. I kissed her passionately, not wanting to ever let her go. They were stolen kisses, worth a million words. If only we were in a faraway land, where we were free to run with the wind, free of all the responsibilities and misery of this world, I would have been the happiest man in this world. I slid down and kissed Loula's stomach, where our child slept.

I kissed it a hundred times, and I said softly, "Little one, this is Papa. I love you so much, and I love your mother just as much as I love you. And one day, we will live together happily ever after."

I heard Loula stifle a cry as she heard my words.

Our time in the garden was not enough. It would never be enough. But we both knew what we had to do, and there was no other way out of it. We dressed quickly and headed back to the palace, and just as we came from around the bushes, Billal was there. His eyes were full of hate as he looked at me. He knew what had just transpired, but he also knew that he could not do a damn thing about it.

Billal stretched out his hand to Loula. "Come quickly. The king is looking for us," he said coldly.

She went to him without a second glance toward me. I wanted to rip out Billal's throat, but I restrained myself. I needed him to play his part. At least it guaranteed Loula's safety. They disappeared inside the palace, and I was alone once again. It was painful to see Loula walking away with Billal. I knew he would stop at nothing to win Loula's affections. I just hoped that she had the strength to keep him at bay.

I wondered what my father wanted Billal and Loula for. I picked up my pace. I needed to be there when the king talked to them so I could hear everything that was being said. I opened the doors to the palace and stepped inside, just in time to see Billal and Loula enter the tearoom. I ran down the corridor, knocking over a pail of water that the servant had just put there. She was getting ready to mop the marble floor, but I had no time to stop and apologize. I needed to get in the tearoom as quickly as possible.

I stepped in the room, looked around, and saw that it was full of people. They had all come to welcome the newborn baby into this world. If only they knew the hard-core truth. I wondered what their reaction would be. I looked into their faces and realized they were just people living their lives. They cared not who sired the baby. They only cared to please the king and be in his favor.

I knew my father had an important announcement to make, and I wondered what it could be. Billal escorted Loula to the empty chair by the window, and she sat in it. Her eyes avoided me as I walked up next to my father and waited patiently to hear what he had to say. The king had a satisfied grin on his face, and the queen sat nervously next to him. At that moment, she looked up sadly at me, and my heart skipped a beat. All the blood drained from my face as I realized what the king was about to announce.

"Ladies and gentlemen," he said as he stood and walked in the middle of the room, "as you all know, my granddaughter came into this world today, and we must celebrate. Everyone, raise your glass. I would like to make a toast to the new addition to our family." The king raised his glass in the air before bringing it to his lips and swallowed the wine in one gulp. He refilled the glass with more wine, raised his glass again, and said with a hint of satisfaction, "I have one more toast to make. Tomorrow, I will give Loula's hand in marriage to my nephew, Prince Billal. They make a handsome couple, and I am pleased to announce that she carries his child. May God bless their union," he said triumphantly. Then he turned and looked at me, arching his eyebrow as if daring me to speak.

If I had a sword in my hand right now, I swear I would gladly have stuck it in his evil heart. He was ruthless, and he was out for blood. I smiled at him, and then I clapped my hands, acting as if I were pleased with his words. Everyone in the room joined me and clapped too. The king looked at me with a lazy grin. He knew me better than anyone else, and he was one step ahead of me. But I too knew him better than anyone else, and I too was one step ahead of him.

Everyone drank their wine and wasted no time wishing the happy couple a wonderful life together. As I lifted my glass to my lips, the wine tasted like poison in my mouth. It burned my throat and settled in my stomach like a ticking time bomb. I did everything in my power to ignore the pain. This pain tightened around my heart and tried to suffocate me.

I looked at my mother. She reluctantly stood, walked up to Loula, and hugged her. But I could tell that my mother was very upset. I would have to explain to her what just happened and why. She was a very strong woman, and I knew she could handle the news without breaking. Perhaps she and I could come up with a plan and outsmart Father.

Billal had a smile on his face, and he looked genuinely happy. He walked up to Loula, took her in his arms, and planted a kiss on her lips. Loula was stiff as a board and did not kiss him back. His hands dropped to his sides, and he silently looked at me as if I were the one stealing his love. He had some nerve. One day, I would kill him with my bare hands. *Let him think that he has won this time around, and when he least expects it, I will pounce on him and rip out his throat!*

Everyone was drinking their wine and engaging in conversation with each other. At least twenty-five couples were in the room, and they all looked suspiciously at Loula and me. They all knew that something was not right, but they did not have the guts to say anything. Everyone in this room, including me, was afraid of the king. But I feared my father because I was afraid he would make good on his threat about Loula. I did not fear him for any other reason. I despised him, and nothing would please me more than to kill him with my bare hands.

Billal held on to Loula's hand as if his life depended on it. *Poor soul, he does not want to believe the truth that Loula's heart belongs to me. Billal is delusional, living in a world of make-believe. He is sleepwalking through life, and he is in for a rude awakening!*

"Son, shouldn't you be with Shaeena and your baby daughter? You have been gone from their side for quite a while now. Go now. We do not want to hold you up. Run along." The king waved his hand in the air and dismissed me from the room, as if I were but a ten-year-old boy.

Humiliated, I was at a loss for words. To everyone in this room, I looked like the bad husband/father for not being attentive to my new family, so I had no choice but to bow and excuse myself.

I felt Billal's eyes on my back as I opened the door and stepped out. I shut my eyes for a second and tried to control my anger. It really wasn't worth it. In all reality, I should not be upset by anything Billal said or did. I knew Loula's heart belonged to me, and deep down, so did Billal. I walked through the corridor, but I did not go to my room. I walked past it and headed back to the gardens. I felt serenity when I was standing among nature's gifts, and at this moment, I needed to be calm and relaxed and get all the poison out of my heart.

The king said that Loula was to marry Billal tomorrow. That was too soon. I knew not what to do. *Tomorrow?* My pulse quickened, and I felt tortured. I could not let this happen. I needed a plan, a quick one. I had to find a way to stall the wedding. There was no way in this world that I would allow the wedding to take place.

I looked around in the rose garden that my mother herself had planted years ago when I was born. It was beautiful here, so peaceful. I looked beyond the gardens, farther down, where the rolling meadows rolled out their carpet of lush green grass. When I was a child, I ran across the meadow chasing rabbits and all kinds of stuff. Life was innocent then. It was not poisoned with hate and greed.

So many things troubled my mind. My thoughts went back to Shaeena's baby. It was a beautiful tiny bundle of joy. *Who is the father? Could it be Billal?* I would never know. For all I knew, anyone could be the father, but Billal seemed the best candidate. I wondered why he did not want to claim the child.

Could it be because he loves Loula so much that he is not willing to lose her? Could the love he feels for Loula run so deep that he is willing to overlook the fact he is now a father? He is willing to give up his parental rights just to have a life with Loula. What kind of a man is he? Maybe he is not the father. In all reality, I have not seen him with the princess in that way. Maybe the father of her child is someone else. It could be anyone. What if the princess is right and I fathered her child? What then?

But deep in my heart, the only baby I wanted to claim as mine was Loula's. The only reason I did not claim Loula's baby as mine now was because I was afraid of the king's threats. I wanted to ensure my baby's safety.

But what ails Billal so that he does not want to claim his own child? Is he even the father? I cannot tell for sure, and if he is not, then who else could it be? I could not imagine there being anyone else. The princess is a smart lady. She would not sleep around without a reason. Could I be the father of her child? I do not remember sleeping with her. I would never sleep with her willingly. The three days I slept at her house, I don't remember a single thing. I blacked out. How odd that those three whole days of my life have been wiped out of my memory. How can that be?

As I walked back to the palace, I thought of Shaeena. *What drives her to claim me as the father? Is it because she loves me, or is the real reason because she wants to be queen one day? Is she love-hungry, power-hungry, or both? Or could I really be the father?*

This thought sent cold shivers up and down my spine. *If I were the father, it would be a sad day because I feel no bond with the baby. She is not mine. Shaeena is hiding the truth, but one day, the truth will come out. I would not stop searching for the truth until I found it.*

I took the steps two at a time, and when I reached the double doors, I opened them just in time to witness my father come out of my room. *Was he visiting Shaeena and the baby to wish her well, or did Shaeena and my father plot against me?*

I had to find out the truth. I hurriedly walked to my chamber and opened the door. The baby was still feeding off Shaeena's other breast, and if it were not for all the craziness that was happening around us, I could easily have said that I had not ever seen a more beautiful sight than a mother and child bonding in this way.

I closed the door behind me and walked up to the bed. I looked down and could not help but smile. The baby looked content in the warmth of her mother's arms. Shaeena looked up at me and smiled back.

"How are you feeling, Shaeena?" I asked, not really caring for the answer, but just wanting to sound polite.

Shaeena hesitated before she spoke, as if she were trying to choose her words very carefully. "The baby and I are doing well. As you can see, Nidal, your daughter is enjoying her dinner. If you had come a few minutes ago, you would have had the chance to hold your child," she said wearily. "The king was just here, and he gave us his blessings. Where were you, Nidal?" she asked, waiting patiently for an answer.

"I was in the gardens, taking a stroll. I had a few things on my mind, and I just needed some space." I didn't care for her response, which I knew was coming anyway.

I walked to the other end of the room and sat on the couch. I was frustrated with my life. I just wanted all this to end.

Shaeena was struggling to stay awake. I knew she was really tired from giving birth, and it was only a matter of time before sleep took her. The baby wiggled in her arms and started to yawn as its little body stretched. This little person was related to me. She had royal blood running in her veins. But even so, she was not my daughter. She was Billal's. I was almost sure of it. My baby was in my lover's womb, and I was going to do whatever it took to keep her safe. Shaeena and the baby finally fell asleep.

I walked out of the room and lightly closed the door behind me, lest the baby wake up and then Shaeena would not get the rest that any mother who just gave birth deserved. I headed toward the dining room. It was almost dinnertime. I was the first to arrive. The servants scrambled to set the dining table as they threw a tablecloth on it that was probably worth more than all the furniture in this room put together. *Why would the king squander his money like that? Why not put that good money to better use? Like rebuilding the orphanage and bringing in the children who are orphaned from around the country? I'm sure more of them need warm beds to sleep in and hot soup to fill their tummies.*

I pulled out my chair and sat in it. I put my elbows on the table and rested my head on my hands. I was really tired of life. One would think that I, the crown prince of Arabia, with everything at my fingertips at the snap of a finger, would be pleasantly pleased with my life. But that was far from the truth. I was handsome, rich, famous, loved by all the females of this country, and envied by all the males. I had Loula, the love of my entire life, the reason for my existence. Without her, I was nothing, an empty shell of a man who would cease to exist. I had everything a man could desire, and I was not happy. I was miserable and lonely, and my heart was tortured.

A tear escaped, rolled down my face, and landed on the silk napkin that was neatly folded on the table, just as the servant put an empty plate in front of me, a plate that was of fine bone china with gold trimming around it. This plate alone easily cost a peasant's monthly wages. *A stupid plate worth so much! One plate alone could feed a family for a month!* I looked around the room at all the other riches. Tapestries and famous paintings decorated the walls. Crystal and porcelain decorated the table. I saw silver water pitchers, fine crystal goblets, and utensils made of silver and gold. All fit for a king, a king who was selfish and greedy, a king who was not worthy to wear the crown.

At that moment, the door burst open, and people started to pour in. The king and queen came first, followed by several of the king's men. The second- and third-in-command came in next, and then my heart started to beat faster. Billal walked in, holding Loula's hand as he gently pulled her around the table to their usual seats, across from where I sat. Loula stole a quick glance at me and then lowered her eyes to the table. My heart skipped a beat. I loved this woman so much, and it hurt to be across the table from her instead of next to her. She was mine, and I had no rights to her according to my father. I sighed. This was not as easy as I thought it would be.

Billal acted as if he had every right to be sitting next to Loula. One day, I would wipe that smirk off his face. *Son of a bitch!* He deliberately pushed my buttons. He got a high seeing me suffer. *Well, how about I play his game for once?* Slowly, I pushed my leg forward, and my foot was next to Loula's, rubbing her ankle. It took her by surprise. Wide-eyed, she looked over at me nervously. I raised my foot a little higher, and Loula squirmed in her seat.

Billal was having conversation with the man who sat to his right. The man kept wiping his sweaty bald spot with his napkin, obviously nervous about something as he chatted away. He had Billal's undivided attention. Billal was oblivious to my actions. I brought my foot between Loula's legs and rested it on her private part, and her eyes opened wide with fear. I almost laughed aloud. This was hysterical. But as I continued to rub her most private part, my shaft was taking control of the situation, and it wasn't funny anymore. I could tell that Loula was getting turned on too. Her eyelids were half-closed, and her hands were pulling the napkin she was holding. She closed her legs tight around my foot, and I almost lost control. This was a very dangerous game that I was playing. I immediately pulled away my foot, and I saw Loula's eyes open as she shot a glance my way, questioning my motives. I looked away from her before I gave myself away and every person here tonight found me out. It would place us in a very dangerous situation. I hoped Loula was able to read my mind and understand why I did what I did.

I looked at her now. My face was somber, and I noticed she was spaced out. She was coming in her underpants. I could tell by the expression on her face. I wanted to be inside her at this very moment. She was having her moment without me. I was jealous of her underwear that got to touch her skin, while I was at the other side of the table. I wanted to reach over and take her here and now. I could feel myself getting ready to explode.

I must stop this immediately. I made eye contact with Loula and winked. She lowered her head, but not before I motioned with my eyes toward the door, letting her know that I wanted her to meet me in the gardens tonight. I knew my moves were very risky, but I could not help myself. I needed to touch her body. I needed to make love to her tonight. My shaft was hurting. I needed to release it from its pain, and only Loula could do that.

Dinner was served, and I suddenly lost my appetite. I glanced over at Loula, and I saw she too was nibbling at her dinner. With trembling hands, I reached for my wine goblet and drank, washing down my sorrows.

At that moment the king asked, "Nidal, how is Shaeena and the baby?" There was a nasty look in his beady eyes. I wanted to spit in his face. I wanted to tell him to go to hell, but I held my tongue and plastered a fake smile on my face.

"They are faring just fine, Father. They are resting now."

He looked pleased with my answer, and finally, Father geared the conversation away from me. I was glad not to be the center of attention. It was just like my father to always want to make me feel uncomfortable. He was a master at destroying lives.

At that moment, the king hit the table with his fist and demanded more wine to be brought to him. My poor mother was startled, along with everyone else who sat at the table. The servants were shaking in their boots as they poured wine in the king's goblet.

The king raised his glass. "Let's drink a toast to the new member of the royal family."

Everyone raised their glasses in the air.

"God bless the baby and its mother," they all said cheerfully.

I too raised my glass and thanked everyone for their warm wishes. Then I rested my eyes on Loula, who was trying to hide her tears by this time. She swallowed, turned to Billal, and asked him to pass her the salt, and as Billal did as he was told, Loula quickly glanced at me and nodded lightly before she turned and grabbed the saltshaker from Billal's hand.

I felt a warm rush inside my body. She had just let me know that she accepted my invitation to meet her tonight in the gardens. I would wait for her all night if I had to. I needed her to touch me like no other woman ever had. Only she could clench my thirst. My shaft was swollen, and it hurt. I placed my hand on it, trying to cover up the evidence, but it was no use. It was throbbing with pain. I stood quickly, excused myself, and practically ran out of the room.

Out in the hallway, I headed for the nearest bathroom. I had to relieve some of the pain my shaft was feeling. I opened the door and stepped inside, and I quickly pulled out my swollen shaft and started to play with it. Almost immediately I came, and I felt such relief. As I was washing my hands, I looked in the mirror and saw my face. It was red from the heat of the moment, and a wave of anger took over my heart and mind. I played with myself like a jack-off. I was a jack-off. I punched the mirror and watched it shatter to pieces as it fell into the sink. My hand was throbbing with pain as the blood rushed down my arm. I took the towel that was folded neatly next to the sink on a cherrywood table and wrapped it around my hand to stop the bleeding. This had to stop. I was going crazy. I needed to have a talk with Loula tonight. We had to come up with a plan. I needed her. I wanted her badly.

I walked out of the bathroom, and a couple of servants were standing outside the door with a broom and a dustpan in their hands, waiting for me to leave so they could clean up. *They knew*, I thought wildly. They had that knowing look on their face. I marched outside the palace and walked straight to the back of the gardens where my hiding place was. I threw myself down on the grass and cried like a little baby. I had become someone else. *Whatever happened to my ego? Where had my self-esteem gone? Who have I become?*

I was always so sure of myself. I was strong and proud of who I was. Every man wanted to be me. I was envied throughout the country. I used to chase the women from a young age. Now I barely noticed them. I used to wet my pants thinking about screwing all of them, and now I only desired Loula. *Am I a fool, or am I a man in love?* I lay there waiting, frustrated and hoping that Loula would come soon.

Hours later, when the lit torches were about to let go of their flame and diminish what little light lit the pathway to where I lay, I awoke from a brief sleep that I must have slipped into. I heard bare feet walking softly on the grass heading where I lay. I squinted and tried to make out the face of the onlooker, making sure it was her. When I confirmed it, I jumped up and grabbed her, pulling her to me. She collapsed into my arms as we kissed passionately. We dropped to the floor and undressed, shedding our garments quickly as we panted for breath. Naked, I wasted no time plunging into her with such force that I almost forgot she had my baby inside her womb.

Loula cried out like a wanton woman as I slammed deep inside her. We both climaxed at the same time, and our bodies shuddered in ecstasy as we lay now in each other's arms, sweating and out of breath. I whispered my love for her in the dark. This was what I lived for. This was what I would one day die for.

My eyes drifted over her breasts and down her belly, and a strangled sound escaped my lips. I was still aroused, and my shaft was still throbbing. I wondered if Loula felt the same as I did as my hands reached between her legs and I skillfully played her until she screamed for me to take her one more time. I was bewildered as to why fate wanted to punish us by keeping us apart. This was what I was born to do. This was my fate. This was my sweet obsession. I waited and entered her slowly this time. I wanted her to beg for me to take her. And beg she did.

She cried for me to make love to her, to take her to new heights she had never reached before. She cried my name again and again until tears rolled down her face. I shuddered wildly inside her as I came, spilling my seed once again inside her. She purred like a wild cat and collapsed in my arms. We both lay there, our bodies still trembling from our lovemaking. I trailed kisses along her long, slender neck, and she intertwined her fingers in my hair and pulled my head down until my lips reached and sucked at her breasts. She moved in rhythm to my body. I was still inside her, and she could not get enough of me or I of her. How many people could say that their love life was as powerful as ours? No one could because it didn't exist anywhere else in the universe. We had it all right here under the stars, and that was why I could never let her go. She was my match in every way. I would die for her if I had to.

The moon cast its moonbeams on Loula's body, and she looked like a goddess as she lifted her body to a sitting position and her hair fell down her waist. I held my breath. Her beauty was above and beyond anything I had ever seen. With trembling hands, I reached up and caressed her breast. They were much fuller than I knew them to be. It was because she was with child, my child.

I closed my eyes and pulled her to me. As she lay on top of me, I asked hoarsely, "Do you love me?" I held my breath as I waited for her reply. I knew the answer, but I still wanted to hear it from her lips. It had been a while since she last told me, and I yearned to hear it again.

"You know I do, Nidal. I love you desperately with every fiber of my being. I love you more than I love myself, but not more than I love my child, Nidal," she said passionately.

And I looked at her and said hoarsely, "Our child, Loula. It is our child." I claimed her mouth before she uttered another word.

Hours later, spent and exhausted, just before the sun rose, we reluctantly got up and walked back to the palace. We promised each other that we would meet like this many times again. Neither of us mentioned the wedding that was supposed to take place today. In our hearts, we pretended that it was not happening as we kissed each other one last time before we entered the palace.

We both tiptoed down the corridor, not wanting to make any noise, lest the servants or, worse yet, Shaeena or Billal hear us. And as we parted, my heart went with her up the stairs to her room. I slipped inside my room quietly and found Shaeena breastfeeding the baby. She followed me with her eyes to the bathroom. Minutes later when I came out, she said not one word to me as I lay next to her in bed and fell asleep as soon as my head hit the pillow. I had nightmares all night, and when I woke up early the next morning, it was to a little baby crying. The tiny little bundle of joy was not happy, and her mother was not able to calm her down.

I jumped out of bed and headed straight for the bathroom, closing the door behind me. I went to the sink to wash my face and remembered that today was the day my beloved was going to marry Billal. My heart hammered against my chest at the thought of Loula married to that man. I needed to find a way to stop the wedding. At that moment, I heard commotion in the room. Concerned, I opened the bathroom door just in time to hear the servant shouting in tears that the king had had a heart attack. My heart pumped fiercely at the announcement, and I wasted no time as I raced out of the room wearing only my underpants and headed toward my father's bedchamber.

My mother was crying, and she begged God to spare her husband's life. I wrapped myself with my father's silk robe that lay by the chair next to his bed. I took my mother in my arms, and tried to comfort her. The doctor had just arrived and was seeing to Father. I heard the ringing of the bells in the tower. They were letting the people know something serious had happened. My father looked dead as he lay there, but I could see his chest rising and falling slowly, a sign he was still alive. I walked over to my father, and a lump formed in my throat. I was mad at him, but I still loved him and did not wish him ill. I dropped to my knees by his side, and my mother joined me. We both prayed to God for his well-being.

Moments later, the doctor completed his check-up. "The king will survive the heart attack. He needs rest and by no means is any one allowed to stress him out in any way. His heart is weak and it needs to regain its strength back," he said firmly.

The doctor and I left the room, leaving Mother and the servants behind to watch over the king.

"Doctor, would you mind kindly if you stayed at the palace until Father is out of danger?" I begged.

"Of course I will stay. It is my duty to make sure the king is out of danger," he said without hesitation.

The doctor's quarters were just down the hall from my father's bedchamber. He had been given his own space here at the palace ever since Loula and Shaeena had been with child. In case of an emergency, he had to be on call all day and all night until the babies were born, but there were times where he left for days at a time to attend to things that needed his attention at his home where his practice was located.

I leaned against the wall for support, allowing the tears to stream down my face. They were not all painful tears. They were happy tears as well. Although I did not want any harm to befall my father, the heart attack he had suffered meant there would be no wedding today. This would allow me some time to come up with a plan, one that would ensure the safety of Loula and our baby. I wiped away the tears and thanked the good Lord for helping my father stay alive and for allowing me more time to figure out what to do.

The palace was full of people, yet there was not a single sound to be heard. It was for the king's benefit that all was quiet. He needed his rest, and everyone did his or her best to comply. I stayed with my father the whole day, and I even slept in the room at night to keep an eye on him while my mother went to her chambers. She was exhausted, and I sent her away to get some rest. She reluctantly left, and I promised her that I would send for her if anything changed.

Sometime in the middle of the night, sleep had not claimed me yet. I thought I heard a noise in the hallway, and I slowly opened the door to my father's bedchamber and peeked out in the hallway just in time to see my mother slip into the guest room where the doctor was staying and close the door behind her. I was baffled, not understanding what she was doing in that room.

When like a bolt of lightning, it hit me. She was having an affair with the doctor. No wonder he always showed much concern about my mother's welfare. I always thought it odd that he was always around at a moment's notice. Thinking back, I remembered the secret looks he gave my mother when he thought I was not looking. I remembered many times his hand resting on my mother's hand, and I always thought it was a friendly gesture. Now I knew there was more to it.

I could never be angry at my mother if she had been having an affair with him. My father deserved everything he got. He was not an attentive husband. Years ago, he ordered her a different bedchamber, saying he needed space. But I knew that every night thereafter, he brought many women to his bed. He never asked for her to return to his room all these years. It was just recently that I noticed she had been visiting him at night. All those years ago, my mother had been lonely, and she had looked elsewhere for comfort. I blamed her not! I slowly closed the door, tiptoed back to my father's side, and sat in the chair. I was wide awake the rest of the night. Sleep eluded me.

Right before daybreak, I heard my mother's soft footsteps, and I immediately ran to the door. I opened it and I saw my mother quietly enter her own room and close her door, none the wiser. I snuck out of my father's room, and I went to my mother's. I tapped on her door lightly. A second later, the door opened slightly, and she was surprised to see me standing there.

"Is something wrong, Nidal? Did something happen to your father?" she asked, concerned, motioning for me to enter.

I knew not what to say, so I just looked at her in silence. A few seconds later, she mouthed the word "oh" and slumped against the wall. I pulled my mother into my arms and held her tight. She started to cry, and I comforted her.

"Mother, I do not pass judgement on you. Father has mentally abused you for many years. I understand completely your need to take a lover to your bed. Your choice of a lover is a wise one, Mother. The doctor is very discreet, and above all, he is kind and affectionate. He has dedicated his life to the throne, and I for one like him immensely," I told her, hoping to make her feel better.

"Mother, do not feel ashamed. Any woman in your position would have done the same. I hold no grudge against you. In fact, I think you are a very brave woman, and you deserve to be happy. I know Father could never give you the love you need and deserve, so you looked elsewhere." I tried to ease her embarrassment. "I, for one, think you should have taken many lovers. If I were in your shoes, I would have done just that." I smiled down at her. Then I took her hand and pulled her to the couch. We both sat down and tried to make sense of our lives.

We talked until the sun came out and the birds started chirping playfully outside. It was a glorious morning, and I knew that somehow everything was going to be fine. We had the talk of a lifetime. I told her my deep innermost feelings and explained to her that I could not and would not make a life without Loula. I had her blessings, and it was a good feeling to have at least one of my parents on my side.

"Thank you, son, for not passing judgement on my trespasses. You know that I love your father, but there is a huge void in my life. I feel lonely and unloved by your father. The doctor fills that void with so much love that I feel complete when I am with him."

I understood. Loula did that to me too. She fulfilled my every desire.

"Be careful, Mother, if Father suspects your affair, he will scream treason, and place the doctor's head on a silver plater, not to mention what he will do to you," I warned her.

"Do not worry about me. I am being super careful." She said, "Son, please don't think ill of me. I never wanted to go behind your father's back. It just happened, and I have never been happier." She started to cry again.

I took her in my arms and wiped away her tears. "Mother, did I ever tell you that you are my hero?" I said very emotionally. "You are a brave woman. You stand on your own two feet and have never wavered. Even after Father threw you blow after blow of heartaches over the years. You survived and overcame it all." I was proud at that moment that she was my mother.

My mother searched in my eyes for a hint of truth to what I said, and when she felt that I meant every word, she hugged me so tight that I almost suffocated. We took a few more hours enjoying each other's company before we hightailed back to the king's bedchamber. The doctor was already there, and he stepped backward when he saw us and allowed us to get closer to my father.

The king was awake, and he looked at us, smiling weakly as he padded the bed for Mother to sit next to him. I threw a stolen glance at the doctor and saw him stand stiffly behind us, quietly observing the king and queen with a frown on his face. He was clearly irritated with the whole situation at hand. I felt no resentment toward him. As a matter of fact, I was grateful that he made my mother happy.

My father motioned for my mother to lean in closer to him, and when she did so, he kissed her on the mouth. There was silence in the room at that moment. My father apologized for all the years of misery he had caused her. My mother was in tears, touched by his words. I too was very emotional at this time, but the doctor was clearly distressed. He shuffled his feet back and forth and unconsciously took a deep breath. I could not blame him at all. We all knew that, once my father got back on his feet, he would go back to the person he really was, an old, miserable fool.

The day flew by without a hitch. I took charge of all of my father's affairs. By the end of the day, I was exhausted. I never knew that my father had so much to do in one day. He was a slave to his crown and, with that, came certain obligations. At the end of the day, I was worn out. I realized I did not even have time to think much about Loula today as I walked into my apartment and closed the door behind me.

Shaeena was already asleep, and the baby was in her basket next to the bed. She too was sleeping like an angel. I washed up, went to bed, and passed out almost immediately. I think it was the first time I slept without Loula on my mind.

Chapter Sixteen
Loula

*K*issing Billal was pleasant. He was good-looking, and I knew he loved me. I kissed him hungrily and wrapped my arms around him. I was turned on in a weird kind of way. I did not understand it. It was different than when I kissed Nidal. A whole different feeling, but it was still good. I even allowed Billal's hand to trail inside my gown and touch my breast, but I didn't know at what point I started to believe it was Nidal caressing me and not Billal.

Right about that time, Billal and I heard the loud cheers in the halls of the palace, and we looked at each other, wondering what all the commotion was about. Billal reluctantly jumped off the sofa and ran to the door, opening it slightly. The cheers came again, a little more loudly this time. A servant was passing by our room, and Billal asked her what was happening. The servant responded excitedly that the new member of the royal family had arrived. Billal closed the door abruptly, walked back to the bed, and waited patiently for my reaction.

I did not know how to respond to this news. The room felt like it was spinning as I clutched my pillow and threw my face on it. The gut-wrenching sobs that tore from my throat sounded like they were coming from someone else. I cried a river. Life wasn't fair. It should have been me giving birth to Nidal's child, not Shaeena.

Billal's hand was rubbing my back, trying to comfort me, but nothing in this world could bring me comfort at this time. I needed to be left alone. I did not want Billal touching me, so I lifted my head off the pillow and looked at Billal.

"Don't!" The bitterness of my own voice startled me.

Billal pulled away his hand and looked at me steadily, not knowing how to respond. He cast a curious sideways glance at me, and silently, his eyes were searching for answers. I could tell his patience was running thin with me, and this observation startled me. There was a shuddering tension about him, as if he were on the brink of exploding. I held my breath and shut my eyes, not knowing what was going to happen next. Then I heard Billal's footsteps walk away from me, and I took a deep breath and let out a sigh.

When I opened my eyes, I saw Billal looking out the window. With his back to me, he announced, "I am going to go and congratulate the princess. I shall not take long. When I come back, we need to have a talk." His voice held a dangerous softness as he walked away with supreme confidence.

He walked out of the room and slammed shut the door behind him. I wondered what he wanted to talk to me about. I was not in a mood for talking, especially not with him. I did not need to wait here for his return. I had nothing to say to him. I quickly jumped out of bed and headed straight for the bathroom. I needed to freshen up and take a walk in the gardens.

Dressed, I checked myself out in the mirror and pulled my hair back in a ponytail. I looked much younger than my twenty-nine years. Satisfied with my appearance, I marched out of there, and once out in the hallway, I went down the stairs two at a time. When I landed on the main floor, I raced down the hallway and headed straight for the back doors. My gown made it impossible to walk any faster than I did. I knew the guards and the servants were all staring at me, and as I pushed open the doors and the fresh air caressed my cheeks, I felt the tears rolling down my face. I quickly wiped away the evidence that revealed my pain.

I strolled in the gardens and saw Nidal standing with his back to me. I walked up to him and placed my hand on his shoulders. He turned and looked right at me. I do not remember exactly what happened next. All I could say was that I somehow ended up in his arms. Every fiber in my body was screaming for him to touch me. I melted in his arms as he kissed me passionately.

"Shaeena's baby is not mine, Loula. The baby you carry in your womb is mine, and do not even try to deny it," he said.

He knew the truth, but I did not admit it or deny it. I was speechless. All I wanted to do was lie down on the grass and have Nidal make sweet love to me. When he was inside me, all my pain vanished, as if I had not a care in the world. Nothing else mattered to me besides this man. Nothing.

Spent, we lay in each other's arms and whispered sweet nothings to each other as lovers do, promises we knew we could not keep, but at the moment, it was just what we needed to hear. When it was time to go, we quietly dressed and headed back toward the palace, but not before promising each other that we would meet again here in this spot whenever we had a chance.

As we walked around the bushes and we were almost near the water fountain, Billal stepped in front of us. His hands folded into fists at his sides, and his piercing eyes sent shivers through out my entire body.

"The king has asked for our audience," he stated coldly.

He took me by the hand and led me away, marching the both of us to the palace. It was hard for me to leave Nidal behind, but I knew I could not say a word. *Billal knows*, I thought as my heart sank. *It's only a matter of time before he accuses me of having an affair.*

In the tearoom, the king and queen greeted us when we entered. I could tell that the queen was not happy about something and guessed it had to do with the announcement that the king was about to make. When Nidal walked in, the king announced that Billal and I were to get married on the morrow. My heart stopped beating. I plastered a fake smile on my face. *What am I going to do?* The rest of the time spent in the room was a blur to me. I was too overwhelmed with sadness to even react to anything.

Later on, during dinner, Billal and I entered the dining room and sat in our usual chairs across from Nidal. Shaeena's chair was empty. Nothing prepared me for what happened during dinner. Nidal had his foot up between my legs, and I lost myself in ecstasy as he caressed my most private part. I was oblivious to my surroundings as the tingling feeling had already started from the top of my head all the way down to my toes, and just as I was at the point of no return, Nidal pulled his foot away, as if he were punishing me for the turnabout in his life, as if it were all my fault. I stared at him, stunned, not believing what he had just done to me. Even though he had pulled his foot away, my body continued its course, and at that moment, I came so hard and so fast that I almost screamed.

I checked myself just in time as the electricity coursed throughout my body and almost knocked me off my chair. I clamped my lips shut, fearing my passion might escape my lips unknowingly. My fingers tightly pulled on the napkin I held. And slowly as the beautiful feeling started to dissolve, I looked over at Nidal and saw him staring at me with a knowing look. He motioned toward the door, and I too let him know without words that I would meet him later that night in the gardens.

It was hard to play the waiting game. Billal and I left the dining room and headed toward our room. As I climbed the stairs alongside Billal, he brushed my bottom lightly with his hand. We entered the room silently, and Billal turned me around and kissed me passionately. I allowed him to. I closed my eyes and pretended it was Nidal, my prince, who held me and kissed me. And it worked. My imagination took over, and I allowed Billal to continue kissing me until he had enough of my lips.

Finally, he stopped abruptly and looked at me, not understanding why I so easily allowed him to kiss me. I stood there silently until Billal figured out the truth and stepped back in disbelief. Embarrassed, I sighed, turned, and walked away. I wished this drama would end fast and he would just sleep and I could run to my lover in the gardens. I knew he waited for me there, and I trembled with lust at the thought of him.

Finally, Billal shut his eyes and fell asleep. I waited until I heard the slow rhythm of his breathing that assured me he was sleeping. Then I slid slowly out of bed and ran barefoot to the door. I swung it open slowly and closed it behind me softly, afraid I might awaken Billal. Then I ran as fast as I could down the stairs. The marble floor was cold against my bare feet, but I couldn't have cared less as I ran past the sleeping guard who was posted at the front doorway. I smiled at the sound of his snoring, thinking that, so far, it was easy to sneak out of the palace. I pushed open the back doors that led to the gardens and ran as fast as I could through them until I reached the bushes where I knew Nidal would be waiting.

And he was there. I could see him. Even though the torches were almost ready to burn out, I could see his beautiful face. The moon was full tonight, and it cast its beams on my lover's face. My heart skipped a beat. We made love all night. It wasn't the kind of sex that everyone has. Ours was different. When we made love, it was like we were two artists who were creating an art that was unique. Our hands brushed each other's skin, and with each stroke, the art got more colorful and more creative. It was like we were creating a masterpiece. As we blended all the right colors, our bodies melted and became one creation under God. It was magical. It was one of a kind, this love of ours. And I felt ecstatically happy.

Finally, the time came for us to go back inside the palace, each to our room. My heart sank at the thought of parting from Nidal, but the moon was lost in the sky as it made way for the sun to rise. It was crucial that we did not get caught. Too much was at stake if we were found out. Reluctantly, Nidal pulled me to my feet and kissed me tenderly one more time. Then we walked back to the palace.

Entering the palace, I ran up the stairs, and my heart was thumping so fast that I thought it would burst. I slowly opened the door and walked inside my room. I closed the door quietly behind me, and then I slipped back into bed. As I lay my head down on the pillow, I thought I saw Billal's eyes open and look right at me. The dawn's light was enough for me to see him looking at me, but when I blinked my eyes a few times, Billal's eyes were closed. He looked like he was sleeping peacefully. Alarmed, I stared at him for what seemed like hours, waiting to see if he would open them again. I wondered if I were just paranoid and thought his eyes were open when they really were not. But I was not sure now what the truth was. To make matters worse, I was going to marry Billal today unless by some miracle something happened to prevent the matrimony from taking place. Tears rolled down my eyes as I tried to be still and not make a sound. I did not want Billal to wake up and start asking questions. At some point, I fell asleep and rested my troubled mind.

What seemed like only a few hours later, Billal awakened me with a warm kiss on my lips. He took the liberty and caressed my exposed breast as his mouth continued to kiss me. I did not have the power to withdraw, feeling guilty from the night before. I kissed him back because my body was responding to his touch. My body betrayed me as I slid closer to him and wrapped my arms around him. I might as well get used to him touching me because I was to become his wife today.

A few minutes later, we heard the banging on our door and jumped up from our little experiment. I heard Billal say, "Enter." The door swung open, and the servant walked in excitedly as she said almost out of breath that the king had suffered a heart attack. My mouth dropped at the news I just heard. *Could it be? Could it be true? Is the king dying?* I didn't know what to make of it. I heard Billal behind me shuffle around the room, collecting his belongings, dressing quickly, and running out of the room.

"Billal!"

Billal stopped in his tracks for a brief second and stuck his head through the doorway. "Loula, I must go and see for myself if what the servant claims is true. Then I have to take control of the palace because Nidal will be by his father's bedside. I am sorry, but I need to leave immediately." He left, and I heard him running down the stairs as he yelled orders to the guards.

I slumped on the bed, a little dizzy from all the excitement. I did not know what to make of it all. *Am I happy the king might die and I could be free to marry Nidal, or am I sad for Nidal that his father might pass away and he would be left with only one parent?* My heart played tug-of-war with those two options. To be free of Billal and Nidal free of Shaeena. We could marry and live a life full of happiness. I spent the rest of the morning daydreaming of a life with Nidal by my side.

In the afternoon, the servants brought me my lunch on a tray and placed it next to my bed on the bedside table. There was chicken and potatoes, a salad, and freshly squeezed orange juice, but that was not what caught my attention. Next to the plates of food, there was a single rose and a folded piece of paper. With trembling hands, I reached over and grabbed the note, thinking it was from Nidal. But the note was from Billal, telling me how much he missed me and how he looked forward to tonight. I did not touch my food. I had suddenly lost my appetite. I knew what Billal meant by his words. He thought I finally accepted him as my betrothed and he wanted to claim my body tonight.

I stayed in my room the entire day, not wanting to show my face around the palace. This was a depressing day for me. When the servants came and removed the tray, I asked them of the king's health. They told me that he survived the attack. My heart was heavy with sadness. Not that I wished him dead, but my life would have been a lot less complicated had he died.

I needed to speak with Nidal, but I knew it was impossible to do so. First, he was probably at his father's bedside. Second, he was going to take charge of the palace until his father got better. This thought made me sad. Nidal was going to be busy the next few days, and that only meant that he would not meet me in the gardens. But the bright side to all this was that there would be no wedding for me anytime soon. Relieved, I smiled for the first time since yesterday, when I had been lovingly wrapped in Nidal's arms.

For the first time since the announcement that the king was sick, I thought of the queen. *Poor lady, how she must be hurting, knowing her husband is suffering. But then, is she really in pain, or is she secretly happy that she would be rid of him if he does not survive the attack?* If the latter was true, I did not make judgment against her, for she was living a life of torture as his wife. The king was a miserable man, and he hardly ever smiled at her. He was not a man in love. He looked more like a man full of greed and poison. Venom came out of his mouth when he spoke. He clearly was not a good person. It made me sad to know this because I knew the queen was the opposite. She truly was a good queen and deserved better than what life had dealt her.

By dinnertime, I was exhausted from waiting for some word on the happenings of the palace. I relied on the servants. When they came to me to bring me dinner, I asked if they had heard any news concerning the king, and they reassured me that all was good. I did not dare ask them anything else, for I did not trust them. They were loyal to the king, not me. When they left, I looked hungrily at the food on the tray. My mouth watered at the steak that rested on the plate. The vegetables looked mouthwatering, and the bread was hot and crispy. I devoured everything, for I was starving. I drank the small glass of wine with one gulp and poured another from the bottle that was conveniently sitting on the edge of the side table next to my bed. *It would be nice*, I thought, *to get drunk and forget all my problems.*

And as I sat there content with everything I had just eaten, I felt a tiny little flutter in my stomach. My mouth gaped open at the realization that my baby was finally kicking inside me. Tears of joy welled up in my eyes. My baby was playing inside me, and I rubbed my stomach happily. I thought Nidal should know this, but I did not know where to go looking for him. *Is he at his father's bedside? Is he in meetings with the members of the royal team, giving orders and running the palace because his father is bedridden, or is he by Shaeena's bedside comforting her and her child?* The thought of Nidal by Shaeena's bedside made me want to barf.

It was time for Nidal to claim my child as his and demand I become his bride. He needed to stand up to his father and not take no for an answer. I would tell him so when I next saw him. I did not know when that would be, but I hoped and prayed that it would be really soon. I ached for his touch. I suddenly felt lonely. I pushed the tray aside and jumped out of bed. I paced the room back and forth nervously. I needed to get in touch with Nidal, my prince, whom I suddenly missed with all my heart. I needed him, and I knew not how to find him.

Then as if by some miracle, the door swung open, and in he walked. My heart skipped a beat as I looked into my lover's face. He closed the door, locked it, came swiftly to me, and pulled me into his embrace. I melted in his arms and kissed his lips, the lips that burned mine as they marked their territory. I pushed my body hungrily on his, and he pulled me tighter into his arms. I lost all control, and I ripped his shirt open, slid my hands on his chest, felt his beating heart, and called out his name. I untied the strings to his pantaloons, and they dropped to the floor. He moaned hoarsely and pulled my gown off my body, and I stood there naked to his touch as he lifted me up in his arms and carried me to the bed.

Our bodies fit together as one as we made love and reached to great heights of passion. At this time, it was just him and I. Nothing and no one else mattered. We made love so fiercely, so passionately, that I lost control of all my senses. His eyes were blazing with tender love as he whispered how much he missed me. His lips trailed kisses down my neck. I could feel his heart hammering against mine. I had felt so happy that I thought I would burst from the excitement of all the joy that I was feeling at this very moment.

Nidal's hand caressed my stomach, and I told him that I felt the baby inside me flutter earlier. We both cried, feeling that life was not fair. We were both at a loss for words. But words were not needed at this time as Nidal's hands caressed my stomach, gently rubbing it and waiting to feel his child kick. But our baby did not respond to his father's caresses, and Nidal was disappointed.

I smiled and said, "Don't worry, Nidal, there will be other opportunities to feel the baby kick."

Nidal lowered himself until his lips were on my stomach, and he kissed every inch of it. I was just beside myself with adoration for this man, for whom I would give my life for.

Nidal pulled himself up and kissed me hard on the lips. "Loula, my life, my soul, my everything, I love you so much," he said passionately and claimed my lips one more time.

I could not get enough of him. I held on to him for dear life. This was what I lived for, and this was what I would die for. And I knew without a doubt that Nidal felt as I did.

"Nidal," I said as I pulled my lips away from him, "we need to talk. I know time is against us today, but we must talk." I mustered up the courage to tell him how I feel.

Nidal stopped kissing me and, with a questioning look, waited patiently for me to speak my mind.

"Nidal, we have to find a way to be together. I need you, I love you, and I can't go on this way. The baby and I need you to be more active in our lives. You need to express your thoughts to your father. You need to stand up to him. I cannot go on this way. I am in pain. My heart bleeds without you." I pleaded for him to understand and take some action to reassure me that he would fight for our love.

Nidal said nothing. He only stared at me with what looked like pain in his eyes. He pulled himself up into a sitting position, and then he pulled me up next to him. I saw the look in his eyes, and I knew I would not be pleased with what he was getting ready to tell me.

Nidal took a deep sigh. "Loula, how can you ask this of me at this time? You know what the consequences would be if I spoke up and claimed my love for you. You and the baby would be in grave danger if the king finds out the truth about us." He cupped my face with his hands and whispered, "Please, don't do this to me. Please be patient until I figure things out. I need you to be a little more understanding. I am doing my best to find a solution to our problem. I have a lot on my plate right now."

Nidal's eyes searched mine, and I did my best not to cry.

He said, "Loula, please give me more time."

I did not have too much time to give him. Billal was becoming more demanding, and I knew not what the outcome would be. I could not tell this to Nidal. I did not want him to kill Billal. I knew Nidal would not stand for his cousin touching me. So I kept my mouth shut and said not one word. I would have to take care of this one on my own.

Nidal immediately noticed my mood swing and, with his fingers, tipped my face upward. "What are you thinking now, Loula? Do not keep me in the dark. Tell me," he demanded lightly as he waited patiently for my response. I did not know what to tell him. I could not reveal the truth to him.

"Nidal, I will do as you say. I will wait patiently for you to think of a way to fix all this," I lied, smiling to throw him off the truth.

But Nidal was smarter and quicker than I was. He raised his eyebrow and looked suspiciously into my lying eyes and knew instantly that I was keeping something from him. He was no fool.

"Tell me now what you are thinking, and this time, the truth, please," he warned, fighting to keep the anger out of his voice.

I averted my eyes, not wanting him to read the truth in them, but it was too late. He was smarter than I thought, and he roared through his teeth. There was a shuddering tension about him as if he were a hairbreadth from exploding.

He drew his head back, and his voice held a dangerous softness as he said, "You have three seconds to tell me the truth before I go looking for Billal and kill him with my bare hands."

I winced as I looked into his eyes, and I knew he was going to do as he threatened. I tried to think of a response that would satisfy Nidal, but I could not come up with a single thing.

With a hint of sarcasm in his voice, Nidal said, "He tried to make love to you, didn't he?" When I did not answer, Nidal's eyes widened, and he jumped out of bed, naked in all his glory, and said recklessly, "Tell me, Loula. Did he accomplish his goal?" he asked breathlessly, waiting for an answer.

I stared at him, speechless. I could not believe what he had just asked. I carried his child inside me. I waited patiently for him to come to me. *And this is what I get?* His accusations took me aback, and the words spilled out before I could stop them.

I said regretfully, "Well, at least he wants me badly enough to want to marry me. He does not hide his love for me. He does not accept Shaeena's child as his own. You, on the other hand, have no balls! You hide your love for me. You hide the fact that you have fathered a child with me again! And you sleep in the same bed with the woman that you will wed one day! Because as you say, it is your duty to marry her, since she had your child, since your father says so, since you are not man enough to claim me as your wife!" I spat angrily.

I knew instantly that I had said the wrong things, but it was too late to take back my words. I wanted to tell him that he was a fool for not realizing after all this time that he was the only man that I loved. But I stubbornly kept my mouth shut. He needed to stand up for me, and he needed to claim me as his wife. I would not yield. I would not be his puppet anymore.

"You suck the very life out of me!" he said.

I could tell he was trying to keep the anger out of his voice. Then a miserable silence followed, and we both stared at each other. Both of us were angry out of our minds.

"You have found my weakness, Loula, and you use it to hurt me!" he said callously. "Your words were brutal, Madam, and you have accomplished what you wanted. You killed me in every way possible!" His voice held a note of finality.

I froze, realizing too late that I went much too far this time.

"You open your mouth and throw words in the air, without thinking of what they mean. You want things done immediately when you know it cannot be done in that fashion. I am the crown prince of Arabia, and I am but a servant to my crown. There are certain expectations the people of Arabia expect from me! I have fallen in love with you, against my people's wishes, against my father's wishes, and against everything I have ever believed in! I have become a jack-off. I play with myself when I can't have you, when I am going crazy with want for you, when I do not have you near me. I do this because I cannot substitute you with anyone else, and I have come so low that I touch myself! I am ashamed of myself, but I can't help it. When I think of you, I go crazy! You have made me into a crazy man! I have done everything humanly possible to make you mine! Now the most powerful man in Arabia is threatening your life! The king wants your head on a silver platter. My baby's life is at risk! I have been wrongfully accused of fathering a child that does not belong to me! I have to stand by and see my cousin touching the woman I love! How much more of this do you think that I can take?" He ran his fingers through his hair.

I knew that what he said was true, but it was hard for me to accept it all. I was running out of patience, and it seemed he was too. He was yelling again. Nidal was slowly changing into a different person. I looked at him. *What is really in that mind of his?* He looked stressed out. I knew he had a lot on his plate. *But what am I to do?* My tears slid down my face, and I did not even realize it.

Nidal immediately ran to me, took me in his arms, and held me tight. I wrapped my arms around him, not ever wanting to let him go. Sobs ripped through my throat, and I cried my heart out. Nidal cupped my face, and his lips brushed gently over mine, sending shivers through me. But I knew this had to stop. We could not continue in this way. I had to make him see my point of view.

My eyes were shining with tears, but my back was straight, and my voice was firm and unwavering when I opened my mouth and said, "Nidal, this has to stop now. I am suffering. Do you understand? You brought me to this land, a place I knew nothing about. You took me from the only family I had, and you promised me many things, of which you did none! You have not kept your promises, Nidal!" I pulled away from his embrace as the tears threatened to spill once again. "I am pregnant with your child, and I have never felt as alone in my life as I do at this very moment! I sleep in someone else's bed at night, and every night, I pray he does not rape me! Every night, I dream of you, and every morning when I wake up, I am alone again. Just knowing you are in the same bed with Shaeena kills me. I die a new death every day! Nidal, I cannot take this anymore." I threw myself back in his arms and wept.

I knew I had accomplished nothing tonight. But at least he knew how I felt. Nidal looked into my eyes and said passionately, "Loula, I love you. You know I do."

I nodded numbly as I tried to blink away my tears. *And is that his shaft that I feel hard against my body?* I placed my hand over it and lightly caressed it.

Nidal shut his eyes and moaned under his breath, "Don't, Loula. Please. This is not the right time. I have to get back to my father's bed. I need to see him about a few things before he falls asleep," he said miserably.

"Yes, Nidal, you are right. Go now, and do not worry about me. I can handle myself. Even if Billal tries to make love to me tonight, I will try to stop him. And if I do not accomplish it, then at least you know that I tried," I said sweetly, my eyes averting his. I knew he was going to explode any minute now. I held my breath for what was coming.

Nidal growled loudly, and he picked me up and slammed me against the stone wall. His body pressed against mine as he said hoarsely, "If Billal lays a finger on you, I will rip him to pieces. Do you understand that? And you will have the same fate as him if I so much as suspect that you allowed him to touch you in that way," he said angrily, shaking me lightly. "Tell me that you will never allow him to touch you in that way, Loula! Promise me that you would never allow it, please," he begged breathlessly.

I was truly exhausted now. Nidal raised his eyebrows, waiting for me to say something in response to his question. I remained silent, and he made an agonizing sound, unable to withhold his patience with me anymore.

I kept my eyes averted, and with a sharp edge of anger in his voice, he asked, "Promise me that you will not allow Billal to touch you, Loula." His voice was full of anguish.

That struck a chord of fury inside me. I was enraged. *What does he think? That I would so easily give myself away like that? How dare he even insinuate that!*

The bitterness of my own voice startled me when I responded, "You think highly of yourself, don't you? You think the universe revolves around you. That you even ask me such a question only reminds me that you have changed. You are not the Nidal I have come to love. I am carrying your child in my stomach, and you dare ask me to promise you such a thing! I am not a whore, Nidal! I do not sleep with Billal or any man besides you! If you question my loyalty, then you are not worthy of my love! Go, leave me in peace, and do not come back until you learn to respect me!" I was very emotional, and I felt disharmony at this time.

A startled look flashed across Nidal's face as he stared at me in silence. He studied my face to see if I meant what I had just said. His hands dropped to his sides as he turned and walked away from me.

When he reached the door, he turned and looked at me. "Good night, Loula." His tone was dismissive.

He opened the door and stepped out into the hallway. I ran after him, but it was too late. He had already disappeared down the staircase. Pain tugged at my heart. I was emotionally broken at this moment. I closed the door, walked over to the bed, and collapsed on it, and I cried myself to sleep.

❧ ❧ ❧

In the morning, I awoke to find Billal sleeping next to me. I studied his face and saw all the tiny fine lines and dark circles under his eyes. He looked tired as he lay there in deep sleep. My heart went out to him. He had a lot on his plate now with everything that was happening in the palace. He stirred a little, and I held my breath, not wanting him to wake up. He desperately needed to sleep some more.

As I lay there watching Billal, my baby started to kick in my stomach, and I was beside myself with love. The tiny miracle in my womb had awakened and was playing. Automatically, my hand caressed my stomach, and at that moment, Billal woke up, and he reached over and gently caressed my face.

"Good morning, beautiful," he said, smiling. "You have a happy smile on your face. To what do I owe the pleasure?" he asked teasingly.

I smiled back. "The baby is kicking."

He placed his hand excitedly on my stomach and tried to feel it for himself. And just about that second, the baby kicked really hard, and Billal burst with laughter. His eyes were sparkling with love, and I could not help but love him back. He was a beautiful person, and I was glad that he was here with me at this time. I placed my hand on top of his and dragged his hand to where the baby kicked next, and we both laughed with joy.

I heard a soft knock on the door, and the servant walked in, carrying the tray with breakfast. She placed it on the table and quickly exited the room. I was famished, smelling the bacon, sausage, and eggs, alongside the hot rolls with a rich butter spread. The baby and I were so hungry. I devoured everything on my plate and even tried to steal a piece of bacon from Billal's plate. He playfully slapped my hand away, and we both laughed aloud like two little children having fun. At that moment, he looked at me, and I felt something in my heart that I could not explain. I sobered up and looked away, embarrassed.

In a serious tone, Billal asked hoarsely, "What is it, Loula? Why all of a sudden do you look away from me? Have I overstepped my boundaries? Have I disrespected you without knowing?" With genuine concern in his voice, he continued, "Loula, please, tell me what is wrong."

I turned, looked at him with tears in my eyes, and said softly, "No, Billal, you did nothing wrong. As a matter of fact, you have done everything right. I am the one I am mad at. I play with your feelings, knowing I can never love you the way I love Nidal. You are a good man, Billal, and you deserve better." I let out a big sigh.

Billal just sat there looking at me, as if I had just slapped him on the face. I wondered why he looked stunned. I had never told him that I carried feelings for him. On the contrary, I had told him the opposite. But at that moment, something was tugging at my heart. I realized something that I could never admit to anyone, let alone myself, before now. I loved him, and as I tried to accept this new realization, I stared at him wide-eyed and openmouthed.

Billal was confused. "Madam, release me from my pain, pray tell. Let me in on your secret." He placed his hand on mine and waited for me to respond.

And without thinking, I blurted out the three words that had the power to ruin everyone's lives. Three words that were better off never being said. But it was too late now. The damage was done.

"I love you." I whispered, lowering my gaze from embarrassment. Billal jumped out of his chair, knocking it to the floor, and lifted me up. He took me in his arms and squeezed me tightly. Almost immediately, I knew I had made a huge mistake, but the damage was already done. Billal's lips eagerly landed on mine, and he kissed me tenderly.

When the kiss ended, Billal drew his head back and held me at arm's length as he tried to study my face. He seemed very emotional at this very moment. "Loula, you have found my weakness, and you have hypnotized me. I am at your mercy," he said with trembling lips as he dropped to his knees. I looked down at him, not understanding what he was about to do.

He looked up at me, and he took my hands in his. "Loula, you know I have loved you since the very first time I laid eyes on you. You are a delightful creature, and you have stolen my heart. And now to hear you say to me those words, you blow me away. I kneel before you, Loula, not as a prince, but as a man in love. I declare my love for you. Marry me, Loula. Marry me now. Today. Let us go and get married right now! Please, Loula," he begged.

He looked so handsome, and I was a lucky woman for him to love me. But I knew in my heart that, even though I really did love Billal, I loved Nidal more. Nidal was my first choice, and in this lifetime, he was the only man for me. I hated to wipe the smile off his face, but he must know the truth. I spoke hastily, and now I had to hurt him without wanting to.

I took a deep sigh. "Billal, I am so sorry. You misunderstood me, but it is my fault, not yours, for I did not clarify for you what I meant. I do love you dearly. I've come to realize this now, but I love Nidal more. He is the man I wish to spend the rest of my life with. He is my true love. I know I cannot and will not live without him. I am sorry if I have hurt you. I did not mean to. Forgive me, please, Billal," I pleaded, hoping against hope that he would be understanding.

I could see his lips trembling, his eyes watering, and his hands shaking as he stood up from his position and straightened his back. He towered over me as he looked down into my eyes.

He squared his broad shoulders. "You played with me, Loula. You used me, and I, the fool, believed you." He laughed aloud now as he stepped back, away from me, as if I had some kind of disease. He pointed his finger at me. "I love you so much. It hurts knowing that you love Nidal. I am your match in every way, Loula, yet you choose him! You have always chosen him! You think me a fool!" He grabbed the tray with the plates on it and threw it across the room, shattering everything on it.

Fear struck me, and I placed my hands on my stomach to protect my baby as I stepped backward, away from Billal. At that moment, the door swung open, Nidal came running inside our room, and Billal made a fist and punched him squarely on his jaw. Nidal swayed backward from the unsuspecting blow and crashed into the stone wall, stunned. Billal slammed the door behind him as he exited the room, and I ran to Nidal and hugged him.

"What happened here, Loula?" Nidal rubbed his jaw, now red and swollen. "Why is Billal so mad? What did you say to him that got him so upset?" he asked suspiciously, expecting an answer from me.

I knew not what to say. I feared a lot of trouble would happen if I told him the truth. But I could not lie. *What if Billal were to tell him the truth?*

I looked down at my feet. "I told Billal that I love you and want to marry you and not him, and he got really upset." That was not a lie. I just withheld some information from him. That was all.

A miserable silence followed, and I slowly tipped my head back and saw Nidal analyzing what I had just told him. I held my breath, knowing he would explode at any moment. Nidal was not stupid. He would figure it out, and then I would be in trouble again.

I stood there all tensed up, playing the waiting game. Finally, Nidal said in an unfriendly tone, "What else did you say that angered him, Loula? He already knew you love me. It has to be something more than that."

Theodora Koulouris

I noticed the anger in him starting to build. I looked away, lest he read the truth in my eyes.

But Nidal was clever, and he walked up to me and grabbed me by the shoulders gently. "Pray tell, Loula, what else did you tell him that caused him to get this upset? I demand you tell me now before I go to Billal and get the truth from him. I must warn you, Loula, if I hear it from him first, I will be angry as hell."

Swallowing hard and with quivering lips, I told him the truth. "I told Billal that I loved him." I held my head up high, and then I added quickly, "But I also told him that I loved you more, and it was you whom I wanted to marry, not him." Then I braced myself for what I was sure would follow.

"You told Billal that you loved him?" Nidal whispered softly.

And it was like the calm before the storm. At this point, I was ready for anything. I knew this revelation would destroy our relationship, but it was too late. I had said it, and I took full responsibility. Nidal threw his head back and laughed aloud. I watched in horror as his throat rumbled with laughter, not understanding any of this. Nidal continued to laugh until tears were in his eyes. And when the laughter stopped, a dangerous look was on his face, and I took a step backward and placed a protective hand on my belly.

"You told Billal that you love him? Who else have you told those words to? Tell me, Loula. Why do you lie to me and to yourself? Tell me why you told Billal that you love him!"

Nidal took a step forward and grabbed me by my shoulders. Terrified, I froze in my tracks. I knew I was in the wrong, and I knew not what to say. Tears rolled down my eyes, and as I looked at Nidal, tears were rolling down his face too. I tried to reach over and wipe his tears, but he slapped away my hands.

"I am so sorry, Nidal, but it's not what you think. I did tell Billal that I love him because I do love him, but it is not the same kind of love that I feel for you. You are my life, the very reason for my existence. I love you with all my heart. I could never love

310

anyone the way I love you. Billal has been good to me, and I love him for that. Please, don't confuse my feelings with what you think I feel. Do not underestimate the love I feel for you, Nidal. You would be cheating yourself out of great happiness. Billal got angry because I told him that I loved you more. I told him that I wanted to marry you and not him, and this is the truth, Nidal." I waited to see if Nidal would accept my words.

After what seemed like a lifetime later, Nidal grabbed me and held me tightly in his arms. "Loula, you are mine, and I will never allow you to marry anyone but me," he said passionately, and then he kissed me hard on the lips, bruising them, as his hands pulled on my gown.

I heard the ripping of material. I gave myself to him in total submission as he tore my gown off my body and stripped himself of his clothes. He took me hard and fast to heights of passion where only mad lovers go. I yielded to his touch and trembled in ecstasy.

Life was beautiful. Nidal was beautiful. I was finally collecting what life owed me, true happiness. Our bond could never be broken. We could not move forward without one another. When we danced our lives away, Nidal let me lead. Our love had transformed into a rare jewel, so precious that no one was able to separate us. Only God himself had that power, and he was being generous to us.

🞛 🞛 🞛

The days came and went, and I was happy. Days turned to months, and my pregnancy was going well. It was toward the end of my second trimester. The baby kicked wildly, and I loved every minute of it. Nidal came to me every chance he got. I was blissfully happy. The king's health was getting better, and I suspected that, once he got back on his feet, he would make plans for Nidal to wed the princess. Until then, Nidal was completely committed to me. Billal was busy with his own stuff. He had

311

taken over many duties since the king had gotten sick. He was second-in-command, and certain responsibilities came with that. I could not have been happier. By the time Billal came to bed each night, I was fast asleep. Before I woke up in the morning, he was already out the door.

Shaeena was too busy with her infant to make any kind of demands on Nidal. So for now, we had each other, and we enjoyed every minute of it. We took strolls in the gardens, we made love behind the bushes at night, and Nidal snuck in my room whenever he knew Billal was out and about. The servants had a field day with us. They knew, but they learned to keep their mouths closed.

I had not seen the queen for a long time. I suspected she was busy with the king and helping him recover. I wondered what the queen had done with Natalie. I had not seen or heard of her since the fire. I finally overheard the queen tell the servants to prepare Natalie for departure. She was to go and stay at the doctor's home. What business did she have to go there? Why would the doctor take her to his house? She was not related to him. I thought that was odd, but I was too preoccupied with what to do about Nidal that I quickly forgot about her.

Today, Nidal promised me a picnic in the meadow. I loved going there. It was so magical this time of year. Banks of colorful flowers flanked it, and I saw trees that danced with the wind, lush green grass, and animals playing without a care in the world. But most of all, it was the memories I loved the most. Under the willow tree, we made love each time we went there, and I was looking forward to being with Nidal again.

Finally, the door opened, and Nidal walked in all smiles with a picnic basket hanging from his right hand and a bottle of wine in his left one. I grabbed my wrap, and ran to him, and planted a kiss on his warm lips. We headed out the door and down the stairway, and as soon as we landed on the first floor, there was Shaeena, who had just come out of her room. She stood in front of us with her hands on her hips and she looked at us angrily. We stopped in our tracks, speechless, and we looked at each other nervously.

Nidal studied her for only a brief moment, and then he barked, "Step aside, Madam."

She ignored his request and rested her gaze on me. I swallowed and looked away from her, not knowing how to handle the situation. I was not about to let her spoil my day, so I ignored her totally.

"Step aside, Madam. Do not make a fool out of yourself again," Nidal said sarcastically.

And that only infuriated the princess even more. She was huffing and puffing and was about to make a nasty remark when Nidal gently pushed her to the side and she almost lost her balance.

"How dare you lay your hands on me in such a manner? You will regret it soon enough, Nidal!" she screamed.

But Nidal only laughed. "Behave yourself, woman. Your claws are starting to come out." Then he looked at me with tender, loving care. "Let's go, Loula. Just walk around her and follow me out of the palace."

So I did just that, and I heard Shaeena stomp her feet on the marble floor behind me. I did not turn to look. I just kept walking behind Nidal and exited the palace. We walked about a half mile, and finally when we came to the willow tree, Nidal dropped the basket and the wine on the grass. He grabbed me and kissed me sweetly on my lips. All was forgotten as we kissed and made love, right there under the willow. Nidal caressed my stomach and talked to his child, telling the baby how much he loved me and how he could not wait for his boy to be born.

"Nidal, how do you know it is a he?" I asked playfully.

Nidal just ignored me and continued his conversation with the baby. "If you are a baby girl, little one, even better. I will give you the world on a silver platter. I would love to have a little girl who looks just like her mommy, a little girl I can spoil." He gently rubbed my stomach.

I could not be happier than I was at this precious moment. I felt complete. Nothing in the world could bring me more joy than this. We stayed in the meadow all day and had our picnic, and we made love again until we were fulfilled with each other. It was late in the evening when we gathered our belongings and headed home. The servants had lit the torches and were putting the animals away as we reached the palace. I saw Billal standing outside the doors of the palace with his hands on his hips, and he looked mad as hell.

His frown deepened as we approached the palace. He stood rigid, and his eyes were bright with hatred as he looked at Nidal. Then his gaze swept over me, and he looked back at Nidal and growled, "If you ever, and I mean ever, leave the palace with Loula again, I will rip out your throat!" he threatened.

"You don't give me orders. Do you forget that I am the crown prince, and next to me, you are nothing! It will do you well to remind yourself next time before you open your mouth and sound like a fool. Loula is mine. You will never have her, and as a reminder, if you ever touch her again, I will kill you with my bare hands!" Nidal sneered. And he pulled me alongside him inside the palace.

Once inside, Nidal kissed me tenderly with the guards and a few servants present, looking right at us, stunned at what they were seeing, but I did not care. I kissed him back hungrily as I wrapped my arms around him and melted in his arms. After we were done kissing, Nidal looked around at the servants and the guards and barked orders to them, and they all scrambled to their duties. I could not help but laugh at the scene I had just witnessed. But Billal wiped the smile off my face as he stepped into the palace and looked at me with eyes that looked as if they were in pain. He walked right past us and went flying up the stairs two at a time. We heard the door slam really hard, and I knew that, when I went to my room, Billal was going to put me in my place.

When I looked back at Nidal, I found him regarding me silently. Then he cupped my face and kissed me one more time.

Before he sent me to my room he said, "I promise I will come to you as soon as I can."

I reluctantly left him and walked up the stairs slowly. I was in no hurry. I knew full well that Billal was waiting to give me a piece of his mind.

When I reached the room, I opened the door gently and entered. He had his back to me, and he was looking out the window with his hands in his pockets. I braced myself for his words that were sure to come. Billal turned swiftly around and fastened his eyes on me. He walked over to me. I could feel his breath on my face. He was that close. Billal blinked and remained silent for a moment. His eyes were bright with anger. Then he pushed past me brusquely, walked to the bathroom, and slammed the door shut, but not before muttering that I was a worthless whore.

I just stood there, stunned with what had just transpired. I could not blame him for feeling the way he did. I did not play fair with him. But I felt it was not my fault that life had dealt me this misery. I walked over to the bed and sat on it, and I tried to figure out what I would tell him. He was in there for quite a while, and finally when he opened the door and walked toward me, I stood and addressed him.

"Billal, I apologize for everything. My intentions were never to hurt you." I meant everything I said to him. "Please believe me, Billal. I love you, and I do not want you to suffer in any way." I took a step closer, reached out, and touched his face.

Billal took a step backward. "Madam, contain yourself. You have no right to touch me! You gave up your rights outside the palace a few moments ago. Release me from this pain in my heart, and then leave me in peace," he pleaded emotionally, and he turned and walked back to the window.

A miserable silence followed. We were both left speechless. I did not know what to do next. It was as if time stood still. I never anticipated that the day would end like this. I guessed it was unavoidable because Billal saw us coming together from the meadow, but I never set out deliberately to hurt him.

Billal broke the silence. "Have you ever felt love for me, Loula?" he asked in a choked voice. He still had his back to me, and my heart skipped a beat.

"I love you, Billal," I whispered back to him.

I wanted to put my arms around him, but I was afraid of rejection. Again, there was silence. He placed both hands on the edge of the window and leaned his head out for fresh air. I was right behind him, waiting for him to turn to me. After what seemed like a lifetime later, he pulled his head back in and turned. His eyes were wet with tears. *Dare I think it is because of me, or is the sting of the air causing the tears?*

He walked past me to the bed and sat on it. He looked defeated. My heart went out to him. I ran to him, dropped to my knees right in front of him, and put my hands on his.

"I beg your forgiveness, Billal." I took a deep breath. "I never meant to hurt you. I really do love you." I hoped against hope that he believed me.

"I believe that you love me, Loula, but it's not enough! I want you to feel for me what you feel for Nidal! You love him more, and that revelation hurts me. You are my match in every way, Loula, yet you choose him. I have done everything I could to get you to love me, but it was a losing battle from the start. I ask you now. Please release me from this pain. I am suffering, and I do not know how to make the pain go away. Please, Loula, release me from my pain!" he pleaded again, and the tears rolled down his cheek.

I felt inclined to answer him, but I did not know what to say. *What could I say? He is right. I love Nidal more. Much more. I could never love another the way I love Nidal. He is my life. He is the very air that I breathe. But I had to say something to Billal to help him out of his misery.*

"Billal, please, understand this. Had I met you first, you would have been my first choice. You are handsome and kind, and you love me so much. But it was my fate to meet and fall in love with Nidal. He is the one I must be with. I do not say this to hurt you. I never want to hurt you, Billal. But I say this because it is the truth." I hoped he understood what I was telling him.

My words were not getting through to him. He stared at me like a lovesick puppy that was in tremendous pain.

"Billal, why do you love me? You deserve better than me. You deserve a woman who can give you unconditional love, a woman who would die for you. I know this country has many maidens for you to choose from. They would kill to spend one night with you. Go find yourself a wife and be happy, Billal," I begged him.

"I do not want anyone else. I want you! If I cannot have you, I do not want another. I'd rather stay single." Another tear escaped his eyes. "I will wait for you to change your mind, Loula. Nidal will never marry you. He cannot marry you even if he desires to. He is the crown prince of Arabia. Shaeena has his child. By law, he must marry her! He will make you his mistress and nothing more. You will spend nights alone while he sleeps in Shaeena's arms. He will come to you on rare occasions, and if he gets caught, your life will be in grave danger, not to mention your child's. The king will kill you and the baby! Is this what you choose? Is this what you want for your life? You throw away my love and choose a life full of pain? Why, for what, for who, for a man who can never claim you as his? Is that what you want, Loula?" he asked desperately.

I closed my eyes. My tears rolled down my face freely without shame. He was right. Everything he said was the truth. I dropped on the floor and wept like a child. I pounded the cold floor beneath me until my hands turned blue. I cried until my eyes had no more tears to spill. Billal just sat there watching me, holding his breath and waiting for the results he was hoping for. And he won.

I rose off the floor and went to him in total submission. I chose him because he was right. Everything he said was the truth. I clung to him, and he held me tight. We both cried like little children. My pain was unbearable. I now knew and felt the pain that Billal did. Our fates were sealed. There was no going back.

We lay in the bed that night silently in each other's arms. No words were spoken, for there was nothing to say. We both knew what we had to do. The Loula that Nidal knew died tonight, and she buried herself in his heart. The shell that was left of Loula knew what she had to do. Come morning, all that I knew would seize to exist. I closed my eyes and slept, for there was nothing else for me to do.

When morning came, Billal asked if I wanted to go for a walk with him. I said yes, wanting to get some fresh air. After we cleaned up and dressed lightly, Billal held my hand as we exited the palace. My heart was heavy with pain, but I ignored it, reminding myself again that I was now the new me. The old Loula was buried in Nidal's heart.

Our walk brought us to the meadows. I did not know how we ended up here. All I knew was that I was dead inside and someone else was standing here with Billal.

Billal bent his head and kissed my lips. I responded immediately. It was a hungry, heated kiss, and I knew exactly what I was doing. Billal started to unbutton my gown, and I let him. When it dropped to the floor, I was standing stark naked in front of him. Billal feasted his eyes on my body, and I could tell he was on fire. Some kind of stirring was inside me too. I reached and pulled the strings to his pantaloons, and they dropped to the floor. Billal pulled off his shirt, and he too stood naked in front of me.

My eyes roamed over his broad shoulders, traveled down his chest, and continued down his lean waist. His muscled, masculine thighs were spread apart, and I licked my lips when I lowered my gaze to his manhood. It was erect and massively big. A groan escaped Billal's lips.

He was a handsome man with a beautiful body, and I had the honor of touching it. Billal took a deep breath and closed his eyes as I lightly stroked his chest, and when I lowered my hand, Billal grabbed it and looked in my eyes.

"Loula, are you sure you want to continue?" he whispered hoarsely. His breath was lightly teasing my face as I nodded in response to his question.

Billal slammed my body to his, and as our bodies touched, I felt his huge manhood piercing my thighs. He pulled me down on the grass with him and kissed me tenderly as his hands explored my naked body with expertise. He was a skilled lover. I stroked his shaft, and his body jerked violently at my touch. He inhaled sharply and lost all control, immediately positioning himself between my legs.

I wrapped my legs around his waist and cried, "Take me now, Billal. Please make love to me."

Billal entered me with such passion that I almost came immediately. When we both reached our peak almost at the same time, it was pure heaven. Now I knew I was beside myself at this moment, not realizing the damage I had just done, not understanding I had just changed the course of my life at this moment and headed straight for the destruction of my soul. But even so, I ignored all reason and continued making love to Billal.

Billal held me in his arms so tenderly, and I knew at that moment how much he loved me. He was still inside me and unwilling to pull away. At that moment, I heard a horse galloping toward us, and I heard Nidal's voice loud and clear as he yelled, "Oh my God, Loula! What have you done?"

At this moment, I realized that I had caused the damage that sealed our fates. I pushed Billal away from me and looked around for my clothing to cover up. I was ashamed of myself. I could not look into Nidal's face. I dressed quickly and kept my eyes to the floor, not saying a single word.

Billal stood up, naked in all his glory, and yelled back, "What in God's name are you doing here?"

Nidal jumped off his horse and punched Billal square in the face. Billal stumbled backward and fell on the grass, rolling a few feet away. Nidal turned to me, raised his hand to strike me, and stopped it midair. He looked at me disgustedly, spit on my face, got back on his horse, and rode away. I stood there, watching him leave. My knees were trembling, and they buckled, and I fell to the floor and passed out.

Nothing would ever be the same again. I had sealed everyone's fates. I had done it singlehandedly with no one to blame but myself. I had made my bed, and now I had to lie in it. I would never smile again.

Chapter Seventeen
Nidal

Where do I start? Where do I begin to talk about the misery in my heart? It all started on the day I snuck into Loula's room and made love to her. Then Loula told me off. She complained I was not man enough to claim her as my bride. She knew not what she was talking about. I explained to her that it was a very dangerous thing to do under the circumstances. The king despised her. Her appearance at the palace threatened him. Her life and my baby's life were in grave danger. *How could I claim her as my bride when it meant severe punishment, possibly even death, if I so much as admitted that I loved her and she carried my child in her womb?*

Then, to make matters worse, Loula admitted to having feelings for Billal. I'd rather have someone stick a knife in my heart than have her tell me that she loved Billal, but even then, she fixed things, and our love flourished. My baby was growing inside her, and I was beside myself with great joy. We had stolen moments together, and we lived in our own world.

On the day of our picnic at the meadow, we made love again under the willow tree, not knowing it would be our last time ever that we touched each other in that way. Walking back to the palace, Billal saw us together, and after that, things were never the same between us again.

The next day when I awoke, the princess and her baby were sitting on the chair by the window. The baby was sucking her mother's breast. I walked to the bathroom and washed up, and then I walked to the couch where my clothes were, and I started to dress. I felt Shaeena's eyes on me. It was unnerving knowing that she was staring at me.

When I was finished dressing and I was about to leave the room, Shaeena words stopped me in my tracks. "Where are you going, Nidal? Are you going after Billal and Loula? They are by the willow tree making love. Billal told me yesterday that he was going to seduce Loula there today. Your precious Loula is going to have a taste of another male inside her. They are probably doing it as we speak," she said with a satisfied grin.

My mind was blown away at this moment. *Is it possible? Is Loula with Billal at the willow tree making love?* I threw the door open, startling the servants, and marched hurriedly out of the palace to the stables. I grabbed my stallion and rode so fast that my horse almost collapsed on me. I could not think straight. I was very angry, and I could not accept the fact that there was a possibility that Loula would give herself to Billal. My horse galloped at a fast pace, and I saw from a distance two bodies on the grass, entangled in lovemaking. I could not make out who they were, but deep in my heart, I knew.

From that moment on, I was a broken man. As I rode closer, I saw them clearly. My heart broke in half, my mind froze, and I placed my hand on my chest, fearing I was about to suffer a massive heart attack. When I punched Billal and he fell, I was about to finish the job and beat the living fuck out of him, but at that precise moment, I realized it was not his fault. It was Loula's fault! It was all her fault. I looked at her, and I saw a wanton woman in front of me. My father and Shaeena had told me so many times, but I would not listen to them. Loula had blinded me with her love. I was about to strike her, but I restrained myself. I did not want to stoop so low and hit the woman I loved. Instead, I spit in her face. I was disgusted with her, and I was done. *Finished! Kaput!* I released her image from my mind as I rode away from her and threw caution to the wind.

I reached the palace, gave my horse to the servants, and marched inside the palace and headed straight for my father's room. My mother was sitting next to him, and he looked a whole lot better. His smile faded when he saw the mood I was in. I could only imagine what I looked like. My hair was disheveled from the wind, my face was red from the anger in my heart, and my hand was throbbing from the punch I had thrown at Billal. My parents both stared at me, waiting for me to speak.

"Father," I said, loud and clear, "I have come to the decision that I want to marry the princess. She is my perfect match. You were right, Father. I will arrange for the wedding in one month's time."

My parents looked at each other, each with a different look. My mother was stunned at my revelations, and my father looked pleased. I did not wait for their response, for I wanted to run upstairs and tell Shaeena my decision.

Upon opening the door, I noticed that the baby was fast asleep in her basket and Shaeena was standing by the window, looking outside. I walked up behind her, and my hands wrapped around her breasts cupping them over her sleeping gown. A moan escaped her lips, and she pressed her body onto mine. I ripped the gown off her body and slammed her hard against me. She pushed her ass hard against my groin, and I lost my senses. I continued caressing her breasts with one hand as my other hand glided down to her womanhood, and my fingers played her until her body trembled in my arms and she moaned in ecstasy. I put my hands around her waist and turned her around.

Shaeena panted breathlessly as she pulled the strings to my pantaloons, and as they dropped, she kneeled down and, with her lips, worked wonders on my manhood. I was delirious, wanting desperately to be inside her. My shaft was swollen, and I needed to spill my seed fast. My fingers intertwined in her hair, and I pushed harder into her mouth as she continued playing her magic.

Seconds before I came, I pulled her up, grabbed her by the waist, and slammed her hard against the wall. Her eyes feasted upon my naked body, and she reached and grabbed my shaft and played with it hard and fast. My body shuddered, and unable to hold off anymore, I flipped her around and entered her with such force that she cried out with lust. Her palms were up against the wall as she cried out for me to move faster and deeper. I grabbed her by the hips and slammed into her ass, savoring the electrifying feelings that violently coursed throughout my entire body. I growled with pleasure.

At that moment, the door crashed open, and I saw Loula standing there with her mouth agape. Without thinking, I slammed harder into Shaeena while I still had my eyes on Loula. The princess moaned with pleasure, and I lost it and reached a second climax, so intensified and so powerful that it was like nothing I had ever experienced before. Shaeena and I both called out each other's name in the heat of the moment.

I turned and looked into Loula's horrified eyes, and it brought me great pleasure knowing that she was hurting. I wanted her to see me screwing the princess. I wanted her to die a thousand deaths as I had when I witnessed firsthand the love of my life screwing my cousin. I started pushing inside Shaeena again, moaning with lust as I looked with a satisfied grin at Loula. At that time, Loula left the room and closed the door behind her.

I was confused and did not know which was the greater satisfaction: the enjoyment of having my shaft inside Shaeena or the wonderful feeling of the revenge I got when I climaxed inside Shaeena right in front of Loula. I could not make up my mind. Both ideas were powerful enough to make me want to spill my seed again inside this beautiful woman I held in my arms. I lifted Shaeena in my arms and brought her to our bed. I enjoyed another round of lovemaking with the princess, and this time, it lasted a whole lot longer than the first time.

The next morning as Shaeena lay asleep in my arms, with a smile on her face, I lay there next to her, staring at the ceiling. *What the hell have I done?* My remorse came unexpectedly and hit me like a ton of bricks. Never mind the tears that rolled down my face or the pain that tugged at my heart. Every part of my body, every inch of it, was hurting from the remorse I felt. The guilt and the regret I was feeling at this moment was hurting so much that I wished I were dead, for that would have been a better option at this time.

I was disgusted with myself. I was above and beyond saving myself. I wanted to die. I wanted to disappear from the face of the earth. Fresh tears rolled down my face, tears that spoke of shame and regret. I died inside, a thousand deaths, over and over again. I was so ashamed. I could not believe that I had climaxed in front of Loula while I was inside Shaeena. I wasn't even drunk. I was sober! *What was I thinking?* I thought I was taking my revenge on her, showing her that I too can have sex with another. But what I really did was kill any love left inside her. I knew that nothing could turn the clock back, but I would give my life to undo what I had done.

Now it was too late. The king would definitely kill Loula and my child if I backed out of the wedding to Shaeena.

Oh my God! What have I done? How can I fix the hurt I have bestowed upon Loula? How can I take back what I have done to her? My heart cries out for her, even now. After everything, I still love Loula desperately. My love for her is even stronger today than any other time. I will never have sex with another woman ever. I don't deserve Loula, but from this moment on, I will stay faithful to her, even if I marry Shaeena and even if Loula marries Billal. I will not sleep ever again with any woman unless it is Loula who lies beneath me.

Chapter Eighteen
Loula

When I was naked under the willow tree with Billal, making love, I sealed everyone's fate. It was the beginning of the end. It is my fault entirely, and I took full responsibility. Even when I walked in on Nidal, my beautiful Nidal, the love of my life, the very reason for my existence. Even when I saw him having sex with Shaeena. Even when Nidal continued making love to her right in front of me. Even then, it was my fault and no one else's. I will never get over the picture of my Nidal inside another woman, reaching his peak in front of me. I knew he was taking his revenge on me in the worst way possible.

Everything was my fault. I created the situation, and I did this and no one else. I would never get over it. I would suffer for the rest of my life. It had begun. The suffering had already started. The poison was dripping little by little. It would continue dripping until I died. My only concern at this point was my child. I must do everything to protect it. I had no desire to go on in this life, but I would push myself for the sake of my baby.

I sat on my bed, day and night. I did not talk to anyone, for I could not say a word. I knew I had fallen into depression, and

I could not stop the process. The poison that dripped slowly into my system controlled me. I did not know what day it was. I did not know what time it was or what I was to do. I did know that I loved Nidal with all my being. Every fiber in my body was in love with him and begged for his forgiveness. I was waiting for him to come to me, but so far, he had not. Nidal is probably still angry with me. Maybe he doesn't love me anymore. I did do the unthinkable to him. He probably just wants to move on with his life with the princess. He does not want me anymore, for if he did, he would have come to me by now.

Billal sat with me day and night. I saw and heard him cry every day. He does not leave my room. He feeds me, washes me, and lays me down to sleep. He talks to me all the time, telling me the love he felt for me. I loved him too, in my own way. I did appreciate all he had done for me, but I wait for Nidal, the only one who could wake me up from this depression I was in, and as the clock ticks away the minutes, I fell into deeper and deeper depression. Only Nidal can stop it from happening. All he has to do is come to me and tell me he forgives me and that he still loves me. Those words would awaken me from this sleep that I had fallen into. Only he can do it.

Nidal is the air that I breathe. My soul has left me, and my heart is about to stop beating. Already I have the poison so far in me that I am about to die. The baby is one of the reasons I hold on. The baby is innocent of sin. I am the guilty one. I deserve to die, not my baby. I think it is only a matter of time before he comes into this world. I hope Nidal comes to me before then, for I fear I will not make it after the birth.

I was in the last month of my pregnancy. I was big with child. Billal had already sent for the doctor because today my pains in my stomach have gotten much stronger, and still, Nidal has not shown his face. He doesn't love me anymore. Billal was right when he told me that Nidal doesn't care anymore. Tomorrow might be the wedding. Tomorrow, Nidal is to wed Shaeena. *Maybe he will come to me tonight. I will wait for him. I will always wait for him until the poison takes me.*

The pain intensified now. I could hear my screams. The pain was unbearable. I closed my eyes and prayed for Nidal to come. If only for one last time, I just wanted to ask for forgiveness. That was all I wanted. The baby was kicking hard. It felt like my stomach was about to burst. The doctor just arrived. I saw the queen with him. She and Billal were crying. I screamed again, and then I passed out.

I did not know how many hours had passed. I was in and out of consciousness. I could hear the doctor's worried voice. I heard Billal telling me how much he loved me. I could hear the queen's sobs, but I did not hear Nidal. *He had forsaken me.*

Finally, I woke up in the morning. The sun was shining through the window, bringing bright light in the room. I looked around and saw Billal. He was fast asleep on the chair next to my bed. The room was quiet. I looked around for my baby, and I did not see it. My hands automatically went to my stomach, and it was flat, empty. No baby was there. Maybe the queen had taken the baby to bathe it. Maybe they want me to rest and she will return my baby when she knows I am awake.

"Billal?"

He opened his eyes and grabed my hand. He looked down to me. A lot of tears spilled from his eyes.

"Billal, where is my baby? Can you tell them to bring my baby here? I needed to hold him in my arms," I said, already guessing why Billal was crying.

Billal would not stop crying.

My screams sounded like they were coming from someone else. They were loud screams that ripped into the air and echoed throughout the palace. Billal was sobbing now, and I heard my name being called from outside the door. It sounded like Nidal, but I was not sure. I heard the pounding and the screaming and the guards arguing outside the door.

I turned and faced Billal. "Was it a boy or a girl, Billal?" Already, I could feel the lump in my throat as I waited patiently for Billal's response.

Billal looked at me tearfully and said softly, "It was a boy, Loula. A beautiful baby boy."

He started to cry all over again. I let out a big wail. My heart burst with pain. I screamed and cried and cried and screamed, and the pounding on the door got louder. My name was being called over and over again, and I just could not hold on anymore. I lost my zest for life, and at that very moment, everything went blank.

Hours later, I awoke from the bells that were ringing in the tower. I realized it was probably time for Nidal and Shaeena's wedding. He was going through with it after all. I could not understand how things had turned out this way. Nidal has chosen marriage to her. And that was fine. I was fine. We would all be fine. Slowly, I got out of bed and walked to the window. When I looked outside, I saw the wedding guests arriving. I felt so sad. I felt empty, like I had nothing inside me, like I had nothing else to live for.

I slowly walked to the door. The cramps had gone away, but I was in a different kind of pain. I opened the door and peeked outside. I saw the guard down the hall chatting with the servant girl. He had his arms around her. They looked like they were madly in love. A smile formed on my lips. I envied them. The pain tugged in my heart. I placed my hand on my chest and took a deep breath. I needed fresh air.

I tiptoed out into the hallway and went around the corner to the back staircase. I slowly walked down the stairs, making sure that no one saw me. This stairway is secluded. Grateful that no one is around, I continued my journey. I reached the bottom of the stairway and walked down the back corridor to the back doors that were located on the east side of the palace. I pushed them open, and the sun hit my face, warming it. It was a good feeling.

I took a deep breath and allowed the fresh air to travel down my lungs. I closed my eyes and hugged myself, and just then, the feeling came back. It was the poison in the pit of my stomach. It twisted with pain, and my tears came again. I started running as fast as I could, like a crazy woman. I ran through the gardens with my eyes closed, allowing the wind to blow on my face. I ran until my feet gave up and I could not run anymore.

Finally, I stopped and wiped the tears away from my eyes. I then saw where I had run to. It was the other side of the huge palace, almost a half mile away from everything and everyone. I remember the queen had once mentioned this place to me. She said it was dangerous because it was near the cliff, a very steep overhang. I was curious to see what was at the bottom of it, and I inched my way to the tip of the cliff and looked down.

All I saw was a deep opening that was about a mile in depth. Rocks were everywhere, and I do have to say it was inviting me to jump. I backed away and steadied myself, and that was when the poison left me. At that time, I felt all the anger and pain go away. I was left with a peaceful feeling. I looked around and saw the beauty of nature in all its glory. It was God's world. *Too bad, it is too late.*

I sat down on the dirt and made myself comfortable. I closed my eyes and thought of a time, long ago, when I first had met Nidal, my prince. He was so beautiful, and he had loved me so much. I thought of everything he ever said to me and everything he ever did to me. I know in my heart that he loved me unconditionally. I brought the poison into the relationship. It was my fault. I lost my baby. I lost both my babies, and it was my fault. My tears started rolling down my face, and I thought of Nidal and Shaeena getting married today. I had lost Nidal, and it was I who had done this. I do not blame him. I knew he loved me I brought the poison first into the relationship and now he has chosen Shaeena instead of me. I blame myself for this.

Suddenly, I remembered something, that day long ago when I had gone to the village with Billal. The old lady who followed me around, the one dressed in black. She had warned me, but I did not listen to her. She said Nidal and I were soul mates and that we were heading for disaster, but we could save ourselves if we stayed away from each other. She was not senile. She spoke the truth. I did not listen to her, and my fate is sealed now. A tear rolled down my cheek.

I stood now and allowed the wind to play with my hair, and I stepped closer to the cliff, knowing exactly what I must do. If I go back into the palace, I will only bring more pain to Nidal. I wanted him to find happiness in his new life and not grief. The only way to give him this gift was for me to disappear. All I had to do was jump, and then all would be fine. I would do this for Nidal. I loved him so much, and I would give him back his happiness. If I killed myself, Nidal could have a better life without me. The poison would be gone. I would do this for him because I loved him very much. It was my gift to him, to give him back his life. I would go and meet my babies in heaven, and Nidal could live a happier life without me.

My right leg swung toward the open space of the cliff. I closed my eyes and jumped. I heard Nidal's voice behind me. It was echoing through the wind as I was falling to my death. I was smiling because Nidal had me in his arms and we were making love under the willow tree. We were so happy.

Chapter Nineteen
Nidal

*hey say that real love is a strong and powerful feeling.
He who said that lied. Love is even greater than that.
Love is the very existence of everything. Love is the very
foundation of life. Without love, we really do not exist. But love can
also be poison, the kind of poison that fills your veins with grief.*

It had been three long months since I last saw Loula. I had
tried numerous times to see her, and I had not succeeded. Many
guards under the king's orders had kept me away from Loula. At
least ten guards bar the door to her room. I had not been allowed
to even climb the stairs. There are guards there as well, closing off
the entrance and preventing anyone from using the stairway.

I was mad with grief. I could not function properly. I had
to find a way to see Loula. I knew that, if I did so, I could fix
everything. My mother told me of Loula's pain. She told me that
Loula was in a world of her own. She had fallen into depression.
Why doesn't anyone listen to me? I knew that, if I went to her, her
poison would go away. She needed me now, just as I needed her.
I must find a way to go to her. All this is my fault. I did this to
her. I put the poison in her, and now she suffers because of me. I
would never forgive myself. *Never!*

I found out today that my love was having labor pains. She would have my baby today. This should have been a happy day for the both of us. Instead, it was very painful because I tried to go to her and I was not allowed entrance to her room. I heard her behind the door scream from pain. My heart tore at the pain I knew she was feeling. I had snuck past the guards on the stairway, and I even got through the guards by her door. I banged on her door and called out her name, but the guards pulled me back. They were following my father's orders. I was barred from entering her room.

I called out to her. I wanted Loula to hear my voice so she could know that I was there for her and I had not abandoned her. My tears rolled down my face and burned my skin. The guilt and remorse that I felt was the worst. If I could give my life for her happiness, I would in a heartbeat. If I could turn back the clock, I would do everything differently. But I knew that nothing could be done now. I had destroyed her because I loved her too much. I could not even claim my baby as mine. If I did, the king would take it away and maybe even kill it. I closed my eyes at these possibilities. My hands were tied. There was nothing I could do.

I went to my room and sat on the bed. I was alone today. Shaeena and her baby were taken to another room because it was the day before our wedding. I was told that I was not supposed to see the bride until our wedding day tomorrow. *This is bullshit! I am not going to marry Shaeena! I do not love her! I despise her! I hate her!*

I opened my mouth and let out a big scream. I pulled my hair in anguish. I pulled my shirt and ripped it. I screamed again and again and again. I cried my eyes out.

A few hours later, my father entered my room with a grin on his face. I froze. He was the meanest motherfucker I had ever had the honor of meeting. I knew he came to me with important information. He was going to threaten me again. There was a glint in his beady eyes as he looked at me. I stood and walked right in front of him. I wanted to show him that I was not afraid of him. He was ruler of this country, but he was not ruler of my heart.

The king studied my face for a few minutes before he spoke. Then he said without an ounce of pleasantness, "Loula had the baby." His words were cold as ice.

I did everything I could to refrain my lips from trembling and I asked him, "And Loula, how is she faring?" My body was tense. My heart stopped beating as I awaited his answer.

"She is in mint condition. Son, you would do well to concentrate on your life and not on Loula's. Tomorrow is your wedding day. Nothing is more important than that."

Before I could snap back an angry retort, he turned quickly and walked to the door, but not before throwing over his shoulders, "Oh, by the way, the baby boy did not survive." He walked out of the room and slammed the door behind him.

I reached out to the wall for support. My body was shaking, my mind was spinning, and my heart was bleeding. *My baby is dead! Oh my God! My baby is dead!* I could not breathe. I fell to the floor. My feet could not support me anymore. I clutched my heart and screamed as loud as I could. I cried for this baby whom I did not even claim as my own. A baby I did not even get to see, a little life that was not able to survive on its own. My baby! This was my baby, and I had not the balls to claim him as mine. A baby boy, an angel from heaven, a piece of me, my son!

It was my fault. I did this. I made this happen. With my stubbornness and my jealousy, I put the poison in Loula, and my baby died. I shall never forgive myself. I knew I would never get over this. I must see Loula. I must speak to her and beg her for forgiveness. *Oh, God, help me, please.*

The torture in my heart was so strong that I was not able to get up on my feet. My voice abandoned me, and I could not say another word. I was sick to my stomach. I did not want to live anymore. I could not go on without Loula. I had to go to her. I had to tell her that I loved her. I would think of a way to take her away from here. We could run from this country and find a home elsewere. Then I could give her the love that she deserved.

I wiped my eyes and stood up, and I promised myself that, from this day forward, I would live and exist only for Loula. No one and nothing could stand in my way. If Father or his men tried to stop me, I would kill them with my bare hands. I should have done this from the beginning. Maybe then my child would have been alive. *Oh, how that hurt, dear God.* My heart tightened at the thought of my child. *I swear from this day forward that I will do everything I can to undo what I have done. I know the grief will take years to go away, but I will try my best to rectify my mistakes.*

As night fell, I tried thinking of a plan. The plan had to be a good one. If it failed, then Loula's life would be in danger. With trembling hands, I reached for the glass of water that was sitting on the table next to the chair that I sat in. I swallowed hard and tried to wash down my pain. But I knew that nothing would take away this growing pain. It is fate, and fate has tricked me into believing in her. I would take fate into my own hands now and never again allow it or anyone to destroy me or mine.

I stayed up all night. I was not able to fall asleep. Nor did I try. I paced the floor all night, trying to figure out what to do. As the sun rose in all its glory, shining its way into my room, I wondered if Loula had awakened. I looked in the mirror and saw circles under my eyes, evidence of a sleepless night. The servants came and went all morning, bringing me breakfast and all the clothing I would need to wear for my wedding.

The wedding was to take place at four o'clock in the afternoon, and that gave me ample time to figure out what to do. Around lunchtime, a disheveled Billal threw the door open to my room, walked inside, and locked the door before he turned and faced me. Anger sprang forth from my heart at the sight of him. I jumped up from my sitting position and sprang forward like a mad dog. I wanted to kill him with my bare hands. I wanted to strangle the life out of him. He needed to pay for all the anguish that he had caused Loula and me.

Billal barred his face with his arms, and I took that opportunity and punched him in his gut. Billal doubled over in pain, and as he bent forward, my knee came crashing on his jaw and he fell backward and landed on the floor.

"Get up, you piece of shit!" I snarled, running out of breath. "Get up and fight like a man, you motherfucker! Get up and fight for your human right to live, because I swear by all that is holy that I will kill you now!" I growled.

I lifted him up from the floor, and with my left fist, I threw him a punch, and I heard bone cracking.

"Nidal, wait. Stop!" Billal wiped his bleeding lips that were threatening to swell up. "I come in peace, Nidal. I am here to help you and Loula. I promise that I come in peace." He fell against the wall for support. "Please listen to what I have to say. It is imperative that you hear it all. I promise it will be worth your time." He gasped for air. "I will start from the beginning. Do not interrupt me until I am done. Please, sit down and listen. I am here to help you, cousin." He pleaded for me to allow him the audience he requested.

Intrigued by what he had to say, I fell silent and waited to hear his words. Looking into his eyes, I knew he really did have serious stuff to say. So I sat down on the couch and waited.

"Cousin, I will start from the beginning. When you told me about Loula, I thought you were chasing after a skirt who was not worthy of you. I thought you to be a silly young prince with an innocent heart. But when I set eyes on Loula, I realized why you were so in love with her. I fell in love with her the instant I laid eyes on her too." He waved his hands at me trying to make sure I did not jump up and attack him again. "I did not know what to do. I fell so in love with her that I could not function without at least looking upon her beauty once a day. The only thing that stopped me from claiming her right away was the fact that you had already staked your claim on her, and I respected that in the beginning, but as the days turned to months, I was beyond thinking clearly. The love I had for her impaired my judgment, and I made a fool of myself over and over again until I looked like an idiot." He gasped for air.

"I was a fool in love and did not know what to do, Nidal. One day, Princess Shaeena came to me and asked me to visit her at her palace. My curiosity was piqued, and I went. She told me of her love for you and how displeased she was that you had chosen a commoner from another world over herself. She asked me to help her to win your love. She told me that she wanted to have your baby, but you were not interested in her. She seduced me, and I slept with her. Within a month's time, she found out that she was pregnant with my child. She told me to tell no one and that she would find a way to pass the baby off as yours. When you went to her palace and stayed there for three nights, she drugged you, and you passed out. That is why you do not remember a thing. You never slept with her. I did, and the child is mine," he said very emotional as he looked at me, waiting to see if I would pounce on him.

But I just sat there, trying to understand everything he was saying to me, and I tried to put what he was telling me into perspective.

Billal continued bitterly, "At first, I thought she was insane, but as I considered what she was saying, against my better judgment, I thought that, if she claimed the baby as yours, then I could have Loula all to myself. I made a huge mistake, Nidal. Loula's heart belongs to you. It always has, and it will always be that way. I know she loves me too, but I also know that the love she feels for me is not as powerful as the love she has for you. It hurt me to come to that realization. And in the beginning, I thought I could change her mind if I played my cards well, but try as I might, I never accomplished it. I have come here today, not as a prince, but as your cousin who loves you dearly, to ask for your forgiveness," he said sincerely.

A miserable silence fell as I tried to stomach everything that he had admitted to me.

Billal's voice sounded bitter as he continued, "When Shaeena pushed Loula down the stairs and Loula lost the baby, I had no idea she would do that. When I found out, I was devastated that she had hurt Loula in such a way. I went to her palace and slapped her so hard that she was bruised for days." Then Billal sat on the chair, the one opposite the couch I was sitting on. He dropped his head in his hands and wept.

Alarmed, I wait for him to continue. I knew he needed to tell me more. A few minutes later, he continued, "Listen carefully to my next words, Nidal. They will be very hurtful, and you will suffer a pain that no one before ever has, but I must tell you everything and warn you before it is too late." He averted his eyes and started to cry, and I knew that what he was about to say would impact me in a big way. I braced myself for his next words.

"Nidal, Loula has fallen into depression. She has been sick for three months now. From the day she witnessed you and Shaeena having sex. The king told me that, if I so much as uttered a single word to you, he would exile me from Arabia. I knew not what to do," he muttered as he ran his fingers through his hair and swept them away from his eyes.

I regarded him, and I knew he spoke the truth, but I could tell more truth was about to be told. I knew in my heart that what he was about to say next would kill me, and I blinked and waited patiently for him to continue.

"Nidal, Loula gave birth to twins this morning, and they lived. The king took them and swore us to secrecy, saying it would be treason if we told you the truth. He took the babies and left. I told Loula that she had only one child and that he was stillborn."

My heart stopped, and I let out a loud scream. It did not even sound as if it is coming out of my mouth. It sounded as if it were from somewhere far away. I lay back on the couch, my head rolled to the right side, and I wailed like a little baby. I wept for Loula, I wept for my babies, and I wept for the love that was almost lost to me. More screams tore from my throat as my head rolled from side to side. I pulled my hair, and I ripped my shirt. I cried and cried until my voice disappeared and my tears were all wasted, and I was left with nothing, absolutely nothing, but an empty feeling.

"Nidal, listen. We are running out of time. You must listen to the rest of the story. The queen took the babies from your father and took them to a hiding place. They are safe. No harm will come to them. She went against your father's wishes and stole the babies and hid them. Do not worry about them. It is Loula I came here for. She is dying slowly, a death beyond the doctor's help. You need to go to her and take her away from here. I fear there is not much life left in her. You must go now! Only your presence has an effect on her. Only you can save her. Please go now. Do not waste any time. She is not doing well, Nidal." He ran out of breath. Billal placed his hand on his heart and tried to calm it.

"Why do you tell me this now, Billal? Why do you run to me with all this information and go against my father's wishes, knowing full well the consequences of your actions? The king will excommunicate you. He will punish you in the worst possible way." I got up from the couch and stood on my wobbling two legs, fearful that they were not able to carry my weight.

"Cousin, I feel remorse. I feel guilty for coming between the two of you. I never wanted all this to happen. The love I felt for Loula blinded me. I did not know that my game would kill her. Please, Nidal, go to her now before it is too late."

Alarmed by the tone in Billal's voice, I ran out the door, raced up the stairs, and headed straight for Loula's room. I pushed past the guards, and I kicked the door open and ran inside to an empty room. Fear gripped my soul as I looked around. Loula was nowhere to be seen. I run to the window, looked outside down below, and saw that the guests had started to arrive. *Is it time for the wedding? Where is Loula? Where has she gone?* I walked out into the hallway and demanded to know where they had taken Loula. The guards looked at me confused, and pushed past me to see for themselves if what I claimed were true.

I wasted no time as I sped to the back stairway, not wanting the guests to see me. Running quickly down the stairs, I pushed past a couple of servants who were in my way and reached the back doors. As I opened them, the fresh air caressed my face, and I closed my eyes and swallowed the oxygen. As it flowed down my lungs, the tears rolled down my face, and I just stood there and allowed myself a few minutes to meditate and clear my head.

Two men who worked the gardens came up to me and asked, concerned, if I were feeling all right. I reassured them that I was fine and asked them if they had seen Loula. The taller of the two men pointed east and said he saw her a while ago, walking toward the cliff. I started to run as fast as I could in that direction, and my lungs are about to burst, but I could not afford to slow down. Just then, I froze in my tracks. I saw Loula. She was standing on the edge, and she was looking down the cliff. I called out to her, and I ran as fast as I could to her. I called her name over and over again, but she did not turn to me. And as I got closer, I saw Loula put her right foot out and step forward into thin air. Right there in front of my eyes, I saw my Loula take the leap.

I screamed at the top of my lungs, "No!" But it was too late. I collapsed on the dirt floor and wept like a child. I knew my life was over at that moment. There was no reason for me to go on.

My mind took me back to the very first time I saw Loula. She looked like an angel from heaven. She stole my heart from that first day. I thought back to all the times we made love. Each time I touched her, it felt like the very first time. I was born to love her. She was mine, and I did not take good enough care of her. I did this to her. I killed her. I was the reason she killed herself. I pushed her over the edge. It was all my fault.

I lifted myself up from the ground, and walked slowly to the cliff, and looked down. Loula's body was broken among the rocks. The sobs tore from my throat and I screamed like a crazy man. My voice echoed back from the rocks. And then everything went still. My heartbeat slowed down, and I was calm. I inhaled, and the fresh air traveled down my lungs. I heard my name being called and I turned around and saw my mother racing toward me. Billal followed not far behind her. He too cried out my name. Everyone was coming. My father and even Shaeena were running behind them. They all called desperately out to me, but I heard only the calling of my love. And as I fell to my death, I thought of my babies and knew that my mother would watch over them.

There was a peacefulness as I was falling that came to me. I knew that I was going home. It was time. And I smiled and released all the poison out of me before I hit the ground.

The Burials

The rain came down lightly as the two bodies were put into their graves. They were laid to rest next to each other. It was an awful sight as the queen, dressed in black, threw herself on the ground next to her son's grave and wailed so loudly that everyone started to cry with her. It was her right as a mother to release her feelings in such a way. The onlookers held each other for comfort, for they too were in torment. The bells rang loudly and echoed throughout the air. It was the sound of death. Death was in the air.

The king stumbled to the ground next to his wife and cried for the first time in his pathetic life, but no one matched the wails of the queen. No one felt such pain as she did, as she pounded the dirt that covered her son. Her fingernails scratched the surface of the dirt, and her fingertips bled.

The king clutched his heart with one hand, fearing another heart attack, and his nephew flew to his side and kneeled next to him for support. Billal was also mourning both deaths. He loved his cousin Nidal, and Loula would always be the love of his life. His tears rolled down his face with great pain and remorse. He felt responsible for the deaths.

Blinking away the tears, he looked around the graveyard. Thousands were lined up around the graveyard. They were all dressed in black and mourned their prince and his love. Billal's eyes fell on the princess. She too was dressed in black from head to toe. He looked at her with hate. She was the poison that dripped in everyone and caused all this. Her jealousy and greed brought forth all the poison that caused this outcome. She singlehandedly master manipulated everyone when she threw her net and caught them all in her web.

The princess caught the look that Billal gave her. She was wearing a black veil that covered her face. No one saw her dry eyes. No tears were in them, only hate and poison. She hid the poison well behind her veil. No one suspected the anger in her heart. She looked at the graves, and even now, jealousy coursed through her entire body, shaking her to the core. She hated losing, and the thought of Loula winning even though she was dead ate at her nerves. She knew now that she would never be queen. Her child would never have the chance to become the queen of Arabia either. Knowing Billal, he would come and acknowledge his daughter, and that would spoil all her plans.

She grieved for Nidal. He was the only one who could have given her what she so desperately wanted, to sit on the throne and be worshipped. Her eyes fixed on the queen who lay on the ground weeping her heart out. A grin settled on the princess's face. *Cry, you old crow*, she thought. *And cry until you croak!* Then her gaze fell on the old king.

Shaeena licked her lips. Her head hung sideways as she swept her gaze over the king's body. *Fat, old, but very powerful*, she thought. The wheels of her mind started spinning, calculating her next moves. Nidal was gone, but there was still the king. *He was easy prey*, she thought as her eyes settled on the king's manhood.

Shaeena's gaze swept over to Billal. He was still staring at her with tears rolling down his eyes. *So melodramatic*, she thought with distaste as her gaze focused and settled back to the king. She licked her lips and thought of all the different things she could try on the king in bed. *He is nowhere near as sexy as his son was, nor would his manhood be anywhere near as huge as Nidal's*, she thought dryly. Her forehead crinkled with distaste at the thought of the king's naked body on top of hers. But she did not have any other choice. The king was her only way to ensure that she wore the crown one day, and if she got lucky enough to get pregnant by the old geezer, then her child would ensure her position on the throne permanently. A smile formed on her poison lips as she looked down to her feet and pretended she too was crying.